How to
Knit a
Love Song

How to Knit a Love Song

A Cypress Hollow Yarn

RACHAEL HERRON

AVON

An Imprint of HarperCollins*Publishers*

HarperCollins books may be purchased for educational, business, or sales promotional use. For information please write: Special Markets Department, HarperCollins Publishers, 10 East 53rd Street, New York, NY 10022.

First Avon paperback edition published 2010.

Designed by Diahann Sturge

Library of Congress Cataloging-in-Publication Data
Herron, Rachael.
    How to knit a love song: a Cypress Hollow yarn / by Rachael Herron. —1st ed.
        p.   cm.
    ISBN 978-0-06-184129-3 (pbk.)
    1. Knitters (Persons)—Fiction.   2. Ranch life—Fiction.   I. Title.
PS3608.E7765H68   2010
813'.6—dc22   2009045028

10 11 12 13 14   OV/RRD   10 9 8 7 6 5 4 3 2

*For my mother,
Janette Frances Herron,
who always believed.*

Acknowledgments

My deepest thanks to Bethany Herron for her cheerful willingness to keep reading and editing before this was even a real book, to Christy Herron for believing in me and for perfume samples, and to Dan Herron for instilling in me a love of cowboys. My love and thanks to Lala Hulse for being my best cheerleader and for opening the champagne, again and again. I am so grateful to my wonderful, amazing agent Susanna Einstein, who believed in me first, to Jenny Arch, who pulled me out of the slush pile, and to my fabulous editor, May Chen, who made it all possible. My thanks to Eddie Dwyer and Bonnie Terra of the esteemed Alameda County Fire Department, for their help with research, and to Charlie and Marilyn Foscalina of Livermore, for regaling me with sheep tales. To the Providers of the Desk, thank you for that beautiful vote of confidence. My thanks to Elizabeth Sullivan for taking my chicken-scratch notes and making Cade's sweater pattern readable, and to Kiyomi Camp for being my super-speedy test-knitter. To Oakland's own Chris Baty, thanks for starting NaNoWriMo—you've changed the world. And to the readers of Yarnagogo.com, over all these years, I couldn't have done this without your love and belief. I have the best readers in the world. Thank you.

Chapter One

Sometimes the hardest part is the first stitch. When you don't know what you're doing, the very thought of starting can be terrifying. Put down my book. Refer to it only if you must. Cast on bravely, now.

— E.C.

Abigail gave the metal latch a giant twist, shoving all of her body weight behind it. Her hand slipped off it at the last moment, and her whole arm slammed through the bars in the gate.

"Damn it!" That hurt. She pulled back her arm and rubbed the elbow that would probably be black and blue tomorrow.

The gate was still closed.

Abigail would get this thing open if she had to use her teeth to do it. It *was* the front gate, she was pretty sure, and it looked like the only way up the dirt drive. There weren't any locks, and she could get the long bolt to turn halfway, but she didn't know how to jam it over and out of the way. She sweated in the late October sun and felt her hair starting to curl against the nape of her neck.

She stood straight and took a deep breath. Her hands burned.

Her red pickup idled behind her, mocking her attempt to drive it through the gate. She should have turned the engine off, at least.

A man sat on horseback on the brown ridge above her. She could just see him under a cluster of eucalyptus trees, far enough away to make out that he was male but not much more. Was he watching her?

No, he couldn't be. He probably couldn't see her clearly from up there. If he could, he'd have come down, at least to see what she wanted. Instead, he must be looking over the valley, down to the ocean behind her.

Abigail was covered in sweat and panting. This wasn't quite the way she wanted to meet anyone, but she wished that cowboy would come down and help her with this stubborn gate. If sheep ranches even had cowboys. What did they call them?

She looked up the hill at the man. He gave every impression of watching her, so she summoned a smile and gave a cheery wave.

No response.

She waved again, this time a little more frantically, although she tried to keep the desperation out of her body language.

She *had* to drive through this gate.

Abigail hopped a little and circled her arms in wild motions. He couldn't miss it.

Could he?

The cowboy's head turned, and the horse started to turn, too, and it looked as if they were headed uphill and away.

"No! Please!" Abigail yelled, as loudly as she could, all shame now tossed to the ocean wind. "Come back!"

She didn't think he'd be able to hear her, but his head swiveled back toward her. Then the horse's body followed that motion.

Abigail rubbed her now dirty, scraped hands on her brand new Wranglers. She hoped a little dirt would take that new-jeans sheen off of them. As he got closer and closer, she could tell the cowboy riding at her was the real deal, the kind that might have opinions about jeans that weren't broken in. She rubbed her palms one last time against her thighs and then waved.

"Well, howdy!" she called.

As soon as the words left her mouth, she wanted to take them back. *Howdy?* The shape of the word in her mouth hadn't felt right and she could tell by his pained look that it hadn't sounded right either.

He was striking, in the way that anything carved from nature is. His cheekbones looked chiseled, high and tanned. His eyes were as green as the grass on the hill behind him, and the long planes of his body seemed as strongly muscled as the horse he rode.

Abigail's mouth opened, but her voice only squeaked.

Then she managed, "Wow! You're real!"

And she realized that there was, indeed, a worse thing to say than howdy. "Umm. I mean, hi."

She stuck out her hand, and then realized that not only was he still ten feet away, but the fence and gate still separated them, not to mention that he was still sitting on the horse, and she was standing on the ground.

She shook out the offending hand, as if it hurt and she was trying to loosen the muscles in it. Then she stuck it in the pocket of her jeans that might be a *smidge* too tight.

"Do you work here? Do you think you could help me open this? Is it locked and I didn't see it? Is this the front entrance? Is there another way I should go?" Abigail paused. "Is that too many questions in a row?"

She smiled, and waited for a similar response.

Nothing. The cowboy's eyes widened at her barrage of questions, but he didn't smile, nor did he attempt to answer a single one.

Instead, he pulled the horse up to the gate, and leaned over. With one hand, he flipped the offending latch. The gate swung freely and fast, directly at Abigail.

"Hey!" she scrambled backward. "Okay! I'm out of the way now, thanks."

She jumped in her idling pickup, drove through the gate, and hopped out to close it.

The cowboy just sat and watched.

She swung the gate, heavier than it looked, back into place, and slammed the latch home. The metal had taken off several layers of skin and she knew that her palm was probably bleeding, but she didn't look at it, just smiled up at him and said, "Thank you."

She got back into the truck and was about to head up the gravel driveway when he said loudly, "What is that, anyway?"

She took the truck out of gear and stuck her head out the open window. "What is what?"

"That thing you're driving?"

Abigail didn't understand the question. "It's a Nissan?" Was that what he wanted to know?

"Is it supposed to be a truck?"

Great. He was going to be a jerk. Maybe she and the other owner could fire this guy, as soon as she got her bearings.

"It's my truck. Got a problem with it?"

"Kind of a silly-looking little thing. What does it haul?"

"It's my silly-looking little thing, and it's always done the job. I'm sorry it offends you."

"No, really. Have you ever put anything in the back? Besides grocery bags or your friend's couch, I mean?"

"It suits me just fine, thanks." The words came quickly and for that she was grateful, but she felt small and disappointed. She had driven up here, her feelings a huge balloon of happiness and excitement, and he'd pushed a pin into them.

Well, forget him. She put her beloved red pickup back in gear and shot up the driveway, spraying gravel. She didn't want to startle the poor horse that had to carry him, but she hoped that she scared the guy a little. What an ass.

But now! Now was the time she'd been waiting for, now she was going to see her brand-new home, her brand-new start.

She drove up and over the low hill, past live oaks and more eucalyptus, past flocks of sheep—real, live sheep! They dotted the hillside as if they were part of a perfect painting, placed there just for her. She passed a small pond that looked more picturesque than useful, but really, what did she know about living in the country? Nothing, that's what.

All that was about to change. Right here, right now.

Abigail caught her breath when she saw it. A two-story 19th-century wooden ranch house, painted white with dark green trim, it looked loved and well worn, a place that could be truly called home, something she hadn't had in what felt like forever. It sat nestled next to three or four huge, old oaks, their limbs sheltering and low to the ground.

A place to feel safe.

Behind and to the right of the house stood a matching cottage, a miniature version of the bigger one. Abigail's heart swelled with happiness. She wondered if that delightful spot would be where she slept. Or would she sleep in the house and work in the cottage?

This was really it. This was the place. Home.

As Abigail's feet crunched up the gravel driveway, she could hear a soft breeze making the drying oak leaves crackle. Other than the low roar of a distant plane overhead, there was no sound but the blood rushing in her ears and her heart beating quickly in her chest.

She willed herself to calm down as she climbed the four shallow steps up to the white wraparound porch. But it was no use, really. This was too good to be true.

Abigail knocked on the door, already slightly ajar.

No answer.

Was this the doorbell? She turned the wind-up key in the door, and it set off a jangling ring inside.

She waited, the breeze on the back of her neck giving her shivers. The good kind.

She knocked again.

Still nothing.

Abigail pushed the door open.

It felt deliciously like breaking and entering, but it wasn't, not really. She had Eliza to thank for it.

She was in a tiny foyer, with large sunny rooms opening up to either side. Directly in front of her a set of steep stairs went up, the fabric runner deep red and worn with use. To her left was what looked like a small dining room, in it a heavy dark table decorated with a silver teapot and dark blue napkins dotted with yellow flowers. Paintings of the local landscape hung in wooden frames.

To her right appeared to be a parlor, a real, old-fashioned parlor. A huge bay window looked onto that next-door cottage. Abigail stepped into the room. An antique sofa, a somewhat worse-for-wear grand piano, a redbrick fireplace, a flat-screen TV. Old and new, it all went together, giving the room a feeling of home and continuity. Books were everywhere: on shelves that looked built in, stacked on end tables, piled on the rocking chair in the corner. A huge yellow cat slumbered in an overstuffed wingback chair in a ray of sunlight and barely opened his eyes to look at her.

Heaven.

A slam and footsteps from behind her. Abigail stifled a scream and turned.

The cowboy. Looking furious.

"What the *hell* are you doing in my house?"

Chapter Two

Knitters don't give away stash easily. If you are offered something, be it wool, angora or alpaca, take it. That knitter knows you'll need it someday. (This, of course, doesn't apply to acrylic. Run from acrylic.)
—E.C.

"This is *your* house?"

"You mind telling me exactly who you are?"

"Abigail Durant. The new part owner. And you are . . . ?"

Abigail hoped against hope that he would say he was her new ranch-hand or neighbor or something, anything, but she already knew by his attitude what he was going to say.

"I'm Cade MacArthur, the *only* owner. Seems like we have a few things to settle, and quick."

Abigail turned her head at the sound of a car spitting rocks up the driveway. This was either going to be the lawyer who told her to meet him here for the reading of the will, or this was Cade's backup. She hoped it was the former.

"For the love of . . . Who's that?" he said, whipping his hat off his head and slapping it down on a sideboard. Something that sounded like china rattled inside.

"Didn't you get the letter? About the reading of the will?"

"I know it wasn't today."

"It's the sixteenth."

"Damn."

At the knock, Cade opened the door to a small, pale man in a suit who smiled at them both. "Afternoon, Cade. And you must be Ms. Durant, nice to meet you. John Thompson, at your service. Through here? Won't take a minute. I'm not fussy about these things."

He walked past them and into the next room, which turned out to be the kitchen. A blend, again, of new and old—a stove that had probably been installed back when the new-fangled gas ones first came out sat next to a gleaming black refrigerator. Well-loved-looking pots and pans shone from an overhead rack. A silver-and-red Formica table stood in one corner under a farming calendar advertising some sort of grain.

The smiling lawyer pulled up a chair at the table and gestured for them to join him. He took out a collection of paper and gave them each a stack. Abigail sat next to him.

"We can do this the old-fashioned way, with me reading it to you verbatim, or I can go over it broadly, and we'll read the fine print later," he said.

Cade, standing next to the stove, said, "Yeah, that. Do it fast."

"Eliza Carpenter died two weeks ago today. She asked me to . . ." He stopped when Abigail held up her hand.

"Hang on a sec, if you don't mind. The funeral? Where were you?" Abigail asked Cade. He hadn't been there, she was sure of it. She would have remembered him. Even through that pain, she would have noticed him, would have remembered his eyes or noticed the breadth of his shoulders.

"I couldn't go. I had to run this place."

"You couldn't take a day off to go to your great-aunt's funeral?"

"Nope."

"Wow. I bet she would have liked it if you'd been there."

"She was dead. I don't think she noticed."

"I'm sure other people did."

"I don't care about other people. I care about this place. And I don't owe a stranger any explanation, that's for damn sure."

"Got it," said Abigail. Okay, he was going to keep on being awful. She turned her back to Cade. "Mr. Thompson, I'm sorry. Please go on."

"Yes, of course." The lawyer seemed to be fiddling with something on the table that didn't exist, his fingers twitching. Under any other circumstances, Abigail would have offered him something, a soda, some coffee. But Cade wasn't offering, and she could only watch.

And wait.

The only thing the lawyer had told her on the phone last week was that she had a place to live. She came here knowing nothing else. Now she wasn't even sure of that.

The suspense was killing her. She ground her nails into her palm.

"Well, all right. So, going over it in the broadest of terms . . . " The lawyer flipped some papers, frowned, found the one he was looking for. "Eliza wanted you to have the cottage, Abigail, and the land it stands on, as well as everything stored inside it. Cade receives the house and the land it stands on with all belongings found inside, as well as all land, excluding the land upon which the cottage stands."

"Wow," Abigail breathed.

Cade's mouth opened, then closed. It looked like he couldn't even talk—he turned to face the stove, and the sound of his breath hissing through his teeth made Abigail's palms sweat.

Great. Now she had to deal with him.

"Look, Mr. MacArthur, let's talk about it."

"The cottage," he said through gritted teeth, back still turned, "is completely uninhabitable."

"What?"

"Crazy old broad filled it with crap. And I mean *crammed*. Ceilings to floors, out to all walls. It was her dumping ground for years."

"Well, you see," started the lawyer, but Cade cut him off again.

"No one could live there. And aren't we forgetting the most important thing?" He turned around, quickly, the muscles under his denim shirt straining as he pushed against the stove.

"I live here. On this land." His eyes sparked at Abigail, and if looks could kill, she'd need paramedics in another minute.

He repeated, "I live here. This is my home. I can't believe she did this. God*damn* her. She always thought she knew what was right for me. Only I don't get this. I take care of her ranch, I save it, so she can leave and move south, where she meets scammers and con artists." He shot a look at Abigail and went on, "I don't even buy her out, so she can feel like she still has a home even though she never *comes* home, and this is what I get?"

Abigail opened her mouth, but he held up a hand.

"Don't. I turned this ranch around. It was going downhill, bleeding money. She would have lost it all. Now it's one of the most respected in the valley. This is my place, my home. And you're just . . . "

"I don't want your house, Mr. MacArthur."

"Like hell. You want it all. I'll fight this."

"Look, you don't know me, but I'm not the kind of person who takes pleasure in making someone else miserable. This morning when I woke up, I owned no property. I'll be more than happy with the cottage."

Cade pulled up a chair and sat, suddenly too close to Abigail. She smelled hay and sunshine and something rougher. He placed his hand, weather worn and huge, on the table next to hers.

Through his teeth he said, "It's not your cottage." He turned to the lawyer and stabbed a finger at the papers. "John, how real is this?"

"It is all in writing, Cade. Legally witnessed, notarized. I don't think you can fight it. That's my friendly opinion, but we can go over it in detail anytime."

"This is the stupidest crap that crazy old lady ever did."

Abigail's heartbeat quickened. "Don't you *dare*! She was the closest friend I ever had. Say what you like about me, but don't ever talk like that about her. I *loved* her."

"And I didn't? Is that what you're implying?"

"This is how you talk about someone you love?"

Cade turned and looked at her, so close that she felt his breath on her cheek.

Her own breath stopped for a moment.

She stood. "This has all been a lot for right now. Hasn't it?" She filled her lungs to prove to herself she still could. "Mr. Thompson, is there anything more? Anything else we should know?"

"There are inheritance taxes and some forms I need, but they can wait . . ."

"Besides those."

"No."

"I see."

Abigail felt like running to her truck and sitting in it for a minute to find some of the excitement and daring that had gotten her here today, but she couldn't. She'd stick this out. Even if this man made her hands shake.

"So." She turned to face the cowboy. "May I get the keys to the cottage? I'll need to fix myself a place to sleep tonight." She didn't feel half as brave as she hoped she sounded.

The lawyer, helpful again, for which Abigail was grateful, offered, "There are two bedrooms upstairs. You could have your pick and start work on the cottage tomorrow."

"She could *what*? This is my house! Would you mind very much staying the hell out of my business, Thompson? In fact, you can leave right now."

The lawyer's face fell, and he gathered his paperwork. "Thought I was helping. I guess I'll get out of your way."

Abigail walked the lawyer to the door. As she did, Cade opened a drawer that sounded like it had cutlery in it and slammed it so hard the pans rattled on their hooks. Abigail jumped.

She kept her voice low as she spoke to the lawyer. "You've been very helpful. I didn't expect it to be like this, and I'm not quite sure what to do now, but I'll keep you posted."

"You do that," Thompson said, and he smiled at her, a small man with a big, sweet grin. "If you have any questions, or if you need someone to show you around town, well, you know, I'm usually not busy in the evenings, and there are a couple of really good restaurants in town that I'd be happy to show you."

"Thanks," Abigail said, shaking his hand. "I'll keep that in mind, but I really think I'll be staying close to home for a while so I can get settled."

From behind her in the kitchen, she heard a roar.

"This is not your home!" Cade yelled, and she heard another door slam farther away.

Abigail closed the front door behind her and leaned against it. She shuddered, thinking about going back in that kitchen. She took a deep breath. This was safe. That awful cowboy was just mad. Angry. That was natural, right? This was so much more than she had bargained for. But she had needed to escape San Diego, and she needed a home.

Somehow this was going to work out, wasn't it? Didn't it have to? Eliza meant her to be here. When Abigail fled San Diego (it felt like so much longer ago than just this morning), she only packed what she could fit in the truck. She took her computer, a hard-copy draft of her latest book scribbled with red marks, her clothes, and her best fiber: the alpaca and cashmere, of course. She'd given away the rest, offloading some of her stash of yarn, most of her books, and all her furniture. A new start. She had a little money in the bank and a truck that apparently wasn't worth anything to a rancher. It was all she had, really.

It wasn't much. And she didn't know how it would fit here. But she deserved a new start.

Chapter Three

When you cast on, don't count your stitches more than twice. If the numbers don't match, hope for the one you want, and knit across. If you still have to add or take away a few stitches, do it then. Don't fuss so much.

— E.C.

C ade had heard of people being too mad to see straight, but he had always thought, up until now, that it was just a saying. It didn't really happen.

But walking out the back door, he actually couldn't see for a moment.

Blind with rage. It wasn't just a cliché.

He stumbled over his own boot on the way to the barn, didn't see the dirt clod in his way. Couldn't see it.

How could Aunt Eliza have done this to him?

The woman, who he would have sworn didn't have an ounce of guile in her anywhere, had cried over her knitting needles and asked him to leave it all in her name. *Don't buy the house, Cade,* she'd pleaded with him, tears pooling in her huge, blue eyes. *Let the house and the cottage and the land stay in my name, so even when I'm five hundred miles south of here, I'll know my home is still my home. When I die, it'll all come right.*

It's all coming right, he thought. Right out the window.

Give the cottage away? To a stranger? Who did that? Who broke up a piece of land like that?

Who did that to their family?

He had work to do. But Tom would be in the barn, and he couldn't face his friend and ranch manager giving him the third degree right now. Tom had grown up around here, knew Eliza, knew her well enough to perhaps be able to give Cade some words of advice, some piece of knowledge that would make this all fit, make this all right.

But Cade didn't want to talk to Tom. No matter what he might say, it wasn't all right. Some city girl had waltzed in, if you could call driving a stupid girl-truck waltzing, and scooped up a big piece of his land from under him.

It wasn't his place anymore. Wasn't only his.

In truth, it never had been.

Now it was hers, too, and he didn't even remember what she'd said her last name was. Or where she was from, although he assumed— hoped—she was from San Diego, since that's where Eliza had been for the last ten years. He didn't know what she did.

For all he knew, she was a lawyer. She looked like a lawyer. She was pretty, that was true. In that citified, glossy way.

Okay, she was more than pretty.

Kind of gorgeous, actually. What a waste.

That thick, shoulder-length brown hair the color of coffee, those strikingly bright blue eyes, that perfect mouth. And her body, all breasts and hips and curves and long legs, in proportions that guys didn't usually see in real life.

In any other situation, he'd be interested, all right. It was the first thing he'd thought, seeing her wrestling with the gate, that she was his type. Hell, she was any hot-blooded male's type.

It took him only seconds to realize that this was the person the lawyer had told him about on the phone, the person who might be sharing his aunt's estate with him, and one second more for him to loathe her with every fiber of his being.

He'd made her truly uncomfortable, he knew that. And at the same time that he'd hated acting like a jerk, he couldn't change his attitude. Even if she hadn't planned on being one, she was a thief.

Cade walked past the barn, hoping that Tom wouldn't glance out the office window. Cade headed for the hills, literally. The land sloped up just past the barn, and a short walk would lead him to his favorite place in the world, an oak-studded knoll that looked down to the ocean. He needed the view and the wind to blow some sense of perspective into him, because otherwise, he was going to . . .

He didn't know what.

But he'd rather not find out.

He started hiking up the hill.

Who did she think she was? He was goddamned sure that if someone had left him property, he'd make certain that it was up for grabs before laying claim to it. She had, at this point, a full cottage. The cottage and land that should be his. She had them free and clear, no mortgage, probably fifteen hundred square feet of California history, part of an old stagecoach stop, a beautiful home.

Even if it was uninhabitable.

God, she wasn't going to be able to live there yet. Not for a while.

But he wasn't going to tell her that. She could figure that out on her own.

Cade was used to his own space, his own company. It made him, he knew, a better businessman, better around the sheep. He was used to a calm life. Serene. Pastoral.

This girl was going to destroy his serenity. Already had.

Goddamn Eliza. Cade took a deep breath and wiped his brow. He was sweating more than he usually did on this climb. Anger.

And betrayal.

His grandmother's sister, his great-aunt Eliza, had been the one to whom he had run when he ran away as a teenager. Eliza had told him he could stay and work with her sheep, and had talked him into calling his parents, acting like it was her idea that he come and stay a couple of months—things weren't working with his mom and dad, even before his mom flew the coop. Eliza gave him a place to be, away from the never-ending arguments.

He *had* loved that woman. He had worked his ass off, going to school, getting his degree so that he'd know how to do it right. At twenty-two, he'd moved in with Eliza and taken over running the ranch. Eliza had been delighted. Since her husband Joshua died, Eliza had been running the ranch by herself. It had been her husband's passion, never hers. Eliza's sheep wandered off and she forgot to shear them in the spring, only remembering when she was low on fiber to spin. She wasn't physically strong enough to do the heavy lifting required, and she preferred to stay inside, knitting with friends and designing her innovative patterns. She'd welcomed Cade with warm, open arms when he moved in, and gave the running of the ranch, what was left of it at that point, completely over to him.

He'd started his own herd: small, mostly Suffolk crosses and a few Corriedales. He started it the way he wanted, growing it bigger and right, until he knew what he was doing and talked the bank into loaning him the money to buy the ranch from her.

Money that Aunt Eliza had refused, asking him to trust her.

A misplaced trust.

Cade was almost there, almost at the top of the rise, and in a few seconds, there it was, he could see the ocean, the long line of it below him—silvery, almost too bright to look at. He sat on his favorite old stump.

He tried to breathe, but his lungs felt heavy. The air felt thick. He scuffed his boot in the dirt.

Cade had to get her off his land. And fast.

Chapter Four

Unless you learned to knit in early childhood, it's natural to feel out of your element and clumsy. It's natural to think everyone else makes it look easy.

—E.C.

Abigail put the key to the cottage in her pocket and walked outside. Cade had practically thrown it at her as he'd left the house.

Fine. She could handle it.

Even at a leisurely pace, it was less than a minute's walk across the backyard to the cottage. Abigail stepped carefully up onto the narrow wraparound porch, not sure how run down the place actually was, scared her foot would go through old boards. But it seemed sturdy enough.

Abigail knocked before trying her new key and then felt silly for doing it. But the last time she'd walked into a house without knocking hadn't gone so well.

The lock squeaked as the barrel turned reluctantly. She'd need to get this rekeyed anyway. As soon as possible. She knew people out in the country didn't lock doors, but she always would. Safety first.

The latch finally slipped. She opened the door.

She gasped.

It was like a documentary on the dangers of compulsive hoarding. She could barely open the door; it got stuck on something halfway in and refused to budge again.

Abigail pushed her body through, just clearing the opening. It was dark, and she couldn't make out exactly what it was she was seeing, but she knew it wasn't good.

To her left, a window with its blind drawn. She reached her hand around to release the catch. The blind flew up and a little light filtered into the room. It looked to be a decent-sized living room. Abigail could only imagine that there was furniture in it somewhere, but the room was completely hidden by old cardboard boxes, some looking much the worse for wear, piled almost to the ceiling, on and in every available space, save for a narrow pathway through them.

Abigail moved forward. It was the only thing she could do.

She picked her way among boxes. Once through the first room, she was in what must have been a kitchen at some point but that was now filled with huge, black trash bags. Again, only a narrow path led through the room, and branched out at the back.

One direction led to a bathroom, also full of black trash bags, only the sink and commode exposed. When she pulled back the dark shower curtain, she found the bathtub itself filled with trash bags.

Damn. Did the water work? Abigail twisted the sink faucet. There was an ominous clanking under the cottage and the pipe shook, but nothing happened. She peered into the toilet. There wasn't any water in the bowl.

She flipped the light switch to get a better look. Nothing. Great.

There was a small window over the tub covered with a thick green curtain. When she pulled it back, enough light came through to allow her to lift off the lid of the toilet tank. The whole mechanism inside appeared rusty but completely dry.

There was no water.

There was no power.

Where the *hell* was she going to sleep tonight?

A hotel down the road might work, but she'd seen No Vacancy signs on every one she'd passed on the drive. This was a beach community, after all.

And there was no way she was staying with that guy. Even if he asked her, she couldn't trust him farther than she could throw him. Who knew what he was capable of, especially when he was this mad at her?

Abigail put her hand on the towel rail to steady herself. She would find something good about this place if it killed her. This was the opposite of what Eliza's spare, spotless San Diego independent-living apartment had been. Abigail fought despair. No. Not till she'd seen the whole cottage.

Another path just outside the bathroom led to what must be a small bedroom, also full of boxes and bags.

She battled her way back through the house, trying not to think about the scurrying noise she heard in the kitchen. It was a rodent of some sort, she knew that, but her heart raced nonetheless.

She took a deep breath and stepped over a low box, pushing past three bags.

In the living room, Abigail moved box after box to clear a path just the size of her hips. The boxes weren't heavy, but she noted that they were obviously full of something. She was too apprehensive to look.

A narrow, winding staircase stood in the far corner of the front room. She took the steps carefully, testing each one with half her weight before committing to it. At the top, her head poked up into another small room.

Oh. This room was different.

It was all light—windows on all eight sides of the room. An old-fashioned cupola. From up here, Abigail could see a sliver of the ocean over the tops of the trees. The fog was moving out for the day, and the sky was a silvery gray, dotted with scudding white clouds.

A battered green love seat sat sentry in the middle of the room. A lamp covered with a multicolored glass lamp shade rested on an ornate table next to the love seat. There wasn't enough room to really move around—almost every bit of floor space was taken up by those black plastic garbage bags, as well as odds and ends of furniture, but it was nice furniture, pretty things that Abigail knew Eliza had loved.

The wooden floor had been painted the same dark green as the trim outside, years and years old by the look of the scuff marks. Abigail felt as if she'd suddenly climbed one of the oak trees to find herself in a magic tree house.

She knew without having to ask Cade that his great-aunt sat up here, knitting, for hours on end. This room had the feeling, the spirit of Eliza. Abigail longed to go get her needles and her current project: a man's Guernsey she was designing in dark red handspun merino. Or better yet, she could get her spinning wheel, and sit up here, looking out at the countryside and sea. But she'd have to bring that stuff through the frightening first floor, and then fight to find the space up here to put it down.

Maybe she'd beat a retreat right now and go somewhere to think about all this, about how to start.

Really, she ought to open a box or a bag. Start clearing out all the crap she had just inherited.

As she tried to talk herself into getting started, she heard a loud knock from downstairs. She barely stifled the scream that rose in her throat.

"You okay in there?" Cade yelled into the living room.

Abigail took a moment to breathe, to still the frantic beat of her heart.

"I'm up here!"

"You okay?"

"I'm coming down," she called.

Abigail made her way down the staircase and through the boxes, out to the porch, where he stood.

"I found the house key. You can make a copy of it." He held it out for her, but Abigail was suspicious.

"Why?"

"If something in here doesn't work. Did you check the water? I think it's been off for years." He looked down at his boot and scowled. "You might have to use my bathroom."

Abigail nodded. "Yeah. Water's not on."

"You really going to sleep here?"

"Sure," she said, trying to sound nonchalant. "Especially if I can use your house for the toilet and a shower until I get things fixed up around here. That would be great."

"It's a wreck. She'd come up a couple of times a year, and bring more boxes or bags, loading them in by herself, refusing all help."

"You don't know what's in them? You never looked?"

"Nope. I'm sure it's trash. Just more of Eliza's craziness."

"She may have been a little eccentric, but she was never crazy. If she brought that stuff here, she had a reason."

Cade stepped in the door, and opened the box nearest him. "See? Nothing but newspaper. Saving it for Armageddon or something."

Abigail's heart sank at the sight of the yellowed paper in the box. "Maybe she was a little crazy. But not much. Not really."

"Whatever you say."

Abigail stepped out of the house, onto the porch, into the sun. Cade followed.

He leaned against the railing, then thumped the porch with the heel of his boot. "This place was built thirty years after the big house, about 1904. As far as I know, it's sound, never had any problem with rot, but you should get that looked at. The chimney's cracked and needs cleaning. The toilet isn't seated right, and the tile floor in both the bathroom and the kitchen needs redoing. I think there's carpeting under all that crap, and I can't even begin to guess how long that's been in there. I have no idea about the appliances in the kitchen, but I can guess they're going to need some work."

Abigail took a breath and stood up straighter. She made her voice light. "Well, shoot. That's not too bad, is it? I can have that all fixed by tonight."

Cade looked at her. He didn't smile. Then he leaned forward and gripped the stair rail. "She loved this old cottage. I asked her every time she drove up if she wanted me to start work in here yet. She'd tell me to keep my grubby paws off it, that she was saving it for special."

He stepped off the porch, moving out into the yard, and said, "Really, it's going to take months, if it's just you. You should hire professionals to clean it out and fix it up. I know some guys."

"I can do a lot of it myself. Eliza would like that."

His look of disbelief was clear, one eyebrow raised, his lips pressed firmly together.

Embarrassed. That was the strange feeling she had. But she said, "I know. She's probably gone. But I like to hope she might be around a little bit, somehow, in a way that I can't understand. So I have to act like she might see me, show her that I loved her."

He turned his head away. "Hippy-dippy crap. You going to smudge the place with incense?" He had his jerk voice back and he didn't meet her eyes.

She spun around and walked away from him in what she hoped was an appropriately offended manner. She didn't stop until she was inside the cottage.

She shut the front door behind her.

Then she pulled back the dusty old curtain and peeked out the narrow window. He still stood in the same spot, looking down at the ground, as if lost in thought.

Any other time, any other place, she would want to talk to that cowboy. She'd objectify his rugged good looks. She'd be attracted to his long legs, his strong, wide back. Not here.

But she gave herself another second to look.

Then his head came up, fast, and even across the large yard, their eyes locked through the glass. Abigail gasped and stepped back, out of his sight line.

She took a deep breath. And then another.

Chapter Five

Always knit sleeves first. They act as gauge swatches, and you get the dreaded things over with first, so you can move on to the fun things.

—E.C.

This was awful. Horrible. Disgusting.

Abigail rolled to her other side in the sleeping bag, and prayed she wouldn't hear anything else move. She was lying on the floor next to the dusty divan, in a small body-sized space she'd cleared among bags in the upstairs cupola room. Even without curtains on the windows, it was too dark outside, with no street-lights and no moon, to see anything around her except vague out-lines of stacked boxes. Not sure what the scratching noise had been a few minutes ago, she was too terrified to open her eyes.

If she opened them and saw a pair of beady red eyes staring back at her, be they rodent or something else, she would die of a heart attack. She knew it. Hadn't she already had enough of fear in the recent past?

Cypress Hollow was a tourist beach town. There hadn't been a room available within twenty-five miles. Not that she'd really be able to afford a hotel room for very long. It was an expense she didn't need. But still. It would have been nice to have had one night in a bed before committing to this run-down, junk-filled, rusted-pipe hovel of a cottage.

What had Eliza been thinking?

For that matter, what had Abigail been thinking? On the drive up today, she'd allowed herself to dream, even if only briefly, about a beautiful farmhouse. Or a sweet mother-in-law addition. A hammock, for God's sake.

This squalor wasn't helping. What the hell was in all these boxes? These bags? She pushed the thought of rodent enclaves out of her mind. She would not think of spiders. She would just think happy thoughts.

A happy thought seemed far away.

Sheep outside, grazing. That was happy. More. Tussah silk, unspun. A new pair of Addi Turbo knitting needles.

Abigail squinched her eyes shut tighter and rolled onto her back. It wasn't working.

She would *not* open her eyes. Even with that weird scraping sound above her head.

Damn, she was starving. Somehow, in all the excitement, she'd forgotten to eat anything since this morning on the road.

Also, she had to pee. Of course she'd used Cade's bathroom in the big house before she'd retired for the night. She'd taken her toothbrush out of her bag and scurried through his kitchen to the bathroom, hoping to remain unnoticed. She hadn't seen him, a fact for which she was grateful.

But now, with her usual annoying nighttime timing, she had to go again.

No. She would not open her eyes. She would not make her way through this upper cupola room, downstairs through the crazy piled boxes and out. Her flashlight, although bright, only made it worse. Scarier.

She could just hold it all night.

Abigail suddenly understood the allure of chamber pots.

She took a deep breath and willed her body to relax. This was better. The floor was still as hard as before but she tried to allow herself to sink into it. Everything would be okay. It would all look better in the morning.

A huge *whomp* jolted her upright. She stifled a stream and reached for the flashlight. The noise was directly over her head, and it was followed by another *whomp* seconds later.

Was that . . . *flapping?*

Damn, damn, damn. Her fingers fumbled to find the small button that would light the flashlight. Her breath seemed to be stuck in her throat—she could barely get air around the fear she couldn't swallow.

Abigail directed the beam at the ceiling.

Something large. With wings.

The scream she'd been holding back tore from her throat. As she followed it with the beam of light, the bat flapped around the peaked ceiling.

A bat! A *bat*, probably rabid. Above her.

Without even thinking about what she was doing, Abigail scrambled out from the sleeping bag, shoved her feet into her slippers and ran down the stairs, pushed through the boxes, and stood outside.

She couldn't breathe. In the cold air, it was necessary to concentrate on the very act of breathing in, then breathing out. She bent forward at the waist.

She couldn't sleep in there. She just couldn't.

Tears filled her eyes, and she dashed them away with the back of her fist. So stupid. She'd already failed. Maybe she'd just buy a truck-bed cover and sleep in the back until the cottage was fixed up.

If it ever got fixed up.

She straightened and looked across the yard at Cade's house.

In the upper right corner, on the second floor, backlit against a yellow glow in the window, Cade stood watching her.

Just like he'd watched her this afternoon from the ridge, on his horse.

God, could he see that she was crying from there? Damn him.

She gave a fake smile and a wave, and went back into the cottage. Her purse. She needed just her purse and the sleeping bag. She got both, running as fast as she could through the mess, hearing things scurry as she ran. In the cupola room, she didn't look up, didn't swing her flashlight beam to the ceiling.

She peeked out the window before she exited the cottage. The coast seemed clear—the light in the room she had just seen him in was off.

Abigail raced through the cold night air to her truck. She unlocked it and threw herself inside. She cursed herself for letting her mind wander to the scene in *Cujo* where the people were in the car, hiding from the dog.

If a rabid dog flung its body at the side of her truck right now, she didn't think she'd be much more scared than she already was.

This was going to be just fine. Sure, it was a pickup, so the bucket seats didn't recline much, and she'd have to sleep basically sitting up. But she could do that. She wrestled her body into the sleeping bag, not even bothering to remove her slippers. She used the sweater she'd been wearing earlier as a pillow, propping her head against the glass driver's-side window.

She sighed and closed her eyes. Not a great start.

Moments passed. She felt her body relax. So sleepy. It was going to be okay.

Then something pounded on the glass her head was resting on.

Rabid dog! Cujo! Abigail screamed like she had when she saw the bat, and she couldn't stop the scream, even when she opened her eyes and saw it was just Cade, standing at the window, his hand drawn back from knocking on the glass. Abigail used every ounce of her willpower to stop screaming. She felt tears spring to her eyes. This wasn't fair. She was done being scared.

She swung the door of the truck open, and twisted her body so that she faced him, still in her mummy-sleeping bag. She was an idiot.

Cade's eyes were wide. "I'm sorry. I didn't know I would scare you like that. You've only been out here a few minutes, I didn't think you'd already be asleep."

"I wasn't. You just startled me." Abigail stopped and gripped the steering wheel with one hand. "Oh, hell. God." She gripped the wheel tighter. "But since we're both up, would you mind if I used your bathroom?"

Cade opened his mouth and then closed it. He looked as if he was going to say something, and she hoped like hell it wasn't no. She really had to go now.

"Please?" she said.

He shook his head. "Of course. I just . . ."

Abigail unzipped the sleeping bag, cursing her pink pajamas covered with white sheep. Why hadn't she chosen sweats to sleep in? "Thank you." She almost tripped getting out of the truck. He reached to help, but she flinched away. She was fine.

He followed her into the house. Was he laughing at her pajamas behind her? Snickering at her fluffy slippers on the gravel? She wouldn't blame him.

After she was done, she found him leaning against the kitchen counter. Watching her.

"You can sleep upstairs." His words were slow and deliberate.

Abigail realized that she had no idea who this guy was, or what he was capable of. She had trusted Eliza not to put her in danger.

But she couldn't be sure of anything now, could she?

"You don't want me here."

"You're right. I don't. But making you sleep sitting up in your car isn't right, no matter what way I try to look at it. You can stay until you get the water on in the cottage."

Abigail struggled to consider it rationally. She didn't want to stay here. With a man that she didn't know. Men weren't to be trusted.

But this was Eliza's nephew. If she could trust anyone, wouldn't it be him? Eliza loved her, and wouldn't place her in a dangerous situation, right?

She was just so tired. A bed sounded good. No, it sounded wonderful. She could almost taste the feeling of lying down, prone, in a place with no bats. Eliza would want her to do this, to be brave.

"All right. I accept."

He nodded and looked at the floor.

"There was a bat," said Abigail.

"In the cottage?"

"That's why I was in the truck. I couldn't stand to have it flapping above me."

He nodded. "Makes sense."

She struggled to appear casual. "I'm starving. Is there a grocery store nearby?"

"You going out in your pajamas?" He looked as if he were trying not to smirk.

"I could change. I just realized how hungry I am."

"It's after ten."

"Okay?"

He spoke slowly, as if she were a child. "There is a grocery store in Cypress Hollow, five miles away. It isn't open, because it's late."

"It's only ten."

"The sidewalks roll up around seven, you'll find. It's not really a party town. I hope that'll be all right with you, princess."

"Not looking for a party, cowboy. Just looking for food, but I guess that can wait until tomorrow."

She spun on her heel as gracefully as she could in her slippers, but she realized she didn't know where in the house she was going, where she was supposed to sleep.

"I have a little food."

She waited.

"You could have some."

"I don't want to put you out any more than I already have."

"I won't be able to finish it anyway. You might as well have some."

She would have laughed at his grudging tone, had it been a light moment in any way at all, but his words fell with thuds in the night air.

"Okay. Yes. Thank you. I had breakfast in Santa Barbara when I passed through this morning, but that was a really long time ago. I didn't realize how far north this was, or how long it would take on the coast road."

He opened the refrigerator and leaned in.

"Funny, I thought they still had fast food on the way here. All those joints close up?"

Okay, he was still going to be a smart-ass. That was all right. Smart-ass she could deal with.

"Sure. Like at every exit. But I was too excited to pull over, except for gas. And I hopped on the Pacific Coast Highway for the last few hours, from Morro Bay up. The fast-food options really are pretty limited out there. But the view isn't. It was the most gorgeous drive . . ."

"Well, you've certainly had a good day. A great drive, an inheritance that stripped a man of his home and birthright, and now that same man is fixing something for you to eat. Enchiladas, to be exact."

Abigail had just sat down in the wicker rocker in the corner of the kitchen. But she stood up. So much for this idea.

"I didn't know about all this. Eliza didn't tell me. And I don't need dinner."

"Oh, hell, I'm already reheating it."

Abigail waited a beat before saying, "I'll accept your enchilada, because I think I might die without eating."

Cade hit the microwave buttons until it made a low hum and then turned to look at her.

She returned his gaze.

Neither said anything for a moment. The air in the kitchen filled with the scent of chilies, and something thicker that Abigail didn't want to name.

She held his gaze. And her breath.

"Damn it, I believe you," Cade finally said as the microwave beeped. He took out the food, turned it, and put it back in.

"It's the truth. I never even knew exactly where you lived. I'd heard about you, of course, and I knew you had sheep, and I also knew that Eliza went to see you a couple of times a year, but I didn't know that you lived here, on her land. Honest to God."

"I said, I believe you." He removed the food, grabbed a fork out of a drawer and handed it to her.

"Aren't you eating?"

"I ate at six. Like normal people."

"I was pretty freaked out."

"Yeah? Join the club."

She took a bite. "Oh, wow. This is great." She was ravenous. "Something, there's something in here . . ."

"Chipotle peppers."

"That's it. I'm impressed." Abigail smiled at him.

But he frowned. "Don't be. And tomorrow, if you go left at the gate, five miles down Highway One to Cypress Hollow, go right on Main, there's a grocery store. Stock up. I won't be feeding you anymore. Your room is up the stairs, first door on the left."

And with that, he walked out of the room.

Abigail sighed and took another bite. She could do this. She was brave. She was safe here.

Maybe if she just kept telling herself that, she'd start to believe it.

Chapter Six

*Join the stitches at the cuff in the round. Make sure you
haven't twisted them; that only ends in tears and someone's dinner burning.*

—E.C.

ade had already finished the morning chores with Tom by
the time he saw Abigail moving around the kitchen through
the window. Almost nine in the morning. Cade couldn't remember the last time he'd slept till nine. It might have been five or
six years ago, when he was dating that one girl, oh, what had her
name been? Susie? Margie? Whoever she was, she'd bet him fifty
bucks that he couldn't stay in bed past nine in the morning. Like a
moron, he'd taken the bet, arranging for Tom to do all the impera-
tive chores. He could do it. He'd prove her wrong.

Then he'd stayed in bed with her—the girl, whatever her name
had been, climbing all over him, doing crazy things to him with
her hands, her mouth, doing everything within her power to distract him, to bring his mind back into bed, but he hadn't been able
to stay focused.

He'd stayed in bed until eight, and then he got up, handed her fifty dollars, and was in the barn before she left. He never saw her again.

He strode toward the house through the thin, warm fall light. This was the best time of year—the slight scent of wood smoke mixed with the smell of his neighbors' burning leaves. The air was cool but not yet cold. It would be cold soon, though, he would bet. Just in time for his ewes to start lambing. He preferred to lamb in late November, to make the most of the Easter rush. Children from all over the county got their 4-H lambs from him. His sheep were known for being both attractively built and strong.

High white clouds skittered, their color matching the sheep that ambled below.

Outside. This was his.

He took a deep breath and rested his open palm on the back kitchen door. He'd found this door in a salvage yard in Half Moon Bay. He'd spent two days sanding and varnishing it.

He'd rather stay outside—hell, he'd rather *live* outside than have this next conversation, but they had to talk. He pushed open the door.

"Good morning," Abigail said, sounding careful.

Good. She needed to be careful.

"You found the coffee. When you replace it, I like Ethiopian fair-trade blends. There's a market on Main that sells it by the pound."

"Of course." She nodded and sat at the table. At his table. He'd won that silver-and-red Formica table in a card game the night Lloyd Seelers drank too much Knob Creek and lost everything in his kitchen.

Cade rummaged in a drawer near the sink. "Here." He tossed a coaster at her, but she missed it and it landed on the floor.

Served her right.

She leaned over and picked it up.

"This is nice." She turned it over. "Beautifully crafted."

"Walnut," said Cade. "From a tree that died three years ago."

"You made these?"

He nodded.

She slid the coaster under her coffee mug.

He poured himself a cup, hoping she'd made it strong enough.

"We need to talk," he said.

"Okay. I want to have a few more sips of this, though. I'm not awake yet. What time do you get up, anyway?"

"Four thirty."

"In the *morning*?"

"So the clock tells me."

"By choice?"

"Things need doing in the morning."

"But you have sheep, not cows. I thought cows were the early-morning chore."

"Know a lot about ranching, huh?"

"Not much, apparently."

He took a swallow of his coffee, expecting flavored water and finding instead a decent cup of strong coffee. Huh.

Nor had he expected how sexy she would look in the morning. He was grateful that she had dressed, hadn't wandered downstairs in those silly pink sheep pajamas.

He wondered if she always wore pajamas to bed. Or did she change it up? A camisole? Or a tee shirt?

Or nothing?

He took another sip.

She was wearing a red tee shirt and a soft pink sweater over blue jeans, and she looked young and freshly scrubbed. He could smell a light flowery soap scent in the kitchen along with the coffee.

"Good coffee," he said. He might as well give her that.

"I'm glad you like it!" Her voice was eager, and he could see her trying to rein herself back in. "I mean, um, most people say I make it too strong. I'm glad."

"We need to talk about how to do this."

"I know." She put her hands to her forehead and then back down in her lap. "Eliza really didn't tell me about any of this, you know."

"I told you last night that I believed you. But that doesn't make it any easier, does it, that I'm losing my land?

"Only part of your land, and I told you . . ."

"Let's not go back to that."

"I'm only borrowing that room upstairs temporarily. Very temporarily. I'll fix that cottage up in two shakes of a, well, a lamb's tail?" She grinned. "Get it?"

Cade stared at her.

Her eyebrows drew together. "What, you think I should bow out?"

"It's crossed my mind."

"Legally, I'm kind of stuck here."

"Not a bad place to be stuck, wouldn't you agree?"

"I just inherited something from someone I loved. Something big and unexpected. There's a huge part of me that's mourning for Eliza, and there's a part of me that's flipping out, thrilled that I have a home now."

He opened his mouth to stop her, but she jumped in. *Pushy*, he thought.

"I don't mean your home, I just mean a home. Any home. I've never really had that, and I could make something here."

"Here is mine. This is *my* space."

"Gah! Listen to me. Put yourself in my shoes," she said. "I feel like an ass, but I don't have much choice, because I needed to leave where I was. I needed a new home anyway."

"You seriously want the cottage."

"Yes."

"I don't think you understand what you're in for."

"I don't need a big house. The cottage will be perfect. Someday. I only need a space for me, my desk, and my fiber."

"Fiber?"

"Fiber. Wool. Those sheep running around out there? I spin my own yarn, and dye it, and then I knit it up into sweaters, like this one," she tugged at the hem of her pink sweater. "And then I write patterns and sell them in books."

"Same as Aunt Eliza."

"She taught me everything I know."

"Huh." Cade couldn't picture his great-aunt without sticks and string in her hands—she had always been knitting. And wanting to talk about it.

He'd always been too busy to really listen.

Even when he'd moved onto the property, when he had first tried to help her run the ranch, she had always been trying to talk to him about the crimp and health of the sheep's wool. She wanted to dress them up in sweaters of their own, to keep the ends of the wool safe from sun damage.

He'd laughed at her and talked about the price of meat.

Cade took care of her when she got sick. The breast cancer knocked Eliza down, hard. He'd never seen her like that: weak and in pain. Cade ran the ranch when he wasn't inside nursing her. He became fluent in doctor-speak and learned to make weak broth while still mostly asleep. Eliza recovered well, but when the cancer came back a second time a few years later, when he was twenty-seven, she made the decision to move south.

He'd asked why. He'd been more hurt than he'd allowed himself to let on.

Eliza had said, "The only thing that kept me on this land was Joshua. And then you. But I want to live in sight of the sea."

"Move west five miles, then. At least I'd be close. If you needed me."

"There's a retirement village there. I have friends."

"More of the knitters?"

"It's knitting heaven, they tell me. There's a yarn shop in the middle of the place, and they know me there already. They all want me."

By the letters she'd sent him, she'd been right to go. The nurses had been close by, but she'd been autonomous. She became the queen bee of her social circle, pulling in the younger knitters, too, if Abigail was anything to judge by.

He'd missed Eliza every single day, but he'd never gone to visit her. He kept telling himself he would, that he'd take the time and go. Eliza came up to see him at least twice a year, and it had been too easy to let her do that, to rely on her visits. It hadn't been anything but procrastination that kept him from driving south.

He wouldn't forgive himself for that now.

No one had ever loved him as much as she had.

He turned to face the sink so Abigail wouldn't see his eyes.

But Eliza had done this. Cade brought himself back to the present moment. He cleared his throat.

A silence, thick and heavy. Cade didn't quite know what to say next. He was nervous, a feeling he almost didn't recognize.

And he was still mad.

That's right. Focus.

"We need to talk about how to share this house," he said as he turned. "You have the room you're staying in. I have my room. What I propose is this: I have the run of the downstairs living space until eight A.M. After that, I'll be out on the ranch somewhere. You have the whole house all day until five P.M. I'll then come in and make myself dinner, since we learned last night that I eat much earlier than you do. I'll be cleaned up and out by six thirty, at which point I'll have the parlor to myself while you cook for yourself. I'll be out of the parlor by eight thirty, and then it'll be yours, for watching TV or whatever it is you need to do. Laundry is in the back room off the porch, available any time, first come first serve."

She looked up at him. "Sounds complicated."

"But necessary."

She inclined her head a bit. "Do you have our bathing times defined?"

Crap, he hadn't thought about that. "When you want to do that? You can pick."

"I was joking."

Damn it. "This is serious. You use the downstairs bathroom, and I'll use the upper."

"Fine."

Was that a smile she was hiding? This was no laughing matter to him.

"This is the only way I can manage this situation." He didn't like how hoarse he sounded.

"I'm sorry. I don't mean to joke. It's just so rigid. I can almost picture you drawing lines down the rooms in white chalk, to keep me in the right place."

He'd thought of it. He was glad he hadn't suggested it.

"So. Well, then, so that's worked out. I thought we might divide the refrigerator, but that might be difficult."

"Maybe a kitty?"

"I have a cat. You leave Duncan alone. He's not part of the house-sharing. I told you, this is serious."

"Not that kind of kitty. We used to do it in college. Put an envelope on the fridge, and we each kick in the same amount each week, and make a list, and one of us shops, and we both cook our own things. But that way we don't end up with two separate jars of mayo and two dozen eggs going bad."

"I have chickens."

She smiled, a big grin. "I like fresh eggs. But I only meant that we can share." She paused and then said, "How long will it take me to fix up the cottage, do you think?"

"Honestly? I'd be surprised if you got it done in a month. That's with professional help."

"Can I stay here that long?" Her voice was clear, but he detected a fragility underneath.

"I suppose so." It was the best he could manage.

"We can handle this." She smiled again, but he couldn't smile back at her.

"Well, if we do it that way, with the money on the fridge, then you can help yourself to whatever's in there. I think there's bread in the freezer, if you want toast."

"I already made oatmeal, earlier, actually, but thank you."

"Without asking?"

"We just discussed that. We just worked it out."

"But you took the oatmeal before we talked about it."

"I was going to replace it. I still will. Are we really arguing about oatmeal here?"

"What?"

"You're still angry."

"Damn it!" he said, and she jumped again. She was like a spooked horse. What was her problem?

Then he sighed. He had to do better than this. "I'm sorry. This is a bad situation. Well, it's bad for me."

"It may be better for me, but only marginally. Do you have any other rules for me? Any Bluebeard rooms I need to stay out of?"

She was closer to him now, and the scent of her skin was intoxicating. It made him even more nervous than he already was. He noticed again that she smelled sweet and light and somehow like flowers, but not overpoweringly so.

He shook his head and kept his mouth shut.

She washed her bowl and spoon and cup, and moved to place them in the drainer.

Cade was in her way, leaning with his back against the counter. He knew it and he didn't move.

"Do you mind? Or should I dry them by hand and put them away so you can pretend I'm really not here?"

He didn't move, couldn't. He just looked at her.

She reached behind him to put the glass in the dish drainer.

Without thinking, he put his hand on her wrist, the one not holding the glass. Her skin was as soft as it looked and surprisingly warm.

Abigail gasped and jumped away.

"I'm sorry," he said. What had he been thinking?

"No, I'm sorry, I was crowding you. Damn it, just the thing I'm trying not to do." She attempted a smile, but Cade could tell it wasn't easy for her. "I like your schedule idea. I'll stay out of your way."

"Maybe it is a little extreme."

What was he saying? He didn't want her here.

"No, I think it's good. I'll go shower, and then, let's see," her hand fluttered up to her hair and back down again. "It's only nine thirty, so I think that's my time in the house, but I'm happy to be up in my room."

He should correct her choice of words. Her room.

He could let that go, right?

"No, I'm out of here. I'm going to go up to the north end and check a fence line."

She nodded again, at him, and left the room silently.

Cade took a deep breath and leaned against the sink, looking out the window at the cottage. This was going to be something, all right. He just didn't know what.

Chapter Seven

Knit a sleeve as long as you want, not to the specifications of any silly pattern, even one of mine. If you always roll your sleeves, knit a sleeve four inches shorter. Remember, there are no sleeve police.

—E.C.

Abigail was getting good at acting like she was strong.

She wasn't sure how her bravado held up under his gaze. Those clear, green eyes seemed to look inside her and see way too much. Maybe he wasn't buying her strength act. But she was going to try to keep selling it to him. Besides, she was sick of being scared.

First things first. She told herself her temporary room was going to be fine. She could write for a while sitting in bed with her laptop, but to really think, she needed to spread out. The tiny desk would only work for so long.

It would be hard, leaving her fiber in their plastic bins, but she supposed she could just wait until she was in the cottage. Once her work space was organized, her yarn and fiber up on the shelves in plain view, she'd feel like herself.

Wouldn't she?

The bedroom Cade had given her was small but sweet. A narrow twin bed was covered in a green knitted afghan. The sheets smelled a little musty, but looked clean. She'd wash them later today. Last night, she hadn't felt like looking for the washer and dryer, hadn't felt like putting herself again in Cade's path.

She quickly repositioned the furniture in the room, moving the bed so that it was under the window. She wanted to look up at the sky at night. She moved the small writing desk to the other window on the far wall, so when she was writing she'd be able to look out at the trees and sheep.

She tugged at the afghan, squaring it up on the bed. She recognized Eliza's hand in the pattern of it. She felt silly for doing it, but she leaned down and sniffed. There it was, the slightest scent of the lavender-lanolin hand lotion that Eliza always wore—the smell permanently embedded in the fibers. Abigail felt buoyed.

The house was too deep into the hills to have a view of the ocean, but she could feel the sea. While she unpacked her few belongings, moving clothes into the old dresser, she moved back and forth, to the window and away, taking it all in.

She also kept an eye out for Cade.

Oh, there were too many questions, and each one problematic. Each question would require a conversation with Cade, and she planned on avoiding him as much as possible.

She looked again out the window.

Abigail could barely believe that she wouldn't see her ex-boyfriend Samuel's black SUV idling on a nearby corner under a streetlight, that she wouldn't see his face turned in the direction of her window. She was used to the fear, and had even become good at marshalling it, corralling the trepidation.

But there was nothing out there but the slow dust trailing down the main road where an old beat-up truck had just been. A squirrel raced out from under an oak tree and then did a U-turn and raced back the way it had come.

It wasn't even lunchtime on her first real day, and she wanted, what? Not out, surely, but she didn't want this, this familiar feeling of being cooped up. She was done being kept inside.

She walked resolutely to the door and outside, across the yard back to the cottage. She unlocked the door, hoping that she wouldn't be interrupted this time. She wasn't done with this cottage yet.

A new beginning.

She would start the clean-out today. The faster it was done, the faster she was out of Cade's house, and away from that strange tension.

The box on top of the first pile. That's where she would start. She pulled up a piece of the yellowed newspaper. Was there anything else in there?

Her hand hit a piece of wood. And then another one.

Abigail pulled one out.

It couldn't be. It looked like . . .

It was.

Abigail held up the flyer for a spinning wheel. A gorgeous, dark, wooden flyer that looked antique, or was a very good replica.

She went in the box farther. More flyers.

She carried the box out onto the porch into the sun and brought out the next box.

Bobbins. Scads of them. Made of matching wood.

Abigail smiled.

She opened boxes on the porch until she had found all the various pieces that she needed.

Then she ran to her truck and pulled out her small toolbox. Cade would mock it mercilessly, she was sure, for being small and useless, but she knew it held what she needed.

Less than thirty minutes later, she had a fully assembled spinning wheel in front of her.

It was like a strange, good dream.

And it was beautiful. The wheel itself was hand carved and decorated with carved flowers and vines. The treadle had the same design, and Abigail could hardly imagine putting a foot on such an intricate thing.

All the pieces were there.

And she had a feeling.

Abigail went back in the house and went farther into the front room, over near the stairs. She lifted boxes and shook them, until she found the right heft, the weight she was looking for.

She carried this box out onto the porch and opened it, not surprised to see the newspaper on top. Underneath, wrapped in muslin and smelling of cedar, was a carded batt of wool, a deep heathered green, beautifully prepared, ready for spinning.

"I knew it. You crafty thing, Eliza. You're guaranteeing I don't go anywhere, huh?" Abigail laughed out loud.

She pulled off a hank of the wool, attached a leader to the flyer, and sat on the dusty red chair on the porch. She started spinning. Oh, this was joy. This was right. This was what Eliza had taught her: this was what Eliza had found in Abigail's fingers—this ability to draw the fiber out into just the right kind of yarn.

She stopped and went back into the house. It only took a few minutes of peering into the boxes to realize there were probably a hundred wheels, and hundreds of pounds of wool.

"It's my store, my classroom, my tools," she whispered. Tears came to her eyes. "My dream. Oh, Eliza."

Chapter Eight

*If you don't like how your knitting is going, change it.
Never be a slave to a pattern, especially one of mine.
Make the pattern conform to your will, or burn it cheer-
fully in the grate and write a new one, a better one.*
—E.C.

What was she doing to him? He was behind in a ton of office work, and he had some females that hadn't been acting right. He had to get down to their paddock this morning and try to figure out if they were sick or not. He didn't want to call the vet. He was doing okay financially, but that was because he cut corners, didn't waste anything.

The opposite of how Eliza had been, Eliza who wouldn't kill an animal even if it was making the others sick. That is, when she'd noticed they were sick at all.

The office. He hadn't seen Tom this morning, but he was probably in by now, too. Cade's band of sheep was a good size and required both of them, working hard, all the time.

The smell of coffee greeted him when he opened the door at the back of the barn.

"Tom?"

"Hey, boss. Have a coffee. On the house."

"Generous of you. Your coffee's crap."

"You'll drink it anyway."

"True."

Tom grabbed Cade's cup from the top of a filing cabinet and filled it. "Fix what ails you."

"My coffee would. Yours burns my tongue."

"Don't drink it then."

"You seen the ewes in the third paddock?" Cade asked.

"They look better today. I've been keeping an eye on them. I really think that it was just a cold. They all seem fine, except for that older girl we looked at yesterday. I brought her in."

"Thanks."

"Yup."

Cade didn't know what he'd do without Tom. Of course, he'd never tell him that, not outright. If he did, if he had ever expressed how grateful he was to Tom, Tom would have laughed his ass off. They didn't talk like that. Didn't work that way.

But they didn't have to.

"So the girl's in."

"She is."

"What did Eliza actually leave her?"

"The cottage."

"You got the land it's on?"

"She got that too."

Tom whistled. "Hot damn. You got screwed."

"Yep. It's punishment, I think. For that fight we had."

"About how you date too much?"

"It wasn't the dating she minded."

"What did she call it again? Catting around?" Tom grinned.

"I don't cat around. That was crap."

"If you say so. So that girl over at the house, what's her name?"

"Abigail Durant."

"Sounds fancy."

"City girl."

"I saw the truck. Silly little thing."

Cade nodded. "That's what I said! She didn't like it much."

Tom sat in the brown fabric armchair that had seen perhaps a little too much use and kicked up his feet on the desk.

"She's pretty, though," said Tom. "If I can trust what I saw at a distance this morning."

"Not my type."

"Since when is pretty not your type?"

"Since pretty moved into my house," said Cade.

"I can see the problem."

"Yeah."

"She didn't move into *my* house," Tom said with a lecherous grin.

"You stay out of it. Do not flirt with her. You're too old. I'll have to shoot you to put you out of your misery."

"I'm only four years older than you. Jealous? You know she'd want me."

"You'd have to shower more than twice a year, probably."

"With the water shortage and global warming? Not a chance. She'd have to take me as I am."

"Forget it. No, she's going to stay in the house with me until the cottage is fixed up and livable."

"You better get to work on the cottage then, boy."

"Not my job, it's hers," said Cade.

"You have any idea what's in all those boxes yet?"

"Old newspapers."

"I smell a bonfire in our future."

The thought of it cheered Cade a little. "A big bonfire," he agreed. "With food."

"And whiskey." Tom leaned back in the chair and nodded. Then he said, "What I don't get is why it's happening like this. Eliza worshipped you. This doesn't sound like her. Are we sure that gal isn't playing you? Are we sure she really knew Eliza?"

"I wondered that, originally, but I remember Aunt Eliza talking about an Abigail that was helping take care of her, who knitted with her. I guess I assumed that Abigail was about ninety and toothless. I never figured she'd have a young friend like that, even though if anyone would, it would be Eliza."

"She was something."

Cade nodded. "She always had that knitting in her hands, always with the spinning wheel somewhere nearby."

"Or that thing, what did she call it? The dropping thing?"

"Her drop spindle." Cade raised his pant leg to display blue-green socks sticking up over his boot top. "These are the warmest, softest socks I ever had. I saw her spinning the yarn for it on that spindle while she read a knitting magazine and cooked chili all at the same time." Cade picked up a pencil and put it down again. "We never got into that whole yarn thing. That's why she left, I think. To get closer to the knitters."

"But we raised her sheep."

"I know, and she got first pick of the fleece before we sold the rest."

Tom said, "She was crazy about the fleece."

"Even though it sold for just about nothing." Cade paused. "But she took me in when I wanted to make a real go of it. She let me figure out my ass from my elbow." He cleared his throat. "She believed in me."

"So did I," said Tom. "Don't I get a medal for it, too?"

"You get a kick in the ass."

"You gonna buy the property back from her?"

Cade tapped the bottom of the rusty filing cabinet with his boot. "I was in here until midnight last night, going over and over it. With what the land is worth now, I couldn't ever afford to make an offer. Not that she'd accept it anyway."

He sucked back the rest of the bitter coffee and took his hat off the rack. "Aren't we going up to work on the north fence today?"

"If you say so, boss."

"I hate it when you call me that."

"That's why I do it," said Tom.

Chapter Nine

When the sleeve measures the right length, put it aside and cast on immediately for the second. Don't move from that spot; don't even get another glass of wine before you do. Trust me on this one.

—E.C.

An hour later—three other wheels set up on the porch, fiber all around her—Abigail heard her cell phone ring. She reached in her pocket.

"Hello?"

"Are you here?"

"I am."

"*Finally.* I can't believe you moved fifteen miles away from me. Meet me for lunch." Her best friend and ex-boss, Janet, never wasted time.

"I don't know, I'm kind of in the middle of something."

"No, you're not. Nothing that can't wait a bit longer. Twenty minutes, drive into town, left on Main, Bramblewood Cafe will be on the right."

Thirty minutes later, still picking bits of fluff out of her hair, Abigail walked into the restaurant.

"Darling! You're here! I can't believe it. Sit here, I've already ordered for both of us."

Janet *always* ordered for both of them. Abigail had long since stopped minding, since Janet always ordered her something good, often something she wouldn't have ordered otherwise.

"No, Abigail, I really mean it. I can't believe you actually moved here, to my neck of the woods. God knows I'm only an hour and a half away from San Francisco, but still. No one ever comes to see me, let alone moves to be near me."

"Did it all for you."

"You lie. But you're sweet. And it's going to be so easy to boss you around now."

Abigail laughed. "I don't think you've ever really had any problem doing that, have you? Besides, now that I don't work for you, you can't."

"I will, too! And you should still write a little pattern up for me when you can. My customers would love it . . . And you know I'm good at bossing everyone. Ask that terrified waiter over by the door. I only wanted more lemon but I think he thought I was going to eat him."

Janet was extremely tall and even more striking. She had jet-black hair with one carefully styled white stripe, and she favored clothing with jet buttons and long tassels. She still wore hats in a 1940s way to match her purse and shoes. While her style was dated, she made it work in a way that the twenty-somethings scouring the vintage stores couldn't. She was near fifty, but no one knew how near. She was loud and sometimes merciless and, underneath it all, very kind. Abigail adored her in a way she didn't adore her friends closer to her own age. They were compatriots, whereas Janet was more than that; she had already walked through the fire and now laughed at the heat.

"When I met you, I thought you were going to eat *me*."

"Darling, I would have. I just wanted to gobble you up. You, knitting so seriously, before anyone else was. At least you knew good cashmere." Janet trailed a gloved hand in the air as she laughed.

"That's because you imported the best."

"But I only imported clothing until you asked me for yarn. I thought you were insane, to pay that much for clothing that didn't even exist! That you had to make yourself!"

"It was worth it though. You've made a fortune, selling my patterns and the yarns to the knitters."

"Yes, of course, but I didn't know that was coming. You were ahead of your time, designing those cute clothes, the sweaters that people actually wanted to wear, sexy little knitted camisoles and sassy hats, things that people wouldn't hide in the back of their closets. You came along and took the knitting world by storm."

"It's a small world."

"Not anymore, it isn't, and you're the queen of them all."

"Eliza was the queen. I'm only a courtier still."

Janet's face softened. "I'm so sorry. I barely got to see you at the funeral."

"It was a busy day." Abigail traced the pattern on the handle of her knife with the tip of her finger.

"And now you're living in Eliza's old home. How is it? Are you all right?"

The waiter, looking rather cowed, set elaborate salads in front of them. Janet looked at them, opened her mouth as if to speak, then nodded. The waiter's look of relief was obvious.

"Blue cheese. Best dressing here."

"Fine." Abigail took a bite.

Janet had moved to the central coast after a nasty divorce that occurred in the higher echelons of the fashion industry. Her husband ended up getting the Rodeo Drive storefront she had sold many bolts of cloth and skeins of luxury fiber to buy, and the divorce had been difficult emotionally and financially. Janet moved and started her own online business, something that made her more money now than the store ever had. People whispered that she was a self-made millionaire, but Abigail loved best that the sadness had left Janet's face.

"You've been here for how long now?"

Janet sighed. "Five years."

"That long! It feels like a minute ago."

"I know. And Bill still thinks I won't make it. You know, he was begging to use my name in a new deal he was trying to set up. Obviously, I said no. He sent a note, saying he couldn't believe I'd forget him like I apparently have." She giggled. "I sent a card back asking him to clarify where I knew him from."

"I love it. And are you seeing anyone?"

"Oh, sweetie. I see people all the time. No one special. There's one man, Richard, but he's too recently divorced to have sex without crying, and it's getting tiresome. What about you, though? Whatever happened to that one? Teddy, was it?"

Abigail laughed. "Teddy. He suited his name; he was a doll. But he was in love with me."

"Nothing wrong with that."

Abigail reached into her purse and pulled out her knitting.

"What do you have? Anything good?" Janet peered greedily.

"Just a sleeve." Abigail waved the two circulars in the air. "And no, there wasn't anything wrong with him being in love, if I'd been in love back. But I wasn't. I really, really tried, though. He was perfect for me." Abigail shrugged. "I don't think I'm the falling-in-love type."

Janet reached out to feel the russet yarn. "Yum. Tell me?"

"My own handspun merino."

"And it's going to be . . ."

"You never give up. It's going to be a man's sweater."

"For a new book? Or is this personal? Or better yet, for me?"

"Come on. I don't have a man to knit for. I'll write the pattern up if I like it."

Janet pointed her salad fork at Abigail. "Good. Keep knitting. And don't give me that crap. Of course you're the falling-in-love type. Everyone is, when we get right down to it. What about Jim? Now, that was love."

"You're right. That was. I was down for the count on that one. Only came up to find my bank account empty and my computer gone, with the only copy of my manuscript on it."

Janet groaned. "God, I'd forgotten. That was horrifying."

"It sure was stupid, huh? But you fixed it for me."

"I wish you could have seen the look on Jim's face when he opened the door to find me and Mafia Tony on the doorstep."

"Your *driver* does look like a mob boss."

"He loves playing the part when I need him to. Jim positively gibbered as he ran to get the computer. Sobbed as he handed it over."

Abigail grimaced and checked to make sure her seed stitch was still lined up correctly. "Never saw so much porn in my life as when I opened it up. I put the book on a disc and then wiped the hard drive. I had to take a shower afterward. So much for love. But at least now I back up my work."

"And that other one? Oh, I can't think of his name."

Abigail gripped the needles tighter than she needed to. "There wasn't anyone else."

"Yes, there was. That dark-haired guy you told me about, that you met at ABA. Remember? Asked for your number and you actually gave it to him."

Abigail yanked one of the circular needles too hard, and a dozen stitches slipped off the needle. "Shit."

"What happened?"

"Nothing."

"I know something happened. Tell me." Janet leaned forward again. "I can send Tony to San Diego in a heartbeat."

"I didn't want to tell you."

"Did he hurt you?" Janet bristled like a threatened cat.

"I didn't give him the chance."

"That's my girl."

Abigail leaned her head back and stared up at the multiple broad-bladed ceiling fans. They all moved at the same relaxed pace, the opposite of what her mind was doing. She wasn't going to talk about it to anyone. But Janet was different.

"He was at ABA because his sister wrote some animal book. I thought that was cool, that he was supporting her like that. He called and asked me out, and I met him at his company's boat at the marina. It was a perfectly romantic first date."

Janet nodded.

"He got weird at the end of the night. Insisted that he see me the next day. But I had plans and told him no. He didn't like it."

"Creepy. Go on."

Abigail finally got the last errant stitch back onto the left needle. She didn't have to look at her work to knit, but she kept her eyes down as she went on.

"Turns out he followed me home that night. Kinda went downhill from there."

"You should have told me."

"I was embarrassed."

"Did he try anything?"

"Only once, but I handled it." Abigail felt strong as she said it, but her voice wobbled at the end, and she was horrified to feel her eyes filling with tears.

Janet was up and out of her seat before Abigail knew what was happening. Then she was wrapped in Janet's perfumed arms. "I'm so sorry."

Janet kissed Abigail's forehead. Other restaurant customers watched in interest. "So it's over?"

"I'm here, aren't I?"

"Did you press charges?"

"Oh, yeah. He has a warrant out now, and he hasn't been seen since, not even at his job. They think he fled the state. That and the fact he has no idea where I am make me feel better about it all."

Abigail smiled at her. She wouldn't worry Janet anymore. "I'm safe now. And all that, to say no, I have not found love."

"You'll find it, my darling. Look at me! I'm all wrinkled up and I find it all the time!"

"Is that what the kids are calling it these days?"

Janet laughed. "Oh, I'm glad you're here! Was it hard to leave?"

"No, you know I hated that apartment. So close to the freeway, so loud. I got rid of everything, put it all up on Craigslist. Had a virtual garage sale. I only brought what I love. Didn't take up much space, actually. I feel freer than I have in a long time."

"I knew Eliza's old place was out here somewhere, but I never thought that anything would happen like this. How are you doing? Are you overwhelmed? What did she leave you, exactly?"

"Her cottage. And the land it's on. And everything in it."

"Wow! I knew she loved you, but damn. Is her nephew that gorgeous boy, the tall one who looks like every girl's fantasy walking?"

"Do you know him? Cade?"

"Cade, that's it. I know *of* him. A friend of mine dated him last year, until he broke it off."

"Really?"

"She was crushed. I remember hating him and then she pointed him out at a restaurant—he was there with another woman, and they'd been broken up for a month by this point, I thought he was a slice of heaven. Worth a broken heart, that one."

"How long did they date?" Abigail felt a keen interest that she decided not to examine.

"I think only a month or two." Janet leaned forward across the table. "She said the sex was amazing. But that doesn't surprise me. He looks like sex on a stick. Or on a horse. Or in the sticks. Whatever quaint phrase they use out here."

"These aren't really the sticks anymore, I don't think."

"They'll always be the sticks, darling. But they're *my* sticks. So anyway, the sex was amazing, and she said she was *tres* smitten, and she dreamed of a ring and wearing bandanas at the wedding. Then he pulled the hay out from under her, and she was left crying on my doorstep. Isn't that just the way?"

"I can see it. He's seems, rather . . . callous."

"Mmm. Do I sense a note of interest, my little one?"

"Absolutely not. The opposite, in fact. I don't like him at all. But I have to live with him for a while."

Janet waved away a water refill and leaned in again. "This just got good. What do you mean?"

"I got the cottage, but it has no water."

"How awful."

"And it might have rats."

Janet went pale. "Darlin, . ."

"It for damn sure has bats."

"Abigail! You can't live there."

"You're right, I can't live there until it's cleaned out and fixed up, and then it'll be just fine. Wonderful, even. But I have no idea how long that's going to take. In the meantime, I'm living in Cade's house."

"Tremendous." Janet clapped her hands. "Fantastic!"

"Do you think so?" Abigail paused and knit a few stitches. "I mean, Cade, he may be the local heartbreaker and all, but . . . "

She didn't need to put it into words. Janet said, her voice soft, "Cade is just a good old local boy who looks good in his jeans. He may break hearts, but he'd never hurt anyone. I've dated three of the local deputies: I'd know if he was a bad guy. And he's Eliza's nephew."

Abigail nodded. "That's what I thought. All right, change of subject. I've found something today, in the cottage."

"Tell. Ropes and chains?"

"It's a gigantic mess, totally crammed full of stuff that looked like trash. Boxes everywhere. But the boxes are full of fiber and spinning wheels. And who knows what all else is in there?"

Janet raised her eyebrows.

"Think about it!" said Abigail. "Eliza Carpenter's treasure trove. Do you know how many people in this country would freak *out* if they found out they could come to her home and use her things, take classes, perhaps?"

"They *are* passionate about her, yes."

"She's a religion. I think I could use this to jump-start my little workshop, my class space. I think that's what she meant me to do."

"So it's all yours?"

"Yes. I'm just not sure how Cade'll feel about having something like that on, or near, his land."

"Look at you, love. He'll give you anything you want."

"I don't think so. He thought he was going to get everything."

"He shouldn't have assumed."

"I would have, too. I feel kind of sorry for him."

Janet reached over and patted Abigail's cheek. "That's why I'm the businesswoman, darling, and you're the writer. Now, tell me when I can come see this little ranch."

Chapter Ten

While you cast on all those stitches for the body, have someone tell you a lively story. Even better, make them count the stitches for you.

—E.C.

bigail spent the next week settling into a routine. The house division was working: she rarely saw Cade, and if she did, it was only from a distance. He didn't seem to notice her at all. He didn't even glance in her direction if he passed through the kitchen while she was at the sink. He went to bed much earlier than she did, and she was surprised, when she sat in the parlor to read or knit, how companionable the house felt, knowing he was asleep upstairs. It felt more like home than any place she'd been since her mother died. And even if Cade couldn't stand her, his cat, Duncan, seemed to like her company, resting on her knee at night, purring up a storm.

She was taking her time going through the cottage. It was going to take a lot of work, but it wasn't as hopeless as she'd thought, now that she knew the bags and boxes weren't trash. A good cleaning was going a long way toward renovation. True, she'd need a new roof before winter settled in, and a couple of windows needed fixing, but the toilet was going to be fine if it was reseated, and the kitchen seemed to be okay.

She'd had an exterminator in about the bat. He fixed the hole in the wall where it had come in and promised her that he had taken care of the problem. She prayed he was right.

Abigail drove into Cypress Hollow to talk to a plumber about the toilet. She made an appointment with him, and he welcomed her with a warmth that seemed genuine. His wife invited her to a book group the library was starting. It felt good, this beginning.

Driving back to the house, Abigail passed a sign that said, "Alpacas. Going out of Business, All Must Go. Sweet Animals."

Alpacas.

The best, finest, softest fiber, one of her favorites to work with. Maybe they were selling fleeces.

She pulled over and drove through the open gate in the direction the arrow on the sign pointed.

An older man wearing overalls and a railroad cap waved at her.

"Want a couple of alpacas?"

She shook her head and smiled. "Only interested in the fiber. Have you sheared lately?"

"Eh, never got into all that, just sheared and threw it out. Supposed to make money on the babies, but it wasn't the money she thought she'd get." Abigail tried not to look horrified. He threw the fiber *out*?

He went on. "These were my wife's animals. She's dead now, and they gotta go. You can have 'em cheap."

"I have no place to put them."

The man looked at her closely, then looked out at her truck. "Ain't you the gal that moved in with Cade MacArthur up to Eliza's old spread?"

"Wow. The jungle drums are beating. Yes, I am."

"Cade has room. He told me once he loved the 'pacas, and he

wanted a couple. He has that extra room off the back of his little second barn, out at the cottage, that would be perfect for them."

He looked at her closely. "Make a nice gift for him, probably."

Abigail narrowed her eyes. Was she being taken? She *did* have that little shed thing out behind the cottage, but she hadn't really looked at it yet.

"If you take the male and female, I'll throw in the dog."

"The *dog*?" Abigail had wanted a dog for a while now, but was now the right time?

"That one over there." He pointed over to the porch. "I'm gonna have her put down if no one wants her, and no one does. Border collie, y'know. Best dog made."

"If she's the best, why don't you keep her?"

"Wife just died." His voice broke. "I'm outta here. Going to sail to Hawaii. Don't need a dog. But you'll need a dog with the alpacas."

"Really?"

"Well, maybe not. They're pretty good and quiet. I'll just have the dog put down, then."

Abigail felt her control of the conversation spiraling. She sighed. "Let me see the dog."

Chapter Eleven

*Don't take your knitting so seriously. It's supposed to be
fun, remember?*

—E.C.

Cade heard Abigail calling his name, and it sounded frantic.
Was she hurt? He left the barn at a run, down toward the
house.

"Cade! Help!"

Cade ran faster. Had she fallen? Did she have a medical condition
he didn't know about?

Where the hell was she?

He rounded the corner of the house, and saw her, over by her
truck, parked near the cottage. An old trailer was pulling out of the
driveway—was that Mort's truck dragging it?

He kept running, but slowed a little when he noticed that she appeared
to be smiling. Grinning, actually.

And what was next to her?

Good God. She hadn't.

"Alpacas! Look!"

"Are you *kidding* me?"

"No! They're the cutest things ever!"

"I thought you were hurt."

She had the good grace to look chagrined. "I'm sorry. I just thought the boy here was getting away, but Mort put him on a tighter lead and tied him to the fence."

"You got alpacas."

"You don't like them?" Her smile faded.

"I don't know much about them. I know enough to know I didn't want any on the property."

"But I'll keep them in my little barn. You won't even know they're here."

"What do you know about livestock?"

"Not very much. But Mort told me what I had to feed them, and he gave me some stuff to start off with, and he said they were gentle. And then I can shear my own alpacas."

"And do what?"

"Spin the fiber into yarn! It's the softest stuff. I'll make you socks."

He snorted before he could help himself. "Alpaca socks? I can't even imagine."

He heard something from her truck and turned to look at what was causing the bumping noise.

"You got a dog." She didn't do anything halfway, did she?

"Not just any dog. She's a border collie."

"And let me guess, you don't know much about border collies."

"You do? Can you tell me? She's the sweetest thing ever."

"And probably the smartest thing ever, too. I've got two of them that live in the barn and work the sheep. They're smart enough that I wouldn't leave out a can opener near a can of tuna."

"Mort said she was smart!"

"How did he talk you into all this?"

Abigail smiled and reached to pet the head of the female alpaca, but the animal shied away and moved away as far as she could on the leash.

"His wife died," she started.

"Three years ago," said Cade.

"What? He made it sound like it was yesterday. But he's sailing to Hawaii soon, so he had to get rid of the dog."

"He's no sailor. He just bought a new tractor. He's not going anywhere soon. And he's been trying to get rid of those beasts since Mary passed."

"He told me you wanted alpacas. That you would think they were nice."

He couldn't help laughing now. It was too funny: her earnest, excited face, Mort taking her for all she was worth. "A nice gift? I've been giving him a rash of shit ever since he let his wife buy them. They're always getting loose and running down the highway. She said she was going to raise and sell them, but he never saw a dime. And where are you going to keep the babies? You can't fit more than two out in the shed."

She glared at him. "I don't need baby alpacas, not yet, anyway. Two is enough to start with. Their fiber will keep me happy and busy. They're sweet and wonderful and I love them."

He was surprised she didn't stamp her foot after saying this.

"They have names?"

"Yes."

"Wanna tell me?"

"You'll laugh at me."

"Would I do that?"

"Yes, but I'll tell you anyway. Merino is the boy here, the darker one. Tussah is the pale girl. She's the sweet one, but they're both wonderful and I love them."

"Merino, like the sheep? And Tussah I'm guessing is something in your fiber world."

"A kind of silkworm."

"You named alpacas after a sheep and a worm?"

"You said you wouldn't laugh." She turned her back on him and moved to start untying the male from where he was attached to the fence.

"Where are you going to put him?"

"I told you, in my shed."

"You already set it up?"

"Mort said that they only need a little space and an overhang to get out of any weather that might come along."

"Have you checked that fence back there? I haven't used it in a long time."

She looked at the ground, her cheeks flushing. He couldn't tell if it was in anger or not, and he didn't like it. He was used to being able to read women at a glance. They didn't usually challenge him. This one, she was a challenge.

None that he couldn't handle though.

"I looked," she said. "I can't see any holes in the fence."

"Want me to look for you?"

Her eyebrows drew together and the smallest crease appeared between her eyes. It satisfied him. He'd gotten under her skin. Finally.

She didn't want to say yes. He knew it.

"Okay, I guess. If you want. But I think it's fine."

Cade smiled and went around the back of the small barn, leaving her to deal with the alpacas and the dog, which was now barking its head off inside the cab of the truck. He could hear his dogs barking in the barn in agreement.

God, this shed. When Eliza had lived here, she'd used it for chickens, although when Cade had taken over, he'd built a real coop farther down the hill. He didn't like to hear and smell chickens early in the morning—he preferred a little distance between him and the roosters crowing.

Not that they ever got up before him, come to think of it.

It was an adequate shed, though. Even though he'd been giving her crap about it, it was a fine little building to shelter two alpacas. Any more than three and they'd be pushing it, and he figured she'd have three before long, since there really wasn't a way to separate them in this tiny shed.

The fence line did look all right, he thought, testing several places with his hand, and then his boot. That was Tom's doing, not his. Cade stayed active and on top of all the areas they were working, but he tended to overlook places like this, places not in use.

Vanity pets. On his ranch. He supposed he was going to have to accept it, at least until she gave up and left, which hopefully would be sooner rather than later, but alpacas! On his land!

God. He'd look like a pyramid-scheme fool if anyone drove the top ridge road and looked down.

He came around the shed and met her back at the truck.

"Looks good," he said.

"Hmmph," she said, which sounded an awful lot like an I-told-you-so.

"Where are you going to keep their feed?"

"In the shed with them." She sounded uncertain, though.

"They'll get to it."

"Oh. Um. What about that shack over there?" Abigail pointed to the old shack a hundred yards away. It was still faintly purple from a paint job Eliza had him put on it when he was a teenager.

"No room. It's junk in there, just tools and stuff. And, by the way, that's my shack. Not yours."

"Big Rubbermaid containers? Would that work?"

He inclined his head. It would probably work. If she got *big* containers.

"So you're breeding them?"

It was a low blow, and he knew it. She already looked completely overwhelmed, holding a lead in either hand, glancing back over her shoulder at the increasingly frantic dog in the truck.

"No! At least not for a while."

"I give you until tomorrow."

"Oh, God, will they really?"

"Alpacas are induced ovulators."

"That doesn't sound good."

"Adults go into estrus during sex. Sex makes them receptive, actually fertile. Then you'll have a bouncing baby cria in about eleven months."

"From tomorrow."

"Tonight, if you're lucky."

"Mort kept them apart?"

"I never saw them together, let's put it that way."

"But I have no way to keep them apart."

"You could make money on a baby, pay for your . . ."

"My overenthusiasm. I know. I'm used to it, don't worry." She looked at him and brushed the heavy hair out of her face, her blue eyes lighter than he'd seen them before.

"Well, okay, then," said Cade lamely.

"Thank you. I'll put them away." She spun away, taking the male, Merino, with her, leaving the female tied to the fence, gazing after them.

They really were kind of cute, he figured, with those big eyes and fuzzy topknot.

Not that he would ever admit that out loud.

He had work to do.

Cade put his head down and walked away, refusing to look back to see how she did.

Chapter Twelve

The body of a sweater is the most delicious part. You can sink into it and feel the personality of the pattern and the yarn marrying in your talented hands.

—E.C.

Abigail got the animals inside the fenced shed area. They followed her willingly, and while they were both head-shy and didn't appear to want to be petted, they didn't seem afraid of her. They were much more unsettled by the sound of the dog's barking, and appeared to relax when they got around back, away from the truck.

Rather reluctantly, not knowing whether she'd ever get control of them again, Abigail took them off lead when they were inside the fenced enclosure.

"You're free!" She looked around. "Kinda."

She went back to the truck and smiled at the dog, who appeared to be chewing on the seat. "Hang on, I'll be right there," Abigail called to her.

Mort had set her up with everything she'd need, he said. He'd given her vitamin supplements ("free, I'm giving you these 'cause I

like you") and feed buckets. He'd filled the back of her truck with
hay, on the house, courtesy of his late wife. "Feed 'em the grass hay,
no alfalfa, that's too rich for 'em," he'd said.

She now stood back from the truck and looked at its bed with satisfaction. Not that she had any idea of the difference between grass
and alfalfa, or even if he was feeding her a line of bull, but it sure
felt good to be using her truck for something that wasn't moving a
couch, as Cade had put it.

She went to grab a bale and bring it to the critters, who had to be
hungry from their ordeal.

She pulled.

Damn. Apparently hay was heavy. She used her hands to pull
some apart from the top level. The stuff was coarse. She'd need
gloves.

She'd probably need a lot of things.

She did her best, leaving food in a low tray in the shed, and filling
the water buckets after making sure they were clean. She'd need a
book on alpacas. Or better yet, the internet would surely answer all
her questions.

Did they even *have* the internet out here? She hadn't opened her
computer once yet, and she realized that this was the longest she'd
gone without staring at a computer screen in years.

It wasn't a bad feeling.

She double-checked that everything looked okay with Merino and
Tussah, tried to touch them again—which they roundly rejected—
and went to deal with the dog.

The dog had seemed to love her on the drive over. They'd made
a fast friendship, the dog drooling and licking her face ecstatically
while she drove. Abigail knew it was good, this was right. Her new
best friend. A dog to keep her company while she tried to avoid Cade
as much as possible.

A dog to keep her safe. A dog that would bark and growl and bite
if she needed it to. Abigail remembered falling asleep some nights in

San Diego, hearing noises outside her apartment. She'd just lie there terrified, convinced it was Samuel out there, creeping around again, trying to peek in windows, but she'd been too afraid to even walk across the room to call the police, let alone look outside. She had wished for a dog then, a sturdy dog with a loud, frightening bark.

But now her new dog was freaking out, and Abigail knew she herself was not long to follow. Every time Abigail approached the side of the truck, the collie barked ferociously and threw herself at the window, snarling, baring her teeth.

"It's okay. Remember me? We were pals a few minutes ago. I swear."

Abigail put her hand on the passenger door handle and then jumped back two feet when the frothing mouth hit the glass, coming at her.

"No! Stop it!" This was definitely not the way it was supposed to be. The dog, whom she hadn't even named yet—Mort hadn't had a name for her—was supposed to love her, like she had on the drive over here.

The barking and thrashing intensified, and Abigail realized the dog was going to hurt herself.

"What's wrong with your dog?"

Startled, Abigail screamed and jumped, tripping over her own feet, landing on her backside in the dirt. God, she had to quit screaming every time he startled her.

"You scared me! What are you doing? I don't want your help."

"You don't want my help, I can see that." Cade had to yell over the din of the dog, who had now escalated to howling. "But you might need it."

Abigail stood and brushed herself off, turning to try to see if she was covered in dirt, hitting her jeans with her hay-scratched hands. Muttering to herself, she said, "I don't need any damn cowboy to help me, I can handle this myself, thank you very much."

While she was talking to herself under her breath, Cade went around to the driver's-side door, popped it open and released the dog.

"No!" yelled Abigail.

"Hi, baby. Oh, who's a good girl?"

The dog, traitorous thing, clambered all over Cade, trying to climb up him in her eagerness to lick his face. What had looked like vicious, rabid slaver turned out to be nothing more than eager slime. Abigail watched him kneel in the dirt as the dog hurled herself into his willing arms.

"Are you kidding me?"

"Were you really scared of this puppy? This cute little thing?" Cade rubbed the dog's head and scrunched her ears. "Who could be afraid of this, huh? Huh?"

He glanced briefly at Abigail, and then turned his full attention back to the dog.

"What's her name, anyway?"

"She doesn't have one yet."

"I think she's a Clara."

"No, she's not."

"Clarabelle. Clarabellerina." The dog danced in front of him and returned for more love. "Is that you? Is your name Clara?" The dog barked in happiness. "Yes," Cade said, rubbing it in. "Yes, I knew that."

"For Pete's sake. Give it up. Give me the dog." Abigail jerked the leash out of his hand and started to walk up the steps of the cottage. She was glad she'd moved the treasures she unpacked earlier back inside. Cade didn't need to know about her find just yet.

"Do you have food for her?" Cade asked.

Abigail's footing slipped a bit on the step. She clutched the stair rail. "Weak step," she snapped. "Of course I have food for her."

"And food and water bowls?"

She didn't say anything. She couldn't bear to admit that she hadn't thought that far ahead. Crap. She'd have to drive out again, and find a pet supply store. It was as if she had moved in and left part of her mind at the gate, as if she'd used her brain up in getting here and hadn't gotten it back yet.

He said slowly, "I'm sure you have all that, that you're all prepared. But if you find you've forgotten something, there are some extra old food bowls in the back of the big barn, by the grain storage. There's dry food in a plastic bin. Help yourself."

Sure. He welcomed the *dog*. Too bad *she* wasn't a dog. He'd have been happier to see her then, wouldn't he?

He walked away. Again. Leaving her with a dog who was pulling against the leash, straining to follow him, with two alpacas in the back that she had no idea what to do with, with a cottage that was probably falling apart.

She didn't want to overreact. This was all wonderful, on the surface. An inheritance! A home of her own, away from San Diego. Sure, the man didn't want her here. But she had a tougher skin than that, didn't she?

Even when her little apartment had that fire, years ago when she was in college, when she had been sleeping on friends' floors, keeping her toothbrush in her backpack and having her mail sent to a post-office box, she hadn't felt as homeless as this.

Home was everything to Abigail. She had to know where her things were, which direction the bathroom was when she awoke in a strange place. She unpacked in hotel rooms, using all the drawers. She unpacked in tents, laying her clothes out for the next morning. Even as a teenager, after her mother died, when her father was moving them around every year or so for work, she did the brunt of the packing and unpacking because she liked it. If she had to move around so much, at least she always knew where everything was.

And she did have a lovely room upstairs in the house. In the house that wasn't hers, that she was sharing with someone who liked a strange dog better than her. Honestly? If she had a home that she was suddenly forced to share with a stranger, she'd hate them, too.

But she'd be nicer about it.

Well, he *had* offered the dog bowls and the food.

Offered them to the dog, who was pulling her through the boxes, through the house.

"Clara! Stop pulling!"

Clara looked up at her and gave a happy little bounce.

Great. Now she'd done it. The dog's name was apparently settled.

"Clara?" A lick on her hand was the answer.

"I really meant to name you myself. I was kind of looking forward to it, actually." Abigail paused, looking around the living room. It was still dark in here, even with the curtains pulled back. The windows needed washing. It smelled funny—musty and old.

How would she make this home?

"Let me show you something," she said to the dog. "It's upstairs."

Abigail led Clara, panting and slobbering with excitement, up the narrow staircase into the rooftop room. Without being encouraged, Clara ran through the clutter to the center of the room and hurled herself onto the little divan, looking intensely out the windows at the trees.

Abigail sat next to her. "It's nice, isn't it?" She looked around the little room. No bats. She took a deep breath. "And oh, it is mine. It's mine."

Clara licked her cheek.

She spent several more hours out in her shed, before the sun went down, working on making the alpacas comfortable. They were nervous about the dog, so she left Clara tied up on the other side of the fence, and Clara watched their every move with fascination. Abigail had a rudimentary set of tools out in her truck and had discovered the immense satisfaction to be gained in hammering fence boards. Even though Cade had checked the fence line, she walked every step of the small outside pen area, pushing and pulling boards. When she found one that wiggled a little, she smacked it, hard, with the hammer until the old nails sunk back into the weathered board.

Only once had she hit her finger, and even then, she hadn't cried out. She lived on a ranch now. She owned livestock. She was tough.

She could so do this.

She managed to get close enough to Tussah to pat her on the side. She was as soft as she looked. Neither looked like they'd been shorn anytime recently, which, on the one hand, was a good thing, because she'd be getting their fleece that much sooner. On the other hand, she'd have to learn to shear them.

She wouldn't think about that now.

After making sure and doubly sure that her new livestock wasn't going anywhere for the night, she led Clara around to the house. They went up the stairs quickly, Clara nosing into corners, Abigail pulling her so they'd keep moving. "I know, we'll explore when he's not here. Keep going, baby."

True, he'd been nothing but nice this afternoon, offering information on the mating habits of alpacas, and helping her get the dog out of the car.

But he'd been mocking her, she was sure of it. He'd enjoyed telling her that not only had she bought two animals that she didn't understand, but she'd let herself in for progeny, too. Great.

Alpaca sex. She couldn't even think about what that looked like.

And he'd gloated when he'd released Clara from the truck. Abigail's face must have been terrified. How stupid she'd been. Clara'd only been excited. On any other day, Abigail would have known that. But today, well, a lot had happened today. And she was still jumpy.

She would have remembered the dog food. She felt stupid for not having thought of it earlier. It had been kind of him to offer some. He had a soft spot for dogs, that was all . . .

Abigail brought up some of the offered kibble, and a bowl for water. Clara ate as if she'd been starved all her life and then jumped up onto the bed. She was asleep on her back and snoring within minutes.

Abigail got under the covers and pushed Clara to the edge. The two of them didn't really fit in the old twin bed, but it was nice. Warm. Abigail put her arm around her dog and waited for sleep to find her.

Chapter Thirteen

Making stitches twist around themselves, making them cable their way up the body of a sweater, is the knitter's alchemy.

—E.C.

It was a good morning for a drive: clear and cool, the fog hanging back as if reluctant to push onto the land.

Cade hadn't been to Tillie's Diner for two weeks, not once since Abigail arrived. He hadn't wanted to leave her alone on the property. He wasn't sure what he thought she might do, but it had taken this long to trust that all she was going to do was avoid him in the morning and then spend the rest of the day cleaning the cottage. Then she'd avoid him at night, too. He'd been aware of her presence in the house, but it was like living with a ghost—she was always just around the corner, or he'd just missed her and could only smell her perfume still lingering in the room she'd just vacated.

It'd be good to get to the diner. He'd missed Tillie's.

As he passed over the long, curved bridge that went over the river, he drummed his fingers on the wheel. Stupid tourist in a rented RV in front of him was driving too slowly, like they always did here. Mills Bridge was a frightening and magnificent spectacle. It curved so much that while driving over it one could look ahead and see the bridge curving to the right, the river rushing underneath, the sea below the far side.

The waves out there were high today, he noticed. Promise of more bad weather, even with the clear skies. He felt pleased. At least it would match his mood, which was swinging like the bikes hooked to the back of that RV. It was one thing to have lost some of his land to that girl. He was *really* trying to reconcile himself to that. What choice did he have? But then he'd remembered the damn alpacas on his way out. Alpacas!

Everything would be better at the diner.

The local ranchers hadn't acknowledged him at first when he'd started coming here fifteen years ago. Wouldn't even nod to him at the feed store. But he kept it up, having coffee near them at Tillie's. He never jumped into conversation, just listened.

After a few years of Cade's stubbornness, they started giving him a little bit of ground, nodding their heads a bit when he came into the diner instead of outright ignoring him.

It was when they began teasing him that he knew he'd made it. They took bites from his toast as they walked past his table, they teased him about the latest waitress that he was seeing. They seemed to delight vicariously in his conquests, and they laughed if he got dumped, which was rarely. They complimented his flock and deferred to his opinion when it came to Corriedales, since he was the only one running that breed in the valley.

Cade tore past the RV at his first opportunity, gunning the engine to its maximum. He sped down the canyon, around the big curve, and into town. Traffic was suddenly heavier, and he remembered, as he always did, that Cypress Hollow was and always would be a touristy beach town. A pleasure destination, not just a place for him to get groceries.

Tillie's was located on Main Street, a block from the beach. Surfers and farmers alike loved the diner for its cheap eats and good, strong, plentiful hot coffee. Old Bill had run the place for just about forever and never aged. Some of the oldest regulars swore that he'd been leaning heavily on the cash register since they were youngsters. He manned the register every moment of the day, never appearing to take even a bathroom break. He wasn't married, had no kids, and lived above the diner in an apartment whose windows faced the breaking waves. "Not a bad life," he'd say, when people asked him. "Not bad at all."

Cade parked in a free spot and strolled in.

"Bill," he said. "They back there?"

"'Course," said Old Bill, leaning on the register. "Might be surprised to see you though."

"It's been a while, but not that long."

Old Bill shrugged.

"It's not like I went anywhere. Damn."

Bill picked up a rag and wiped the glass-topped counter.

Cade strode through the diner to the side room, which was reserved for parties in the evening, and unofficially, for the farmers in the morning. It had four tables, a commanding view of the street, and its own coffee carafe, which Shirley kept full most of the time. If she was too busy, the guys would brew their own, but they grumbled about it.

Most of the regulars were here. It was a good time for it. Nine thirty: all their chores were done. Some of the guys had hired help that did the grunt work now that they could finally afford it, but they still kept the real hours, waking at four or four thirty. The meal they met over looked like breakfast, but acted more like lunch.

The core group was here: Pete, Jesse, Landers, Hooper, and Stephens.

And every one of them looked startled as he walked in the back room.

Cade sat in his usual seat, next to Stephens.

It remained quiet. Stubbornly, Cade didn't break the silence. He helped himself to a cup of coffee, and when Shirley came for his order, he pointed at his regular plate of eggs and sausage on the plastic menu. "And a blueberry muffin. Please."

Shirley nodded and bustled back into the main dining room.

Finally, after another long silence, Pete said, "Alpacas?"

The entire room broke into guffaws. They roared. The higher the volume of their laughter got, the redder Cade's face became.

"You've been just waiting for this, haven't you?"

"Man, we thought you was *never* gonna come in here. We been dyin' for you to come by. It's been weeks!" Stephens raised his coffee cup as if toasting Cade.

Landers said, "So Mort finally got to you, huh?"

Hooper said, "I knew he'd get someone to take those critters, but I never woulda figgered it to be you, son."

Jesse laughed so hard he went into a coughing fit. He hid his face behind his blue bandana.

Cade shook his head. "Hell, no! It wasn't me."

The men's laughter rose again.

"No, really! It wasn't me! Mort suckered the girl who's taking over the cottage."

The laughter died, leaving only Jesse spluttering.

Landers said, "We heard something about that, but we didn't believe it. Did Eliza really give away the ranch?"

"Not the whole thing. But yeah, the cottage. And its land."

"But that's smack in the middle of your property."

"It's only mine since she died. It's not like it was always mine."

Pete slammed his coffee cup onto the table, coffee spilling over its sides. "That's been your land for ten years, ever since she left. We all knew she was never coming back."

Landers said, "And now you have alpacas?"

"Like I said, that's all her. I'm not touching them. If they die, she'll have to hire someone to cart them off."

Stephens said, "I hear she's cute."

Cade nodded. "The female alpaca is kinda cute, yes. I'd agree. But I still don't like her."

Jesse folded his handkerchief. "But do you like the girl? I saw her down at the Laundromat. She's just my type, if I do say so."

Landers poked Jesse with a fork. "Just your type if she likes eighty-year-old men with consumption."

"I'm only sixty-five. And it's asthma."

Stephens said, "So, Cade. Is she? Pretty?"

Cade inclined his head in a half nod. They weren't going to let this go, so he might as well meet them halfway. "She's pretty. I guess you could call her really pretty. But she's annoying. Way too excited about everything. Why was she at the Laundromat? I have a washer and dryer."

"Excited is a good thing, son."

"Not like that. She's just a little . . . enthusiastic. And I don't want her there."

"She's moving into the cottage?"

"As soon as she can fix it up."

"You helping?" Landers winked at Cade.

"No, sir. I'm avoiding her as much as possible."

Jesse sighed. "What if your gal looked like her?" He pointed out the window with his spoon.

Two of the men wolf-whistled as Abigail walked past the window, her hair swinging behind her in a long ponytail.

"Now, that's what I call a looker!"

Cade slumped further into his chair.

Pete noticed his posture first. "Is that her? You gotta be kidding me. Really?"

Cade rubbed the bridge of his nose and shut his eyes. "Damn."

"Oh, sweet Mary, I'm gonna handle this." Stephens scooted into the main dining room and out the front door before Cade could move to stop him.

"Hell."

Less than thirty seconds later, Abigail was escorted into the side room on Stephens's arm. Her eyes were wide.

"Yes, I've only been here a couple of weeks . . . Am I being kidnapped?"

"You probably haven't even had time to meet many people. Let me introduce you to some of our local ranchers and farmers." Stephens started to move her around the room. Cade wondered what his chances were of making it out of the small room unnoticed.

Too late. Cade knew he'd been spotted. He didn't actually see Abigail look at him, but two pink circles flamed on her cheeks. By the time Stephens was saying, "And I believe you know our boy, Cade?" Abigail's cheeks were completely red. She nodded.

"Funny, real funny, Stephens," said Cade.

"And you know what?" Stephens went on, "I'm all done with my breakfast. You just sit right here, next to Cade."

"Oh, no . . ."

"That's right," Cade said. "I'm sure she's busy. . . ."

"Don't be rude, son."

Oh, hell. Cade gave up. He knew when he was outnumbered. "Go ahead, sit."

"How gracious. How could I say no?"

Was she laughing at him?

Cade said, "We were just talking about your alpacas."

"Oh, my God," she said, leaning forward over the table toward Pete and Jesse. "Did you know they hum?"

Pete's bushy eyebrows shot up. "Pardon?"

"I thought I'd read that it's only the mothers who hum to their young to keep them calm, but I heard them humming to each other three days ago. They were all settled in to go to sleep, and they were humming. It was the cutest thing ever. I've been listening for it since, but I haven't heard it again."

None of the men had an answer for this, just puzzled smiles.

"Cade won't tell you this, but he really wanted alpacas."

"He what?" Jesse started coughing again.

"That's what Mort said, when I got them. He said they'd make a fine gift, but I think I'll do one better than that. I'm going to keep these for myself and just give Cade the babies."

The men were falling for it. And her. Cade could see each one of them going a little goo-goo eyed at her. She was charming, he had to give her that. She took the time to smile right at each one as she looked around the table.

"No, you're not," said Cade. "They're vanity pets. A pyramid scheme."

Abigail down turned the wattage noticeably and looked at him. "How can an animal possibly be a pyramid scheme?"

"People just raise them in order to sell the babies to other people who will raise them and sell *those* babies to more suckers. They're not good for anything else."

Abigail shook her head and the ponytail bounced. Cade wished she didn't smell so good. It was distracting. "Are you crazy? Alpaca fiber is insanely wonderful! I can't wait to spin my own, from my own alpacas." She grinned at Landers. "Doesn't it sound like we should say *alpaci* or something, for the plural?"

All the men's heads nodded, up and down. Cade knew they had no idea what she was talking about. They were smitten.

Shirley came back to refill coffee. She splashed coffee on the table when she noticed Abigail.

"Whoa. I had no idea there was a lady back here. I'm so sorry. What can I get you?" She cleared Stephens's plates out of the way.

Abigail shrugged. "I'm not that hungry. I wasn't planning on eating. Just a latte?"

Cade waited for it. Shirley and the men always mocked tourists who came in asking for a fancy espresso drink, the ones that plain old coffee wasn't good enough for.

"I'm sorry, dollface, all I have is coffee. But I could have Emilio in the kitchen steam you a little milk, if you want."

All right, Abigail did look adorable, in her green-and-white gingham blouse and still-new Wranglers, but did Shirley have to fall for her, too? Cade snorted.

"Oh, no, don't go to any trouble."

"Emilio wouldn't mind," said Landers.

"Regular coffee's fine by me."

"Well, okay. Something to eat?" Shirley asked.

"Maybe just a blueberry muffin?"

"Oh, shoot, honey. Cade here got the last one this morning."

Quick as a snake, Pete's arm shot out, took Cade's muffin off his plate and set it on the table in front of Abigail. "There you go. He wasn't gonna eat it."

"I was, too!"

"I'll get you a lemon scone, Cade. And hold tight, honey," Shirley said to Abigail. "I'll get you a fresh cup of coffee from the front. The pot out here is old now."

"Scone. What the hell's a scone?" Cade grumbled, but no one was listening. They were busy asking Abigail questions about the alpacas.

He listened to her charm them. It was impossible, really, to sit near her and *not* be charmed. She gave each man her full attention as he spoke, and responded immediately, enthusiastically.

She wasn't faking it either. Cade sat back and watched her. Abigail really was excited about the idea of coming to see Pete's peacocks, and she really did want the recipe for Jesse's wife's apricot jam. She smiled at Shirley when she got a refill, and Shirley beamed back. Abigail's face lit up every time the men brought up something new, something else to learn about their valley.

She turned to Cade. "Do you know where that is?"

He hadn't been paying attention. "Um, run that by me again?"

"The falls? With the hot spring at the base?"

"Smythe Falls? Yeah, of course. It's kind of between here and the ranch, just after Mills Bridge. If you take the little dirt road to the right after Mort's place . . ."

Abigail cut him off. "Can we go there?"

"Maybe."

"Now?"

Cade spluttered on the sip of coffee he'd been taking. "Now? No way."

She shoved the last bit of his blueberry muffin in her mouth and talked around it. "Why not? It'sch a boot'ful mornin'."

"I have things to do."

Pete said, "Nothing important, though."

Landers said, "Nothing that can't wait another hour or two."

Jesse said, "Are you insane? Show her the falls, you idiot."

Stephens said, "I'll take you, Abigail."

Oh, hell, no. He wasn't going to be upstaged by a man pushing seventy who would probably use the opportunity to shuck off his overalls. "Fine, I'll take you," Cade said. "Someone has to protect you from him." Cade pointed at Stephens. Stephens leered at Abigail.

Abigail stood, smiled at everyone, and then leaned over to kiss Stephens's cheek. "I don't need *that* much protection."

Stephens looked ecstatic.

Chapter Fourteen

Rest in the stitches. Rest in the yarn. Rest in the motion.
—E.C.

She was a good follower, he'd give her that much. She drove behind him, but not on his tail, nor did she follow so far behind he was worried he'd lose her entirely. His truck rattled down the dirt road toward Smythe Falls, and he wondered for the twentieth time what he was doing.

Going to the falls? In the middle of the day, a day in which he'd planned to move some irrigation pipes that needed moving before the rains came. And he'd been going to check the hens. They weren't laying enough, and he wanted to check for signs of coyote. Maybe the chickens were stressed out. If coyotes moved toward the chickens, they'd be after the lambs soon enough.

But now here he was, with Abigail.

He pulled over into the makeshift parking lot, a dirt circle ringed by trees. On the weekends it was packed with cars, but now it was deserted.

He'd only take a minute to show her where to go. Then he'd go back to work.

She bounced out of her truck, her ponytail bobbing behind her. "Is it this way?" She pointed.

"That's the only trail, so, yes."

"Let's go!"

"Um, no, I think I'm going to get on the road. I just wanted to make sure you could find your way here. Now just follow this path up about a quarter of a mile, turn left at the oak bench and you'll be there. Enjoy."

Cade turned, but then felt a hand on his arm.

Abigail said, "Please? Come with me? I love waterfalls, and I'd love the company."

Cade heard something in her voice, something different from the friendly tone she'd used at Tillie's Diner. She sounded like she was trying to be brave, which meant that she was scared of something.

She was scared of him. She'd been avoiding him like the plague at the house, and he'd been doing the same to her.

He didn't want her in the house or on his land, no, but he wasn't a monster.

"Okay, I guess. Yeah, okay."

Her smile was so bright it lit up her whole face.

The hike to the falls was short but steep. It was dark under the trees, and he pointed out tree roots to avoid. She thanked him politely every time, but there was no hiding the excitement in her voice.

The creek ran next to the trail, and the riparian smell of wet leaves and natural rot hung in the cool air.

"Almost there." Automatically, he held out his hand to pull her up onto a huge fallen tree that had blocked this portion of the trail for years.

She slid her hand into his.

Damn, her hand was soft. He pulled Abigail up and they stood there, balancing on the fallen tree. He knew he should let go of her hand, that it would be the sensible thing to do, but she teetered a little, and her hand tightened in his.

His heart raced. He dropped her hand and jumped down. This was a stupid idea. He'd just get it over with and then get back to the ranch.

"We're almost there." Cade heard her clambering off the tree behind him but didn't look back.

He turned left. The narrow trail opened up into a bright, open spot. The waterfall poured down the rocks from above, splashing into a wide pond at the bottom.

Abigail, now beside him, gasped. "It's incredible."

She brushed his arm with hers as she moved in front of him, and his whole body reacted to her touch. He felt like a fifteen-year-old, unable to control himself. He took a deep breath.

"Can we swim? It's so weirdly warm today for being almost November. It would be a shame to waste it. Do people swim here?" she asked.

"People do. Now that you know where it is, you can come back anytime."

"Now? You want to?"

Cade couldn't quite believe what he was hearing. She wanted to skinny-dip? The idea both aroused and surprised him. "Naked? Now?"

Abigail looked horrified, and he saw her get nervous, all over again. She was as tense around him as he was around her. "No, no, I meant . . . I guess I thought underwear kind of looks like a bikini, but . . . oh . . . I'm sorry. I don't know what I was thinking."

Was she kidding? An opportunity to swim almost naked with a gorgeous girl? Even if it was with her, this might make the trip worth it.

Cade took off his shirt. "Why not?"

Abigail gasped again.

Cade stepped out of his boots and shucked off his jeans and socks, leaving only his boxer shorts and his cowboy hat. "I'm even taking off the hat. Don't tell anyone." He set his hat carefully on top of his boots.

Abigail's peal of surprised laughter rang through the trees. Cade ran forward and cannonballed into the middle of the pond, right where he knew the hot spring met the cool water cascading from above. He came up with a yelp and turned to look at her.

Cade lost his breath, and it wasn't because of the water.

Abigail was moving quickly, probably trying to get in the water before he saw what she was wearing, but he saw, all right. Pink panties decorated with a ribbon bow and a matching pink, lacy bra. She might have thought it would look like a bikini, and she was right in that it covered the same amount of skin that a bikini would have, but it looked like underwear. No, scratch that. It looked like lingerie.

Cade tried not to stare, but she was stunning. Why had he been avoiding her, again? Why was he not trying to see more of her, like this? Maybe if he could think straight, he'd remember.

Abigail looked at him quizzically, and he tried to adjust his face. He must be leering at her like Stephens had at the diner.

She ran toward the water and did a cannonball like he had, but in the wrong direction. It was deep enough there to be safe, but that was the cold end. The super-cold end. That was the end no one ever went into because the hot mineral water didn't make it that far.

Abigail came up screaming. "Wow! Oh, holy hell, this is cold! How do you stand it!" She panted and dog-paddled toward him. "Why didn't you tell me?" Then she said, in a different tone of voice, "Oh!"

She'd reached a warm part, he could tell. He watched her face relax, and a part of him that should have been relaxed very suddenly wasn't.

"Oh, this is wonderful." She kicked and flipped herself upside down and came back up. Water streamed down her face, over her eyes and lips. Her sexy, full, very wet lips . . .

Sadly, he'd probably have to stay right here until she got out and drove back to the ranch. Or maybe he'd have to stay here forever. If he got out of the water now, she'd be able to see what she'd done to him.

She swam closer to him. "Oh, it gets warmer the more you go this way."

He nodded, unable to trust his voice.

"This is amazing!"

She was amazing.

He had to stop thinking like this.

She swam past him and got out, climbing onto the large, flat rocks next to the pond. "Do people ever jump from up there?" She pointed up to the rock overhang above them. Cade could barely drag his eyes away from her underwear, now almost see-through, to look up. She seemed less self-conscious now, and he was glad. Really glad.

"Oh, yeah. Some do."

"Have you ever jumped from there?"

"Sure."

"I want to."

"Then go for it."

"But I'm scared of heights."

He laughed. "That's not a height, so you should be fine. It can't be more than ten, eleven feet."

"No, that's okay. That's too high for me." She looked nervous.

"If you want to, you should do it."

"I'm not good with scary things. I hate roller coasters. And I'd never bungee jump, even if you paid me."

"You moved up here, alone. And now you have to live with me, and I'm no prize. I'd say you're all right with scary things."

Abigail smiled. "You are scary, that's true. But maybe that just means I'm at my limit for scary things. I've hit my quota for the month."

"Well, if you're not brave enough, then you're just not brave enough."

It worked. Abigail flushed and stood up, dripping water onto the rock. She surveyed the narrow path around the side of the pond that led up to the ledge. She walked up it, her hair still streaming water down her back. Over her buttocks. Down her legs.

Cade didn't know being aroused could hurt this much. He moved into the colder end of the pool. Maybe that would help.

"Cade?" Abigail had reached the ledge. "I think this is a bad idea." Her voice shook.

Good, maybe she'd take her time up there, and he'd recover a little. "You can do it!"

But instead of dithering and making him talk her into it, like the other girls he knew would have, Abigail just nodded. Then she closed her eyes and jumped. Her shriek cut off abruptly as the water closed over her head.

She came up laughing. She didn't say anything; she just swam and laughed her way back to the big flat rock. Then she lay there, giggling.

Cade moved into the even colder water.

They fell silent. Cade was content to float.

After what must have been half an hour, Abigail stirred. She rolled to look at him.

"You must be a prune."

"Yes."

"And cold."

"Thank God, yes. I'm cold."

"I think I fell asleep." She stretched. "Should we go?"

Cade nodded. This was a good time. Before she stretched again. He dashed out of the water and up the side of the pond. He grabbed his clothes, keeping his back to her. Once he pulled his jeans up his still wet legs, he was uncomfortable enough that he could safely turn back to face her.

"I hate putting on dry clothes when I'm wet," he grumbled.

"You should have come up onto the rock with me."

"That wouldn't have been a good idea," Cade said, his voice low.

"Why?"

Cade cleared his throat.

"Oh," she said. She went shy all over again, and turned her back to step into her own jeans. She didn't turn around again until her shirt was on and completely buttoned up.

"Thank you for coming out here with me," she said.

"No problem."

"I'm sure you had better things to do at the ranch."

"Don't worry about it."

But the moment was broken. The words hung awkwardly between them. He had to hurry to keep up with her as they walked back to their trucks. She was up and over the fallen tree before he could offer to help.

In the dirt parking lot, she only nodded at him. She gave a small smile, but Cade didn't know how to return it. He should say something, anything, but by the time he'd figured out a few words that might not be completely idiotic, she was in her truck and backing out of the lot.

Screw fifteen years old. He felt more like twelve. Idiot.

Chapter Fifteen

How talented you are! How clever!
—E.C.

There were two bathrooms in Cade's house. Abigail had been using the one downstairs for the past two weeks, even when she had to walk there quietly in the middle of the night. She tiptoed when she went, not wanting a floorboard to creak and wake Cade up.

But tonight, she really, really wanted a bath. She felt like she still had the pond water in her ears, behind her knees. And the only bathtub was upstairs. She was going to use it, but first she was going to make good and sure that he wouldn't be around when she made her way there.

It was still his time to use the kitchen and downstairs area. As strange as she'd thought it at first, she was grateful for the schedule. Every time she saw him, she struggled with her feelings. She wanted to be friendly with him, wanted to be herself, but also to remain at a . . . what should she call it? A professional distance, yes, that was it. They were going to share land, share a driveway, share space, for the foreseeable future. It sure would help to have an amicable relationship.

Would he ever be able to have that with her? Everything he said seemed laced with something more. Today, at the pond, she would have sworn he'd been implying that he was attracted to her. That couldn't possibly have been what he meant. She felt foolish for even wondering about it.

But the way he'd looked, for that moment, when he was still wearing his cowboy hat, naked except for his boxers? She'd lost her breath. She'd been glad when he'd jumped into the pond. It gave her a moment to gather her courage to take off her clothes.

She'd been wrong. Underwear was nothing like a bikini. It just wasn't. If she set that awful tension aside, though, it had been fun. Exciting. She was so happy she'd jumped off the rock. In the past, that would have been too hard. But here, now, it was all different. And his voice, strong and steady, telling her she could do it . . . She had believed him. And he'd been right.

Abigail looked at her watch. It was after eight thirty. According to the schedule Cade had made, she could have been down in the kitchen cooking dinner since six thirty, but it was too risky. She had seen enough of Cade today to last them both for a while.

She waited a little while longer before curling up on the bed and putting an arm over Clara.

Abigail wasn't sure who needed a bath more, her or the dog.

She might have slept a little, because her eyes flew open in the dark room. Clara jumped, but kept snoring.

Abigail heard Cade's door close.

She waited.

And waited some more. Nothing.

She took off her clothes and put on her robe. Gathering her toiletries, she tiptoed to the bathroom down the hall.

This was a man's house, so she expected black towels and chrome details, toilet tissue on the floor and a stained bathtub. But she had to have this bath, even if the tub needed a good scrubbing first.

What she entered was a pretty bathroom, not feminine, but definitely not all guy. It had to be Eliza's doing. The tub was an old claw-foot, chipped but satisfyingly clean. A dark green shower curtain went with the old wooden pedestal sink that had green trim. As she looked at it, she realized that it actually might be the same green as the trim on the outside of the house.

Abigail smiled. That seemed like Eliza.

She turned on the hot water and waited. Lovely and hot. Now, a touch of cold water.

A cup of tea would be nice.

And maybe a piece of toast.

Abigail padded downstairs. She put the kettle on and popped a piece of bread in the toaster. Then she sat in the rocking chair and closed her eyes for a moment while waiting for the toast to pop.

Then she heard a roar from upstairs, followed by wild barking.

She ran upstairs as fast as she could. Had Clara lost her mind and attacked Cade? She didn't even know where Cade kept a phone so she could call 911 if she needed to.

At the top of the wooden stairs, she slipped in warm water. By wheeling and grabbing the stair rail with all her strength, Abigail avoided falling backward down the stairs. As she made it to the door of the bathroom, she heard Cade roar again.

"What *happened*?"

"It's flooding! How did you do this? Get towels!"

"Where?"

"Hall closet. Now!"

Abigail grabbed as many towels as she could carry and ran through the water again. It wasn't deep, but it seemed to be moving fast.

"Turn the water off!" she yelled as she came running back into the bathroom.

Cade was wearing nothing but his blue jeans, kneeling in the bathroom. He looked at her incredulously. "Water's *off*. What, you think I'd leave it running?"

"How did that happen? I just left the room a couple of minutes ago. Does the bathtub leak?"

"Yes, it leaks. It leaks right over the top of the bathtub if it overflows! Start mopping! This is going to go straight through the floorboards. . . . "

"What about the overflow valve?"

He glared. "It's a clawfoot. Where would the water go?"

Abigail opened her mouth and closed it again. "Oh."

She fell onto her knees, grasping at the belt of her robe, making sure it was firmly tied. He was practically naked already. She didn't want to join him.

She'd had a sneaking suspicion that his chest would be good, not that she'd been consciously thinking about it. And this afternoon at the waterfall had confirmed that she was right. But she hadn't seen this, hadn't seen the muscles.

She guessed working a ranch was good exercise. She could see his bare back as he swept the water from the floor with a sopping towel. His muscles rippled across his back. She hadn't ever known that muscles could actually do that. But his did.

"Here," she said in a small voice. "This one's dry."

"You'd better have a towel for yourself, too."

"I do."

"Start drying."

Abigail went out in the hall and worked backward, tracking the water to its farthest reach, mopping back toward the bathroom. She went through four towels by the time she got back to where Cade was.

She crawled toward him in the hall through the puddles, drying the floor, conscious of how her robe was hanging. Cade was being thorough, it seemed, and was still on his hands and knees in the bathroom. In all good conscience, she should join him and help him in there.

But it was such a small room.

She entered. He barely glanced at her, then pointed to an area under the tub.

"Get the water back there. You're smaller, you'll fit better."

It was a tight squeeze, and Abigail had to get as low as she could without showing off anything she didn't want to display. The towel she was using was almost full of water, and she wasn't sure she was actually getting anything drier.

"Here, use this one," Cade said, and took the wet one away from her. He threw it with the rest piled in the drained tub.

Then he sat on the floor near the door and watched.

He watched her dry the spots under the tub, and then watched as she scooted backward and got the puddles under the sink.

He watched her as, trying to be surreptitious, she adjusted her robe so that she was still completely covered.

She was, but he stared at her anyway.

He sat with his arms crossed against his broad chest, still that glare on his face, but his eyes were darker than she'd seen them.

Maybe it was a trick of the dim light.

Abigail finished under the sink, and looked around.

"I think we did it."

She threw the last towel into the bathtub, then moved carefully so that she was sitting on the floor opposite him. Her legs stuck straight out. She made sure they didn't touch his. One hand clutched her robe closed at her throat.

"I'm sorry."

He cleared his throat and shook his head a little. "How did you manage that?"

"I don't have any idea. I only went downstairs to make some tea. I was only there for a minute."

"I heard you walk by my door and then down the stairs. Then I didn't hear anything for fifteen minutes, until I heard the dripping."

"That's impossible. I was only . . ." Her voice trailed off. "I must have fallen asleep. I sat down in the rocker; I must be more tired than I thought."

He sighed and leaned back against the wall. Still seated, he let his arms uncross. He looked tired, she thought.

"I am really, really sorry. Have I done any permanent damage?"

His eyes, which he'd closed for a moment, opened slightly and looked at her, then closed again. "Not to the bathroom, no."

"I mean, the floorboards . . ."

"Nothing that can't be dried out. I've done it myself."

"You take baths?"

He frowned. "Even out here on the range, we take baths. You'd be surprised."

"I didn't mean . . ."

"That's the problem. You didn't mean. You didn't mean to get in my way, you didn't mean to flood the bathroom, you didn't mean to take over my house with your footsteps and your perfume . . . You just didn't mean."

"I . . ."

"Don't say you're sorry. If I were you, and I were in your shoes, I'd *feel* sorry for me, too, but I wouldn't *be* sorry, so don't say it again. It's getting really old."

Abigail could think of nothing else to say, so she remained quiet.

He sat, eyes still closed. She wanted to get up and get out of his way, but he was blocking the door. In order to leave the bathroom, she'd have to step over him, and in her short flimsy robe, stepping over him would show off more than she wanted to.

She'd wait. She couldn't apologize anymore; she'd wait him out instead.

They sat.

After a couple of minutes, Abigail started getting cold. Was he playing a game?

She waited a little longer.

The game was getting old. How long would he keep this up? Then she noticed that his breathing was getting steadier, deeper.

He was taking longer pauses between each breath. His arms relaxed as she watched. His head, against the wall, drooped slightly, hanging to the side.

He was asleep.

She stood, as quietly as she could, touching nothing in the bathroom. She tiptoed toward the door, stepping over him, ever so carefully: one leg, then the other one. Almost out.

A hand wrapped around her wrist and pulled. She fell off balance, falling backward. Another arm came up and snaked around her waist, and she fell all the way down.

But she didn't land on the ground. She landed square in his lap, as he'd obviously intended, his arms pinning her in place.

Abigail opened her mouth to speak, to protest, but nothing came out.

They looked at each other.

"I must have tripped," she said, her voice much smaller than she'd meant it to sound.

"You must have. It's good I was here to catch you."

"Yes," she said and tried to pull her arms out of his grasp.

"But we should take a moment and make sure you're not hurt."

"Not hurt," she whispered.

"Are you sure?"

She nodded.

He nodded once, and then pulled her tightly against him, one hand releasing her wrist and going to the back of her head. His head lowered, and his mouth was on hers, hot and rough and persistent.

And she was kissing him back. Good Lord, what was she doing? The hand that he'd released was moving of its own volition, up to the back of his neck, pulling him down so that he kissed her harder. His tongue touched the inside of her mouth, asking, and then before receiving an answer, plundering.

Their mouths moved against each other: He requested, she granted. She'd never been kissed like this. This was more than a kiss. He was making love to her with the kiss, her body responding in ways that were shocking her, and she did nothing to stop him.

Instead, she pressed against him more.

She didn't want to stop him.

Cade shifted, still kissing her, his mouth warm, his tongue insistently pressing, teasing, licking. She matched him, shifting with his body, not sure what his intent was, but knowing she couldn't move her lips from his.

His arm, now free of holding her, came between them, and she felt his fingers at the top of her gown. He slipped a finger down, and the robe parted with a silken whisper.

She felt him gasp against her lips, and could tell by what happened under her, his hardness against her hip, that he was far beyond aroused.

Her breasts, exposed to the cool air, felt more vulnerable than they ever had. Her nipples grew tight and high.

He had to touch her. She would die if he didn't touch her.

One finger brushed one of the rosy peaks, so softly she wondered if she'd imagined it. A throaty groan, was it hers? His? She couldn't tell.

And then, without any warning, she was sitting on the cold bathroom floor, Cade towering over her.

"What the hell?" she said.

He said, "Godammit. I didn't want that."

He turned and was gone, his bedroom door slamming behind him.

Abigail took a gulping breath and pushed her hair back. She closed her traitorous robe tightly, and stood up. Her knees were wobbling and she noticed her hands were shaking.

She hadn't wanted that either. But now she didn't want anything else.

She was in trouble.

Chapter Sixteen

If it makes you feel better to think you're in charge of the yarn completely, then go ahead and do that. It won't change the truth.

—E.C.

The next morning, when Cade opened his eyes in the quiet, still darkness of predawn, he knew something had happened, and struggled to remember what he'd forgotten while sleeping.

Then he got it.

He'd kissed Abigail in the bathroom.

He groaned and rolled over, putting his face in the pillow. He was rock hard the second he thought of her. Again.

Yes, she was attractive. Hot as hell. No, he couldn't get her out of his mind, even though he desperately wanted her off his property.

But he'd never dreamed he would grab her like that, wrench her down on his lap like he had.

It was something he hadn't been able to control. He wouldn't have believed, an hour before he kissed her last night, that he would ever kiss her. Much less ten minutes before he did, when he'd been so furious about the water all over his house, the house that had flooded because she'd been an idiot and had fallen asleep with the tub running.

No, he'd been the idiot. She hadn't meant to flood the bathroom. He *had* meant to kiss her. With all his body, he had meant that kiss last night.

Abigail had kissed him back, he knew it. He'd grabbed her, pulled her down, but she'd kissed him back as hard, harder, perhaps. Her hand had been in his hair, twisting, pulling him closer, so that their breaths were interchangeable and that breathing was as fast as if they'd been running.

Oh, this was agony. He had to get out of bed, fast, and get out of the house before he saw her.

How was he going to avoid her until she got the cottage in livable order?

It might be impossible, but he could try.

Cade showered, dressed, ate his instant oatmeal, and was out of the house in under twelve minutes. He had most of the barn chores done by six thirty, when the sun was peeking up and Tom was walking in.

"You look like hell," said Tom.

"I need you to check those ewes again today. Get the vet, just to be sure."

"No 'good morning, old buddy'?"

Cade wasn't in an old-buddy mood. He scowled.

Tom said, "Okay, then. I'll make my own coffee, I guess?"

"There's some in the office. Go ahead."

"Anything you wanna talk about?"

"Nope." Cade kept raking out a stall that had held until this morning an older ewe that had been struggling with pneumonia. She'd died sometime in the night, and he'd already dealt with her body this morning.

"That ewe gone?"

"Yep."

"Damn. I thought she looked better yesterday."

"I did, too. We were wrong."

"You upset?"

"That sheep cost me money."

"Have anything to do with that girl up at the house?"

Cade stopped raking and glared at Tom. "No."

"Okay." Tom held up his hands and started backing away.

"Why would you ask that?"

"Forget I asked."

"It's not about her."

"I believe you."

"But why would you ask about her?"

"I'm thinking you have more you want to say to me about it. But I'm going to get some of that coffee. If you want to talk about it, talk. Otherwise, I'm going to get to work."

"It's not about her."

Tom nodded and walked toward the office.

How had Tom known? Why couldn't Cade just be upset about the sheep? This was his livelihood, after all. It would make any rancher upset.

But Tom was right, and Cade figured they both knew it. Tom knew him well. Cade dealt with death on the ranch the same way Tom did, with regret it couldn't be avoided, and a stoic conviction that humane and healthy treatment of the livestock would go a long way toward a strong, sturdy fold.

A simple ewe dying of common illness and age—that wasn't enough to make him look like this, act like this. Cade knew his face was reflecting the exact way he felt—Eliza used to beat him so soundly and regularly at poker that he'd never even played anyone for money. He knew he'd lose.

He'd just have to avoid Tom today. Wouldn't be so hard, not if he moved those irrigation lines he'd meant to do yesterday, and not if he went up to the ridge line and worked up there—he hadn't been up to that end in months, and there was some brush he wanted cleared. He'd check to see if it was a burn day in the county; maybe a good bonfire would make him feel better.

And he'd avoid Abigail, too. Forever. Wouldn't be that hard, would it?

She'd been shivering in that skimpy robe last night. Wait until she saw how cold it could actually get out here. A couple of cold winter storms would probably drive her out. 'Course, they were still so close to the ocean that it never snowed or anything like that, but the nights could still drop down below freezing. The cottage wasn't well insulated. And the chimney was blocked.

Humanely, he'd have to tell her to get that chimney fixed, at the very least. But that was it. She could think of and install insulation on her own.

Unless that made it take more time for her to get out of his house. Her and that ridiculous robe. Dammit. He needed to distract himself.

As Cade drove the ridge in his truck, he noticed heavy clouds looming to the north. He got out, pulled on his leather gloves, and started hauling brush. He took a break a couple of hours later and walked up to the one point, where, through the trees and over two valleys, he could see the ocean. It was dark slate, and he could tell, even from here, that the water was rough and whitecapped.

From up here, he could see only nature, only trees and ocean. Not even a power line marred his line of vision, though he knew that if he turned his head a little to the east, he'd see an electrical grid of lines marching across the low hill that his neighbor Tuttle owned.

He loved it. Close enough to town. San Francisco within range, if he needed it. There were people around if he got lonely. There were women to date, plenty of them. And Cade liked to date.

But he'd been alone since Eliza moved south, leaving him in charge.

Matter of fact, now that he thought about it, he'd never lived with another person in his life. He'd gone from his parents' home and then bounced from apartment to apartment, finally to the ranch, avoiding entanglements from every side.

Not that there hadn't been women who had tried, sneaking lip gloss into his bedside tables and extra pairs of panties into his sock drawer. Every time a woman started that up, he didn't merely bag up her stuff and return it to her—he got rid of the girl. He didn't have time for a relationship, no time for love. So he sidestepped it, religiously. People didn't find that movie-perfect love like Eliza and Joshua had every day. His parents certainly hadn't. He didn't want to follow in their footsteps.

And he certainly wasn't going to let some perfect stranger, a beautiful one notwithstanding, walk in and wreck his solitary happiness.

Mostly Cade preferred to be up here on the hill, looking down, knowing he could be down there and choosing not to be. He knelt and took off a glove. He touched the dirt. Eliza's husband, Joshua, had loved this land the way Cade did. He'd died when Cade was eleven, of a massive heart attack, but before he died, Cade had seen him kneel down and taste the dirt. Cade had tried it, too. They'd grinned at each other and proclaimed it the most delicious dirt in the world.

A sudden cold wind, wet with ocean moisture, hit his cheek, and the oak leaves clattered behind him. The clouds above him were moving more slowly, heavily, massing.

It was going to be stormy tonight. Something was moving in.

By the time Cade got back to the house to make his dinner that night, he was body-and-bone exhausted. He'd thrown himself into clearing brush, and had made such a good bonfire with the stuff that even though he'd notified the local fire dispatch agency, neighbors had called, thinking it might be out of control.

An off-road fire engine had chugged up the fireroad to check on him, but since he'd gone to school with Tim, the captain on the rig, they hadn't given him a hard time. They'd all stood there and watched, and they seemed as mesmerized as he was, staring into the flames, not saying much except about the incoming storm.

Now Cade smelled like smoke; his chest and throat ached from it. His muscles burned, and he was exceedingly dirty.

He needed a shower, food, and a good, strong drink, in that order.

The shower he got.

The food he made, a quick grilled steak and a salad from leftovers. He ate at the kitchen table, defying Abigail to come in, breaking their schedule.

She didn't. Of course she didn't. She must be avoiding him like he'd been avoiding her.

The first drops of rain hit the gutters outside the kitchen window. The silvery drops on the window were still hitting slowly, but they'd get faster as the night went on. They were in for it tonight.

After fixing himself a scotch and water, he grabbed the suspense novel he was reading from upstairs and went to the parlor.

He'd had his first bonfire of the season today and he'd light the first fire in the chimney tonight. Fitting. Maybe he'd burn the image of her, bare breasted, lips swollen, out of his mind.

Wasn't working so far.

After he started the fire with kindling and wood from the back porch, Cade sat back and brushed off his hands with satisfaction—no matter how many times he lit a good fire, he never got over feeling like an accomplished Boy Scout.

No, *Man* Scout, that was it. He felt better than he had all day.

His favorite chair was an overstuffed purple monstrosity with an overstuffed ottoman to match. Eliza had loved to sit here in front of the fire, knitting. The chair wasn't anything he ever would have picked, but it went with the feeling of the old room. The parlor had been the ladies' waiting room when the house had been a stagecoach stop in the late nineteenth century. Through the big leaded panes of glass in the front windows, one could look out at the two remaining hitching posts. Cade had four horses for working and driving the sheep, and he'd never felt the need to hitch either of them in front of the house. But he liked sitting here, looking out into the dark, knowing that more than a hundred years ago, other people had sat here, looking out into the dark from this very room.

He cracked open his book with a snap, breaking the spine.

Took a sip of his scotch.

Sank into the words. Perfect.

Almost. His scheduled time for clearing out of here was just fifteen minutes away.

But he might not even leave when his time was up. This was still his house, wasn't it? She could go somewhere else. Or if she came in here, which she wouldn't, she'd leave if he didn't.

Cade pushed the thought of her out of his mind.

Again.

Chapter Seventeen

Always add an inch of length to any sweater you're making, before you reach the armhole. You'll want it later if you don't.

—E.C.

Abigail stood, her knees aching. She'd been sitting in this spot for at least two hours. She dug her cell phone out of her pocket to check the time. She noticed she'd missed five or six calls, but they were from a blocked number, and she had no messages. It was probably time to change her phone number.

And it was her time of evening for the kitchen.

She'd gone out this morning into town to get food. After her quick shopping trip, two bags full of necessities like peanut butter and ice cream, she'd taken a stroll down the boardwalk. It was mostly closed up for the season, but people still walked along in groups, drinking coffee, watching surfers, and fishing off the end of the pier.

People had smiled at her, like maybe she fit in already. She didn't have to look over her shoulder all the time, and when she did, only friendly faces met her gaze.

Now Abigail locked the front door of the cottage, carrying a huge armload of boxes out to the recycling bin. She'd been working for hours, unloading bits and pieces of wheels and boxes of fiber, filling all the empty bookcases she could find and making makeshift cases out of cardboard as she had to. She wanted the rooms cleared out, so she could see what she was working with. But even though she'd worked all day, she wasn't even half done with the front room.

The more she opened and unpacked, the more she realized Eliza's intent. In her gently controlling way, Eliza was pushing Abigail, even now, to open a public space.

A classroom in her old cottage. A store.

Box after box, Abigail was finding everything that she'd need to start her dream business. She had enough spinning wheels to teach classes and still have overstock to sell. She had enough fiber in carded batts and rolags to spin into hundreds of skeins. There were boxes of plain, sturdy wool in all colors, with the manufacturer's contact info on each box, in case she wanted to reorder, even though there was so much that she couldn't imagine ever having to do that.

She'd even found an old cash register and a receipt book. Each box she opened answered one more of the questions in her head.

Abigail hadn't fully asked herself yet whether she was really going to open a shop here. She hadn't worked through it in her conscious mind, but in her unconscious mind, the one that really made the decisions, she knew she would.

Her dream a reality.

With a handsome cowboy nearby, no less.

She hadn't thought about him all day. She'd been great at not thinking. At all. Every time he came into her mind—that mouth, those large, strong, knowing hands—she thought about the shop. Her cottage. The classes she could offer. The alpacas.

Anything but him.

She dropped the cardboard off at the garbage cans, which were between the barn and the house, and clapped her hands to call Clara, who was under her truck, gnawing on something.

It was getting cold out here. And windy. She felt her hair being lifted and thrown in front of her face. Was that a drop of rain? She called Clara again, but the stubborn dog just looked out from under the truck and ignored her.

Fine—she needed to check that she'd gotten all her shopping bags out of the cab of the truck anyway. She looked in through the window. No bags were inside, but her glove box was open.

Abigail frowned. She'd thought she'd locked the doors. It was a habit that two weeks in the country hadn't been able to break yet. Yes, the doors were locked. She used her key to open the truck.

The glove box was hanging open. It was a tricky glove box, too. It was easy to close and almost impossible to open. She'd always had to bang on it just right. And she knew it had been closed when she got out of the truck with her groceries earlier.

Abigail rifled through the contents. She didn't keep much in her glove box for the very reason that it was so difficult to open. Registration, owner's manual, a tire gauge, two sixteen-inch circular needles and a small ball of sock wool for emergency knitting, nothing else. Nothing was missing.

Of course nothing was missing. No one would break into her truck in order to open the glove box. The sticky latch must just be acting up, in reverse. Abigail closed it and tried to shake off the creepy feeling that had settled on her shoulders. She looked up the gravel drive. Nothing. Back the other way, just the barn. Nothing out on the county road, what she could see of it.

It was the isolation, that was all. She'd get used to it.

As the rain started in earnest, she knelt next to the truck and pleaded with the dog, offering the treats that she'd stocked up on earlier. Clara finally came out after snarfing three treats, dragging what looked like an auto part out with her. She had grease on her muzzle.

Fantastic. A car-eating dog.

They went into the house. Abigail prayed Cade wouldn't be in the kitchen.

He wasn't. The coast was clear.

She made a quick sandwich. After working in the cottage and not thinking about Cade all day, she didn't have the brain for much more.

She sat at the kitchen table, ate her sandwich, and watched the rain. Clara sat under the table and leaned heavily against her leg.

What Abigail *really* wanted was to sit and knit. This was the kind of weather that was best for knitting—windy and cold, wet and getting wetter, good for being warm and safe inside. If only there were a fireplace in the kitchen.

There *was* a fireplace in the parlor. She looked at her cell phone again to check the time. Wasn't it her turn for the parlor now? He should be cleared out, and if he wasn't, he sure would when he saw her.

She went upstairs to grab her knitting and was down again in a minute, Clara following close at her heels. At the bottom of the stairs, instead of going left back to the kitchen, she went right, into the parlor.

She found Cade sitting in the overstuffed chair, book in hand, as squarely in front of the roaring fireplace as one could be. Duncan, his enormous yellow cat, sat on his lap. Somehow Cade made even the purple armchair look rugged.

Crap.

Well, it was her time. He'd made the rules. She would play by them, even if he wasn't. She entered with her head high, ignoring him. Perhaps she'd nod to him in a moment, once she was set up on the couch. But she'd give it a minute.

But Clara ruined her entrance by racing ahead, all wiggles and tongue, circling Cade ecstatically, as if he were a huge juicy piece of steak.

The cat exploded into a yellow puff of smoke as it screamed its way out of the room in protest.

"Duncan!" said Cade.

"Clara!" Abigail was horrified. She hadn't considered this possibility. Would he think she'd sicced the dog on the cat on purpose?

Cade grinned and set down his book, the dog's head in both his hands.

"Who's my girl? Who's a good Clarabelle? Who's a good dog?"

Judas. Abigail scowled at the traitorous dog. Clara was too busy making love to Cade to notice.

Abigail sighed and took a spot on the long couch. It looked antique and uncomfortable, but she should have known better. Eliza wouldn't have had anything in her house that didn't soothe the soul and body. Abigail sank into its depths comfortably. A good knitting spot.

Even better would be the chair in front of the fire currently occupied by the guy who needed to go to bed. Soon.

"Long day?" she asked, attempting for a casual tone.

"Nope," Cade said. His voice was ten degrees cooler when talking to her compared to her dog.

"Well, that's good."

Abigail pulled out the sleeve she was working on. She was almost done with this one, and in her mind she was playing with the idea of the next one—would she maintain the motif of this small zigzag, or would she leave it off the next sleeve? It was going to be a man's sweater, perhaps a new design for the next book, but Abigail knew men were sometimes put off by asymmetry. It would be a risk.

This was the kind of decision making she usually loved doing.

She wasn't enjoying it a bit.

She stared at the yarn as it wound through her fingers and onto the needles.

Wasn't he getting the hint?

Nope, he was still playing with the dog, who was now rolling from her belly to her back.

"Lie down."

Clara lay down.

"Roll over."

Clara rolled over, almost knocking over a small end table.

"Now, sit." She did.

Cade pointed his fingers at her in the shape of a gun. "Bang!"

Clara rolled her eyes in ecstasy right before she threw herself onto the ground, limp.

Abigail stared. She'd had no idea. But she wouldn't let him know that.

"What else does she know?" Cade asked.

"She knows, um . . . shake." Abigail guessed.

"Shake, Clara," said Cade, and Clara lifted her left paw for him to shake.

Good girl, thought Abigail.

"You got a good one," said Cade, and laughed as Clara tried to get in his lap like a puppy and lick his face.

"Well, she seems to like you."

"I like *her*. I always have, even when she was Mort's."

Gah. Abigail tried to put her face back into neutral.

"You knew about her tricks."

He grinned. "Maybe."

She'd fallen for it. Time for him to go. "So, did you get up at four thirty again today?" she asked.

Cade looked at her as if she'd grown a third arm. "Yeah."

"Wow. That's a long time to be up. Huh. What time is it anyway?" She lifted her bare wrist. "I don't wear a watch."

"Neither do I," he said coolly.

Damn. He was playing the game, too.

Abigail spent the next half hour in a state of frustration. Oh, she wanted him out of this room. She wanted to knit. Listen to that rain: It was perfect, a perfect night for sinking deeply into the repetitive motions of knitting. She wanted to be able to think about her plans for the future, for the cottage.

She wanted to be in front of the fire. She wanted to sit in that chair he was planted in so firmly it was as if he had grown roots that went through the leather, through the wooden floor, down into the soil beneath.

Go to *bed* already.

She yawned. Watched him.

Nothing. He turned a page and took a sip out of the glass that apparently never needed refilling. Maybe he was faking it. Maybe he was taking false sips to out-sit her.

But she watched intently the next time he drank, and she saw the liquid level go down incrementally. She felt stupid. Cade was obviously just sitting here, enjoying the night storm as she was.

She should be able to do the same thing. She was a grown-up, after all, and he wasn't a kid taking her ice cream. They were two adults in an awkward situation. They could work this out. Right?

Right.

Ffft. She threw her knitting down on the couch and went to the large windows. She couldn't see anything, not a light, not the rain, nothing. Just herself looking back, strangely wide-eyed.

She cupped her face with her hands and pressed the outside edges to the glass. Now she could see what was out there. The rain and wind whipped the trees closest to the house; the puddles that had already gathered were pummeled with raindrops. One sheet of rain followed the next.

"It's pouring," she said to him, more to break the silence again than actually to speak to him.

He nodded without looking up from his book.

Oh, he was a stubborn one.

And she was tired of it.

"Isn't it my time to be in here?"

He shrugged and held up his bare wrist. "Don't know."

"It's nine."

"Already?"

"I'm not sure what you're trying to do here, but I'm not going anywhere. I want to knit tonight. I'm not going to sneak off to my room in order to avoid you."

"Neither am I. Why would I do that?"

"But you wanted to avoid me. That's why you made the schedule."

"No," he said slowly, putting his book on his lap and looking at the fire, not at her. "I made the schedule because I thought you might be uncomfortable with me here in my house. I wanted to stay out of your way."

"And now?"

"I'm over it. I figure I'm doing you a favor by letting you stay here. We can share, can't we? We're adults."

Abigail walked back to the couch.

She didn't want a fight, not tonight. Not here. Not where she was alone, with most of her friends far away, not where she was trapped in a house with a man who obviously couldn't stand her, even if he *had* kissed her last night.

That kiss.

She blushed, remembering it. She'd done such a good job of pushing it out of her mind though she was sitting so close to him. Until now.

Cade cleared his throat and shifted in his chair.

She blushed harder. She prayed he wouldn't look at her right now, not until the color left her face.

The only sound in the room now was the crackle of the fire and the pouring rain outside. The low whoosh of the rain was punctuated by metallic clanks as big drops landed on something outside.

What was wrong with her? And why wasn't she knitting? Abigail sat back down.

Knit through everything, that was her motto, as it had been Eliza's. Always knit. Knitting was Abigail's meditation, her entertainment, her solace. Knitting was everything. Her needles talked to each other, and with that tiny sound, she felt better.

She breathed.

Cade turned pages.

She picked up the chart she'd drawn on graph paper, studied it, and then knit some more.

The rain came down.

Abigail grew so used to the silence that when Cade spoke, she jumped and lost a stitch off the end of her needle.

"Did she teach you to do that?"

"Hang on." Abigail poked at the work, pulling at the stitch that threatened to make a break for it. "Okay, I caught it. What?"

"My aunt. She teach you?"

"How to knit? No. My mother taught me."

"Where is she?"

"She died when I was ten."

"Who raised you?"

It felt blunt—she'd never been questioned about her parentage as if she were being challenged.

But she answered him. "My dad, mostly, when he wasn't at work. But we moved around for his job, and I was home alone most of the time. I knitted a lot."

"That must have made you super cool."

Was that humor in his tone?

"Coolest kid ever. Big coke-bottle lenses, knitting. Kids called me 'granny' from the time I was about seven." She smiled. "But I kept knitting. The best gift my mother ever gave me."

"Where's your dad now?"

"He died about five years ago. Fell off a ladder on a roofing job, landed on his head."

"Damn. I'm sorry."

"Me, too. He was all I had left, except for Eliza."

"Don't you have friends?" Cade looked startled by the way it came out of his mouth. "I mean, wasn't it hard to leave?"

Abigail laughed. "Don't worry, I have plenty of friends. But besides Janet, I have no friends that I call my family, now that Eliza's gone. But now I'm near Janet."

"But didn't you have a home down there? Roots?"

"I've never really had roots anywhere. Dad moved us a lot, and I kind of kept it up. I stayed in San Diego the longest, and that was because of Eliza. She became home to me." Abigail touched the seat of the sofa with her fingertips. She wouldn't tell Cade that's why she felt at home here, as if her roots were already growing, that it was because of Eliza and how present Eliza felt here on this land. He wouldn't understand.

She looked at Cade. He was still staring at the fire with his eyes half closed. "Do you knit?" she asked.

He barked a laugh. Clara, who had been snoozing at his feet, jumped and pulled her ears back, then closed her eyes again. "No, I don't knit. Eliza always threatened to make me learn, but she never got to me."

"That's sad. You must wish now that she had."

"Nope, I can't say that I do."

"Your great-aunt was a knitting genius. Beloved by generations. Her books are in print in dozens of languages. She was a legend."

"She was just my aunt."

"Wow." Abigail couldn't understand how anyone could have known Eliza as "just" anything.

"Don't get me wrong," he went on, "she was incredible. She was one of my favorite people. She could do anything she put her mind to here on the ranch. She could drop a pole in the ground and string barb wire and birth lambs and fell trees by hand. When she remembered something needed doing, she did it. Otherwise she was knitting."

Abigail smiled. "I love imagining that."

"What do you remember about her?"

Abigail sighed. "I remember everything. I remember how we met.

It was maybe seven, eight years ago. I was knitting in a café, not caring that everyone was looking at me. It was before knitting was cool again, and no one knitted in public. Some people seemed annoyed by it, and I wondered if I should put it away. But I didn't.

"Then this woman came up to me, this tall, striking woman, with the most amazing long gray hair I'd ever seen, and I thought for sure she was going to ask me to stop. Instead she reached a hand out and felt the drape of the fabric and said, 'Wool and angora?' Then she sat down and pulled out her needles and we started talking." Abigail took a breath. "She was one of the best friends I've ever had."

"Did you see her a lot?" Cade's face was softer than she'd seen it before. She would bet that he didn't know it.

"Every single day. She introduced me to the craft world, told me I could sell my patterns. She was basically the one responsible for me being able to leave my desk job and write knitting books for a living. Once I could do that, I had time every afternoon. I'd drive to her apartment and tell her about what I'd worked on in the morning."

"It was a residential-care home, not so much an apartment, right?"

"That's what she called it. But she had her own place, she was autonomous and always made sure people knew that." Abigail shot him a look. "So I cared enough to listen and call it what she wanted. It's not like a nurse was in there with her—they only checked on her and made sure she was okay and that she'd taken her meds."

"Nursing home."

"Nothing like it. You'd have known if you'd visited."

"She told me she was fine making the trip to see me and the house twice a year."

"You believed her."

Cade looked down at his book and fiddled with a bent corner. "Didn't cross my mind not to."

"She told me that you were the busiest person she knew, which was funny, because I've never known anyone more busy than she was. She'd be up at dawn to sit with her coffee and knit. She'd write letters. She'd sketch out ideas for her next book, and maybe write a little, and then she'd get in her little VW and trundle down to either her yoga class or the local yarn store."

"She did yoga?"

"She was good. She got me into it."

"Wow."

"If she was at the yarn store, it never failed, someone would enter the place, recognize her, and start babbling. She never felt comfortable around those people, the people who thought she was a hero, that worshipped her."

Cade frowned. "Seriously? I mean, I knew her books were popular, but really?"

"They stuttered. They couldn't talk. I saw one woman leave the store in tears after getting her autograph."

"She was a knitting rock star?"

"A knitting rock star. That's it exactly."

"And you were a groupie."

Abigail nodded, knitting her cables, trying not to stare at him. His face, when listening to her, was mesmerizing. His green eyes were gorgeous, glinting in the fire's dancing light. She looked down, focusing harder on a difficult decrease.

"I was, at first, and then I stuck around. Then I was her friend."

"Because you wanted an inheritance?"

The words were like a blow.

Abigail dropped her knitting into her lap. "You win. You get the parlor tonight."

She had given it her best shot, but she was done.

"I'm sorry," said Cade, quickly.

Abigail put her knitting into the fabric carrying bag she had next to her.

She paused. Then she said, "I cried for two days straight when she died. I couldn't get out of bed. I made myself physically ill. Besides my mother, I've never loved anyone as much as I loved her. And she loved me. That's what I know, and I don't care what you think."

He stood, the book dropping to the floor. "I didn't mean . . ."

"I know what you meant. I can't change your mind. Good night."

"Don't . . ."

"Don't what? You're getting what you want. Excuse me."

He moved, stepping sideways so that he blocked the door.

"Excuse me," she repeated.

He didn't move.

She wanted out of his parlor.

He wanted her out of his house.

Abigail looked up into his eyes, and saw that what he really wanted was to kiss her again.

Crazy as it was, as angry as she was at him, she knew she'd succumb to his desire if she stood here even one more second.

She knew her cheeks were flushed, that her eyes held unshed tears.

"Would you please move?" Her voice was breathless. He leaned toward her to hear it.

Then he leaned just a little more, and brushed the softest of kisses over her lips.

"I'm sorry," he whispered, against her mouth. "I didn't mean to say that."

Then he stood back. She knew this was her moment. He would let her walk by, he wouldn't take advantage of her. This was all the apology she was going to get.

But she looked up at him and stepped forward the last short few inches, closing the gap between their bodies, drawn toward him as if there was a string pulling them together.

His eyes were greener than she'd ever seen them, suddenly warm. With what? Lust? Friendship?

"I don't know what I'm doing," she said.

"Me, neither," he said.

She put one hand on his chest, went up on tiptoe, and kissed him, her turn this time to brush her lips against his.

"Good night," she whispered.

But instead of stepping away, she kissed him again.

As soon as she did, she knew it was a mistake. What had started out as a low rumble in her body, a dull heat, flared up into raging flames that she knew she wasn't going to be able to put out with just one kiss.

She could actually *feel* his body temperature rising along with hers. She had one hand on his arm, and she felt both her hand and his skin flush with heat, a sudden slickness under her palm.

She struggled to breathe, to regain control. His arm went around her, and he slipped his hand under her shirt, touching the small of her back where she was suddenly damp with heat.

He breathed as raggedly as she did. Their mouths moved, licking, tasting, tongues commingling, touching, and when she drew her head back to look at him, his green eyes had gone dark. His mouth was wet and slightly parted.

"You don't want me living here."

He groaned and pulled her back to him, "No, I don't. But I do want you." Then he kissed her again, and led her hand down to the front of his jeans where the fabric strained. Abigail gasped. Desire flooded her brain in a way she'd almost forgotten.

He took a few steps forward, leading her, guiding her backward. His mouth never lifted from his.

She wanted him, too. It was just sex, her body needing release in this stressful situation. She could choose when and where she received that release. Nothing wrong with that.

A tremor rocked her body.

She closed her eyes and saw Samuel. Smelled him for a moment. No.

The back of her calf hit the edge of the sofa. She could do this.

Abigail sat, and Cade followed, kneeling in front of her. She leaned forward, both hands going to his face, leading him in for another kiss. He placed kisses on every inch of her cheek, down her jawline, and farther.

His hands went to the hem of her shirt.

She gasped. Her hands moved to still his. *Wait.* She couldn't. The fear rose up in her throat. Cade's mouth against hers was suddenly too rough, too harsh. She stiffened under his touch.

"Stop."

Cade's reaction was instant. "What's wrong?"

"Nothing." Abigail's breathing was ragged, and she wasn't sure if it was from Cade or from the feeling inside she was trying to push down. Trying to smother.

"Something happened," he said.

"It's just . . ."

"Too fast?"

Abigail gave a half laugh that broke in the middle. "No. The speed is fine." She raised her hand and pressed it to her lips. If she could just slow her heart, for one second, she'd be able to think, to figure out where she was. The dark thrums of panic still threatened to rise up and blind her. If she could just breathe.

"You're shaking." Cade, still kneeling at her feet, took her hand and held it between his. His hands were warm and wide. Solid. Something to grasp. She held on.

Abigail closed her eyes.

But she saw Samuel again, against her eyelids. No! She wouldn't close her eyes, then. She held them open, but avoided Cade's gaze. She looked over his shoulder at the fire, still snapping sleepily in the grate.

"What's going on?" Cade touched the side of her face.

"I'm sorry. I'm just having a hard time."

"With me? Is it something I did?"

Fighting to keep the heat from stinging her eyes, Abigail shook her head. She would *not* cry. "Not you."

"Who was it?"

Abigail's hands shook harder.

"Did he hurt you?"

Oh, God. "Not much," said Abigail.

"Son of a bitch." Cade rose and sat next to her. His arms folded around her, and it wasn't the same embrace of just moments ago—it was close and strong. No expectation hung from the feeling.

A long moment later, Abigail couldn't tell how long, Cade said, "You want to tell me about it?"

Abigail tried to speak, but her words caught and stuck in her mouth. She tried again. "It wasn't that big a deal." She cleared her throat. "I don't know why I'm reacting like this. He was crazy, actually literally crazy." She blinked, hard. "Him and his damn pink roses. He tried to . . . but I didn't let him."

"The kiss reminded you of it?"

"I haven't kissed anyone since him."

"Nothing to be sorry for." Cade's voice was very quiet but steady.

Abigail moved deeper into his arms, and he pulled her closer. He said words into her hair. She didn't pay attention to what they were—she could tell by the tone what he meant.

This was the cowboy? The jerk? The guy who wanted her gone?

This was someone else. She'd never felt like this. She fit against him. He was strong. She relaxed into him as if she were melting.

The soft words continued raining into Abigail's hair, against her cheek. She felt them enter her body and move into a place she hadn't known needed filling. Outside, the storm eased, the downpour changing into a mist.

Chapter Eighteen

If you can believe one thing, believe this: No one will ever notice your mistakes later.

—E.C.

His arm was killing him. And his back hurt. Why was he on the sofa?

But something moved under him, something warm and soft, something that made him jerk open his eyes.

It wasn't a dream.

Abigail was underneath him, sound asleep, her head turned to the side on a knitted pillow, eyes screwed tight against the sun starting to come up.

The sun was coming up.

He hadn't seen the sun rising from a prone position in years. It must be after six already.

But instead of being in a hurry, instead of ripping his arm out from under her, instead of rolling to his side and taking his weight off her, he took a moment.

She was gorgeous, even in sleep. Her hair was tousled, her nose buried in the couch cushion. She took his breath away.

Of course he'd noticed that she was pretty, but this was amazing. The perfect body that fit his, as if they were sculpted from the same piece of clay. The hips that fit his hands. Her mouth that kissed his as if it was made to do so. Those eyes.

He longed for her to open her eyes. He willed as hard as he could for her eyes to open.

Nothing.

He joggled her a little with his arm.

She sighed.

He kissed her, the lightest sweep of his lips across hers.

Her eyes opened. That lightest of blues, that color of sky . . .

She opened her mouth and screamed. Then she scrambled up and over him, not seeming to notice that she'd knocked him off the sofa in her haste.

"Hey!" Cade yelled as he unceremoniously hit the floor.

"What the hell did we do? Did we . . . no. Why am I here? I don't remember!" Her voice sounded on the edge of panic again.

"Look at me," he said, hoping she would look at him again, that way. Like she had last night.

But she didn't. Her eyes darted to him and away, out the window, anywhere but into his eyes.

"Aren't you getting up kind of late?"

"I don't mind." The strange truth was that he didn't.

He watched her struggle to regain her dignity. "Why don't you go upstairs and change your clothes, and then I'll make you breakfast."

"I . . . Okay." She was out of the room like a shot.

Eggs, he thought, with bacon. And maybe biscuits. Did he have time to make gravy? He had to get out to the chores eventually, but for the first time in memory, he was okay with letting them wait. Tom would pick up any slack he left.

He hummed on his way to the kitchen.

This wasn't the way to kick the woman out of his house. He knew that. He still wanted her out.

But maybe, just maybe, there was the tiniest possibility that having her in the cottage so close by might not be that bad.

That guy. That asshole that had hurt her. Cade felt his neck flush with anger again as he walked into the kitchen. Men like that gave everyone a bad name. Thank God she'd gotten out of whatever it was that she'd been in.

His heart felt light, surprisingly light, as he prepared the breakfast, clanking and banging pots, the sound of eggs cracking and bacon popping in the cast-iron pan. He didn't usually feel this chipper this early in the morning unless getting laid had been part of the previous night. And he hadn't gotten that last night. He'd sure as hell wanted it. But after she got scared, it was enough just to hold her. No, it wasn't very manly; he admitted that to himself. But his heart stayed light.

Breakfast was ready in quick order. He didn't hear the shower anymore. He didn't hear anything, actually.

He gave it another couple of minutes.

The eggs were getting cold. He called her name.

No response. He went to the bottom of the steps.

"Abigail?"

Nothing.

He started to climb the stairs and was met by a shout.

"No! I'm coming down!"

"Well, hurry up!"

Abigail entered the kitchen. She was dressed in a black V-necked tee shirt, black pants, and black heels. Her hair was brushed into a low, smooth knot at the base of her neck. Her lips looked bee-stung.

He supposed that last could be partially his fault. He smiled.

"Good morning, gorgeous."

"We have to forget what happened last night. I mean"—she paused, looking at the ground—"I know it's hard to forget, but it would be better if it didn't come up as a topic of conversation, and please know that it won't happen again. I apologize for my part in it."

While ladling eggs onto her plate, Cade said, "I don't want your apology, Abigail. I want you to take it back. And I want you to eat."

She held her head higher. She looked like a bank executive—that was it. A really hot bank executive.

"It looks lovely. But I'm not actually very hungry. I have to go to town this morning."

"Already talking like a country girl. Going to town. Come on, just eat." He put the plate in front of her. She pushed the plate back at him.

He nudged it again, down the counter toward her.

She pushed it back, with more force than he had expected, and it flew off the counter and onto the floor with a loud crash. The plate flew into hundreds of pieces, eggs and bacon and biscuits hitting the floor.

"*Shit!* I didn't mean to . . ." she said and knelt down.

"Wait," he said, "be careful. Don't cut yourself."

"I won't. I'm used to it. I break everything. All the time." She sat back on her heels. "I'm sorry, I didn't mean to."

She was so upset that every part of her body radiated unhappiness. Cade didn't know how to fix it. He didn't know her at all, and couldn't even begin to guess what the magic words were to make her feel better.

"I don't care about the plate. I have a million of them in boxes upstairs. No idea why she had so many, but she did. And there's more food. Now, come on."

He took her elbow and lifted her gently, guiding her to the table, pulling out a chair and seating her in it. "I don't want you to get food on your good clothes. I'll clean that up, and I'll fix you another plate."

"Why are you being so nice to me? This is about last night? Being pathetic is all a girl has to do?"

"Well, it wasn't a bad idea, let's put it that way." He shot her a grin, aiming for lightheartedness, but it missed the mark, as she looked down at her hands.

"I'm sorry. I guess I'm in a good mood."

"I'm still in your house. You're upset about that."

He nodded. "Yep. I still am. This is my house, and I feel like Eliza bamboozled me, big-time. However . . . " He slid another plate of food in front of her.

"However," he continued. "Eliza did it by placing a gorgeous woman here, so I guess it could be worse."

She flinched.

"Last night was . . . " he said.

"I said I don't want to talk about it."

"Fine. Eat. Talk about whatever you want."

"I have to tell you something. I should have told you before now. I'm going into town to get a business license this morning." She took a bite of bacon.

"I don't know about San Diego," he was fixing his own plate now, and he could feel his stomach rumble, "but around here I don't think you need a license to write books like you do. I mean, maybe when you file taxes or something, but you probably don't need to be in a big hurry about it."

"It's not for writing books. I thought I should tell you myself so you don't hear it from someone else."

Her voice sounded nervous. Was it shaking?

"What's it for, then?"

"I'm going to open a business."

Cade tried to process the words.

"A business for writers? What's that?"

"A workshop. A place to teach people about fiber and yarn and spinning and knitting, mostly teaching space."

"Where?"

"In the cottage."

Cade thought about it, processing the words as fast as he could around his disbelief. "You can't do that. Not on my land."

"Technically, it's mine."

"No. You don't have an access road, I control the driveway."

"I can put in a small driveway through the back of my alpaca run, out to that county road if I have to. It would be nicer to use your driveway, though, if you would consider letting me rent it from you."

"You don't have the zoning." Cade leaned on the counter, gripping the edge tightly. His knuckles turned white.

"Your land is already zoned for it, since your neighbor apparently has some kind of produce stand? This area has multiple zones."

"You can't."

"I can. It won't be bad." Her voice slipped back to the eagerness and speed that he now recognized. "You won't mind, knitters are lovely people. They'll be quiet. They'll love coming to a ranch, a working ranch, and they'll all be fans of your aunt." She took another bite of her eggs. "This is delicious, by the way. Are they your eggs? I mean, from your chickens? I'm sorry I dropped the plate the first time." She was talking quickly now. She was nervous. And she had every reason to be.

No way in *hell* was he going to have a goddamn knitting classroom on his property.

"Eliza's fans are rabid. You have no idea. And I have my own fan base, strange as that may seem. People like my books. They'll come, they'll take classes, they'll look at your sheep."

"No, they won't!"

"Well, maybe I can convince you to let them. And once they see your sheep and find out their names, then there's this amazing thing that happens to knitters—they want the fiber or yarn straight off that animal, and they'll pay almost anything to get it. So if they see Rosebud in the field, then you can sell them Rosebud yarn at a great price."

"Are you listening? No classroom. No Rosebud. My sheep don't even have names, for the love of God."

"So let me name them! I'd love to do that."

"No shop. No classes."

"It's my dream. I know it's sudden, Cade, but . . ."

"Is that how you work? Now I get it." He nodded.

"What?" she said.

"You kiss me last night and make me feel sorry for you, and I spend all night with you with our clothes *on*. And the whole time you *know* that you're going to do this in the morning, that you would have to tell me about it before I heard it from someone else. You were just using me last night. Paving your way. Or should I say, paving your driveway?"

"It wasn't like that, I never thought . . ."

"You're a smart lady, Abigail. You're smarter than I gave you credit for. I thought you were some city chick, dumb enough to accidentally buy two alpacas and a herding dog, dumb enough to want to live in an old cottage on a ranch in the middle of nowhere."

He nodded as he scraped his own food into the trash. No point, really. He was too mad to have an appetite.

"But no, you bought the alpacas to breed them, so your classes can tour the ranch and ogle the crias, and then you sell that fiber to them at a premium. You have the border collie so you look like a genuine ranch girl. You're going to sell them the whole package, aren't you? Trap them in your tourist's web, and they'll never know the difference.

"And you thought you could get me on your side, is that right? That if you cried a little and batted those blues at me, I wouldn't notice when you hung out a sign on the front gate and paved the front yard as a parking lot."

"I didn't plan it that way. You kissed me first last night! And in the bathroom, too!"

"That just means you're good at what you do."

"You think I planned it this way?"

"It's obvious. You set me up. But it's not going to work."

He watched as her eyes filled suddenly, brimming with tears. She stood and turned, brushing off her pants.

She walked to the front door and turned. "Eliza, when she came up here to see you . . . those bags and boxes . . ."

Then she stopped and opened the door. She left, her head down. Clara followed at her heels, her head also lowered, as though the dog thought she was in trouble, too.

Damn.

He had caught her. She was really, really good. He was amazed at how *slick* she was, how he hadn't seen this coming.

Cade cleaned up, went out to the barn, discussed the workday with Tom. Felt like he'd been punched in the gut. Did his chores. All the while, the slow burn of rage in his chest grew heavier, a thick braid of anger lodged in his body.

The more he pushed on fence poles, the harder he drove the tractor into the mulch pile he was working on, the more his body temperature soared. Under the scent of his own heat and sweat, he could smell her, that light, sweet smell, that scent that had masked what he'd found today. She was machinating, conniving. Was there even a guy who had hurt her in the past? He wouldn't put it past her to just make that guy up. To get the sympathy.

The girl who had been on the couch with him last night—he had no idea who she was.

What she could be.

God, it just proved everything he believed about women. He grimaced as he pulled a burr out of the palm of his hand. He should be using his gloves now to move this pile of brush, but he didn't want to.

All women. Just the same.

Just like his mother. She'd left his father after taking him for all he was worth. She'd used his father to move up in the world, out of her trailer and into his house. She'd given birth to Cade, and then left with all his father's money, and most of his pride. Every couple of years she'd show up and move back in again, all tears and remorse. His father would fall back in love, then they'd start to fight. Cade hid under his blankets until he was old enough to run to Eliza's. Every time his mother left, she took more of his father with her, until there was nothing left. When his dad died, he was nothing but a pathetic shell.

God, what a sucker Cade'd almost been.

That moment last night, when he had been drowning in Abigail's eyes, in what had felt like her soul—that had been an act. A well-played role.

He'd fallen for it.

He wouldn't make that mistake again.

Chapter Nineteen

When you join the arms to the body, make sure you're in
the mood to concentrate. Leave the play knitting aside,
just for this row. This is serious.
—E.C.

Janet's black town car crunched up the driveway. By the time
Abigail got to the car itself, Janet had gotten out and was standing, hand over mouth, looking around.

Janet stage-whispered to Abigail, "Is it real?"

"It's real."

"And this little house? This is the new place? This is where the
shop is going to be? Where you'll live?"

"Theoretically. Although you'll tell me if it is or not, I think."

Janet grabbed Abigail and squeezed her, hard. Abigail responded
by holding her and hugging back so hard that Janet gasped.

"Anything wrong, honey?" Janet took a step back and looked at
her. "Everything all right out here in the wilds? It's been two weeks
since our lunch and I haven't heard from you once. You're one step
away from home-brewing liquor in a still, aren't you? I knew it."

Abigail shook her head. "It's only twenty minutes from where you
live in town."

"But think of the *town*, honey. It's no metropolis."

"You left that all behind years ago anyway. You should be used to it."

"I suppose I am, but I am not used to *this*. Now, show me everything. Oh, my God, you have a dog?" Clara tried to jump on Janet, but Janet stepped to the side in a practiced move.

She was wearing an orange-and-fuchsia low-cut blouse that clung to her curves and showed to great advantage the chest that she had bought and paid for years ago. Her outfit was completed by a tight brown skirt with a long slit up the side and high-heeled brown leather knee-high boots.

"I can't show you everything. Believe me, you don't want to walk around the barns in those heels. I can barely manage it in tennis shoes."

"I can go anywhere in these, darling. Lead the way."

"The cottage first, then. It's really all I can safely show you anyway." Janet's perfect eyebrows went up, but didn't ask.

They went up onto the porch, Janet making appreciative noises. Abigail opened the door.

"Oh," said Janet. "Wow."

"It needs a lot of work."

"Understatement of the century. What *is* all this stuff?"

Abigail's voice became lighter as she told Janet more about what Eliza had left for her. She showed her the partially set up wheels, and opened boxes to show her the stored fiber.

"Spinning wheels!" Abigail pushed four boxes aside to show her the Lendrum, already put together. "Tons of wheels, all kinds. Fiber in rolags and batts, all gorgeously prepped. Yarn, lots of it, from a vendor in Maine. Dyes, all natural. Look! There's even a cash register, over here. Oh, it's somewhere. But isn't it amazing?"

Janet cocked her head and said, "It's something, all right."

"You have to admit that it's awesome, right? Eliza is giving me not only the cottage but my dream as well."

"Your dream was to sell yarn on a rural road twenty minutes from a decent cup of coffee?"

"I can make my own coffee here."

"What does the cowboy think about all this?"

Abigail flushed, and she knew Janet noticed. She turned to close up a box. "He's not too happy about it."

"I'm sure. Will he get used to it?"

"He'll have to, won't he? I mean, he doesn't have that much choice. This is my land, my place, my property, and I can put in a driveway out to that county road behind my pasture, if I have to. I got the license this morning, and met with the local business bureau, and it's all set to go. As soon as I'm ready in here, I can open the shop."

Janet put a finger to her cheek. "You have a pasture? Oh, darling, it's too much. Show me your pasture."

"I have alpacas, too."

Janet's mouth dropped open, and for once, she didn't appear to have anything to say.

Abigail thought Janet did well, the next half hour, as she led her around the property. She made it across the dirt and into the shed just fine in the spiked boots. She seemed to adore the alpacas, although they didn't look like they knew what to make of her, and shied away every time she approached.

Tussah, the female, was making great strides. She let Abigail approach her neck and touch her back. Merino didn't shy too much from her either. Abigail figured the twice-daily feeding she'd been doing was starting to work.

Abigail made sure Cade's truck was nowhere in sight and then showed Janet the main house. Janet loved the parlor the best.

Of course she would, thought Abigail. The one room she didn't want to reenter, Janet swooned over.

"That *lamp*! And those windows! That piano! The whole room is perfect. It's like something out of *Little House on the Prairie*."

"Oh, please."

"And just look at that fireplace, can you ever imagine anything more romantic? What you need to do, honey, is get that Cade in here one night, you give him a little whiskey or whatever it is the cowboys are drinking these days. A little smooch, and you get a little hot-cha-cha, right here," —she paused, looking over the room—"right over there on that sofa, mmmm-hmmm."

Abigail rolled her eyes and tried to sound nonchalant. "Cut it out."

"Oh, honey, I'm only teasing you."

"Didn't you want to see the barn?"

"Of course I do. Lead on."

Once outside, Abigail again carefully searched for Cade's big old truck, but didn't see it. She'd found in the past few days that the barn was a wonderful place to visit if she could sneak in by herself. There was always a sheep or two in one of the pens, not with the fold. Cade had four horses that he rode and used in herding the sheep, and they were kept either in the pasture to the immediate rear of the barn, or in their stalls. Two other working dogs lived out there, too, dogs that seemed completely flummoxed by Clara's inability to do anything work-like.

Before she came here, Abigail hadn't ever known how nice it was to hear a horse's puffy breaths coming over a wooden door. She'd snuck in several times already to hear it.

"Horses! Oh, divine," exclaimed Janet.

Well, at least she was an appreciative audience.

"Oh, look at the big beasts," said Janet. "Look at how handsome you are, what a big boy you are, how gorgeous, that big soft nose, and those huge eyes . . ."

"Thanks. I love getting compliments like that from beautiful ladies."

Both women spun around to find a man standing behind them, his arms crossed, a smile across his face, a cowboy hat on his head.

"Oh, *divine*," breathed Janet.

"I'm Abigail. You must be Tom. Cade's mentioned you." Abigail stuck out her hand. His palm was huge, callused and rough.

"I've seen you up at the house from a distance. Been meaning to come up and introduce myself, but it's been busy down here lately. I'm sorry for that."

Before Abigail could respond, Janet stepped in front of her.

"My name is Janet," she said, batting her eyes. Abigail hadn't ever actually seen anyone do that before, and she was amazed.

So, it seemed, was Tom.

"T-Tom," he stuttered. Then he cleared his throat. "Are you Abigail's sister?"

"Aren't you the sweetest? No, I'm in fashion. Imports."

Tom looked confused.

"Luxury fibers, darling. That's how I know our girl here. Actually, I'm the one who convinced her to write her first book. Now, you—you look like someone with a book inside you, just waiting to burst out."

Tom grinned and stuck his hands in his pockets. "Well, that's somethin'. I've been thinking a little bit lately that I'd like to write a book someday. Maybe a Western. Like Louis L'Amour."

"Show me more of your horses, and maybe I'll see if I can pull that book out of you."

Tom grinned bigger. They wandered off down toward the other stalls.

Abigail called after them, "I'll be at the cottage, then, okay? Cleaning!" Neither looked back at her. "By myself! Don't worry about me!"

Janet gave a jaunty wave without turning around.

An hour later, Abigail was covered in dust, grime, and sweat. She had moved the bulk of the boxes into one half of the front room, culling the junk from the stuff that would be stock, marking on the sides of other boxes what the contents were. She had a plan for moving the boxes out of the hall and kitchen. While she did the grunt work, in her mind she was designing her bedroom-slash-writing studio upstairs, in the cupola.

It almost worked to take her mind off Cade.

She had, however, managed to decide that she would sacrifice having a big bed upstairs and just get a small one—it would be hard to get a big one up there anyway—in favor of having a larger writing desk in front of one of the many windows. The octagonal room itself had windows on all sides, and Abigail had chosen yellow walls with red-checkered curtains. The red would help keep the light out in the morning, and looked as cheery as the landscape outside.

Maybe she'd see Cade from up there, when she was working.

Not that she'd be looking.

She would give the rest of the cottage over to her new workshop. She didn't really know what to call it in her head—store, shop, classroom? She wanted a limited amount of retail product available—some spinning wheels and oils, things like brake bands and bobbins. She pictured baskets in the corners with wooden bobbins that customers could poke through and pick from, bins of loose fiber that people could pull out, bundle, and measure on the scale that would stand on an old dark wooden desk. She didn't have the desk yet. But she could imagine it.

But really, more than a store, Abigail wanted a place for knitters to gather, for people to be able to come and knit or spin in a beautiful place. She wanted couches and tables piled with books and coffee cups, and colorful walls, light and flowers. A sense of place.

She would change the downstairs bedroom into a small classroom. She wouldn't have big classes, never more than seven or eight people—there was room for a large table or two, and comfortable chairs. Yesterday, when she'd been cleaning in there, she'd been surprised when she pulled back the old, heavy drapes and found a pair of French doors that opened onto a small deck, overlooking the alpaca pasture. The doors, along with the three windows, gave the room all the light they'd need to spin even the finest of downy fibers.

She wondered if Cade had ever seen anyone spinning, wondered if Eliza had spun anything for him.

No, maybe not. Eliza didn't like to make things for people who wouldn't appreciate the gift; she wouldn't make handspun socks or hats, much less handspun sweaters, for people who would carelessly toss them into a hot washing machine. So Cade probably had little from her.

But Eliza had loved him. So he *might* have a store-bought-yarn hand-knitted sweater or two, she supposed. Eliza had always glowed when speaking of her nephew. She had been so proud of him, proud that he'd done so much with her land, with his life. She had been so proud that he'd taken after his father and not his mother, who had been a piece of work, apparently.

What would Eliza think now?

"Where are you?" whispered Abigail, wandering through the rooms littered with boxes. "Are you still here?"

She threw open the French doors again and wandered out.

Janet's voice calling her from the front made her jump.

"I'm out here, " she called. "Come through the bedroom."

Janet came out onto the deck, Tom following at her heels. He looked a little confused, like he'd been hit on the head with something. He didn't seem to mind.

Actually, he looked besotted, his eyes locked on Janet's face.

"We're going to lunch. We just wanted to tell you, in case you were looking for me, or in case Cade looks for Tom."

Abigail noted she was not invited.

"We're going to talk about literature," said Tom.

Janet shot her a cheeky grin, and they popped back through the French doors and out of sight.

She supposed that was what she got for taking Janet through the barn.

She would check on her livestock; that would cheer her up.

Chapter Twenty

I've always found it's better to keep my fingers moving,
knitting always. It keeps me out of trouble.
—E.C.

Abigail called Clara, who dragged herself out from behind a
pile of boxes. It looked like she had been chewing a sponge.
Great. Now the dog would be sick on top of everything else.

They walked out and around to the pasture. Abigail had left the
door to the shed open to the field behind it. That way the animals
could wander in and out at their whim, eating or drinking water,
with the freedom that any alpaca deserved. Or at least, that's what
she assumed an alpaca deserved.

Tussah looked up when she opened the gate, did a small head toss,
and backed up a bit. But she let Abigail approach her, not moving
away as quickly as she had yesterday.

"What a good girl." Abigail looked around. "Where's Merino?"

He must be in the shed, perhaps taking a nap.

It was dark inside, and Abigail strained her eyes. She peered into the corners. There was a dangling lightbulb overhead, but no matter how hard she looked, she couldn't see Merino.

"Tussah! Where's Merino?" Yeah, asking the other alpaca would work.

Clara, on the other side of the fence, cocked her head to the side, watching Abigail closely.

Then she saw it. Damn.

There was a rip in the fence so big it looked like it had been cut with wire cutters—Abigail wasn't sure if it was new or if she'd missed it. Cade had checked also, hadn't he? Had he missed it, too?

Or had he seen it and not mentioned it? It wouldn't bother him much if she lost the alpacas.

She didn't quite know what to do. She'd lost cats before, but beyond searching the backyard and calling their name around the neighborhood, there wasn't much to be done about a lost cat.

She'd had a dog run away when she was a kid, right after her mother died, and she'd had a doubly broken heart. She knew that if her mom had still been around they would have found Lucky. Mothers were good at that sort of thing. She remembered being so furious at her father for not being able to find her lost dog.

It was nice that Clara was sticking to her so closely, like a shadow most of the time, unless she was chewing on things she wasn't supposed to, like that sponge.

But now—yeah, now she had a problem.

How to look for an alpaca.

Should she drive? Should she look for tracks first?

Yes. Wasn't that what they did out here on the ranch? Search for the tracks? She really had no idea what to look for, but she figured an alpaca footprint couldn't be too hard to figure out.

She ran back past a startled-looking Tussah, to where the break in the fence was. Yes, here were prints. They were distinctive and clear, narrow, notched ovals, and they were on both sides of the hole in the fence. Abigail wished Tom hadn't left with Janet; he could have helped search.

But as she headed up the hill, following a dirt track that Merino had apparently found appealing, she thought it was just as well. Tom would tell Cade, who would get a huge laugh at her expense. They'd sit around all guy-like and chortle. Probably spit off the porch.

No, she'd do this by herself.

It was a gorgeous, cool, foggy day. The ground was still slightly wet. Thank God. Merino wasn't proving hard to track at all.

Or maybe she was just good at this. Sure, she was a city slicker, or at least not a country girl, but these tracks were easy. They seemed purposeful—Merino was headed in one direction with what seemed like intent. He didn't veer from the track he was on. His clear footprints led her forward, to a stand of oak trees.

Once in the trees, it got a little harder to follow him. Her newfound confidence didn't flag, though, and she was prouder by the moment each time she found the disturbed place in the leaves that signaled where her animal had stepped.

The oak leaves crunched under her feet as she went, and looking back she realized that even her own footprints were evident, now that she was trying.

She glanced up between footsteps to survey the land around her. She wasn't even sure this was still Cade's property, although since she hadn't had to climb over a fence, she assumed so.

The track veered now to the left, going a bit downhill. Abigail skidded on some leaves and almost fell.

Easy. This was no place to fall.

The signs were harder to find now. She struggled, taking minutes at a time between track identifications. There were other markings now, and she had no idea what kind of animals they belonged to. She hoped they were nothing that liked alpacas for dinner, though. Did mountain lions live up here?

Then she lost Merino's tracks entirely. They were suddenly gone, the earth too hard or the leaves too thick for her to pick anything up.

She sighed and pushed her hair out of her eyes. She'd probably been following a deer for the last half mile, anyway.

Now, to figure out which way was back to the cottage.

She stood in one spot, then headed a little bit uphill.

Yes, this was the way she had come.

But she hadn't noticed that stump with the red paint before, and surely she would have, right? Why would a stump be painted red, all the way out here? She turned again, looking behind her.

She couldn't identify anything.

This was ridiculous.

She walked farther. She kept walking, clambering over fallen logs, praying that she was avoiding the poison oak she knew was all around. Nothing looked familiar in the slightest. But why would it? Trees looked like trees, and she hadn't been paying any attention at all to the land around her while she was tracking Merino—her head had been down, eyes focused only on the ground.

Maybe it might help orient her if she went uphill. She had gone downhill, after all, for quite a while, and if she got up high enough, maybe she'd be able to see the cottage or the ranch—anything.

Panting, legs burning, she climbed up. At the top of a hill, she turned all the way around, but the trees still blocked her view.

Nope. No earthly idea where she was. And she knew that Cade's land was bordered to the north by conservation land, which could stretch on forever.

She might die in this forest.

Okay, she could admit it wasn't really forest. At all. It was rolling hills thick with live oaks and eucalyptus.

The redwoods! She remembered that there was a stand of redwoods to one side of Cade's ranch, and those should be easy enough to spot if she got high up enough. If she climbed one of the trees . . .

One oak had low, spreading limbs, and it looked like the kind of tree she had loved to climb when she was a kid. Of course, that had been years and years ago. But wasn't it like riding a bike?

It had been years since she'd ridden a bike, too.

She took off her shoes—she'd always been better at climbing in her bare feet—and started up the trunk.

The hardest part was the first bit—jumping up to grab the lowest branch, swinging her feet up onto it at the trunk. But it got easier after that, as if her body remembered just what to do, how to lean to the next branch, to trust it would hold her weight. In what felt like no time, she had scaled her way to the top of the tree, to the highest limb that she had determined would have the best, most unimpeded view.

And there, down and to her right as the crow flew, were the redwood trees.

Thank God, she knew which way to go. She breathed a sigh of relief and started climbing down.

She slipped.

Her foot skidded off the branch she stood on. Bark peeled off in strips. Both hands tightened around the limb she was holding on to, but she couldn't balance herself, and then she was hanging on to the limb with both hands, her feet flailing below her. She couldn't reach with her feet the branches closest to her—all were just a few inches too far in front or behind her. She couldn't fall—there was a limb below her that she'd break something on if she fell, not to mention the fact that the ground was still ten feet below that.

She tried to bring her foot back up on the branch that she'd slipped off, but the little jump she'd made had been too much, and the branch broke under her weight, dropping to the ground.

Now she was dangling. Abgail was going to have to fall, but she had to do her best to avoid the limb directly below her. Her heart was racing, and she threw her fear into motion—swinging with all her strength, as she had on the jungle gym as a child. As her legs flew out far enough, she gave a high scream and let herself sail.

It was a split-second's relief as she cleared the branch below, and then she was hitting the ground, letting her knees bend as she hit, going down on her side, and rolling, rolling, until she came to a painful stop.

Abigail lay on her back, looking up at the blue sky through the oak leaves, taking assessment.

Her neck wasn't broken; that was good. Her spine appeared to be intact. Her hands were skinned from clutching the branch, but she could wiggle her fingers.

The part she really didn't want to think about was her left foot.

She moves her toes and gasped. Well, at least she could control them. But she couldn't bend the ankle at all, and sitting up slowly, she reached for her foot.

It wasn't at a funny angle, and she could press the bones with her fingers although she gasped from the pain. It was most likely a good old-fashioned ankle sprain.

But she was really damn far from the house now.

She stood, using her right leg and foot, placing no weight on her left, and took a step, placing the slightest bit of pressure on her left ankle.

She almost wept with the instant rush of pain. The shock of it was already wearing off, and the throbbing was moving in.

But she could handle it. She was strong. She was tough. She had endured worse than this before.

She took another few steps.

No, she was wrong. This *was* the worst pain she'd ever felt. She sat for a moment and let the sharpness of it subside to a dull thudding, and then stood again.

She wasn't going to make it.

Thank God Janet was with Tom. That made it all so much simpler. She got out her cell phone; four bars of reception, even up here. God bless technology.

"Darling!" Janet answered on the first ring. "I'm sorry we're still out, do you want us to bring you back a doggie bag?"

"I need help. I've hurt myself, up in the hills above the ranch. I need to be picked up—I need Tom to drive up here or something and get me." She could barely keep the sob out of her voice. She would not cry.

Abigail heard a shuffling noise and then Tom was on the line.

"You're hurt?" His voice was tinny in her ear. "How bad? Do you need me to call an ambulance?"

"No, I think it's just a bad sprain, but I can't walk on it."

"Are you sure? We could get the air ambulance started your way . . ."

"A what? Do you mean a helicopter? No way in hell. Just come get me, can't you?"

"Where are you, exactly?"

"Um. I'm above the ranch."

"What does that mean?"

"I climbed a tree because I was lost, and all I can tell you is that if you leave the back kitchen door and climb straight up from the house into the trees, I'm somewhere in there."

"Don't suppose you have any better description?"

"I'm on the top of one of the rises. A lot of oak. Less eucalyptus on this hill than the others."

"All right. I'm too far away, but I'll call Cade and send him."

"No!"

"Don't you worry. He'll find you."

Tom dropped the line, leaving her phone quiet and dark.

God, if there was any way now she could get up and hobble, even hop out of here, she would. But every time the ankle moved, even the slightest bit, she felt queasy and the pain went straight to the top of her head.

Two minutes later, her cell rang. She didn't recognize the number, but she knew who it was.

"No, I don't know where I am."

"Sounds pretty stupid to me. How did you manage this one?"

"Sheer talent."

"Tell me how to find you."

"Leave the house through the kitchen door, and go out in the hills. Go straight up from there."

"Straight up how? North? Northwest? Northeast?"

"Oh, let me get a compass. Hang on for a really long time while I make one from these leaves."

"Okay, smart-ass. Tom said you're on the top of a rise?"

"Yes."

"Are there any hills higher than yours?"

"I'm below the trees right now. I can't see."

"But when you climbed the tree, bring it back into your mind. Was there anything around you?"

"Trees. Trees were around me. Oh, yeah, I passed a red stump. So I guess I'm not lost."

"You're a pain in the ass, you know that? Think about it. Did you see a radio tower? Mowry's cell site? Any redwoods?"

She was quiet while she tried to remember. "I could see the redwoods by the house. And I think, to my left, there were a couple more, very tall, maybe a quarter mile away. And to my right, kind of between the ranch and the cut in the hills where you can see the ocean, I could see a metal tower, but I'm not sure if it was radio or cell."

"Tall and triangular?"

"Yes."

"I'm coming. Sit tight."

With little else she could do, Abigail scooted backwards until she could rest her back against the offending tree. She stuck her tongue out at it and felt immediately stupid. She was glad no one could see her.

No one could see her and she guessed it was all right if she had a little cry. Just a quick one.

She let the tears come, hot and fast. This wasn't supposed to happen. She'd only been looking for her lost alpaca, and climbing the tree had been a good idea. Coming down was the hard part, that was all. That hadn't really figured into her thought processes while going up.

After what felt like four hours but was probably more like only one, Abigail heard a very faraway voice calling her name.

"Here!" she yelled with all her lungs. "I'm here!"

Cade's voice yelling her name got closer and closer.

Abigail felt crazy with relief—she was saved!—and she had never wanted more to be anyplace else. Anyplace that wasn't here, where she wouldn't be waiting for rescue from a cowboy who hated her. She strained her ears for the sound of his truck approaching, now that he knew where she was, but she couldn't hear any kind of engine, except for a whine of a small plane, very far overhead.

Crash, crackle. The rustling that she'd thought she heard was getting closer. "Here! Over here!" she yelled.

He couldn't have . . . could he?

Oh, yes, he had. The rustling she heard was almost upon her, coming up from behind, and then she could see them both—Cade on his horse.

He'd come on horseback to rescue her. The irony of it wasn't wasted on her. Cade knew it, too—the sour look on his face confirmed that he felt the same way.

"Thanks for stopping by," she said.

"Wasn't doing much else today anyway. Only running a sheep ranch without any help because my foreman left for lunch." Cade drew the horse up close to her. "Tom doesn't leave for lunch."

Abigail was briefly terrified of the huge beast above her, even though she knew it was stupid to be scared.

"He won't—he won't step on me, will he?" She wanted to draw

her legs out of the way, but she was loath to move them at all. The pain was bad enough when it wasn't white-hot with motion.

Cade only rolled his eyes. He swung off and landed almost at her feet. "Will you be able to get up on the horse?"

"Of course."

"You do know how to ride, don't you?"

"Are you kidding me?"

"No."

"Okay, no, I don't," she admitted. "But it can't be that hard, right?"

"I'm going to have to ride with you, then."

"Both of us up there? I don't think so."

"You don't know how to ride."

"I can figure it out."

"And I'm not risking my best horse to your poor judgment. Can you stand at all? Is it just the one ankle, or do you have more injuries you didn't tell Tom about?"

"Just the one, and I can stand by myself." Why this stupid need to impress him? She wanted to appear strong.

So she stood, quickly and firmly, using her arms braced behind her on the tree trunk, placing weight only on her good leg, using her thigh muscles to go straight up. So far so good.

Then her left foot brushed against the ground. She could actually feel herself going pale, the blood draining out of her face, and she slumped for a second while she tried to take a shallow breath around the pain.

He was next to her in that short second, his arms around her, holding her up.

"I'm fine," she whispered. She cleared her throat. "I don't need your help."

He tightened his grasp on her, raising one arm and placing it over his neck. "You do, if only to get on the damn horse. Shut up and do what I tell you."

Abigail opened her mouth to retort, but realized he was right.

She'd never get on that horse without his help, and she'd never get off this hill without that horse.

"Now, hop a little bit over here." He held her with one arm and steadied the horse with the other.

"I have no idea how to get up there," she said.

"I'll throw you."

"Excuse me?"

Cade's hands went to her waist. He lifted her up and twisted her so that her good leg went over the horse. At the end of the same motion, he caught her bad leg at the knee, stopping its motion. He caught the leg at the calf, and lowered it to the side of the horse.

She gasped.

"I know that hurt. But it would have been worse otherwise."

"I know." She should thank him, but she couldn't speak through the pain.

"This might be bad, too, but only for a minute, and then we'll get you out of here. Scoot forward if you can, and hang on."

Hang onto what? The reins? She didn't understand their configuration. Did one rein mean go and the other stop? The mane? That couldn't be right. She was sure she'd seen people ride like that, but that had been in the movies, and this didn't feel like a movie beneath her. It felt like a massive warm rock. Her legs straddled it, and her fingers dug tight against the muscles of the horse as Cade slung himself up and behind her.

She gasped. Something had hit her foot, possibly Cade's boot, and she saw stars for a moment. His arms came around her, tightly.

"I'm sorry. I tried not to do that. Okay, hold your legs out in front of the stirrups, and I'll try to avoid joggling you as much as I can. It might be a little bumpy, though."

"Aren't you going to give me a bullet to bite on?" she asked, her voice strained.

He laughed, and she felt the laughter in her chest. It was more of a bark than a laugh—as if he hadn't expected it to happen. Then he cleared his throat.

"What the hell fool thing did you think you were doing all the way up here? Taking a hike?"

"Yeah, that was it." She turned her head to the side to talk to him, but he spoke right in her ear.

"Bring your trail mix? Next time bring a map, would you? It was damned hard to find you—I've been calling your name up here for almost an hour. I went from ridge to ridge before I got the right one."

"I was looking for stupid Merino."

"What?"

"The male alpaca. He got out."

"Mort said he always *was* good at that."

"Alpacas aren't supposed to be good at escape."

"The exception to the rule, I suppose. Why did you think he'd have come all the way up here?"

"I followed his tracks."

She waited for the inevitable laugh. She was not disappointed.

"Alpaca tracks? Up here? Lady, even I couldn't do that, and I've been practicing since I was a boy. They're too light, hardly weigh a thing, and these oak leaves move so quickly in the breeze. Maybe in mud or something, but I can't believe you followed him up here. Can't believe he was ever up here at all."

"I think I was doing okay. I really think I was following him."

"Sure. Go ahead and think that."

They rode out of a copse and onto a hillside. Far below them Abigail could see the house, the barn, the cottage, the ocean gleaming in the far distance. "Look how pretty that is," said Abigail.

Abigail could hear the smile in his voice. "The prettiest sight in the whole wide world."

Abigail shifted her hips so that she could keep her ankle forward, away from his booted foot, and in the process, she ended up scooting her rear end against him. He'd been starting to say something else, but he stopped, abruptly.

"What?" she asked.

"Nothing." But it was suddenly quite clear to Abigail what the problem was. She felt something behind her, something that wasn't his jeans. He was hard against her. Her mouth went dry.

It would happen to anyone, she thought. Anyone put together like this, on a horse that was swaying, their two bodies rubbing . . . It was natural.

But her body was reacting, too, and she couldn't blame it on being a man.

Could she blame it on the horse thing? She wasn't used to sitting on a moving object like this. . . . But no, she knew exactly what was causing her to heat up like this, what was causing the blood in her veins to throb this hard. His arms around her, his maleness behind her, his lips and voice so close to her ear.

She tried to shift forward, out of his way, but she kicked her foot the wrong way, and winced. He caught the motion and moved a hand to her waist.

He pulled her back, harder against him.

"We have to keep you motionless, or it'll hurt more later," he said, so close that it sent a shiver down her spine.

She flushed red with embarrassment—it was her proximity, after all, she assumed, that was making him react like this. She wished she could move away, but at the same time, she didn't want to move a muscle.

Cade's hand had stayed on the curve of her waist after he'd settled her against him. It rested gently at her hip, and then it moved slightly so that the tips of his fingers brushed lightly against her side through her shirt.

Was he doing that on purpose?

She couldn't feel her ankle anymore. There was nothing in her mind except for thoughts of what he felt like behind her.

Then he tugged the bottom of her shirt out of her jeans and slipped his hand inside, resting it back at the curve of her waist.

"You don't mind, do you?" he murmured. "You'll be better anchored this way. Don't want anything to happen to you."

She shook her head. Did his lips brush her cheek? She turned her head the same direction again and said, "Good idea."

What was this? Didn't he still hate her because of this morning?

Then she let her head drop back against his shoulder, and closed her eyes. She didn't want to figure it out, not right now.

His hand barely touched her skin, fingers skimming the sensitive curves, sliding forward so that his fingers moved around her bellybutton and then back to her side. It was an agony of sensitivity. She wasn't ticklish, but she shivered.

As his hand played up her side, moving ever so slowly toward her breast, she pressed even harder back into him. His hand went higher, pushing her bra up, skimming her nipple with one finger.

He kept his hand moving on her skin, pinching and lightly twisting her nipple. She was as aroused as if he had his fingers inside her instead of on her breast. Her eyes were shut tight, and his breathing was as uneven as hers in her ear.

"Shit." His hand jerked out from under her shirt. He sat up straight and held the reins with both hands in front of her, and she had to follow suit. Her eyes flew open, and she saw that not only were they almost at the barn, which surprisingly dismayed her, but that Janet and Tom were just getting out of Tom's truck.

"The prodigal returns," said Cade, loud enough for Tom to hear as he led the horse up next to the truck.

"I don't get a lunch break? Not allowed? I'll alert my union."

Janet laughed, a high peal of humor that made Tom's eyes light up. He was smitten, it was clear. Men often were.

But then Janet's expression changed, going from high flirt to nothing but concern.

"Sweetheart, how are you? But what? How? Falling out of a *tree*?"

"We have to get you to a doctor," said Tom.

"No, I'll be fine."

They all shook their heads in unison, and Janet said, "We'll *all* go with you. We're off! It's an adventure. I mean, of course, darling, this is hell for you. But for us, we'll fete ourselves as heroes, with Cade being the hero of the day. Of the year! Now get her off that horse, cowboy, so I can give you a kiss for valor."

Cade steadied Abigail in place with his hands, and she tried in vain to forget where his hand had just been. It was no good, though; she still felt the burn of his palm against her skin, her breast.

She took a deep breath and willed her color to go down. She knew she was beet red. Maybe they would blame it on pain. That was for sure what *she* was going to blame it on.

Cade swung off, effortlessly, hardly moving Abigail at all in the process. Then, from the ground, he reached up his arms and told her how to fall from the animal into his arms.

"I'll guard your leg and your foot, trust me."

And even though he was the same guy that had told her just that morning that he would never trust her again, she did trust him. She fell to the side, raising her good foot, lifting it over the horse. She slid into his arms, and he turned at the last moment, raising her body so that her foot didn't hit the ground.

But it still hurt so bad she wanted to swear a blue streak. So she did, raising Tom's eyebrows and making Janet howl with laughter.

"Our little sailor," she said. "Now, let's get you to the car. We'll take mine, since we don't want to have to throw you in the back of a pickup, and it seems as if it's all you people have around here."

Cade started to tell Janet that he'd just take her himself, but she cut him off.

"We're coming, too. You'll need someone to keep you company while she gets X-rays."

Cade shook his head, and leaned Abigail against Tom's truck as if she were a stick of wood.

"Cade, I think we should," said Tom. "It's a nice idea. What if she needs something? Gets lonely in a hospital."

Cade looked at him incredulously. "Tom? When you had appendicitis, you stuck a vial of horse penicillin in your leg and didn't go to the hospital until a week later, when your appendix burst. You were out in less than twelve hours and back at work a day later. You don't do hospitals."

Janet looked impressed.

Tom said, "Just 'cause I'm a stubborn cuss doesn't mean she has to be, does it? And maybe I learned my lesson. Always better to go to the doc sooner rather than later."

"I don't know what you've done with Tom, but put him back the way he was before you leave," Cade said to Janet.

Janet merely snapped her fingers at him and said, "Bring our girl to my car. It's over on the other side of the house, by the cottage."

Cade sighed. "Does everyone always do what she wants?"

"Everyone," said Abigail. "Always."

"For God's sake. Hold on."

And he swung her up in his arms.

"I'm too heavy for you!"

"A hay bale weighs more than you."

"Are you sure?"

"After fifteen years of baling hay, yes, I'm sure. Now, quit kicking around. You'll hurt yourself."

So Abigail relaxed, and let herself be carried. Strangely enough, it felt good. She felt safe. Her ankle hurt like hell, but the rest of her felt just fine.

Chapter Twenty-one

The magic of knitting is that very small acts add up into
something substantial, useful, and beautiful.
                    —E.C.

Cade hadn't been to this hospital since Tom had called him for
a ride after his appendectomy. But he knew where it was, and
he followed Janet's car, grumbling to Tom the whole way.

Janet drove faster than an ambulance loaded with a heart-attack
patient. She screeched into the emergency-room parking lot and
then ran through the open doors.

"She's fast on those heels, ain't she?" Tom was openly admiring.

A nurse ran outside with Janet, took one concerned look at Abigail, shook her head, and walked back in.

"See? It's just an ankle. I don't know why we're all here," said
Cade.

Tom gave him a look before getting out of the truck. He leaned
forward and turned down the police scanner that Cade kept in the
truck to listen for wildfire reports. "I know why I'm here. I bet you
do, too."

Once inside, the staff responded with surprising alacrity, whisk-
ing Abigail off to X-ray.

"I guess that leaves the three of us out here, then." Janet looked happy about it, Cade thought.

Tom, Cade realized, had a similar look.

"Am I going to be a third wheel here?"

Janet said, "You'll just have to be an entertaining third wheel." She patted the seat across from her in the waiting room.

"So, tell me *everything*, cowboy. Tom says you're a great boss, and my friend says you're a great kisser."

Cade's almost tripped over the waiting-room rug. Abigail had *said* that?

Tom made a muffled snorting sound through his nose and wouldn't meet his eyes.

"She, um, what?"

"Dusty Diego. You know her, I believe."

Tom said, "Sounds like a stripper name."

"That's helpful," said Cade. "Thanks, Tom." But he breathed easier. Maybe Janet didn't know everything.

Janet arched her eyebrows. "Do you even remember her?"

"Of course I do," snapped Cade. "We dated quite a while."

"You dated two months. You consider that a long time?"

"For him it is," said Tom.

Janet tucked a high heel under her and said, "I'm not attacking you. I'm only trying to tell you I know how you've been in the past."

"Lady, I don't know you from Adam. Number one, I can't imagine you know anything about me at all, and number two, why would I care?"

"I know sometimes you go for drinks on Tuesday nights at Larry's Grill, and I know sometimes you meet women and then you date them right up to the point that they fall in love with you, and then you dump them."

"You don't know anything about me."

"Really, Cade. I'm not judging. We have nowhere to go right now. We should get to know each other."

Who was this? Why was he having to listen to this crap?

"Tom, I'm going to get something to drink." He didn't look at Janet as he marched away.

She called after him, "Black coffee, darling. One sugar, raw if they have it."

He'd be damned if he got her anything at all. His blood boiled.

He went to the cafeteria, got a coffee for himself and no one else, and then wandered the halls. He was in no hurry to get back to Janet and Tom, none at all.

Going around a corner, he almost stumbled over Abigail, sitting in a wheelchair under the hallway fluorescent lights, wearing a flimsy paper robe. She was knitting something red. Had Janet picked up her knitting for her? Or was it like magic, that she always had knitting with her, like Eliza?

Abigail held the needles up and waved them. "Knit through everything," she said. Then she dropped the yarn into her lap and ran a quick hand through her hair. "Hi," she said in a quieter voice, looking at the floor.

"How are you feeling?"

"They took X-rays and now I'm waiting for the doctor to read them."

"And they're making you wait out here?"

"I don't mind."

Even in the paper gown, she was so goddamn pretty. Even now, he wanted his hands on her.

And he reminded himself, again, for the thousandth time today, that she was trying to start a workshop. In his cottage, which wasn't his, on his land, which he didn't own anymore.

But when she looked at him like that, with those huge blue eyes, he forgot everything for a minute. All he could think about was the shape and feel of her mouth.

No. They were here because of her ankle. Which was an injury sustained on his land, so he was just a concerned landowner who wanted to avoid a lawsuit.

God, a lawsuit. Wouldn't that be something? Him, being sued by her, living together in the same damn farmhouse?

He had to get her out of his house. And fast.

"You're looking better. Don't look as gray as you did."

"Must have looked great." She ran her hand through her hair again. Was it a nervous tic?

She couldn't be self-conscious; she was too pretty. He was sure she knew it, that she'd been told that a million times before, by a thousand men, but he said, without even thinking about it, "You're gorgeous."

She raised an eyebrow at him. "You don't need to do that."

He couldn't push it, didn't need to, didn't even want to, didn't know why he'd felt he had to say it, but she *was* gorgeous, and he could leave it at that.

Maybe that would get this itch out of his system.

She licked her lips, and his blood pressure rose.

Okay. Maybe the only thing that would help would be to get out of her presence.

Or having her again, soft and willing underneath him, moving with him, at his pace, with him in every way.

He almost groaned out loud.

"You okay?" she asked.

"Fine. Hey, you have to sit out here? Or you wanna wait in the waiting room? Tom and Janet are still out there."

She nodded. "Come on, give me a ride."

Then she went fire-engine red.

He almost laughed, but couldn't, not quite. He was too busy thinking about taking her up on the offer.

Janet and Tom appeared pleased to see them, although Cade thought they looked like they might have forgotten why exactly they were there. Both looked mildly puzzled when Cade rolled Abigail up.

"Darling! What do they say?"

"Nothing yet, waiting for X-rays." Abigail waved her hands at them, as if to shoo them off. "I'm still not sure why you all are here, though. Why don't you go out somewhere? Go shopping, or go back to work, for the love of God. It's just my ankle."

Janet shook her head. "We're ignoring you now. Knit, dearest. Sit in that fancy chair and look pretty. I want to hear more from Cade."

"Wait a second. Hang on." Cade wouldn't take any more grilling. "Who are you exactly? I'm still not quite sure how you even know Abigail here."

"Oh! Have I never properly introduced myself? I'm in textiles. I'm Abigail's best friend, and I like to call myself her manager. And I know who you are because—"

"Don't care," he interrupted, not caring if he sounded rude. "How are you her manager?"

"It's a figure of speech. I'm a little bossy."

"I am *shocked* to hear it."

"Is there a specific reason you don't like me, Cade? Or do you just not like the cut of my jib? Substitute your favorite farm phrase—I was raised on boats, myself. We should talk about it, or we won't get through it."

His blood pressure rose again, and not in the same way it had in the hallway when he'd been looking at Abigail. What did Abigail see in this woman?

For that matter, what did Tom see in her? Tom was still goo-goo eyed. Cade wanted to kick him.

Janet said, "Sweetheart, I'm not the bad guy." She laughed and waved a hand at Tom, "I mean, I *am* a bad *girl*, but that's not the point. We've gotten off on the wrong foot. I was being nosy. I apologize. I'm like that."

"She's like that," said Abigail.

"My wonder girl, my favorite writer, and my friend, has moved up from far away, and she's now living in my backyard. I couldn't be more thrilled. However, I don't know you well, and all I've heard are rather colorful things. She's had enough trouble with men, especially lately. So now I'm trying to get to know you myself. I have to make sure you're not a mass murderer."

"Fine." Cade dropped into a metal chair, resigned. "Let me have it."

"Do you have any children?"

He choked. "No."

"Have you ever been married?"

"Not even close."

"Why not?"

"Didn't come up."

"Ever been in love?"

"Of course." How long was she going to keep this up?

"When? Who?"

"I feel like I'm on a date. Who's buying dinner?"

"Darling, I'll buy. You tell me all I want to know though, won't you? So, when were you in love?"

"I don't remember."

Janet laughed. "I knew it! You've never been in love."

"I have felt very fondly about women."

"Have they told you they loved you?"

"Yes, Your Honor."

"What did you say back?"

"I said thank you."

"You never said it back?"

"I don't like to lie."

"Don't you want to fall in love?" Janet asked.

"Do you?"

"Of course. It's my favorite thing in the world to do. I'm *fabulous* at it." She fluttered her eyelashes at Cade.

"You're wasting it on me; send it that way." Cade jerked his chin toward Tom.

"So this whole Abigail-living-with-you thing? In your house? How has that been for you?"

"Janet!" said Abigail.

"Are you an agent or a therapist?" Cade asked. Janet wasn't grating on him as much. She was almost interesting.

"Do you mind sharing your house with her though? Or is it a relief?"

"What do you mean by that?"

"Don't you get lonely? Knocking around that old house of yours?"

"I don't get lonely. I love being by myself in my home."

Janet sighed. "Sure you're not fibbing to yourself? Maybe? Just a little?"

He shook his head, and felt a small smile creep onto his face. He didn't dare look at Abigail. "I don't think so. I like being by myself. I like cooking for myself. I like walking around the house naked when I want to."

"Well, sweetness, I'm sure Abigail wouldn't mind being cooked for, and there's a chance that she wouldn't mind if you walked around naked, either."

"Hey!" said Abigail.

"See?" said Cade. "She'd mind." How much *had* Abigail revealed to Janet? Did she know about the night on the sofa? The tears?

And about how he'd freaked out when confronted with the idea that Abigail might have been setting him up from the beginning?

He bet that she did. He took another sip of his coffee and stretched his neck. "How long does it take to get the results around here, huh?"

Janet continued, "So what about this cottage? Doesn't look like you ever really used it, so you don't mind that it went to her in the inheritance, do you?"

"I mind. I don't know why." He surprised himself with his honesty.

"What's not to know? Are you jealous that you didn't get everything? I think I would be, in your case." She didn't pause long enough to let him speak. "But if I were you, living alone in that old barn of yours, I would have seen this pretty little thing over there, driving up that driveway, and I would have started thanking my lucky stars that our good old Eliza loved Abigail that much."

"I don't live in a barn. And wait, our what? You knew Eliza?"

"She was one of my favorite people in the world."

"Of course she was." Cade sighed. He should probably just give up now.

Janet bounced in her chair and turned to Abigail. "You know how she designed Nordic Curtsey when she lived here? Maybe you can design a modern interpretation, now that you're here."

"I don't really think it needs updating. It's still current, and it's so pretty. And it's already so famous. . . ."

Tom said, "Sweaters are famous? Why would a sweater be famous?"

"Eliza was pretty well known," said Abigail.

"She was known for sweaters?" Tom sounded incredulous.

"You sweater people are kind of crazy," said Cade.

Janet said, "The craziest! And now that we'll have a new store in the area, people can't be more excited. The only good place to go up until now was up the coast, a good hour and a half drive, and that's just too far to drive sometimes."

"A new store?" Tom said, still looking far out of his depth.

"The store Abigail's starting up."

Cade blinked.

"Store?" Janet had to be wrong. It was just some sort of classroom, right?

"Did you not know, Tom? I thought I mentioned it at lunch."

Abigail jumped in, "It's not really a store, not exactly."

"What's the difference between a store and a place where you sell stuff?"

"On the ranch?" Tom took a few steps back.

Abigail said, "I thought I'd have some knitting classes out of my cottage. Maybe some spinning lessons. Sell a few things, like wheels and fiber and maybe a little yarn."

"A store," Cade said, with more venom than he had planned. He wasn't sorry he'd spit it out like that though.

"I suppose so."

"Does it have a name yet?"

Abigail was quiet, and looked at her lap. She was as pale as the wall behind her, but Cade didn't let his compassion be stirred.

"Does it? I bet it does."

"I was thinking of Eliza's, but I wanted to get your approval first. Before I order the sign."

"The sign? That will be visible from the highway, I'm sure."

"Just a little one, you'd only be able to see it from the county road."

"So MacArthur Ranch, which I've spent the last fifteen years making profitable and well respected, but for which I don't have an actual sign, will suddenly become known for its yarn? Its spinning wheels? Its *alpacas*?"

"We can get you a sign. I'll buy you one."

"I can afford a sign. I just never thought I'd need one."

Cade stood. She couldn't do this. He couldn't let this happen, no matter how attracted he was to her. "You won't open a store on my land."

Abigail placed both hands on the arms of the wheelchair and stared up at him. He'd expected to see her hesitate. But there was a flame in her eyes that he hadn't bargained on, even though he'd seen it once before, in the parlor that night.

"I won't. You are correct. But I *will* open one on *my* land."

"I'll contest the will. I'll get the zoning changed."

"Feel free to try. In the meantime, I'm moving forward."

"You'd better move forward where I can't see, then. Because I won't be responsible for my actions."

"Is that a threat?" Abigail's voice was quiet but clear.

"I'm not saying anything I'm not willing to back up. You will not move forward with opening any store. Period. Tom, let's go."

His friend, still openmouthed and stunned, didn't move.

Janet reached out her hand and placed it on Tom's arm.

"Why doesn't Tom stay here with us? I'm sure he'll come in . . . useful. If he stays."

"You're nuts. He's with me. Come on, Tom."

"Well, someone should keep them company." Tom's voice trailed off. "I mean . . . what if . . . "

"Fine. I'm out of here." There was no way he was going to stand for this. "There will be no store. And you should probably avoid me when you get home."

She stood up. She winced a bit, and he knew she shouldn't stand, but she did. She looked him right in the eye and said, "I'm not scared of you, Cade."

There was something behind her eyes, some pulling back, a hardening.

He had caused that.

It was her fault.

He drove home so fast he was surprised the wheels stayed on the road.

Chapter Twenty-two

Now, the longest rows are for rejoicing! Knit on, sail through, you most amazing of all knitters!
—E.C.

Abigail was filthy. She could still smell the dirt from the hillside in her nose, and sometimes caught the scent of left-over "eau de horse" from her jeans. Janet had driven her home from the hospital and dropped her off with a kiss and a promise to come back soon. Tom had watched wistfully as Janet drove away. Then he'd asked Abigail if he could help her with anything, with getting dinner or making it up the stairs in her new walking-boot that she'd have to wear for a few days. Abigail had instead asked him to check the fence at the cottage with her.

They found Merino, her stupid boy alpaca, standing there. Right there, looking at her like she was late to bring him dinner. From the fluff left on the wire of the fence, she could tell that he'd walked back in as easily as he'd broken out. She almost cried, out of both relief and sheer annoyance, when she saw him standing there next to Tussah. She fed them, and got close enough to him to rub his side.

Abigail knew the fence had looked fine when she moved in the alpacas, but it now had a man-sized hole in it. Tom looked at it, too, and shook his head. "That's been cut."

Abigail didn't know how both she and Cade could have missed the hole, but there it was. Just another thing to work on fixing. Tom showed her how to fill in the gaps with wire, then he looked at her exhausted face and did it for her.

Then Abigail hobbled back to the house.

When she entered it, she realized that when she'd told Cade that she wasn't scared of him, she'd lied a little. He'd advised her to avoid him, and she planned on it. She'd be strong and stand up for her rights tomorrow. Tonight she'd hide in her room until she heard him go to bed, and then she'd have a bath.

Abigail napped lightly with Clara by her side and waited until she heard his bedroom door shut before she went into the bathroom. She wished she could take a shower downstairs, in relative safety, but while she was allowed to remove the walking-boot to bathe and sleep, her ankle was wrapped and she wasn't supposed to unwrap it until she saw the doctor again in three days.

Abigail sat on the floor of the bathroom and waited for the tub to fill. She kept her eyes on the spigot at all times. It wouldn't flood again on her watch.

The bathroom was right next to Cade's room. She didn't like being this close to him. She couldn't even close the door all the way: it shut, but the latch-hook that should snap into the door frame wouldn't latch, so a push would open it. There was no lock.

He wouldn't bother her anyway, she reassured herself. He didn't want to see her, either.

The tub was almost full. Abigail stood slowly, pulling herself up using the sides of the tub. She turned off the taps and took off her robe. Using a combination of gymnastic-like moves she'd never be able to duplicate, she managed to lower herself into the water, leaving her foot propped up on the side, out of the water.

She closed her eyes. This was good.

Abigail sighed deeply and slid further in, up to her neck.

Then she heard a creak.

Her eyes flew open. Wouldn't Cade have heard her in here? Surely, he'd leave her alone. She cleared her throat in warning, just in case he hadn't heard her in here.

The floor creaked again, right outside the bathroom door.

Then the door moved, just a touch. It swung as if a breeze had moved it.

"Hello?" said Abigail.

Nothing. The door stopped moving.

"Hey, I'm in here."

There was still no response but silence. Abigail sat as straight as she could while still keeping her foot high and out of the water. It felt like a yoga pose. She'd never been good at yoga.

"Cade?"

The door moved again, a quarter of an inch. Was it a breeze? There was no creaking anymore. Had Cade snuck past the door and made it move just by passing it? But then it moved again. It was open now almost two inches. The door opened away from the tub, so she couldn't see who was there.

Her heart went into overdrive. It would be bad enough if it was Cade, but what if it wasn't? A weapon. Did she need one? The plunger would do, she thought, but she'd have to get there fast, and she had no idea how to get out of the tub.

She willed her voice to be steady and tough. "Do *not* open that door."

As if encouraged, the door swung open just a bit farther.

Abigail held her breath.

A large yellow cat pushed his way in. Duncan.

"Oh, my God. Oh, my God." Abigail sunk back into the water, panting. She'd never been so relieved to see an animal. Good grief, that had been a ridiculous way to react. To overreact, rather. This was home. This was safe. She had to start believing that. It was hard, though.

Damn it. She'd gone almost two days without thinking about Samuel, and now he was back in her mind. She didn't want his memory warring with this place.

A year in a relationship. Wouldn't that have been enough to know someone? Abigail would have thought so, before Samuel.

She'd met him at the ABA conference, standing in a line waiting for his coffee order to be made. He'd asked her what she was doing there, and she confessed she'd abandoned her booth in search of caffeine.

"I'm here for my sister, who wrote a book about an anthropomorphized squirrel. No line at your table either?" His voice was sympathetic, to match his eyes. He was just her type: tall, broad chest, dark hair. Abigail felt her back straightening, and she hoped she still had a little lipstick on. It had been a long, overwhelming day.

"No, there's been a line, all right. I just escaped."

"What do you write?"

"Knitting books."

"Now I know you're joking me. You're too beautiful to be a grandmother."

Abigail raised her eyebrows. "Good line. Have you used that one before?"

"Just been waiting for a chance. Is it working?" He inclined his head toward her, as if whatever she said was going to be the most fascinating thing he'd ever heard.

"I didn't think it would work, but now I'm not sure." She surprised herself with her candor.

"May I have your phone number?"

Abigail took the coffee the barista held out to her. "I'll think about it. Come see me at my table later. Craft-book area."

She tried not to think about him, becoming more sure as the afternoon wore on that he wouldn't find her. But just as her publicist gave her the high sign and started to shut down the signing queue, he showed up carrying a huge bouquet of pink roses. The women waiting watched appreciatively.

He held them out to her. "You really do have a line. One of the biggest I've seen."

"You don't know knitters, obviously."

"Not until now."

He watched her deal with the rest of the women, watched her smile and laugh and touch the knitted objects shown to her. She felt his eyes burning into her.

He had a quiet word with the publicist, left briefly, and then came back. He was the last in her line. He held out a copy of her newest book and said, "Now may I have your number?"

Abigail smiled.

"What's your name?"

"Samuel."

On the flyleaf Abigail wrote, "To Samuel. Not your grandmother's hobby anymore." She followed her signature with her phone number and handed it back to him.

He said, "I'll call tomorrow."

As he walked away, her publicist, Samantha, sighed. "Who's that? Yum."

"I have no idea."

Samuel had called the next day, just as he'd promised. They went on their first date two nights later. A lawyer, he'd borrowed his firm's pleasure yacht moored at the marina. He led the boat expertly out into the still, open waters and then anchored the boat so they could watch the lights of San Diego, the flicker of traffic dancing, airplanes coming in to land along the skyline. He fed her steak and lobster and plied her with wine. They danced under the night sky to gorgeous music she'd never heard before. He kissed her for the first time, a good, wonderful, sparkling kiss. Abigail wanted it to go on longer, to stand like that under the stars for hours with him, but Samuel lifted anchor, motored in, and docked.

"Tomorrow will be even better," he told her.

Abigail laughed. "I wish. But I'm having dinner with friends tomorrow night. Monday night?"

Samuel frowned as he helped her disembark, holding out his hand for her to take. "Cancel."

"No, I've been looking forward to seeing them. They're from out of town. But Monday's free."

He held her hand with both of his. "Please, Abigail, I want to see you tomorrow. Please? Will you think about it?"

Abigail took her hand back with some difficulty. What was going on? She tried to keep her voice light. "I'm sorry, I can't. Call me Monday morning," she said. "We'll talk then."

The next day, when she left her apartment to go meet her friends, he was waiting for her, leaning against her truck.

"Wow." Abigail had no idea what to say, or even to think.

Samuel smiled, his eyes disarming. "I thought you might still want to cancel on your friends. I have tickets to the game. Wanna join me?"

Abigail shook her head and reached her key out to unlock the truck. "How do you know where I live?"

"It's supposed to be a great game." His hand moved to prevent her from turning the key.

"You followed me last night?"

"And there'll be fireworks afterwards. Best seats in the house. Cost an arm and a leg. You have to come with me." His voice was light.

Abigail turned and faced him, her back against her truck's door. She took a deep breath. "Listen up. That's fucking creepy. I've never had anyone follow me before, and I *hate* it. What on earth would possibly possess me to go out with you tonight, or ever again, for that matter?"

Samuel sagged. "I'm sorry. I just didn't know what to do. Last night was the best night of my life. I can't stop thinking about you. There's no excuse for what I did. I just hoped . . ." His voice was small, and his eyes were pools of sadness.

Somehow, even knowing she probably shouldn't, Abigail felt a stab of empathy for him. Was he really that into her? That it had made him follow her? Shouldn't she be more freaked out? Why did it feel more flattering than frightening?

"If I leave now," he said, "can I call you tomorrow? Plan something to make up for it?"

Abigail paused. Then she nodded. She'd give him another chance. He had been so endearing, standing there, running his hand through his thick hair, that worried look in his eyes.

That was about a year before the bad night. A year she wished she could have back in its entirety, a year wasted.

Now. Abigail told herself to come back to now.

Abigail closed her eyes and counted five seconds and breathed in. Then counted five seconds and breathed out.

She opened her eyes and fell back into place. The upstairs bathroom in Cade's house. The tub was going lukewarm, so she used her good foot to push the hot tap up again.

Duncan, who had been prowling the corners of the bathroom, came out from behind the clawfoot tub and jumped up on the rim. He didn't seem to mind the splashing water or the curved porcelain edge.

"Hello, there." Abigail reached out a wet hand. Surely, he'd run if she tried to touch him.

But he didn't. He even pushed his head forward, into her hand. He seemed to love the droplets on his head. His tail trailed into the water, and he didn't seem to notice or mind. Abigail used her foot again to turn off the faucet.

"You're a water lover, huh? Me, too."

Duncan purred harder. Abigail laughed.

Then the floor outside the bathroom creaked again. She jumped and looked over her shoulder.

The door moved again, but more quickly this time. Her dog, Clara, shoved her way in.

"Clara, no!"

The peaceful room exploded. Clara caught sight of Duncan, perched on the tub, and let out a happy *woof* of greeting. Duncan blew up into an enormous fuzzball and twisted his head around, searching for a way out. Clara leaped at the cat, who jumped right into the water and onto Abigail's stomach.

Abigail flailed, but she knew this wouldn't go well.

Duncan looked desperately around the room and dug every claw into Abigail's torso, then used that purchase to launch himself up and over the dog. Abigail screamed in pain as the soaked cat hurtled out of the room. Clara flattened herself to the ground in fear.

"Shit! Oh, damn!" Abigail found that in the commotion she'd forgotten about protecting her foot. It was in the water, the wrapping now completely soaked, and it hurt like hell. "Goddammit!"

Suddenly, there was a bigger commotion. Abigail heard Cade's door bang open and his thundering footsteps. She didn't have time to yell, to shout for him to stop.

"What the hell? Are you okay? What the *hell*?"

Clara scuttled out behind him, her tail between her legs.

"Turn around!" Abigail shouted.

But he didn't, he just stood there looking frightened and angry, staring down at her.

Abigail dragged the towel off the rack next to her and pulled it into the water. She used it to cover herself as best she could, but she knew it was too late. There wasn't anything he hadn't seen.

"Do you mind?" Abigail yelled. The edge of the towel floated near her neck. She used her hands to push it back down in the water.

"Yes, I do! Can you please tell me why you just screamed bloody murder and scared the shit out of me? And why you're bleeding in my tub? And why—oh hell, just start with those two."

"Your cat scratched me."

Cade raked his hands through his hair. He was wearing only plaid boxer shorts, and Abigail had a hard time not staring at him. "You took a bath with my cat?"

"Duncan pushed his way in, and then Clara followed, and the room wasn't big enough for the both of them. He jumped on my stomach and then launched off it." Dang, it hurt quite a bit. She wanted to look at it, but he needed to leave first.

But Cade knelt at the side of the tub. "Let me see."

"Are you completely insane?" Abigail didn't care if she sounded rude. "I'm naked in here, you know."

"You think I don't know that? You think I also don't know that your foot is in the water, and it shouldn't be, and you won't have any way to stand up?"

"I have another leg, you know."

"You woke me up and scared the crap out of me. Let me see the damage. Now." He pulled at the towel and Abigail pulled it back.

"You don't even like me. Remember, I'm supposed to stay out of your way."

"I'm still mad about the store. But for God's sake, I can control myself around you. I'm not an animal."

He tugged the towel up just enough to move it so that Abigail's stomach was exposed under the water. Abigail kept a tight grip on the towel to prevent further exposure.

"Nice," he said.

Abigail peered down at herself. Seven or eight puncture wounds were visible, as were four red stripes. The water was beginning to turn light pink around the area.

"We have to get you out of there."

"We? I can do it myself. Turn around."

Cade rolled his eyes but faced the door.

Abigail used one arm to hold the side of the tub and her other arm to keep the towel around her. She pulled her legs up, trying to ignore the pain from her foot. She used her good leg to stand and steadied herself on the towel rail. The towel, now out of the water, felt like it weighed a thousand pounds. She'd have to drop it so she could use her other hand.

"I need you to leave."

"You don't need help? Fine." Cade pushed his way out of the small room and shut the door behind him, but Abigail didn't hear him walking away. The floorboards creaked only once.

Abigail dropped the towel back into the water. Using both hands, she pulled herself out of the water and swung her good foot up and out. But the floor below the tub was lower than she expected and she slipped. She knocked her bad foot against the side of the tub as she tried to correct her balance.

She hissed in pain.

Cade must have been standing just outside the door, listening. "I heard that. I'm coming in. Ready? Three . . . two . . ."

Abigail grabbed her robe and wrapped it around herself, still trying to breathe around the pain.

". . . one." Cade pushed open the door.

"Careful." Abigail held up a hand to prevent the door from hitting her. "I can't move. Not just yet. Give me a sec." She gripped the sink so hard her knuckles turned white.

"You're an idiot, you know that?" But Cade's voice was softer than normal. He navigated around her, careful not to jostle her. He moved the stool that had been in the corner of the room so that it was next to her. He put his hands under her arms.

"You're green. Sit."

With his hands supporting her, Abigail sank to the stool. "Well, at least the chunks Duncan took out of me don't hurt anymore."

Cade kept one hand on her shoulder while he half turned and rummaged in the medicine cabinet. He pulled objects out as he spoke. "Band-Aids, Neosporin, hydrogen peroxide . . ." He looked down at her. "Ace bandage, two of them . . ."

"Well-stocked bathroom."

"You never know. Now. First the foot."

"Don't touch. Hurts."

Cade knelt in front of her. "You'll be fine." He put one hand on her calf.

"Hurts!"

"You're a big baby."

"I am not."

"Then suck it up." But again, his tone didn't match his words. "Just breathe through it. I'll be done quick."

He removed the soaked bandage, then picked up a hand towel to dry her foot. He used almost no pressure as he eased the cloth over it. Then he wrapped her foot, starting at her arch, rolling the Ace bandage around and around, using his hands to smooth out the fabric as he went.

Abigail breathed. It didn't hurt as much as it should, actually. If she'd done it, she would have made it too tight, she was sure. But his bandaging felt perfect, just like the doctor's had. The snugness of it eased the pain. And the way his hands looked, moving from her instep to her calf, was a distraction all of its own.

"Now for the blood."

What? Oh, that. Abigail loosened the tie on her robe and peeked at her stomach. She'd almost forgotten about the scratches. "They're fine. Almost stopped bleeding."

He held up the tube of antiseptic. "You're getting some of this anyway."

Was he enjoying this? Abigail scanned his face. Yes, he was. It was some kind of game to him.

Was she enjoying it? Abigail was stunned to find she wanted to play along. She'd worry about the why of it later.

"How do you plan on putting that on me?" She tried to flutter her lashes like Janet did. It just felt silly.

Cade said, "The doctor recommends you open your robe just a bit more. Let me take a look at the damage." He was better at this than she was. He had more practice, she reminded herself.

Heat flushed Abigail's face.

She parted the robe at her stomach a bit more making sure her breasts and lap were still covered. "Would you mind?"

Cade's voice was hoarse. "Not at all."

He smoothed the antiseptic cream against the scratched and punctured skin. The cream was cool, his fingers warm.

"I'm sorry about what I said in the hospital. The whole store thing shocked the hell out of me. I was confused. I was rude."

"You were. I accept your apology, but . . ." Abigail's voice trailed off and she shut her eyes.

What should have hurt Abigail didn't. Her brain felt fuzzy. She wanted more scratches, more places for him to touch. She was having a hard time catching her breath.

Cade, still kneeling, looked up at her. In his eyes was a question that Abigail couldn't answer in words.

His hand stilled on her skin. It moved to her waist. Then he placed his other hand on the other side of her waist. He stood, slowly, bringing her with him. He touched the skin just below her breast.

He said, "What is it with you and me and this bathroom?"

All she needed was a kiss. Abigail looked at him but no words came. And his eyes answered her.

Cade's mouth moved to cover hers. His hands held her lightly, but his mouth plundered. Abigail moaned. Arched her back. She moved his hand so that it cupped her breast. He gasped and pulled back, looking at her.

"Wait," he said. "You should go to bed and rest. Yeah, that's a good idea. I should carry you there. And then I should leave you there. Right?" He tripped over the words so that they all ran together.

"You shouldn't leave me there."

"What?"

Abigail wanted this. Suddenly, she needed this more than she needed air. She moved his left hand so that it cupped her other breast under the robe. "You should carry me there. And you shouldn't leave."

Cade kissed her again, hard and hot. Then he made sure the door was fully open before he moved to lift her.

"I'll go slowly. Hold on."

"Hurry," she whispered in his ear as he lifted her.

In her room, he shooed Clara off the bed and set Abigail down. She tried to have a clear thought, just one. But she wanted this.

"We need . . ." he said.

She finished the sentence. "A condom. Do you . . . ?"

He nodded and disappeared out of the room. Abigail breathed. This was the guy who wanted her gone. Who didn't want yarn anywhere near him. Who hated the idea of a yarn store, who'd fought with her twice today already. This was the guy who snapped and snarled.

This was the man who'd held her when she got scared that night. Who'd made her breakfast. Who'd rescued her on horseback. Who'd bandaged her foot so that it didn't hurt.

This was the man who looked at her like no one else ever had.

She untied the belt of her robe and dropped it to the floor. When Cade entered, she smiled at him. She felt a wave of happiness.

She also felt her hands shaking.

Cade laughed, a low sound. "I was going to ask if you're still sure, but I think you just answered that."

"Please?" She held out her hands, and he came to her. His mouth covered hers again. They moved up the bed, carefully, so that her foot wasn't jarred. Abigail used her hands to push down his boxer shorts. He helped, kicking them away.

Abigail smiled against his mouth. "We seem to be suddenly naked."

"Baby, let me show you how naked we are."

Cade nibbled the side of Abigail's neck, his tongue lightly stroking the sensitive skin around her ear. She half giggled, half gasped as he bit her earlobe. He breathed in her ear, and delicious chills ran over her body.

She wanted more. She wanted him.

"Please," she said again, and drew his head to her breast.

He obeyed her wishes; his mouth, hot and demanding, lapped her nipple, his tongue dancing around its sensitivity, then grasping the peak, tugging slightly. He pulled harder with his teeth. His hand was on her other breast, mimicking the motions of his mouth.

She tested the thought of Samuel lightly in her mind.

No. She wasn't scared. She could only think of Cade, what he was doing to her, could only feel her delight in him.

With his mouth still sucking her nipple, teasing it, licking and biting, his hand started drifting down, toward the center of her heat, where she throbbed.

She laughed out loud and then gasped again. "I'm giddy. More, more."

He laughed and whispered, "You sure?"

"Hell, yes," she said. "Please, you have to . . ."

She took his hand and led it down her body, gasping as he touched her. In no uncertain terms, she placed his hand where she wanted it to be.

Cade followed, and moved his fingers slowly, exploring. She writhed, moaning under his touch. When he found the center of her cries, he focused there, making slow circles, using her wetness to his advantage.

Her breathing sharpened, quickened, and she knew she was close. "Don't stop," she begged.

"I won't," he whispered, his mouth still against hers. "I'm right here."

His fingers touched, circled, teased, and did exactly what she wanted them to.

She shuddered, and groaned, and shook. Only a second away, only a breath away, and she needed more, now.

"I want you. Now. Please, please, Cade, please, *now.*"

He followed her, moving swiftly so that he was on top of her, parting her legs with his hips, and with one thrust that took her breath from her body, he was in her, still pressing that perfect spot that let her, brought her—oh, God, that was perfect. She couldn't breathe, couldn't think, could only feel, as he filled her and kept moving.

She came in undulating waves that spiraled around her, around the thickness of him.

He moaned, and cursed, kissed and bit her neck as he moved in her. "I can feel you coming," he managed to say, which made her clench even more tightly.

She moved against him, drawing from him what he had just drawn from her. His breathing grew faster and he gasped, clutching her tightly. In the last moment, when their movements were hard, and slick, and urgent, his hands went to the sides of her face.

She opened her eyes to find him staring at her, and she watched him hit his zenith, his eyes darkening and widening, until she felt herself moving up into him. That moment, those few seconds of falling into his eyes, as he came—those were as intimate as everything that had gone on before. Her heart fluttered—she felt her breath quicken again, in a different way.

"Abigail," he breathed, and then his weight was against her, all of him.

She put her arms around him.

They didn't speak. Abigail felt Cade's limbs go limp, and he grew heavier on top of her. She shifted, easing her hip from under his. He slid to the side.

She faced him, gazing at him in light filtering in from the hall. She felt her own eyes growing heavy, but she stared at his face a little bit more.

The moment of passion. It could hide or show anything, couldn't it?

She yawned. He was so comfortable to lean against, his leg thrown over hers, her back against a pillow, supported by his chest.

Just before she closed her eyes, he opened his.

He looked at her, and it echoed the last moment of passion—his eyes were still so dark, and the look was the same. She felt like she was drifting forward, into his gaze. He leaned forward, caught her mouth, and kissed her, the sweetest kiss that went on and on.

She remembered nothing more.

Chapter Twenty-three

When it comes to deciding what kind of shaping to use, consider the recipient before you choose raglan, saddle-shoulder, or set-in. If he has very wide shoulders, just consider yourself lucky. Then use whatever technique you love best.

—E.C.

Cade's first thought, after he woke, was about blueberry muffins. He knew for a fact Abigail liked blueberry muffins. She'd asked for one at the diner last week and had gobbled his when it was offered to her.

He couldn't see the alarm clock from where he was lying, but he could tell by the way the light was only starting to shift from black to gray that it was still early. Chores. Then to town for a muffin. If he moved fast, he could be back in bed with her in two hours, before she even woke.

He hated to move, though. She was spooned in front of him, her back to him, her body curved into his. She fit him like he couldn't remember anyone else ever fitting him. It was like that kid's story with the bears—what was it? Goldilocks. Not too tall, not too short, not too big, not too small: Abigail was just right.

But the chores wouldn't get done with him lying here just thinking about how she felt. He lifted his arm from where it was draped over her and scooted backward. She murmured in her sleep. Cade leaned forward to listen.

"Rabbits. And helium, with a hat." Abigail's voice was quiet, but the words were distinct. "Carded batts of raisins." She giggled and then was suddenly quiet, her breathing deep and steady.

He slid from the sheets into the cold morning air, shrugged on his workclothes and hit the door running, hoping Tom had made coffee. If he hadn't, he would go without. It was all about speed right now.

It was a gorgeous cold morning, the first real frost still lying on the longer blades of grass. He could see his breath. This was the kind of morning that he lived for. The countryside was quiet, no cars going by on the side road, the sun rising slowly and the air cold. Everything appeared in distinct relief against the palest blue sky.

He worked hard and fast.

An hour later, there was just one last thing to do. He carried pails of water out to Abigail's shed. They had to get her a water hookup soon; those animals drank a ton.

He would finish this, then get the muffins and go back up to the house. He would make good, strong coffee, and pour it into yellow mugs, and bring her a cup. She'd still be tangled in his sheets, eyes closed, soft and warm, everything he wanted to see, to touch in the morning.

He'd wake her slowly, maybe sit next to her and watch to see if the coffee smell would wake her on its own. If it didn't, he'd touch her, lightly. He would stroke that soft part of her cheek, maybe breathe a whisper of a kiss on the top of her hair. He'd run his hand down her side, over the sheet, barely brushing her.

Damn, he was hard again, just thinking about being near her. He couldn't finish watering the alpacas fast enough. What if she woke up? What if she thought better of last night?

The pails sloshed as he jogged to the alpaca troughs. He dumped the water in, and checked on their feed.

Half an hour, if he sped the whole way to town and back. In half an hour, he could be in his room with her, muffins in hand.

The stillness of the morning air was broken by the chugging of a truck, rolling down the dirt road.

Cade sighed. He didn't want to have an early-morning talk with anyone, but he could tell it was Hooper's orange Ford from where he stood. He was caught, a sitting duck out in the open. He didn't have a chance. Hooper was practically a woman, one of the gabbiest men he knew. He was one of the regular breakfast crew at Tillie's Diner. And Cade'd been spotted. Hooper slowed his truck and rolled down the passenger window.

"Morning, Cade."

"Hi, Hoop. Hey, I'm in a hurry, can I catch up with you later?" Cade took a step toward the house, but Hooper held up his hand.

"Just a sec. We miss you at Tillie's. Ain't seen you that often lately." Hooper grinned at him. "So, that alpaca lady, huh? Word is she broke her leg chasing after you? Up on a hill or something?"

"Jungle drums beating too loud, that's all. Not even a broken leg. Just a sprained foot."

"So she still staying with you?"

"As far as I know, Hooper."

"She's not up yet, then?"

"Wouldn't know. And I'm not falling for it, Hooper. You have anything else for me this morning, or can I finish my chores?"

Hooper's face became serious. "I have to say something to you, and you might not like it, Cade."

Cade respected this man. He looked up to him as a mentor: a rancher who had done nothing in his whole life but make his land work. He stood still and nodded.

"You worked hard here, taking the ranch over from Eliza like you did. Just about ready to be sold at auction and you brought it back to something serious. Your sheep are good and strong, and people talk about the way you run this place, like a spread ought to be managed. You only have one guy working for you. You're out there, doing it, making it work. That's what me and the other guys want to see in young guys like you."

Cade looked at his boots. The most he got from the breakfast crew was a punch in the shoulder every once in a while and an admission that his sheep weren't the worst they'd ever seen.

"Thanks, Hoop."

"But."

Uh-oh.

"But we been talking, and we think this yarn thing you're doing is bull-crap."

"Me? *I'm* not doing anything with yarn."

"And you got those stupid alpacas living here. You're on the verge of turning this place into a school field trip. I mean, yarn is good, and my wife makes sweaters for me that I like fine. But she's out-of-her-mind excited about this place. Talk is that it's gonna serve coffee and have retreats or something where the ladies come and stay out here for a weekend to learn about sheep ranching."

"Retreats?"

"You were doing something good out here, something serious. Continuing a tradition. We were proud of you. This new venture you got going, this yarn thing, well, I'm sorry. That ain't us. We've worked hard to get a name for ourselves out here in this part of the valley, and we don't want you to ruin it. We don't want the valley turning into a strip mall. Even if no one else will tell you what they think, I will. I think you're going soft, and you're going to hurt all of us. Think about it."

Hooper tapped his baseball cap, leaned over and rolled up the window, and drove up the road.

Cade felt a burn start on the back of his neck.

This yarn thing. People thought he, Cade, was starting this. They had to know it was her doing, didn't they? Right?

But it was still on his land. Or at least surrounded by it. That was the problem.

Cade shook his head, trying to clear it. This was *not* how he'd felt when he woke that morning with Abigail in his arms.

He thought he had been past this. He thought he'd been starting to accept what Eliza had put in front of him as unavoidable. He stood in place and scuffed his boot in the dirt, as he looked up at the window where she slept.

Those old men would see. Her business would be separate from his. He'd have a successful ranch and she'd run a successful business. The property, all of it, would prosper.

It couldn't change the reputation of the valley. It wouldn't.

He turned his head and looked at the cottage.

When would the big sign go up? Would it be flashy, with neon knitting needles? Or adorable, with a cutesy ball of yarn and a fat kitten batting it?

He imagined the rows of parked cars and women squealing over the adorable alpacas.

Damn Hooper.

There would be no muffins. Really, they weren't that good anyway. They were usually dry.

Cade felt a pinprick of guilt. No, that was stupid. Abigail didn't even know he'd been thinking about getting muffins. She wouldn't miss what she didn't know about.

He would *not* go into Tillie's today. Maybe he wouldn't even go this week.

Cade made the coffee. At least she had good taste and liked it strong.

Men were worse gossips than women.

Upstairs, she was naked in his bed. Sweet, warm, generous, sexy-as-hell Abigail. He had to get these thoughts out of his mind, just for a few hours. As the coffee dripped into the carafe, he shook his head.

She was just Abigail. Eliza had loved her. Abigail wasn't out to get him. What had Hooper said? Strip mall. She wasn't turning the valley into a strip mall. Her business would be more like a roadside food stand. Something to showcase the valley.

Sure.

He poured the coffee into his yellow mugs.

What if they had to put up a stop sign? Or God forbid, a stop-light?

He walked up the stairs.

It was a yarn shop.

Just a yarn shop.

When Cade entered the room, he had trouble thinking a complete thought and stopped worrying about her store entirely.

Abigail lay on her side, one hand under her cheek, the other arm lying the length of her naked body. The blanket and sheet had slipped off. She must be cold. Cade put the coffees on the nightstand and moved to pull the blanket up. Crying shame. No one should cover this, but it was a chilly morning, and she had goose bumps.

So did he, come to think of it. But his weren't from the cold.

As he pulled up the blanket, she murmured something he couldn't understand. He put his hand on her cheek and kissed the top of her head lightly. Her eyelids flickered, then half opened.

"Cade," she said softly. She smiled.

He smiled back. Her eyes were so damn soft. Trusting.

"Good morning, gorgeous," he said. "I brought coffee."

"You're awesome. Coffee . . . " She yawned and stretched, and then she gasped. "Yow!"

"Your foot?"

She nodded. "I forgot."

"You had a big day yesterday."

"A huge day," she agreed. She scooted up, carefully, propping two pillows behind her, pulling up the sheet so that it covered her breasts. Cade handed her a mug and imagined pulling the sheet down again.

Instead, he said, "You tracked an alpaca, fell out of a tree, went to the hospital, and got clawed by my cat. How is your stomach?"

"And I stayed up late, too."

He nodded. "You must be exhausted."

She yawned again. "I think I am. How long have you been up?"

"Not that long."

"I heard voices outside."

"Hooper. From Tillie's, you met him." Cade looked away from her eyes and out the window.

"Mmmm. This is great coffee. Thank you. Now all I need is a blueberry muffin."

"Are you kidding?" How had she known?

"Of course I am. This is perfect."

Cade felt an awkward weight drop onto him as if someone had draped a heavy blanket over his shoulders.

"So," he said.

"So," she smiled.

"Um."

Abigail seemed to take pity on him. "So what are you doing today?"

Relief. "I have to move some more irrigation pipes and work on some others before I can move them. What are you doing?"

"Working on the cottage."

The awkwardness fell again. The cottage. The damn store. Which he didn't want to think about, not right now. He watched her instead. She drank her coffee and stared out the window. She pushed her hair back, out of her eyes. The early sunlight hit the curve of her cheek.

He'd never seen eyes that actually sparkled, but hers did. Maybe it was a trick of the light, but it was a pretty good trick.

"It's going to be fine, you know," she said.

"Your foot?"

"That, too. But the cottage. The store. I'll totally stay out of your way. You won't even know I'm there."

He raised his eyebrows. "I'm still skeptical. But I have to admit, the idea is easier to take when you're talking to me dressed like that."

Pink flooded her cheeks. Abigail looked down at herself and then back up at him.

"I don't usually . . ."

"Usually what? Seduce your men with the blood drawn by their cats?"

"Definitely a first."

He sat on the bed next to her, careful to move slowly. "First time for everything, I guess."

"And this doesn't have to mean anything."

Cade's heart gave a sudden, unexpected lurch. No, of course it didn't have to mean anything. "No, you're right. It doesn't."

Abigail blinked. "I mean, we're adults. Just consenting adults."

"Who are able to have mind-blowing sex."

She blinked harder. "Yes. Apparently that."

"I like that part of being an adult."

"I hear you do."

"What do you mean?"

What had she heard? Was it all from that Janet person? What had Eliza said to her?

"I'm only teasing. I know you have a way with the ladies, and I can personally attest to that. Nothing wrong with it."

Her voice was light, and her eyes were clear as they met his. "I'm teasing you, Cade."

"Eliza hated that about me."

Abigail gave a small nod. "She might have mentioned that she wanted you to settle down."

"Mentioned?"

"All right, it was one of her favorite topics of conversation."

"I *knew* it! I knew she was still stuck on that. Did she tell you about the fight?"

"Not really. I know you had a falling out, what, eight years ago or so? After a trip she made here? But she wouldn't tell me much about it, just that she'd pushed you too hard."

"She actually said that?"

"She felt responsible for the fight, I know that. What was it really about?"

Cade sighed. "She said she wanted me to marry someone. Anyone. That she wouldn't let me buy the land from her, even though I had secured the backing for the loan by then, until I found the one. That's what she said. The one."

"Like her Joshua."

"Like Uncle Joshua. Only a girl, I'd suspect."

Abigail sipped her coffee and kept watching him with those amazing eyes. He was glad she was distracting him with this topic; otherwise he'd be hard-pressed not to launch right back into bed with her for a repeat of last night. He still might.

"The fight really came down to her calling me a slut."

Abigail choked on her coffee, then coughed for a minute. "No way. She did not."

"Okay, maybe it was 'man-whore.'"

"Now, no matter what, I'm not going to believe a word you say."

"Catting around? Will you buy 'catting around'? That's what she actually said."

"I totally buy 'catting.' That's an Eliza word."

"She had this stupid idea that it was all about my mom or something. That since she never stuck around, I couldn't trust women, and I had to learn how. She said I had to quit doing it. Catting."

Cade thought Abigail might break into laughter, but even though her lips twitched, she held it together. "And what did you say?"

"I told her it was insulting to say that to me when I just liked dating. And my mother had nothing to do with my love life. And okay, at that point it so happened that I was dating a few people, but it was none of her business. I told her that, too."

"How many people?"

"What?"

"How many women were you dating then?"

"Maybe four. Or five."

"At *once*?"

"I don't remember. Probably," Cade said.

"Wow. I'd never be able to keep that straight in my head. How did you remember which was which?"

"It was kind of hard sometimes."

Now Abigail really was laughing at him. "Is that normal for you?"

"Of course not. Not really."

"Not really! That means yes! What about now? How many girls are you dating at the moment?"

"Not even one."

Abigail went silent. She looked into her coffee cup but didn't drink from it.

Crap, should he have said something else? "I mean, yeah, last night . . ."

"No, not me, of course," she said.

"Um. No. I mean, we're not really . . . dating." Cade felt like an ass.

"Yeah." Abigail set down her coffee cup and sat up straighter. "Well, I should probably . . ."

"No, don't." Cade, still sitting next to her, put a hand on her leg. "I don't cat around. Whatever that means. I have friendships with girls and it never gets serious. That's what Aunt Eliza hated. I don't think she ever cared what I did with a girl, as long as it meant something."

"Does it ever mean anything to you?"

"No. Not usually." Cade tried to put his meaning into his voice, into his eyes, but she was looking down again. "It's not usually like last night." It was the most he could say. His heart beat traitorously fast.

"You don't have to say that. It's all right."

"The fight had ended with her saying I wouldn't ever get the land that I wanted unless I fell in love. I thought she was being stupid, and I told her so. She didn't come to see me for a while after that. We talked on the phone, but we didn't say much. Then she started driving up twice a year, bringing those bags and boxes with her. We never spoke about the fight, and she didn't ask about my love life ever again. But oh, my God . . ." Cade paused, hit with a flash of insight. "She was meddling with my love life, even then."

"What?"

"Think about it. I just figured it out. I can't believe it took us this long to catch on. Aunt Eliza and I had that fight, she goes home, and a year later starts to stock your store up here."

"My store?"

"She was hooking us up. Planning on it, even back then, seven years ago."

"That's ridiculous. I'd only just met her not that long before . . ." Abigail looked at him, her eyes wide. "Do you think she'd really be that . . ."

"Manipulative? She was the sweetest person in the whole wide world, until she got a burr under her saddle. My love life was a burr, I know that much. She meets you, she starts to make plans."

"Why on earth would she think you wouldn't find someone else in the meantime? Or for God's sake, that I wouldn't? I dated. I dated a lot, thank you very much." Abigail glared at him.

"I'm sure you did."

"And if that was her plan, why not just bring me up here with her on one of her trips?"

"Did she invite you?" Cade asked.

"Yeah, but I kept having to say no. I never seemed to have the time."

"And I was too busy to go see her. I put it off, always." Cade rubbed his hand against his eyes.

"So if she couldn't make us meet in life, she'd throw us together after death."

Cade said, "That's the bossiest thing I ever heard."

Abigail laughed, but the laughter stopped as soon as it started. "Don't worry about it though. Keep up with your ladies. When's your next date?"

Cade smoothed the sheet and didn't say anything.

"Oh, I see. Tonight?"

He nodded.

Abigail sighed. "Okay, cowboy. That's all good. But hey, I've got a lot of work to do today, and I'm going to have to hobble around to do it, so if you wouldn't mind"—she cleared her throat—"passing me my robe over there, I'd appreciate it."

"I didn't mean—" Cade started.

She held up her hand. "There's nothing wrong, Cade. Mind-blowing sex is mind-blowing sex. But I still have to figure out where stuff is going to go in the store, and you've got to work on some water thing for your sheep. Life goes on."

Cade handed her the robe. He couldn't think of a single thing to say.

Chapter Twenty-four

The yoke is like February: it's not really that long, but it takes forever.

—E.C.

Two weeks later, Cade drove up the county road, toward the house. He'd been over at Landers's, helping him with his all-terrain vehicle. Landers needed the ATV to work so he could easily cart his feed around, and Cade enjoyed working on the engines. The fact that Landers's wife made excellent brownies didn't hurt.

He hadn't seen Abigail in almost two weeks. It was like she'd disappeared into thin air. She must be working on the cottage, he knew, but he also knew she was avoiding him.

Hell, just because they'd had sex didn't mean that he was tied to her. It didn't mean anything. He was sorry her feelings were hurt, but he couldn't see much of a way around that.

He drew closer to his property line.

He saw smoke.

On his land.

Black smoke. Vegetation fires put up white smoke and that would have been bad enough. Black was worse.

Cade's accelerator hit the floor.

Cell phone already in hand, Cade fishtailed around the turn that led to his driveway. He was up the small hill in a matter of heartbeats. What the hell was on fire? Not the barn, please God, not the barn. Or the house.

Or her cottage. Not the cottage either, dammit.

One more heartbeat and he was at the top of the drive. Gravel scattered as he shot up past the house. The house and the cottage were fine—the smoke was coming from behind the barn. The only thing back there was the old purple shack that he used for storage, the one Abigail had asked about when she got the alpacas.

He gunned the truck up and around the barn.

Flames roared out of the shack, shooting straight up through the roof, which already looked annihilated.

Abigail stood thirty feet away from the fire, directing a garden hose toward it.

"MacArthur Ranch!" Cade yelled into the cell phone. "Structure fire, fully engulfed storage shack!" It would take the fire department at least eight or ten minutes to get here, and it was obviously too late to save the shed. But the sparks . . .

Jesus.

The tanks of propane.

He stored the propane in there. Abigail wasn't far enough away from the shack.

Abigail.

He dropped his cell phone, threw the truck into park, and launched himself out of the truck and hit the ground running.

"Move! Drop the hose!"

But the noise of the fire drowned out his words. Abigail hadn't even heard the truck pulling up. She kept directing the stream of water at the fire, but the heat was so intense that the water evaporated before it even got anywhere close.

Oh, God.

"Abigail!"

He'd never, ever felt this kind of fear before. Cade poured every ounce of every muscle in his body into racing toward her. He wrested the hose from her hand. She screamed.

"Move!" He grabbed her arm and pulled. He didn't care if he hurt her. "Run!"

"I'm trying to help!"

"Propane!" He dragged her behind the truck and ducked down, taking her with him.

As he did, the tanks blew. The roar of the fire doubled. The noise was deafening.

Burning parts of small bottles flew out of the shack. Spray-paint and lubricant cans halved by the heat, flying like missiles. One blown-apart can hit the side of his truck, and when he looked under the chassis, Cade could see it there on the ground, still smoking.

After long seconds, the rain of metal stopped. The fire still roared.

Cade wrapped his arms around her. Safe. She was safe. He held her more tightly and she clung to him in return. He could feel her heart racing. Or was that his?

All of those pieces shooting out like shrapnel could have done serious damage, at the very least. Not to mention the blast when the fire doubled as the propane blew. How close had he come to losing her?

"I have to . . ." he started.

"Don't let me go," said Abigail in a low, shaking voice.

"Then hold on to me. I just have to get my phone." While Abigail held tightly to his arm, he reached into the truck with the other and found his dropped phone. He called 911 again and warned them about the propane.

"They're just around the corner, sir," said the dispatcher.

Cade heard the sirens as he put the phone in his pocket.

"They'll be here in a minute. Did you see what happened?"

Abigail shook her head. Her teeth were chattering.

"Are you hurt? Burned?'"

She shook her head again.

"Get in the truck. I'll move it out of the way."

Abigail, still silent, climbed in. Cade started it up and backed it farther away from the fire. Sure enough, the grass around the shack had caught fire already, the flames rolling up the paddock, being pushed by the wind. But that field was empty; he'd moved the flock that had been in it into another more than a week ago.

And the flames were rolling away from the barn.

"It's a small-enough grass fire that they'll be able to put it out easily enough," said Cade.

Abigail's eyes were huge.

Cade said, "The wind isn't strong, and we just had that rain a couple weeks ago. The grass is short. This is what the fire guys love to do. And sparks are flying away from us, into the field." He wasn't sure if he was reassuring her or himself.

She still didn't speak, just stared at the inferno that had been his storage shed.

"What happened?" Cade asked.

"I don't know," she said. "I looked out and saw smoke. Then I ran, thinking I could put it out. Oh, God. And I hadn't even called 911. Once I got the hose out, I was just waiting for the fire department to arrive. I have no idea why I didn't think of calling."

"You didn't call 911?"

Abigail shook her head.

Cade parked the truck by the barn. The fire at the shack raged on, but there had been no more explosions.

"Where the *hell* is Tom?" asked Cade.

"I haven't seen him."

Cade's heart froze and he lost his breath. "He was here this morning when we did chores, and he didn't say anything about leaving. Oh, God."

The worst thought flashed through his mind.

Tom was his oldest, best friend. He couldn't even think the words.

But no, Tom's truck wasn't here, and Tom was always with his truck, or somewhere near it. Tom wasn't here. Cade prayed to God he wasn't.

Three fire engines screamed up the driveway and pulled up near Cade's truck. The captain of the off-road engine yelled for Cade to open the gate leading to the field on fire. Damn, he should have thought of that.

He jammed the truck into drive again and led the engine to the gate nearest the blazing grass. Abigail sat next to him and clung to the sides of the seat with white fingers.

Then Cade drove back to the barn. The battalion chief in his red patrol vehicle was just arriving.

Cade turned to Abigail. "Do you want to stay here? Or do you want to come with me to talk to him?"

Abigail's lips were pale. "I want to stay with you."

Cade nodded and then jumped out of the truck. Once she was out, he took her hand and led her to the battalion chief.

Bill Leary spoke rapidly into the two radios he held. The back of his truck stood open, and he was already making marks on a white board. The largest of the three engines had pulled up closer to the shack. Four men piled out of the cab and hit the ground running, pulling hose and starting the pumps. A huge stream of water, followed by another from the next engine, made an enormous whooshing noise.

Cade felt Abigail put her hand in his. She held on tight.

"Cade." Chief Leary nodded at him. "There's no getting that outbuilding back. Anything else in there we need to know about?"

Cade shook his head. "Just the propane, but I haven't heard one explode for about three minutes. They might be all done."

"How many blew up?"

Cade thought. "Seven? Maybe eight. I think that's about all I had in there. They all kind of went at once, like the pressure valves all hit their heat limit at the same time. But a lot of spray cans exploded and flew out. I can't be sure they're all done."

"Anything else?"

"Maybe some paint cans. Only other stuff I kept in there was old tools and a mower with no gas. Some expired medicine that I didn't get around to throwing out."

The chief nodded. Then he said something into the radio in his left hand and craned his head to peer at the smoke from the field.

"They've just about got that fire contained. Less than an acre, I'd guess. You were lucky, my friend."

Cade didn't feel lucky, although he knew he would soon enough. He did feel better, though, as he heard another vehicle roaring up the driveway. He knew the sound well.

Tom's truck was a beautiful sight. He parked and ran to where they stood.

"What the hell? I heard it on the scanner and I could see the smoke from town."

"Where were you?"

"I told you I was going to town, remember? That last working pair of hoof trimmers broke when I stepped on 'em."

"Oh, yeah." Cade had forgotten that.

"Shit. This is awful. And I was only gonna be gone a little while, but when I came out of the feed store, some punk-ass kid or someone had slashed both my front tires. I had to get a tow and then the tire store couldn't even fix 'em—I had to buy two new ones. Took forever."

"I'll pay you for them. You were in town on a work errand."

"Already used your card. But how . . . ?" Tom cleared his throat. "What the hell happened?"

Chief Leary spoke up. "You have linseed in there?"

Cade nodded.

"My guess would be some rags left in a pile started it."

"I don't leave rags out like that," said Cade. "I'm not new at this."

"Well, the fire investigator is on her way out now, so you'll know for sure by this afternoon. Hey, are you all right, miss?"

Cade looked at Abigail. Her face had drained of all color now and she was visibly trembling.

"I'm fine," she said in a very small voice that wasn't convincing.

"Get her out of here, Cade. If I need anything, I'll ask Tom."

Cade led her by the hand back toward the house. It was like leading a tottering child: She didn't seem to be able to see the ground beneath her. Was she in shock? She stumbled along next to him.

Cade opened the door to the house and led her into the kitchen. He scooped Duncan out of the rocker that sat next to the stove.

"Here, sit. Just stay here for a little while." He wrapped a knitted afghan of Eliza's around her shoulders. "I'll make you some tea."

"Coffee?"

"Smart girl."

A few minutes later, Cade kneeled at Abigail's feet and placed the mug in her hands. "You want a shot of whiskey in that?"

She shook her head. "I'm sorry. I'm just so freaked out."

"Natural to be."

"It's your land. Your building. Your pasture that caught on fire. You should be the one freaking out. You shouldn't have to take care of me."

Cade was torn: he wanted to stay right here, kneeling in front of her, looking up into her huge eyes, which were starting to look less terrified, but he also wanted to look out the window to see how it was going. It was like a physical need. Before he'd met her, the land was all he cared about.

He leaned forward and kissed the knuckles of her hand that wasn't holding coffee. He stood and tried to take a small peek out the window.

"Go," she said.

Damn, he'd been too obvious. "No, it's fine. They're good out there. I trust them."

"You have to go. I'll be fine here."

Cade wished they weren't having this conversation right now, while his land smoldered outside. He wanted to take her back upstairs, to his room. He wanted to stay with her all day, to smooth away the fear and worry that still clouded her face. He wanted to make her want to stay, to forget all about moving out of his house.

But even as he wanted these things, he was picking up his hat, which he'd removed when he came in. He twisted the brim in his fingers. Shuffled his feet.

"I have to get out there. I'm sorry."

Abigail smiled up at him, and his heart twisted.

The look of her, sitting wrapped in the afghan on his rocker, in his kitchen, smiling at him as he walked out the door, was so pretty it made his heart feel funny.

Chapter Twenty-five

Watch out! The top inch of a sweater yoke is deceitful. You can measure it again and again, and it will read one inch shy until suddenly you are almost an inch over.

—E.C.

Days later, Abigail still hadn't seen Cade even once.

The same awkwardness between them before the fire still hung in the air, draping the house in a gray shroud. She dreamed of him at night. Once he kissed her in the dream, and she woke, feeling the shape of his lips on hers. But the room was dark—she was alone.

And this morning she thought she heard someone in her room. Someone stood next to her bed and then touched her cheek. But she must have dreamed it. By the time she fought her way awake and opened her eyes, there was no one there, and when she looked out the window, Cade's truck wasn't even parked in its normal spot.

But where *had* he been? She tried not to think about it, told herself she didn't care, but it was like he'd completely disappeared. She heard his floorboards creaking most nights inside his room—the sound traveled along the floor. But when she walked through the kitchen, she saw no evidence that he'd been home at all, no coffee cups in the sink, no glasses standing on the sideboard. Even during his hours for parlor use, he wasn't there.

He'd been working, she knew, because she'd seen his truck up by the barn, and then one afternoon, she'd seen it driving up the hill, up to where she'd gone searching for Merino.

She still hadn't quite gotten on track yet in her sleep patterns. She woke up in the middle of the night, her ears straining to hear anything from his room, from downstairs.

Sleep seemed to be something she could only grab in tiny portions. She wasn't good at holding on to it.

So today she was yawning already, and it wasn't even ten in the morning yet. She'd already had two cups of coffee. And it wasn't like she was really loitering in the kitchen—she'd just taken her time over drinking it.

But he didn't come through looking for coffee. Or anything else.

She wasn't trying to stay out of his way. In fact, she realized that she was actually trying to get *in* his way.

Gingerly, she stood and washed her coffee cup. Her foot still ached, but she didn't have to wear the hard recovery boot she'd had to wear the first few days, thank goodness. She'd hated the noise and heft of it.

She gazed through the small panes of glass for the umpteenth time this week. No sign of smoke, like the other morning. No sign of anything but blue sky. No sign of him.

This was a switch, all right. Abigail was still used to looking out a window for someone, but not like this. During her year-long relationship with Samuel, she'd been used to looking out her apartment window with excitement, checking to see if Samuel had arrived yet. He usually brought her pink roses, and her home was full of teetering vases perched on every available surface. After things went so bad, she became used to looking out with fear, terrified she'd see his black SUV idling under the streetlight.

But here she peered out with hope. Yearning, even. She wanted to see Cade's dirty, beat-up truck, wanted to see him striding, long-legged and comfortable in his clothes, toward the house.

Instead, she leaned on the sink and looked as far as she could see. Hot water sluiced from the tap and over her mug and hands.

Nothing out the window.

Cade's kitchen. The faucet still running. Hot water gone to luke-warm. The land outside that she was staring so blankly into—this was home now.

A wave of gratefulness swelled again inside her. Home. Safe.

And awkward. Uncomfortable. Cade was obviously trying to stay so far out of her way that he'd become invisible. Just because they'd had sex.

Really, really great sex.

Just as well. Today was a day that she actually did want to stay out of his way. Or rather, she hoped he would stay out of hers.

She was having a party this afternoon in his house. Janet had been the one to insist on it. "You have to have a launch party, sweet-heart. A little one."

"A party? Here?"

"You have to have something, people are calling and e-mailing me nonstop."

"Why you? About what?"

"Oh, darling, you should check e-mail and the blogs once in a while. You're the hottest thing in the fiber market this year. Eliza Carpenter's home will be open, will be on view. Not only that, but a yarn shop is in the same space, offering classes. The owner is writing knitting books, carrying on the Carpenter tradition. People are *crazy* for it."

"It's such a small thing, such a small place, so far away from everything else. You really think people will come?"

"They'll come and they'll keep coming."

"But the cottage isn't completely set up."

"They can help. Throw a grand opening, and have them add the final touches."

"You can't ask potential customers to finish setting up a store."

Janet just cocked an eyebrow, got out her cell phone, and started arranging things.

A week later, Abigail was getting ready to host a small party of what she assumed would be mostly women. The beginning of her dream, coming to fruition.

What would Cade think?

The fact that she couldn't get him out of her mind for more than a few minutes could be ascribed to lust. God knows sleeping with him that night hadn't been in her plans. And now her body craved companionship. Well, not just any companionship, but specifically his. That wasn't so strange, she supposed.

Who cared if Cade had been the single hottest experience in her life? Abigail knew that sex was good and healthy. In the past she'd been sturdy, steady, dating, falling in love with very nice men who treated her well and respected her intelligence. Until Samuel, anyway. But he was the exception that proved the rule.

Cade, on the other hand, knew nothing of her books. He had never read an article by her, wouldn't care for the subject matter if he had. He hadn't seen any of her designs. He had no idea how long it took to create something from scratch. He had no clue how much care it took to craft a design and bring it to life. The very sweater she was finishing now: Cade had no idea how long it had taken her to figure out the neckline. Nor did he know that it would look fantastic on a guy built like he was. But the sweater wasn't for Cade—it was for the next book. Obviously.

She dried her coffee mug and put it back into the cupboard.

Stupid crush. Silly, little schoolgirl crush.

But it felt bigger than that.

She refused to admit that.

No more of this. She whistled for Clara and headed for the cottage. At least she could decide what she wanted her volunteers to do. There were still a few boxes that needed unpacking and shelving. Clara would help with the box shredding. Abigail pushed open the door. She supposed she'd have to start locking it again, once it really was a store, but she'd been enjoying coming and going between the house and the cottage, all doors unlocked.

The shop was going to open. Her dream was going to come true. She surveyed the room with delight.

The furniture had arrived last week. It had bitten into her savings quite a bit, but it was worth it. A red sofa was the dominant piece of furniture, flanked by four deep brown overstuffed armchairs. Three tall shaded lamps provided good light, and kept a soft glow in the room. She'd painted the walls a pale butter yellow. It was bright enough to light the room with warmth, but neutral enough that the colors in the unspun fiber looked accurate.

Dark brown wooden bookcases that she'd sanded and polished ran along three walls. The fiber was arranged by type: the cashmere, alpaca, and angora stacked neatly in colorful bundles. Sheep's wool was arranged by breed: Bluefaced Leicester, Corriedale, Jacob, Polwarth.

She'd found a printer in town who'd done a rush job for her. "Eliza's" was printed on paper labels that went around the fiber, wrapped in two-, four-, and eight-ounce bundles. Baskets were scattered around the room, full of bags of wool. There were whole fleeces, too, washed but uncombed or carded.

Next to the baskets were low footstools good for perching on while poking through the fleece or for pulling up into the seating area when more chairs might be needed.

She hoped she *would* need extra seating sometimes.

Near the back of this room, she'd placed a long, low table. She was going to use the old cash register that Eliza had left in the cottage to ring up sales. She'd track sales and orders in an old, blank ledger that was dated 1957. Probably someday she'd get a computer to do it, but for now, it felt right, starting by hand, like Eliza would have done.

The sign was up outside, hanging from the low eave of the front porch.

She'd hung a red velvet curtain in the doorway that led to the kitchen. For classes, she planned to offer light snacks, nice cheese, scones, finger sandwiches. A casual high tea.

Abigail smiled at Clara, who smiled back, her tongue out, panting as she watched the world outside the open front door.

The toilet was functional now, and after an extended, expensive visit from a plumber named Don, so was the shower. She'd painted the upstairs room at the same time she'd painted the walls downstairs, the pale yellow that reminded her of fall sunshine. A full-sized bed arrived when the furniture did, and the delivery guys had put it together. It stood in the middle of the windowed cupola, surrounded by views of the valley, the trees, the sheep, the sky, and a sliver of the ocean in the distance. Her desk was at the window that looked down at Cade's house. She hung curtains as soon as she'd realized that if she could look directly into the top floor of the big house, then anyone in the house could look across and into her space.

When she'd hung the curtains, she hadn't wanted that. Now, she wasn't so sure. Maybe she wanted Cade to be able to look in on her, easily. Maybe.

Her heart gave that funny jump again, that extra syncopated beat she'd been feeling all day.

Work. She had work to do. The pile of boxes full of fiber never seemed to diminish, and there were still books and needles to attempt to arrange. Janet was managing the party—all Abigail had to do was wait for everyone to show up.

A few hours later, satisfied with her progress, Abigail sat out in front, grinning in the sun, watching Clara rip and shake an empty box.

Tom pulled up in his truck.

He leaned out the window and tugged on his cowboy hat. He was a cliché in motion, and he didn't even know it. Or she hoped he didn't.

"Awful cute dog you got there." He whistled at Clara and her head snapped in his direction. Tom woofed, and Clara happily barked back, danced in a small, jumping circle, and went back to her box-shredding task.

"I think so."

"It was good of you to take her."

"I'm beginning to think it was even better of me to take the alpacas off Mort's hands."

"I'll grant that was nicer than most people would have been."

What was he after? They didn't usually exchange this kind of small talk. She'd seen him drive by a couple of times. He'd touched his hat and smiled and driven by.

"What's up, Tom? Something I can help you with?"

"No, just saying hi. Seeing how you're doing. I mean, yeah! Your foot! How's your foot? That's what I wanted to ask."

Ah. Abigail got it. "My foot's doing fine, almost all healed. But what you might be really interested to know is that my friend Janet should be here soon."

"Really? Today?"

"You two hit it off that day?" Abigail loved the look on his face—a mix of eagerness and machismo.

"I think so, I guess so. But that was a couple of weeks ago. She say anything to you?"

"Only that you were a very handsome man."

"She said that?"

"Several times, and she doesn't say things like that lightly."

"I bet she could get whoever she wanted."

"And often does."

Tom looked stricken. Abigail felt awful. "I don't mean that she gets around—I mean, she knows people, and she knows men. . . . But she did seem really into you. . . ." She was making it worse.

She started over. "I bet you she'd really like it if you came by later. She's planning a little launch party. She has a few people coming over to help with the store today, and she'd love it if you lent a hand."

"I just might do that," Tom said.

Abigail screwed up her courage and asked, "Has Cade been around?"

"What do you mean?"

"I haven't seen him in a while."

"Not even at the house?"

"Nope."

"Huh. No, he's been around. Should I tell him you're looking for him?"

"No! No. That's all right. I'll track him down if I need him."

As Tom drove away, hand waving out the window, she tried to think of all the ways she didn't need Cade. She wouldn't track him down.

But would it have killed him to have tracked her down? Just a little bit?

Ridiculous thoughts. She went back to watching Clara. She didn't look up the driveway once, not even out of the corner of her eye.

Chapter Twenty-six

Be careful with your needles. They are magic things. If you're careless, they won't come back to you. Or they can end up hurting someone else.
—E.C.

Six hours later, everyone was exhausted.

They sat in the parlor of Cade's house, perching on extra chairs stolen from the dining room and on edges of the sofa and various couches and ottomans. A woman named Gail sat on the embroidered piano stool. She kept hopping off it to exclaim over the workmanship.

Abigail did have to admit, it certainly was something to see: the lengths to which these women would go for another woman's memory, to honor a woman they had never actually met.

And lengths they had gone. Abigail wasn't really sure where Janet had obtained her guest list, but it included knitting writers from all over the country. One had flown in from New York, one from Boulder, two from Toronto. Abigail knew most of them and considered them friends, had met them at craft fairs and on book tours; she read their blogs, but she had never hung out with most of them in person.

Also in attendance were ten or eleven women who lived on the West Coast. They seemed to be hooked into every yarn happening, every stitch 'n' bitch west of the Mississippi.

A woman named Sarah had tears in her eyes when she lifted fiber out of her first box. "Eliza packed this. With her very own hands."

Abigail looked at its label and saw that it had come straight from a distributor. "Well, she chose what was inside of it, that's for sure."

Sarah had glared at her and hissed, "I can feel it. She packed it."

Abigail had exchanged a look with Janet. A *Star Trek* convention would be less nerdy, less star obsessed than this little gathering. She was glad to be at the center of it, truly honored.

She was also freaked out.

But now it was better. The women were arranged around the parlor, everyone knitting or spinning, some with small portable wheels, some with drop spindles. Janet had performed a small miracle while Abigail hadn't been looking. The sides of the room were lined with small tables covered in lovely foods—small, delicate appetizers and desserts. A short, round woman with pink cheeks circulated with bottles of chilled champagne.

Abigail also felt herself getting more and more rosy with each passing sip that she took. If she were going to make a speech, it would have to be now.

She stood and waited. A quick silence dropped, a quietness that served to make her nothing but tongue-tied. Knitting needles stopped. Wheels whirred to a stop.

"Ladies, a toast." She held up her glass.

"In one short afternoon's worth of work, you have made all the difference. I can see the light at the end of the tunnel. You unpacked and put away and scrubbed and cleaned until I couldn't see which end of the house was up. Someone cleaned the bathroom so that it sparkled."

A brunette holding a plate of cheesecake smiled and nodded at her.

"Someone else scrubbed the kitchen until I can actually picture myself making food on that countertop, using that sink, to—I don't know. Cook something."

Light laughter.

"I'm a knitter. And you're here because you are, too. You're here because you loved Eliza, and you're excited about this project of mine, or because you know me somehow, through my books, or because we've met before, or because you're humoring my friend Janet. I totally understand why anyone would do that."

Janet winked at her.

"But really, this is to say thank you. Both for the knowledge I've gained today, and for teaching me that there are people in this community who want to see this happen." She smiled, suddenly nervous and overwhelmed. Who was she, to be standing here, thanking these people?

"This is all because of Eliza. I design and write because of Eliza, and you're all here because of her, too."

Abigail looked slowly around the room, catching and keeping the eye of everyone there. "To Eliza."

"To Eliza," said all the women in the room, in unison.

Abigail brushed away a tear that had fallen onto her cheek, a tear that she hadn't even been aware of.

"To Eliza," said a breathy voice from behind her.

"Oh!" Abigail hadn't known anyone else had come in. Had she known, she wouldn't have blocked the door while speaking.

"What a beautiful speech," said the new woman. "Who's Eliza? Is she here?"

The speaker was a bombshell. There was no other way to describe her. Her blond hair was swept up in a hairdo reminiscent of the forties, something with swirls and loops, probably done with intricate bobby-pinning.

Her makeup also reminded Abigail of the girl on the side of a World War II airplane, all dark eyebrows and heavy eyelids and deep red lipstick, fair skin, and pink cheeks. She wore a red cardigan—was it cashmere?—and a low-cut black blouse with a red pencil skirt. She carried a red purse that looked expensive. Her heels were chunky, black, and very high.

"Um, no," said Abigail, as the conversation and chatter started up behind her again. "Eliza's not here."

"Too bad. She sounds like something." Her voice was breathy but low, a gorgeous, sexy voice.

Of course, thought Abigail. "Yeah, Eliza was something all right." She stuck out her hand. "Abigail."

"Oh, *you're* Abigail! I was expecting someone older, I think. Because of the knitting. You know."

Abigail could think of nothing to say to this.

"And look! You have all your friends here. Doesn't everyone look constructive?" She gave a bright, polished smile. Abigail wanted to smack her. Who was this person?

Cade approached behind her.

"Betty, I see you've already met my . . . housemate."

"You made her sound older, though. She's pretty. And young!" Betty giggled and looked at Abigail to share the joke with her.

"Abigail." Cade's smile was polite, thin.

Fine. If this was the way he wanted it, she could play along.

"I'm so glad you were able to drop by the grand-opening party." Abigail poured honey into her voice. "Doesn't it look nice in here? Janet did all the work, I have no idea where she found the caterer, but the food is divine. You must have a stuffed mushroom. Or a glass of champagne? It's a celebration!"

Betty nodded and moved toward the table.

"You're having a party. Here. In my house. For your shop."

"Yep."

"That's pretty ballsy. Even for you." His eyes, the green completely gone, only showed dark brown. If they could shoot sparks, they would have.

But Abigail found a thrill in this. She was teetering on the edge of his anger. She found she didn't mind as much as she thought she would have. He had been ignoring her for too long, avoiding her at every turn. This was what he got.

"I was going to invite you, if that's what you mean, but I thought a note hung on the refrigerator would be a little cold. Pardon the pun." She smiled lightly and took a sip of her champagne. "I was waiting until I saw you to deliver an invite in person. Funny, though. Except for after the fire, I haven't seen you at all in two weeks, not since I hurt my ankle."

Betty's face crinkled in either concern or confusion. "Oh, yeah, he told me about that. You fell out of a tree you were climbing because you like to do kid things? Or childish things? I like to do kid things, too, like sometimes, when I'm with my niece, I really get a kick out of coloring books. You know? Oh. Um . . . " She trailed off and stared at the rows of champagne glasses.

"Yeah," said Abigail, unsure of what she ought to say. Cade still hadn't mentioned where he'd been, and even though she knew it wasn't any of her business, her heart twisted at the thought that perhaps the reason he hadn't been around was standing in front of her, talking about coloring books.

"I have a great idea," said Cade, and Abigail scarcely recognized his patently false tone. "Betty, why don't you stay down here at the party while I go up and change? Socialize a bit. I'm sure you'd like that, and Abigail won't mind."

Before Abigail could answer, Cade headed back out to the staircase.

Abigail blinked several times and then smiled at Betty. "Of course. Champagne?"

Betty didn't appear to realize she was a pawn, or if she did, she did a good job hiding it. "I'd love some champagne. It always makes me so giggly."

Of course it did. Abigail rolled her eyes as she turned her back to pour the glass for Betty.

Moving farther into the parlor, where everyone was sitting, Abigail said loudly to no one in particular, "Everyone? This is Betty. Betty," she flapped her hand, "this is everyone."

A chorus of curious hellos sounded through the room, and then it was Janet to the rescue, as usual.

"Darling, what a sweet cardigan that is—you look just like a pinup girl from the forties."

Abigail ground her teeth as Betty smiled and appeared gracious. Of course she was gracious. Shallow, gorgeous people were always gracious. It was bred into them, wasn't it? Like height in horses.

Janet rose and introduced herself, and then said, "Do you spin? Knit?"

"Oh, neither. I'm no good with fiddly things. I'm not very patient."

"Nonsense. That's what I always said before Eliza taught me, and now I'm too fiddly *not* to knit."

"Who is Eliza again? Cade's mentioned her. Is she going to be here?"

Abigail snapped, "If she appeared right now, we'd all run screaming from the house."

Janet shot Abigail a look and said, "She died, not too long ago. We're all very sad. But I see you're here with Cade. That explains why you're here with no fiber in your hands. But we can fix that up in a jiffy. Come, sit over here."

Janet sat her on the couch next to her, and placed a drop spindle in her hands.

Abigail was pleased. This she wanted to see. Abigail hadn't been able to work out drop spindling until she'd learned to spin on a wheel first. Only then had the hand motions made sense to her.

She watched as Betty mirrored Janet's hands, mimicking their movement, fiddling with the drafting triangle until it looked good, spinning the spindle, letting the twist travel up the fiber, and yes, this was the moment. It would hit the ground, living up to its name of drop spindle, Betty would cry or something, and all would be right again.

Really, when had Abigail gotten so mean?

Since Cade had brought this girl into the house.

She waited for the drop. Soon it would happen. Soon that yarn that Betty was spinning would break, and she'd get frustrated and stop. Of course it would happen.

Soon.

Only it didn't happen. The women in the room stopped whatever they were doing to watch the impromptu lesson. "Look at her!"

"It's her first time."

"No!"

"She's doing so well."

"And she's spinning it pretty finely, too."

"She's a natural."

Betty grinned across the room at Abigail and it was such a happy, genuine smile that Abigail was whacked upside the head with guilt.

"Look what I'm doing! I'm making yarn!"

Abigail smiled back and moved closer. It wasn't this poor girl's fault that she was hooked up with Cade—he was gorgeous and successful and single. Who wouldn't want to date him? To live with him?

To fall in love with him?

Abigail reached for the nearest high-backed chair and leaned on it, suddenly dizzy.

"Honey, are you all right? You've been standing too long on that foot. Come, sit over here with us." Janet made another space next to her, so that Abigail would be sandwiched between Janet and Betty.

It was her fault, she supposed. It was where she was meant to sit. Penance.

She wasn't in love. That would be too ridiculous. She tried to push the errant thought out of her head.

It must be the champagne.

Well, talking to Cade's girlfriend would certainly help.

"So, how long have you and Cade been dating?"

"Only a few days now," said Betty, as she expertly twirled the spindle, drafting the fiber into a perfect single. "But it's been going great, and it's been moving so fast."

"You don't say."

"So I was glad when he invited me here. I mean, there's nothing more important to a rancher than his land, is there?"

"That's what I hear. They don't like to lose any of that land either."

"I wouldn't guess so. Oh! That cottage thing he told me about. Yeah, he seems pretty mad about that."

"You think?" Abigail's tone couldn't have been drier, but Betty didn't pick up on the sarcasm.

"I think so, yeah, but I think he'll get over it. Deep down, he likes you."

"Pretty deep, though."

"Well, I can only tell when he's talking about you. He gets all tongue-tied, like he wants to say something else. I think that must mean he really likes you."

"He likes me all right. He'd like me burnt on a stake, or drummed out of town. Maybe he'd like me at the bottom of a lake."

"Don't say that! I don't think he wants a store on his land. But I think"—Betty leaned toward Abigail conspiratorially—"I think you could get him to come around."

"How's that?" Abigail took another sip of her champagne. She was going to be good and drunk by the end of this, but it might be worth it.

"You should sell cow things in your store."

"Mmmm."

"And horse things."

"I'm not sure I see the connection."

"He'd love it."

"He breeds sheep, not cows."

"Okay, sheep things, then, and I know he has a few horses. So think about it—if you had everything he needed, right there in front of him, so he could just walk over and buy the combs or the pills he needed, right there? How could he argue with that?"

"But I'm opening a yarn shop. With a classroom."

"You could carry saddles."

"Next to the yarn?"

"Wouldn't that be the cutest? What do they call that stuff? There's a name for it, all the big animal stuff."

"Tack."

"Tack! That's it. So yarn and tack. Together. You could call it . . . um . . . Tacky Yarn! I love that. That's such a cute name for a store."

Abigail's eyes simply widened, and when she met Janet's gaze she couldn't help laughing.

"It's not a bad idea," insisted Betty. "Don't laugh."

Abigail choked back more giggles.

Janet, tactful as always, nodded and agreed, "That is, indeed, a grand name for a store. It may not be exactly what our Abigail has in mind—she's trying to keep straw and other vegetable matter *out* of her fiber, rather than putting it *in*, but you are just the sweetest thing, aren't you?"

The other women agreed, and oohed some more over her fine spinning. At this rate, she'd have enough for a sock in an evening. She was obviously a natural.

Or a ringer.

"You *sure* you've never done that before?" Abigail asked.

Betty laughed and shook her head. "Never. I'm good, huh?"

Abigail fit her lips together in a thin line and nodded. It was stupid of her to feel this low flame of jealousy.

She had nothing to be jealous of. She and Cade weren't an item—he'd merely slept with her, like he slept with half the women in town, apparently.

So Betty could spin. She didn't have brains, obviously.

"You should learn to knit, Betty. You'd pick it up in a minute."

"I'm sure I would—I have naturally talented hands. People always tell me so."

"Let me guess," said Abigail. "Massage therapist?"

Betty giggled. "No, I teach math. But when I bake, I form my piecrusts by hand, and people always tell me they look great, that I know what I'm doing." She shrugged.

"Math teacher? Where?" Please, oh, please, say at the local grade school or even junior high.

"At the UC. I have a doctorate in applied mathematics with an emphasis in numerical analysis of partial differential equations. But I really love teaching the beginning calculus classes. It's such a rush to see the kids so excited."

"You're a mathematician."

This was horrible.

"I know, I know, I look like a stewardess. I hear it all the time."

Abigail nodded and picked up her knitting. She couldn't believe she'd sat here, her hands not moving, for this long. Knitting would save her. It always did. Knit through everything.

"What are you making?" asked the perfect Betty.

"A sweater. I'm just finishing it up."

"It's big."

"It's a man's sweater."

"Is it for Cade?"

"No!"

"I thought, as a thank-you or something."

"Definitely not."

Betty stopped spinning, tucking the spindle under her leg, as the other women did when they stopped. God, she was a quick learner.

"Is it okay for me to be here? It's okay if it's not, tell me and I'll go find Cade."

Abigail shook her head. "It's my fault. I'm in a bad mood, and I'm taking it out on you, I'm sorry." She really had to pull herself together. She wasn't being fair to anyone right now.

Janet said, "I bullied her into the party, rolled myself in here and threw it all together. She's been working so hard to get the shop up and running. Just ignore her crankiness. That's what I do. Although, darling"—she turned to Abigail—"this is rather unlike you. I don't know if I've ever seen you in such a bad mood."

"Great. I'm sorry. Just a lot still to do."

"I can help," offered Betty. "I work with a homeless people's poetry project on Sundays, but I have most Saturdays free, and I'd love to give you a hand, since I wasn't able to help today."

She really was sweet. Abigail smiled, and this time it was genuine. "I'm almost done, thanks, but I'd love it if you came by or took a class sometime."

"If Cade and I are still dating, I'd love to. I hear he doesn't usually date for long."

"If at all," said Abigail.

"And no matter how you and Cade are doing," added Janet, "you're coming, and that's all we'll hear of it. We'll get you spinning on a wheel next."

Cade entered the room. "Well, look at you. Are you converted yet?"

"I'm one of them now, look." Betty held up her spindle and showed off her single to him. He nodded, looking pained.

"Let's go."

"Don't you want to stay for a glass of champagne? I could spin a little longer."

"Well, I'd love to have a drink in my own house, but the space is all taken up right now."

"Look at this, at the sweater that Abigail's making. Isn't that gorgeous? Hold it up, Abigail."

Abigail did, reluctantly. If only the two of them would leave, this party would settle down to normal again. She was conscious of twenty other pairs of eyes watching this exchange.

The sweater she'd been working on was her own design—she wanted a good, sturdy, attractive men's sweater to hang in the shop. She'd used her own handspun that she'd made last year from a Rambouillet fleece. She'd dyed the skeins a deep russet. Then she'd designed a traditional Guernsey, using the measurements of a friend down south and incorporating several old patterns in the top third. She liked the unconventional zigzag motif she'd lined down the arms, which kept it from being staid. The sweater was almost done—she was about to pick up and knit the neckline, but she hadn't started it yet.

"Look," said Betty. "You could try it on, Cade. She's not done, but it doesn't look like it would hurt anything, would it, Abigail?"

"No, I don't need to do that." Cade started backing out of the room.

"No, I don't think it would fit him." Abigail dropped it back into her lap.

"I think that's a smashing idea," said Janet. "Girls!" She clapped her hands. "Don't you think the handsome rancher should try on the Gansey?"

To a loud chorus of encouragement—boy, the other women had certainly been enjoying the champagne and wine—Cade was cajoled back into the room.

After several more moments of protestation, he looked at Abigail and said, "We're not getting out of this one, are we?"

"I don't think so, cowboy."

"Take it off! Take it off!" yelled the women.

"It's a sweater. It goes over."

"Oh, darling, not over that sweater you're already wearing," said Janet.

"But I don't have anything on underneath."

It was true, Abigail wouldn't recommend wearing the Guernsey over the obviously store-bought dress sweater he was wearing. He was dressed for a date, she noticed. Okay, she'd noticed it as soon as he'd come back into the room, wearing that charcoal sweater and matte-black dress pants. He smelled good, too, a light scent of masculine soap mixed with leather.

It wasn't fair that she thought like this about him. She didn't want to.

So what she really didn't need was for him to strip down right here.

The chant continued, "Take it off! Take it off!"

One woman named Louise who had been quiet earlier, scuttling around with her head down while they were cleaning, was standing on a low table, swinging her sock-in-progress around her head. Abigail saw another woman swigging right from the champagne bottle—she spluttered a bit when she saw Abigail notice her.

Someone did a drum roll on the table with their fists.

Everyone in the room was giggling or hollering, everyone except Cade and Abigail.

"This is ridiculous," said Cade, but he reached for the hem of his sweater.

"I couldn't agree more," she said as she adjusted some longer yarn ends that she hadn't sewn in yet.

"Let's get it over with."

He took off his sweater, and the crowd went wild.

And really, she knew why they were going crazy. Look at him, all abs, tightly defined muscles arranged in the traditional six-pack, curving up to a broad chest lightly covered in dark brown hair. His arms were also defined, large biceps, strong deltoids.

"He looks like a model," stage-whispered Louise from up on the table.

"Give me the sweater, for the love of God," Cade said.

"She's right, darling," said Janet. "You do look like a model. Take your time. Don't hurry on our account."

"Why am I doing this again?" he asked as he pulled the sweater over his head.

"Gah! Not like that!" Abigail jumped to help him pull it on. "I haven't sewn the underarm seams, and I don't want you ripping anything out."

Betty answered his question. "You're doing this for the good of all of us. We like what we're seeing. Plus, Abigail should see it on a live male's body."

What, did she think that Abigail had no access to a man's torso? Okay, she didn't. But she didn't need one, not to simply make a sweater. She could feel herself flushing red.

Cade, too, was bright red. He almost matched the russet of the sweater, which looked wonderful on him.

The sweater looked as if it were made for him.

She swore to herself it hadn't been. Sure, she'd only started to work on it about a month ago, about the same time she'd moved here. She had dyed the wool long before meeting him.

If Cade's body type had flashed through her mind as she'd been knitting and designing, was that really her fault? He was the closest male around, after all. It was natural.

Louise, now sitting on the table, a glass in either hand, said, "He should never, *ever* take that off."

"Unless it's when he's parking his boots under my bed. . . ." Abigail wasn't sure which woman said that, but it set off a tornado of sexual comments and innuendoes. Cade turned even redder and he pulled at the neck of the sweater.

"Get this off of me," he growled at Abigail.

"Don't pull like that." She lifted the hem and pulled it, her hands accidentally grazing his sides as it went up. She felt him shiver under her fingers.

Their eyes met. A sudden heat went through Abigail, and for one moment there were just the two of them in the room. His eyes spoke of fire and passion and reflected her own passion back to her, as if he caught it and amplified it, sending it back doubled. She had to tell herself to breathe.

She worked the neckline over his head. He was naked from the waist up again. During that moment when the sweater was in front of his face, their eye connection was broken.

She tried to catch hold of herself, of her racing heart.

For God's sake, they were in a room full of women, could she at least prevent herself from behaving like a teenager? All giddy and red and blushing. Were her hands shaking?

As he reached for his original sweater, she thought she saw his hands shaking, too.

"Wouldn't you love a sweater like that, huh? What would you do for a sweater like that?" said someone from the back of the parlor.

Another woman called out, "I know how to knit, baby. I'll make you a sweater. I'll help you put it on. *And* take it off."

Cade shook his head, as if to clear it, and said again, with finality in his voice, "We're going. Betty. Come on."

Betty didn't even look at him. She raised a finger and said, "Just a minute. I want to ask about this part." She leaned over to the two women seated on the piano bench and held out her spindle.

Cade cleared his throat and glared. He looked menacing. Betty didn't seem to care, or even to notice.

Abigail realized that she might have really gone a little too far this time. Having a party in his house, without asking, might have been a little much.

Which, really, was why she had done it. A light feeling entered her lungs, and she realized she was close to laughter. Panicked laughter, sure. Bubbling giggles rose desperately in her chest.

She took a deep breath and squared her shoulders again, keeping her expression airy. She looked up at him again.

"Cade, your face is almost purple. Don't forget to breathe, okay?" She looked at him closer, honestly getting worried. Was he breathing at all?

"Are you okay?" Her hand went out to touch his arm, but his hand snaked out and caught hers, instead.

"Kitchen, now," he said, his teeth gritted together.

"I'm coming. Don't pull me."

"Now."

He walked in front of her, faster than she could follow. She could feel the intent interest behind her, from the women packing the parlor, but didn't turn to meet any of their gazes. Janet would smooth things over in there, would quell the gossiping tongues. She was good at that. If she wasn't starting even better gossip, that is.

He was good to follow, she decided, as they entered the kitchen. Apparently, her libido was still lit from that quick gaze in the parlor, because his backside held just about as much fascination as his naked chest had held.

My God, she needed to get hold of herself. Or get laid.

Chapter Twenty-seven

Remember, a woman's knitting needles are sharp, and her eyesight is sharper.

—E.C.

He'd never been treated as such an object in his life, and he'd participated in a wet tee shirt contest in college. The girls had screamed at him then, but tonight had been different. Cade honestly thought that if he would have fit in their knitting bags, they would have scooped him up and run with him right out of the house.

Crazy knitters.

And the craziest of all of them was right on his heels.

Good. He didn't necessarily need the whole world to hear him go off on her about the party, but he was mad enough that if she hadn't followed him, he wouldn't have cared.

"We need to go back to what I was saying," he said and turned around, leaning against the sink.

"I don't actually remember what that was." She tried to hide a giggling sound behind her hand.

"What's so funny?"

"Oh, my God, did you see their faces? They wanted you to keep going!" She leaned forward, giggling, her hair falling in her face. It made her look about eighteen years old. "If only they'd had one-dollar bills, you could have cleaned up. Bought a tractor or something with your g-string money."

It was too late, she was full-blown in the middle of a giggle fit. He knew the signs, and he'd have to wait it out.

He stood in one place, not moving an inch; even though his hip was leaning at an uncomfortable angle against the cabinet door, to move would have been to invite more hilarity. And sure enough, she kept it up for a while, subsiding slowly, after huffing and snorting and hiccupping.

She looked funny enough to make him smile. It lifted his heart to see her like this.

He banished the thought and plastered the stern look back on his face.

This was serious, goddammit. None of this was okay. He wouldn't allow a retail store on his property, even though it wasn't, technically, his property anymore. He'd told her no. He'd made it clear.

Then, not only did she go and have a grand-opening party, she pulled it off here. In his house, which she owned no part of. None at all.

It was enough to make a man . . . Damn it. He couldn't think of anything he wanted to do right now that didn't involve her getting closer to him, and that wasn't acceptable. That was absolutely the last thing he wanted.

He would put more space between them, that was it. He needed to be able to breathe, and she was so close to him.

She wasn't laughing anymore. She was looking up at him, expecting him, he was sure, to light into her about the party. To lambaste her with remarks that would hopefully have the effect of making her sorry she chose to have the party here, sorry that she even ever came here. Sorry enough to pack up her things and leave her dream behind.

But that would mean leaving him behind, too, wouldn't it?

That wasn't what he wanted.

God, what did he want?

He wanted space. He would have to back up. But the sink was behind him. All right, he'd move to the other side of her, around her.

Why didn't she say anything? Why was she standing there, looking at him, so beautiful? His heart felt funny, so odd that it was almost painful.

Screw it. When it came right down to it, even with everything he wanted to say to her, none of that mattered. Not when their eyes were locked like this, not when she was melting into him from four paces away.

There was only one thing he wanted.

He stepped forward. She jumped. Her mouth opened as if to speak, and then his own mouth was on hers, where it belonged. He should have done this at the start. Shouldn't have wasted his time trying to make her jealous, bring Betty here. What had he been thinking? *This* was what he wanted.

She gasped against his mouth, and he touched the inside of her mouth with his tongue. Then more. He needed more, and he couldn't have more, not right here in the middle of the kitchen with two dozen women in the next room, all armed with sharp and pointy sticks.

The pantry. It was behind her and to the left. He maneuvered her as best he could; she gasped again, but it wasn't because of his kiss. He remembered her ankle too late.

"I'm so sorry," he whispered, keeping his mouth as close as he could to hers without actually kissing her. "Are you okay?"

"Yes," she said.

"Then hold on to me for a second."

He put his arms around her waist and lifted, raising her slightly off the ground. He pressed her fully against his length at the same time. He moved forward, kicking the swinging pantry door open with the toe of his foot.

"What are you doing?"

"Here, I'm putting you down." He did it as gently as he could, but as her feet touched the ground, something stabbed him in the stomach.

"Ow! What the hell?" He reached in front of him. "Are you carrying a skewer in your pants?"

"Oh, crap," she said. "It's a double-point knitting needle. Size one. That can do some real damage—are you okay?"

"I think I'm okay, I'm not sure. Am I bleeding?"

The pantry was so small they had to stand against each other. She seemed to want to be as close to him as he wanted to be to her, and he didn't want to lose that—didn't want to spook her.

"Here," he said, taking her hand and placing it under the hem of his sweater. "Feel for me, see if I'm okay."

She bit her lip and nodded. He wanted to bite her lip in the same spot.

She drew her hand across his belly. "Here?" she asked.

"Yes, that's it."

"I don't think it broke the skin. I'm so sorry . . ." she started.

"Maybe you should check lower."

"Did the needle get you . . ."

"Maybe it did."

"Oh, yes, I suppose we're better safe than sorry." She grinned at him, a cheeky grin that made his heart jump.

"How about here?" Abigail's fingers were at the top of his waistband.

"Hmm. Kind of sore. But I think it's just a little lower. You may have to . . ."

"Under your belt, you mean? I suppose I'd better check. You don't want to bleed to death because I haven't done my job."

She unbuckled his belt and undid the button and fly on his pants. But she didn't even graze the front of him, the rock-hard part of him that he so desperately wanted her to touch. She knew exactly what she was doing, and he loved it.

Now her fingers slipped a little into the top of his boxers. "No, I think you're good here, too. I think you'll live."

His voice, when he spoke, was low and raspy. "No, maybe a little bit lower. Please, Abigail. I need you to check."

"Oh, here? That what you mean?"

Her hand was suddenly around him, all the way, cupping and stroking him. He gripped the shelf behind him. He prayed it would hold him.

"How are you doing right here, huh? What if I do this?"

He moaned.

"You don't appear damaged at all. I'm so relieved."

"I'm glad you're happy. But I might be dying." He had a hard time getting out the words.

"Really? You feel pretty strong to me, like you're doing okay."

He dropped his head and ground his mouth against hers.

"See?" she said under his mouth. "You're going to be just fine."

"No, I'm not. You're killing me. Little by little. I need more. I need you."

And he did. There was only one thing in his mind, and that was having her, and soon. He didn't care that the house was still full of people, he needed to be in her. He needed her to be his again, to feel her skin against his, to lie, stretched out against her, in bed.

And by the way her hand was moving against the part of him that needed it the most, she knew how he was feeling.

"God, you have to stop."

"Really?" She laughed, a low sound. It was the sexiest sound he'd ever heard. "Because it kind of seems like you're liking this. I mean, you don't seem to hate it or anything."

"You have to stop touching me like that."

"Like this?"

He bit back an oath. "I'm serious. I can't be responsible for what happens if you keep that up."

"Oh, come on, Cade," she chastised him, never stopping the motion of her hands, never stopping her lips from moving against his neck, stoking his fire that much higher. "You and I are both well-enough educated to know that's crap. You can and will be responsible. I can do anything I want to you, and if I said stop, you'd stop."

"I couldn't."

"But you would."

Cade nodded, took a deep breath and put his hand over hers, holding it tight and still. "If this is a course in women's empowerment, then yes, I admit I'm enlightened. No means no. But shouldn't that go both ways? I say no, you stop?"

"*You* might be enlightened. But maybe I'm just horny."

"I'm shocked." He was, a little.

She grinned at him. "Me, too." The smile dimmed a little, and she glanced away. He watched her take a deep breath.

"I don't know what it means," she said, "and I don't want to think about it, but I . . . I want you."

"I want you, too." He pressed her hand against himself again, but didn't allow her to move, to take more than she already had. He couldn't stand it. "Obviously."

"Okay," she said.

"Would you go out to dinner tonight with me?"

"What?"

"Dinner? The evening meal of choice in these parts?"

"I'm pretty sure I know what it means, but . . . shit. I have a party out there I should get back to. And don't you already have a date tonight?"

Damn. Betty. Yes, he did. Oh, God, he was a total asshole. He should go back to Betty right now; that's what a gentleman would do. But a gentleman wouldn't have gotten himself in this situation in the first place, would he? So instead he said, "Kiss me once more, and then I'll go get out of the date."

Abigail gave him a look that he almost drowned in, and he forgot again where he was. Her hand strained to move against him, but he kept a tight hold on her wrist. He wanted nothing more than to let her touch him. Or to turn her around and bend her over the step stool. Or to lead her back through that clutch of knitters straight up to his bedroom. But he couldn't.

He could kiss her though. He did his best to do that as thoroughly as possible. He brought his free hand up to the back of her neck, and he made sure she knew exactly how much he wanted her.

A click, from behind them, and then a gasp.

"Well, son of a bitch."

Cade spun around, clutching at his jeans, buttoning them in the second it took to turn fully. Abigail's mouth was parted, her lips wet and swollen.

Betty stood in the door of the pantry, looking as if someone had hit her across the face. Both her cheeks turned bright red and her eyebrows drew together.

"Well, that's something, all right." There was anger in her voice, but her lower lip trembled, just the smallest bit, and Cade felt instantly awful.

"I guess I'm glad I drove my own car over here. Even though I'd really wanted you to pick me up. Like a gentleman. Now I know why you didn't."

"I'm sorry. Betty, I'm really sorry." Cade took a step toward her. This was awful.

She held up a hand. "Save it."

Abigail said, "Betty . . ."

"You? No, really, I don't want to hear it. It's been a nice couple of days, Cade. From what I hear, that's all you ever give. So Abigail, enjoy your five minutes of heaven, because that's all you're going to get. At least you won't have to drive yourself home afterward."

She turned on her spiked heel and walked out.

"*Damn* it," he said. Then he looked at Abigail's face and hastened to correct the impression he'd just given.

"No, not damn like I'm sorry she's gone. But I didn't want to hurt her feelings like that."

"I think, no matter what, kicking someone out while they're in the middle of a date is going to hurt their feelings."

"Yeah, but I wish she hadn't seen that."

She sighed and brushed her fingers through her hair, and then wiped her lips with her fingertips. She sidled past him, and while he wanted to stop her, what could he do? This was crazy.

"I guess I'll go back out to my party."

"Yeah, I guess you should do that. Before we get caught by someone else."

"And there are some women in there that would die of a heart attack if they knew what we were just doing."

"Not we," Cade said. "What you were doing to me. There's a difference."

The corner of her mouth twitched. "And you weren't doing anything to me at all."

"Not at all. Nothing. I couldn't be more innocent."

"Sure. Hey, I could go out there and tell them there's a sale at the yarn shop in Half Moon Bay."

"You think they'd believe you?"

"Do I care?"

"So you'll get rid of them?" Cade asked.

"Do I get a date out of it?"

"Hell, yeah." He didn't even bother to try to keep the enthusiasm out of his voice.

"You are already dressed for a date with another woman. That'll save time."

"I know. I'm an asshole. Honestly, I'm not usually that big a jerk though, I swear. Can't we just sneak out without telling anyone?" Cade said.

"No," Abigail said.

"Why not?"

"Because it's my . . ."

"Grand opening, whatever. So you'll take thirty minutes saying thank-yous and good-byes. They'll exhaust you and you won't want to go anywhere at all afterward. Let's just go." Cade stepped back a bit and looked at her. "I want you to myself."

"I have to tell Janet."

"You have your cell phone on you?"

"In my pocket."

"Text her."

He didn't really think she'd do it. She was too responsible. She wouldn't hurt anyone's feelings by disappearing from her own party. Her own very important party.

But she grinned at him, and his heart soared, higher than he thought was possible. She put her hand in his and said, "Let's go."

She was no Betty. She was Abigail. That's all he needed. He held her hand tightly and they ran.

Chapter Twenty-eight

While you're knitting the yoke, if you grow bored, think about buttons. It's always delightful to think about buttons.

—E.C.

What had gotten into her? She didn't make out with and—oh, Lord—give hand jobs to men during her own parties. She didn't even *have* parties. Especially with men who were on other dates. Did that make her the other woman, if only for ten minutes? And she most certainly didn't run out of said party with said man, fishtailing up the driveway at sixty miles per hour. Cade hadn't even turned on the headlights in the rapidly dropped evening, not wanting to attract any attention. Abigail's heart rate increased as they raced up the small hill in the dark. Cade obviously knew every curve of the road, but that didn't slow her pulse.

Or was it him? Sitting in the darkened cab of his truck, she was suddenly at a complete loss as to what to say.

Did he feel like this, too? Was he as nervous as she was?

God, of course not. Look at him. Manhandling the wheel, palming it. Caressing it.

She had to get herself back under control. Abigail put her cell phone back in her pocket.

"You send that text message?" he asked. They'd reached the main road now and he flipped on his headlights. Abigail was relieved to be able to clearly see the road in front of her.

"Yeah, I told her that we were going to the hospital."

"Did you really? That might not have been the best thing. They're all going to show up there looking for us. Did you give a reason?"

"I said you'd tried something in the kitchen and that I'd popped you in the nose and started a nosebleed that I couldn't stop. And that I was going to drop you off and then go get more liquor, since that one woman with the sequins . . ."

"The one sitting closest to the fireplace?"

"That one, had drunk it all."

"You said all that on your phone? Right now?"

"Basically. She knows me well enough to read between the lines."

"Well enough to know that maybe we needed to be alone?"

"That well. She'll do our dirty work for us," Abigail said.

"I don't want her to do *all* our dirty work."

Abigail couldn't respond. She was too busy tightening her hand into a small ball in her lap, releasing it, clutching it again. She wanted to place it on his lap, on that thigh that she knew from experience was exactly as firm and strong as it looked, but she couldn't.

They shouldn't be on a date. They weren't the kind of people that dated each other. Abigail dated white-collar men, men who enjoyed Chardonnays and quiet sex, and Cade, well, he dated women with big breasts who liked to sing karaoke and had favorite brands of whiskey. Okay, and Betty, who was a mathematician. But who *looked* like she probably loved karaoke.

She stared out the truck window. They were getting closer to the shoreline, and he turned south down the coast road. They were going into town. Out to eat. On a date.

She'd forgotten what this felt like.

What it felt like when something was important. When someone was important.

They ate at a small restaurant in Cypress Hollow near the water, an expensive one that she'd heard of but hadn't been to since she moved to town. It wasn't the kind of place you went with friends: the dining room was filled with people gazing romantically into each other's eyes.

Abigail had a hard time not falling into this demographic.

Cade looked so good. He looked like he belonged here. In the candlelight, she could make out small laugh or weather lines around his eyes. They suited him, she thought. He'd be too perfect without them.

They had martinis, crab cakes for an appetizer, steak and lobster for dinner. She went slowly so she didn't get juice all over her clothes. Sometimes her sweater felt too tight, and too low cut. She tugged at the neckline more than she should have. Every time she did, his eyes followed.

"Do you mind if I knit?" Abigail pulled a sock-in-progress out of her purse. It might not be the most polite thing to do, knitting in a nice restaurant, but she had to ease these nerves somehow. He shook his head.

They made small talk.

"Have you ever traveled?" she asked. "Do you like to?"

"Never had time. Been working ever since I got out of school. During school, too." He cleared his throat. "What about you?"

He was only being polite but she clutched at the question.

"I love traveling. It's my favorite thing in the world, I think. Venice. I love Venice best. But Paris is lovely. And Prague. New Zealand! You'd love New Zealand."

"Sheep."

"Yes, sheep."

The food came. She dropped the sock onto her lap.

Cade ate gracefully. Abigail felt like she was all thumbs.

She cracked a piece of the lobster tail with her fork. She hit it too hard and a glob of lobster landed on her sweater. She cleaned it off with her napkin, willing him to look away from her red face. But he didn't. He gazed at her.

Her hands shook.

She told him about her father and aunts who raised her, she asked what he did in his leisure time, and she listened as he spoke of his newfound interest in woodcarving.

It was a quiet restaurant, all dim candlelight and soft edges, the waiters speaking in muted sonorous tones, the patrons matching their tone. But Abigail could hardly hear Cade's voice over the roar of blood pounding.

"And Tom? How long have you known him?"

"Tom's family. I feel like he's been around forever. He worked for Eliza before he worked for me. . . ." He trailed off. His eyes rested somewhere over Abigail's left shoulder.

"Was he ever married?"

"What?" Cade looked back at her. It seemed like it took some effort. "Yeah, married once. She died. He was heartbroken. Um . . ." His eyes left hers again, gazing again over her shoulder.

Abigail turned. A gorgeous woman, dressed in a low-cut little black dress, sat at the table behind them. Her hair was up in a smooth French knot, emphasizing the length of her neck.

Her heart hurt. She turned back to Cade. One more try.

"When was that?"

"What?"

"How long ago did she die?"

Now he wasn't even trying to hide it, openly staring behind her. He craned his neck to get a better look.

Abigail took her napkin out of her lap and threw it on the table. "Take me home."

He barely glanced at her. He half stood, looking over her shoulder harder.

"Seriously? No wonder you can't get a girlfriend!" She sounded as shrill as she felt.

"Sorry, hang on. . . ."

"You've *got* to be kidding me."

Cade pushed his chair out from behind him, not seeming to care that it fell over backward, hitting the man at the table behind him.

"Wha . . ."

"Call 911!" Cade yelled to the hovering waiter.

Abigail turned around again. The man at the table with the beautiful blond was shaking. His lips were blue, the rest of his face mottled. Cade lifted him to a standing position while sweeping his chair out from under him. Cade's arms went around the man from behind, and using both hands, he jerked his balled fist up under the man's ribs.

The man stayed blue. His eyes rolled back in his head. The blond screamed.

Cade jerked his fist up into the man's ribs again. A dark-colored piece of food flew out of the man's mouth. His eyes opened and he gasped like a large fish.

The following moments were chaotic—the man was embarrassed and grateful and wheezing; the blond cried and clung to the man after kissing Cade on the cheek. The paramedics arrived.

So did dessert.

They finished dinner in silence. She was so stupid. He was a hero, and she was a moron.

Cade paid, dismissing her efforts to give him money.

He helped her with her coat.

He opened her door for her, and smiled. He drove in the direction of the boardwalk.

Abigail wanted to scream with frustration. How long was this date going to take? When could they go home, where she might remember who she was?

When was he going to touch her again?

They didn't speak as he parked, and he took her hand as they walked out onto the sand. They both slipped out of their shoes and carried them, still without speaking.

She should comment on the beauty of the night. A low harvest moon drooped in the sky, painting a silvery ladder against the water. She should say something about it, something smart about the angle of the moon, or something romantic about the feeling in the air.

But she had a feeling that if she spoke, she'd either break the mood or she wouldn't be able to control the words, and they'd pour out of her.

And she wasn't sure what she would end up saying.

So Abigail stayed quiet as they walked, as he led her down the deserted beach toward the pier. The moon was so bright she could see the ripples in the sand, the footprints of people and dogs who'd walked here earlier today. Had any of them felt as nervous as she did? Had the setting seemed as surreal to them as it did to her?

Cade took her by the hand and led her under the pier.

Abigail said, "I'm sorry. About the way I was. In the restaurant."

He turned to face her and raised his eyebrows.

"You were amazing. You saved his life. I didn't know what you were doing, what you were going to do."

"Neither did I. But I know what I'm doing now."

He leaned down and kissed her, no part of their bodies touching but their lips. And in the kiss, she could feel every part of him, his strength, his heat. She kissed him back, conveying everything that she couldn't say. This was what her body needed, wanted, craved.

Him. Just him.

For a long moment she was able to hold her body away from his, almost as an experiment. How long could she bear it? To not touch him with anything but her mouth when her whole body craved the intimacy of him pressed against her.

Cade gave up first, and she was glad to give in. He grasped her by the shoulders and moved her backward, stepping forward against her, until her back was pressed against a piling. Then he was against her, full-length and hard as he'd been before, in the pantry.

She couldn't breathe, her head spun. She had no idea where her hands went or where his were going. They moved against each other in the dark in ways that Abigail would have normally found shocking. If she'd been walking the beach and been witness to something like this, she would have been mildly offended. Get a room. Take it somewhere else. Pull your clothes down, up, back into place.

But it wasn't someone else, it was her clothing being moved and rearranged. It was her hand pulling at Cade's belt, loosening the top button. . . .

His lips moved more quietly now against hers, and his hands stilled hers.

"We should probably go," he said.

"Y-yes. You're right." Abigail twisted out of his arms, away from the piling, which, now that she thought about it, had most likely left tar on the back of her clothing. Great. Focus on anything. The tar, the beautiful scenery. Anything but why he was stopping them.

"I'm sorry," Cade said.

"I know. Me, too. I let myself get a little carried away." She shook her head. "No, a lot carried away. I apologize."

"No, don't, there's nothing for you to apologize about."

She walked back toward the stairs they'd come down. "You started it."

"The kiss?"

"The apology. But the kiss, too."

"Right."

Abigail turned to face him. His green eyes in the moonlight were a brilliant surprise. "Why did you take me down here, then? Without talking? And now you want to go?"

He spread his hands out in front of him. "Did I make a mistake? I don't actually enjoy sand in my underwear or other sensitive places, but I'll do it for you."

"Was that the whole plan?"

He walked past her, striding quickly.

"I know you must have a reason."

Without turning around, he called over his shoulder, "I've always wanted to do that."

"Make a girl crazy?" She caught up to him and pulled on his elbow. "It worked."

"No, I've always wanted to take someone here. In the moonlight."

"Nice line, buddy. You can't tell me you never have."

"I never have. I don't take women to the beach."

"So this is like taking me home to Mom?"

"Yep, only you don't have to pretend to like stroganoff."

"It was a test?"

"Don't worry. You passed." He held out his hand. She slipped her hand in his.

This was all right, then. She hadn't made a mistake.

"Now what?" she asked.

"Let's go home."

She had no idea where this was going, holding his hand like this, letting her heart get entangled. She was caught up in his eyes and his hands and the moonlight. But she trusted him.

And she wanted more.

"Drive fast," Abigail said.

Chapter Twenty-nine

Hold bamboo needles firmly, so the yarn doesn't slip.
Move stitches neatly and joyfully, from one needle to the
next. But don't clutch the work too tightly or the needles
will snap and your work will unravel.
              —E.C.

H e drove fast, speeding through town. He took curves ten miles an hour faster than she would have ever attempted, even in daylight. But Abigail felt safe. She felt cocooned inside the cab of the truck, steady and happy in the knowledge of what was going to happen when they got home.

Home. Where they lived.

Under completely unnatural conditions.

But for now it worked for her.

When they got home, she'd be seductive. She'd take her time wooing him, leading him through the house, perhaps taking one piece of clothing off at a time, trailing him, panting, behind her.

Or maybe she'd be really classy, excusing herself and going to change into her little black lace negligee and then coming out, leaning against a doorway. This would be a good time to stand there in the dim light, one hip popped out, holding a smoking cigarette, beckoning. . . .

But she didn't smoke and didn't want to start. And she didn't think she had the patience.

He took another curve, and then shot down a straightaway. Abigail wanted to be nowhere else in the world, except home.

Faster.

Bright blue and red lights lit up the interior of the cab. A siren whooped, twice, three times.

Cade swore. He braked and pulled the truck to the right, skidding on the gravel. "I'm gonna kill whoever that is."

"Killing a cop is generally not a great idea," said Abigail.

"Dammit."

"You were going pretty fast."

"I'm going to die if I don't get you home soon," Cade said.

The cop approached the driver's-side door.

Cade rolled down the window, displaying both his hands. The cop leaned in to look at Abigail. She gave him what she hoped was a disarming smile, although it could have been a set of bared teeth for all she knew.

"Cade," said the cop. He looked about forty, and tired, with prematurely gray hair and dull skin. The uniform fit him too tightly.

"Officer Moss," said Cade.

"I guess you know why I pulled you over."

"That pesky taillight out again, John?"

"I wish I could say that's all it was. But you were speeding, my friend."

"I was? Really? Huh. I was watching the speedometer."

"Then you know you were going seventy in a forty-five."

"Speedometer must be broke."

"As usual."

"Come on, John, I can't afford another speeding ticket."

"Then don't speed."

"I can't believe you'd give me a ticket like this. You're gonna make me look bad in front of my date."

"It's not the first time."

Abigail giggled. The cop smiled at her.

Cade frowned. "Really, please. Don't cite me."

"You got a good reason for speeding like that? The little lady doesn't look pregnant to me, not in any kind of rush to the hospital? You're driving away from it, actually, so that can't be it. Anything better?"

Cade jerked his thumb at Abigail. "Kind of the opposite. She's ovulating."

The cop's eyebrows shot up into his unfortunate bangs. "Excuse me?"

"I said, she's ovulating. We've got things we have to do. And soon."

The cop's jaw dropped. Abigail felt her own mouth open, and her eyes went wide, but she turned her head and looked out the passenger-side window. She bit her lip.

"And who is she exactly? I'm sorry, ma'am, but I don't recognize you, and I know a lot of people around here."

Abigail turned back to look at him, trying to arrange her face into a neutral position. "Abigail Durant. I live with Cade."

"You what?"

"She does." Cade nodded.

The officer took a step away from the truck and pushed back his cap.

"Wow. Cade. I heard you shacked up with someone, but I thought it was just talk. Wow, that's all I can say. And now, I guess, you're trying to . . . "

"We're trying to make a baby," said Cade. "But we don't have much time tonight. Her window, if you know what I mean, is closing as we speak. Got to get her home and do my duty."

"I gotta tell you, buddy, that's one of the best lines I've ever heard."

"It's true, I swear. I want a little Cade from this little lady, and hopefully, he'll have her gorgeous eyes."

"You're still getting a ticket."

"Seriously?"

"I'll be right back."

Cade accepted his ticket, signing for it with one swipe of the pen.

"Good luck to you both. Especially to you, ma'am. You need it."

Abigail laughed the entire way home.

Cade pretended to ignore her, but she could see the corner of his lip twitching, and once he gave a snort that sounded suspiciously like a laugh.

He opened her door for her when they pulled up. She was still laughing but she tried to hide it.

"You're lucky you're sexy when you laugh."

That made her giggle again, just as she was pulling herself together, but with his help, she pulled herself out of the truck.

That slight touch, that resting of his wrist on her hand, sobered her instantly, the giggle dying on her lips. He guided her toward the house, up the shallow steps.

There weren't any cars left in the driveway. "They gave up on me, I guess."

"Thank God," said Cade. "If there had been even one knitter left in my house, I would have shown them my crochet hook collection."

"You *do* know how to offend a knitter, don't you?"

"My aunt taught me well."

Inside. Get *inside*. Every part of Abigail's body was screaming to be indoors with him, inside the house. She could think of other things that incorporated the word *inside*, things that made her flush and made her even more crazy to get in the doors. She was shaking. She hoped he couldn't feel it.

He just had to turn the doorknob. Come on.

Why wasn't he turning the doorknob? He seemed to be trying, but it wasn't working.

Cade frowned. "The door's locked." He sounded incredulous.

"Janet's a city girl. I'm sure she would have locked it behind her."

"Why would she do that?"

"Use the key, then."

"I never use it. I have no freaking idea where it would be. Do you have the copy I gave you?"

"It's in my room, I saw it on my dresser this afternoon. I knew you didn't lock the house, so I haven't been carrying it."

"Fantastic."

"Is there a window open?"

Cade looked at Abigail and touched her cheek. "Baby, I don't have the time to pry a window. But I'll have time to fix a window later." He backed up against the small side window next to the front door and with a small motion, brought his elbow sharply back and into the glass. It shattered with a quiet tinkle.

"Whoa," Abigail said.

He stuck his hand through the opening, moving carefully, and unlocked the door.

"Now," he said.

"Now," she agreed.

It was as if he were a fever that she had, and she couldn't get her temperature down. Instead of doing any of the sexy things she had considered while he'd been driving home, she tripped in the kitchen and almost went down.

His arms were around her, he was lifting her, almost even before she tripped. "Are you all right? What about your ankle?"

Her ankle. It hurt like hell again and she hadn't even noticed it. "It's fine," she lied, knowing she was red in the face. Instead of being the siren, she felt as if she were a twelve-year-old girl with a crush. Instead of having the moves of a seductress, she had the clumsiness of an adolescent. Great.

But her body didn't think she was twelve. The grown-up part of her turned herself around and walked toward the stairs.

He stuttered behind her. "Do you—do you want a drink, maybe?"

"No, thanks."

"I make a mean gin martini."

"Tempting," she said over her shoulder as he trailed behind her, "but I'm not thirsty."

She went up the stairs, feeling the heat of him behind her.

He said, "This wasn't the plan, if you think that's why I asked you out."

"It's okay if it was," she said, as she entered his room and turned to face him.

"But it wasn't."

"I didn't think you had much plan at all, to be honest. We got caught making out in the pantry. Kind of spontaneous."

"But great," he said.

"Are we going to talk all night?" She pulled her sweater up over her head and slipped out of her shoes and jeans. She stood in her bra and panties in front of him, feeling brave and terrified.

"You are so beautiful." His voice shook. He came to her, and he touched her. His hands and fingers moved the scraps of silk aside.

"Why didn't you touch me more, this morning?"

His hands stilled. "What?"

"When you came in my room?"

"I didn't."

Abigail frowned. It had been such a vivid dream. But it didn't matter, as long as he touched her now.

They were on the bed, no words now. His clothes had joined hers in a pile on the floor. She knew she'd helped with that part, but couldn't quite remember how, even now, moments later.

They didn't speak anymore, only motion and heat and low noises that Abigail knew were coming from her but didn't recognize. She used her hands to show him, to lead him to what she wanted. He recognized her desire and used his mouth to lift her up, higher and higher. When she reached the top, she cried out and clutched his head with her fingers and fell back down, tumbling through an intensity of sensation that left her spent on top of the covers of his bed. She was openmouthed, panting, stunned.

He moved up the bed, looked in her eyes. She showed him the yes she couldn't say, moving her legs against his, gesturing, suggesting, moving him with her hips and hands until he was over her. Then he was inside, hard and hot, where she needed him to be.

His mouth took hers as his body did. Her hands dug into his back and pulled him tighter to her. She couldn't get him far enough inside, although he filled her so much that she couldn't breathe. They moved together until his head went back and she watched him spiral out and beyond. She joined him in the ether. They landed together, twisted against each other, eyes locked, their limbs wet and limp and perfect.

He was still on top of her, long, long moments later, the perfect weight, the perfect length, and as his breathing got heavier and deeper above her, she closed her eyes and fell asleep.

Chapter Thirty

Never forget to admire your own handiwork. Drape the sweater over your lap and look at the long, neat lines of stitches. Then make the person nearest you admire your work, too.

—E.C.

He didn't understand how this had happened again, how he'd woken up again with her in his arms. This time yesterday, he'd had a date planned with Betty, and if he had thought about getting lucky at all, it had been with the pretty mathematician.

Of course, that had only been because he had to actively not think about Abigail. At all. If and when he did think of her, images of her lying exactly like she was now, heavy with sleep, naked and warm, smelling of perfume and something deeper, took over his mind.

More than that, he had tried not to think of her in the recent weeks, even clothed.

But while he'd been avoiding her, he'd been unable to stop wondering about her. How was her foot healing? Did she have trouble with the stairs? What did the old cottage look like inside? How close was she to being able to move into it, to moving out of his house?

When was she going to pack her few bags, remove all trace of herself from his upstairs spare bedroom and move into the cottage, leaving his home dark again, and empty? That's what women did—they left. Ever since his mother had left him, when she'd left him and his father for the first time of many, he'd understood that about women. This one lying in his arms even came with a built-in plan for leaving. She wasn't going to stay in this house. That was good. That's what Cade always wanted from a woman.

But this one wasn't going to go far, just across the yard. His heart lifted in a way he didn't recognize.

Her, lying in his arms like this. This was what he wanted.

Her. He just wanted her.

And he wanted her to stay.

She stirred in her sleep and moved against him, cuddling into his shoulder. He felt himself respond viscerally to her motion, involuntarily. Probably not the best way to wake her up, if past experience with women was anything to go by. They didn't so much like being woken up that way, no matter what the male sex thought. Cade knew that.

He kissed the side of her face softly. She made no move, no sound. Good. There was something he wanted to get done.

After his chores, Cade eased his truck down the driveway so he wouldn't disturb Abigail's sleep, and then gunned it and fishtailed onto the main road.

He parked in front of Tillie's Diner, slamming the gearshift into park.

Inside, Old Bill leaned against the counter as he always did. He raised his eyebrows when Cade came in.

"Twice in a month? If the boys recognize you, they'll die of surprise."

"Not if they don't see me. I've just got a quick order."

"I'll tell Shirley," said Old Bill, turning.

"No! I just need . . ." But Old Bill was already waving his towel in the air, catching Shirley's eye. The towel also caught the eye of Stephens and Landers, who had a direct line of sight from the side room into the main dining area.

"Dammit. I don't have time for this. . . ." But Cade knew it was too late. He made his way to where the men sat, watching.

As he entered, the words they'd been saying fell to the floor, and they were silent.

Cade sat next to Stephens.

"Morning, gentlemen."

Usually there was a volley of greetings sent back to him in return. This morning there were silent nods and a grunt or two.

He helped himself to coffee and looked for Shirley. "I just need a muffin. Or two."

Hooper looked Cade up and down. Then he went back to shoveling eggs in his mouth.

"All right, guys, what's going on?"

Pete *humph*ed.

After long, long minutes, the only noise nervous shuffling of feet under the tables, Landers finally cleared his throat.

"So how's it going, Cade?"

Cade placed his hands on his thighs and turned in his seat to face the old man. "I don't know. Why don't you tell me?"

"Huh?"

"I mean Hooper caught up with me a couple of weeks ago, and he told me that you all have a problem with me."

Stephens, the most diplomatic of the bunch, said, "It's not really so much of a problem as a . . . concern."

Pete, the most curmudgeonly of the men, said, "No, it's a problem."

"With my sheep?"

"No."

"With the way I run my place?"

Stephens said, "We've never had any problem with the way you run your place."

"Not till now," said Pete.

"I'm pretty sure it's none of your damn business," said Cade, struggling to keep his voice even.

"It's our business if our valley turns into a strip mall."

Cade spluttered. "A strip mall?"

"You have a yarn store now. That can't lead to anything good. Marla Upbreth up the road from you already sells eggs."

"She has a basket with a plate for money out on the road. It's not like she's set up a shop."

"What's to stop her? If you've got all the women on the Central Coast driving up our shared road?"

"County-owned and maintained," objected Cade.

Pete continued, his face florid. "Up *our* road, with the intention of shopping, they'll look for more to do. We're known for our livestock here. We don't want to be known for arts and crafts." He spat the last words out as if they were dirty. "That belongs in town here. Why didn't you keep that little girl from opening on your land? Even if you're head over heels, be a man about it."

Landers said helpfully, "There's a vacant retail space next to the pulled-taffy store where the bead place went belly-up last month."

Cade took a deep breath. "Number one, I am not doing this because I'm head over heels. Number two, I have no say in this. It's not my land anymore. Aunt Eliza left me the house and the ranch. She left the girl the cottage and the land it sits on. You know that; I *told* you all that. And number three, and most important, it's really none of your damn business. It's only going to get word out about our valley, not entice Wal-Mart. Suck it up."

The others shook their heads.

"Well, it's still low," said Pete. "Pretty damn low."

"It wasn't low, it was her right. It was her land. I'd just been working it."

Landers said, "You'd put everything into that land. It's all yours. She shouldn'ta done that."

"But she did. And I still have the land, don't I? Abigail only has the cottage. That's a pretty small footprint."

Pete said, "Not once all those cars start coming up your driveway. You gonna have to put down a parking lot?"

"Hell, no!" Cade was so vehement the other men broke into laughter. "There won't be a parking lot. The dirt lot is fine."

"How will people find her?"

"She might have put up a small sign."

"How you feel about that?"

"It only says 'Eliza's,' so it's okay. I mean, it was Eliza's, right?"

"But what about the girl?" asked Pete, never one to let anything go. "Word is she's still in the house with you."

"Yeah. Word's right. I didn't have any choice. She couldn't stay in the cottage, not until she's fixed it up."

"When's that gonna be?"

"Dunno. Haven't been helping her, have I?"

"Oh, so you *want* her in the house with you? I would, too. She's a looker," said Pete.

"No! I only meant I'm not helping her . . . " His voice trailed off.

Landers said, "Cops pull you over last night?"

"Just John Moss."

"He had something to say about why you were speeding."

Cade could actually feel himself blushing, and hid his face in his coffee cup. "John's gullible. I thought it might work. I still got the ticket."

"Ovulating?" Pete's voice was almost a squeak.

"It was worth a shot."

The men hooted. Cade felt like he'd come home. This was what he needed.

Then Pete looked at him and said, "But don't take up with her."

Cade sobered. "Why?" It was the only word he dared say without giving himself away.

"Because then she'll stay. And you want her to fail."

All the men nodded. "Yep."

"That's right."

"The sooner the better. Once her business goes down the tubes, you can buy the land back and it'll be okay. And she'll be gone."

Cade felt sick. "Yeah," he said. "She'll be gone."

He looked up and saw Bonnie York entering the diner. She was the local fire investigator. She walked past Old Bill and back to the old room.

"Cade?" she said. "I need to talk with you about that fire you had the other day."

The men moved on to talking about the incoming storm, and Cade felt a different storm building inside his chest.

Chapter Thirty-one

Knit through everything.
—E.C.

Abigail opened her eyes slowly. Where was she? These weren't her sheets. It took her a moment to adjust.

To remember. What she had done. How she had moved against him, how he had lifted and turned her, how he had filled her. How he had held her through the night.

She hadn't slept well, the feel of his skin against hers a constant surprise. She drifted off into sleep, only to be startled awake again and again when he shifted in sleep.

It had been a long time since she'd shared a bed. But it felt good.

She stretched and looked out the window, squinting against the light. Sheep grazed the low rolling hills. It looked like a pastoral print at a gift shop.

Her stomach tightened, fluttered. She felt like she'd had four cups of coffee.

Last night, he had seemed so . . .

Attentive.

Caring. As he'd touched her, as he'd kissed her, over every inch of skin that his mouth could reach, he'd been passionate. As if he'd meant it.

She knew she'd meant it. She'd meant it all.

Abigail sighed and sat up. She swung her bare legs off the bed, scrunching her toes in the sheepskin on the floor.

She *shouldn't* have meant it. She should be protecting herself more. Her last relationship turned out to be one of the biggest mistakes she'd ever made. How could she trust herself to judge the character of a man, when she'd been so devastatingly wrong about Samuel?

Even if Cade wasn't anything like Samuel, look at Betty. *That* was Cade's type. Abigail wasn't, she was just convenient. In the right proximity. Good Lord, if he couldn't get laid in his own house, by the woman living in it . . .

But it still felt like more.

In her heart, a lot more.

Did all his dates feel this way?

Did he touch them the same way, with trembling fingertips, with a mouth soft, then firm, then hot, then sweet? Did he hold them all night the way he'd held her, as if she was precious, even in sleep?

Did they all fall in love with him?

Love.

No. Not that. She looked at the clock. Almost nine.

She stood and moved to the window. She reveled in the feel of cool air against her nakedness.

She yawned, then stretched her arms over her head.

Cade.

She pulled his name through her mind, testing it like she tested fibers, drawing it out under her breath like the fiber drew out toward the wheel.

She tested two other words again: *In love.*

Oh, God. Oh, dammit.

Would that explain the feeling in the pit of her stomach, the nerves, the jangling in her spirit?

Would that explain how even when they avoided each other, she was always so aware of where he was? Her hearing felt fine-tuned. She could hear his truck a minute before he even turned into the driveway. She knew exactly where he was in the house, even if it was four or five rooms away.

She wasn't sure how she felt about her new superpower, but she was beginning to understand it.

In love.

She hadn't bargained on this.

Well. Cade was out and about, doing his ranch things, and she would start moving around, too. It was time to move, really move. It had been a month, the cottage was ready, and it was high time she got out of his space.

She stood, stretched again, and started working. Today would be the day she'd start over, in her new home.

She took her time, but the distance between the house and cottage was short, and really, she didn't have much to move. Abigail had a strange feeling in her stomach, a reluctance she wouldn't name. The stairs, while steep in both places, didn't take that long to climb. She moved slowly and didn't rush the customers that came by, only moving her things when no one was in the store, but by late afternoon, she had moved everything to the cottage. She placed her few possessions on the shelves that lined the cottage bedroom.

Her room in Cade's house was stripped of any sign that she'd ever been there. Eliza's knitted blanket was folded neatly on the bed she'd used. It looked like a spare room again.

Done.

After her last few books were unpacked in her new, upstairs room, Abigail sat on her new bed and stared out the windows. Clara snoozed on her new green dog bed.

Abigail looked across the bright room at the old rolltop desk she'd found in an antiques shop in town. She sighed. It was perfect. It was the writing spot that she'd always seen in her mind when she pictured her ideal office. An endless, gorgeous view, her own space, room for paper and pens, her laptop, her idea notebook. Downstairs, a space for people to come and create their own visions.

Nothing could be better.

But it was missing something. Or someone.

God, it should be enough that she was here, that she had done this, that she had created this space, that she was ready to live the dream. She shouldn't have this burning need to share it.

But she did. And while she was eager for Janet to see it completely done and ready, Abigail wasn't thinking about Janet. Or of any of the knitting enthusiasts she knew.

Cade.

Abigail wanted him here, wanted his approval. She knew in her mind that she might never get it from him, that he might always dislike her venture, her shop, her dream. But to have him stand up here with her, one arm around her, as they looked out on this incredible view . . .

Okay, a girl could dream, right?

Or would he always harbor that grudge, deep down? Would Abigail always be the usurper, the one that came in and took space away from him? The one who took away his silent, solitary life?

She could change his mind.

After last night, she was willing to try.

She raised her hands to cool her burning cheeks.

She wondered if he'd heard back from the fire investigator. As she sat on the bed, she tried not to let her mind go to where it had gone earlier, when she'd almost panicked. She took a deep breath.

It couldn't be Samuel who'd lit that fire.

Samuel didn't have any way of knowing where she'd gone. He didn't know Eliza, didn't know she'd died. Didn't know where she'd moved. Only Janet knew the exact address, and Janet would never give out that kind of information, to anyone.

And it would turn out that linseed or old wiring or something had caused the fire. She shouldn't worry so much.

Dinner. She'd make Cade dinner tonight, and invite him to her place. A date at her new home. And maybe tonight, in her new room . . .

She could barely think about it. So she wouldn't think. She would *do*. She would keep doing, moving, keep herself busy. Keeping Cade out of her mind until he was in her new home. Keeping Samuel out of her mind completely.

Abigail drove to the store in town, picked up groceries, and came home. She wrote on the side of a paper bag, "Dinner, The Cottage, 7 P.M."

She walked over and taped it to the kitchen door. He wouldn't be able to miss it.

This would be good. He'd love it.

Abigail's new kitchen was small but adequate. It had a pie safe built into one wall that made her long to bake pastry. The old stove put out good, reliable heat.

She cooked chicken: chopped it, mixed it with artichoke hearts and pesto, and then made fresh linguine. Making fresh pasta was usually something she loved to do and simple enough, but today she struggled. She couldn't keep her mind on what she was doing.

A few minutes before seven, she pushed a low table out to the porch and set it in front of the swing. She set two places with red napkins and silverware. She got out two glasses and opened a bottle of red wine. She left the food in the kitchen to keep warm. She put bread and brie on a plate. Clara remained well behaved, but never took her eyes off the cheese, and Abigail didn't trust her enough to leave her alone with it on the porch.

Abigail sat on the swing and looked at her cell phone. Seven o'clock. She heard Cade's truck roll up the driveway, and then heard him park. She couldn't see that side of the house from here, but he always entered the house through the kitchen door.

Abigail smiled at Clara. "Soon," she whispered.

She smelled a tinge of smoke in the air—it had been lingering for days, a souvenir of the fire. It was eerie. The way it started so quickly, the way Tom would normally have been around, but was in town with slashed tires . . .

Ridiculous. The fire chief had said it was probably linseed rags. Something like that.

Abigail took a piece of sourdough bread. She spread it with a little brie and stopped herself from having a second piece. Cade would be here soon.

It was just an old reaction, she told herself. Perfectly normal. She'd lived in fear for a long time, and it was probably just built in to her mind now. When something scary happened, the first thing she'd think of was Samuel. Natural.

It was just that the fire had scared her. That's why Samuel was in her mind like this again. As scared as she'd been during the fire, it hadn't been as bad as that night. The bad night.

It happened a couple of months after she'd broken up with him, after she'd told Samuel she wouldn't see him again. The breakup had been bad enough: she'd been in love with him, which had been wonderful, but he wanted more than just love. First, he wanted a copy of her apartment key before she was ready to give it to him. Months after his nagging, she finally handed him one, at which point he wanted to move in with her.

During one of their arguments about their living arrangements, Samuel ended up yelling at her in a restaurant, towering over her while his hands clenched into tight fists. It felt as if the only thing that had prevented her from hitting her was the fact that they were in public.

He'd scared her that night, and no matter how she felt about someone, she knew it wasn't right to be scared. Eliza had taught her better than that.

Abigail ended it with Samuel. A broken heart was better than a broken face. She called herself enlightened and congratulated herself through her tears.

Then he started following her.

Abigail had made a police report about it, of course. She'd even gone to court and obtained a restraining order. The piece of paper said he couldn't make physical or verbal contact with her, and that he had to stay a hundred feet from her, but it didn't stop him from being there, at every turn she made, a hundred and one feet away. The grocery store. The bank. The movies.

She learned there was nothing like fear to mend a broken heart.

Abigail called the cops anyway, every time. Just to be on the safe side. When they arrived, he drove away, smiling and waving at her. There was nothing the cops could do.

She found pink roses on her car's windshield almost every morning, even when it was locked in the garage.

She changed the locks on her doors.

One night she'd come home from visiting Eliza, and as soon as she'd entered, she knew he'd been there. There was a feeling, a metallic twinge of electricity as soon as her door opened. Everything in the living room looked to be in place, but Abigail fled, pulling the door shut and running down the walkway. She got in her car, locked the doors, and called the police.

When they came, they cleared the apartment, making sure he wasn't hiding, and then came out to her car, where she sat shaking. They told her that someone had turned her bedroom upside down. All her drawers had been upended, bookcases knocked over. The bed had been slashed with a kitchen knife, sliced through the duvet and sheets, down into the mattress. Pink roses lined the headboard.

Abigail nodded when they told her. She'd felt him there when she'd opened the door.

After she finished her statement, they escorted her into the apartment. They asked if she needed someone to stay with her while she packed a bag, but she said no, she'd be fine. She'd stay at a hotel tonight and get new locks and an alarm tomorrow.

After they left, she pulled out her suitcase. She wished for the first time for a gun. Or a dog. Maybe she'd get both. For now, what would make her feel better? A knife? No, she'd hurt herself. Something heavy that she could swing. The iron?

Abigail went to the tiny, narrow kitchen closet that housed both the ironing board and the iron. The small door was covered with a hanging tapestry that she loved. It was the only place the police must have missed. When she opened the closet, Samuel, wedged sideways inside, grinned at her and said, "Hello."

Abigail spun and started to run, but he was faster than she was. He lunged out of the tiny space, the ironing board and iron crashing to the ground behind them. He grabbed a fistful of her hair and pulled down, so hard that Abigail's neck snapped backward. She lost her balance and fell. She hit her head as she went down and saw stars. She tried desperately to keep track of exactly where Samuel was, but he was on top of her before she could roll out of the way.

"I missed you, baby."

"You're fucking insane!" Abigail tensed her body under his. Everything she'd ever read about fending off attack flew through her mind. Don't let him take her away from here. Don't let him restrain her. Run. *Fight.*

Samuel used one hand to hold both her hands over her head. He was strong. His other hand held a gun, which he showed to her, holding it in front of her eyes. Then he pressed the muzzle to her temple, traced her eyelid with it, then moved it down her nose and to her mouth. He moved the cold metal against her lips. Gentle at first. Abigail kept her mouth closed.

"Open your mouth, lovely."

She'd never seen him look like this. His eyes were dilated. He had to be on something. Abigail could see the blood vessels in his neck pulsing rapidly. Sweat ran off his forehead and hit her cheek.

"Open."

Not gentle anymore. The metal shoved against her mouth, and he used more pressure to force her lips apart. He scraped the gun on her teeth, until in sheer terror she let her jaw open. He pushed the entire barrel of the gun into her mouth, down her throat.

Abigail willed her legs to be still. She would need them. She tried not to choke, but she gagged against the barrel.

"That's pretty, darling. That's what I like to see. You're a good girl. Will you keep being good for me?"

Abigail tried to nod, but the gun wouldn't let her, so she tried to signal with her eyes that she would.

"What was that?"

Abigail moaned around the barrel.

Samuel licked his lips. He pulled the gun out of her mouth roughly. "Say it again."

"I'll be good," she managed.

"You know I'll shoot you, right? If you try anything, and I mean if you so much as look at me sideways, I'll shoot you in the stomach, then in the legs. I don't plan on killing you, but you never know. Tell me again you're going to be good. If you're good I'll be nice."

Abigail thought she might throw up. Hang on. Hold on. "I'll be good."

"How good?"

"Very good."

Samuel's eyes seemed to shiver in their sockets when she said it. "Say it again," he whispered. Still on top of her, using his hips to hold her down, his arm still holding both her wrists, he ground against her pelvis.

Abigail tried something.

"So good. I'll be so good for you. I'll do anything for you."

Yes, it happened again. When she spoke, Samuel looked like he got almost dizzy. Was it lust? Or something he was on? Maybe this was the weapon she needed.

It would have to be.

"Anything you want, Samuel. I want you." Again, Abigail pushed down the bile that rose in her throat. Samuel ground his hips into her even harder.

"More," he groaned. He ran the barrel of the gun across her cheek, down to her throat. He scraped it along her neck and then tapped her cheek with it, as if testing her.

"Mmmm," she said. "I love that."

Samuel's eyes flared with something that made Abigail's heart race even faster than it already was.

"Have you been bad?"

"So bad." It was a gamble. She was gambling with her life. She couldn't think of anything else. She gauged every word by the way he was shivering against her. If she was right, he was falling for it. If she was wrong, there was nothing she could do about it. "I'll do anything for you."

"Oh, God." Samuel set the gun down and pushed it down by his leg. "Now don't try anything funny. You've already been warned." He put his hand against her face. "I've wanted you for so long."

"I know," Abigail said. She could do this.

He tapped her face. Touched her nose with the tip of his finger. Kissed her on the mouth, forcing his tongue past her lips. He tasted of meat and metal. Abigail struggled to breathe. She kept her legs still, so still.

Samuel sat up, just a little. He took a little of his weight off her hips. "What do you want?"

She looked into his eyes. Yes. She prayed to God this would work.

"In me. I want you in me. Please."

Samuel's eyes narrowed.

"It's what I need." Abigail tried to make her voice sound pleading. It seemed to convince him.

"You want it, I'll give it to you, baby," he said. "I've got what you need." He released her wrists and both his hands went to his belt.

Time. The right time.

Abigail waited.

As he unbuckled his belt, she stayed perfectly still. "I want to see you," she whispered.

Samuel shivered again. His hands moved to his fly. He undid the button. He lowered the zipper. He moved up, taking his weight all the way off her as he pushed his pants halfway over his hips. Pushing down his underwear with one hand, he reached to pull up her skirt.

Abigail exploded. Her knee came up, and she kneed his exposed groin with all her weight. The fingers on her right hand went for his eyes. She hit one; it felt fleshy and full as she stabbed. Her left hand formed a fist and she drove the knuckles into his neck, right into his Adam's apple. As he folded forward in pain, she rolled out from under his now useless leg. She kept hitting and kicking whatever she could reach. She used her arms to scoot backward across the tile floor.

Samuel lunged after her, but she kicked him twice in the head so hard she heard something crack. He screamed. She felt the iron by her hand, where it had fallen earlier. She swung it in the best roundhouse she could manage from her half crouch. The sharp edge made sickening contact with his temple.

Samuel went still. His eyes, still open, unfocused as he fell forward. Blood poured from his head. Both his legs jerked spastically.

It was the last thing Abigail saw before she ran screaming from the house. She didn't remember flagging down the next car, didn't remember the call to the police, didn't remember fainting.

When she came to, she was in the hospital, in a bed, covered by a white sheet. A very nice doctor told her she had to stay for a few hours, for shock. A very nice police officer told her that she'd done a great job, but that unfortunately, he'd gotten away. When they'd arrived, they'd found the pool of blood on the kitchen floor and nothing else. They'd even used their tracking bloodhound, but the dog had lost the scent five blocks away.

Abigail had stayed with Eliza for months after that. She never saw evidence of him. His SUV wasn't around. She didn't get any pink roses. The police told her they had a warrant out and they'd get him the next time he was pulled over for something. They'd keep her posted. He hadn't been at work since it happened. They said he'd probably fled the state.

She moved back into her apartment two months later and installed a security system. Not long after that, Eliza had her heart attack, and weeks later Abigail moved to the ranch. It had been such a relief to stop looking over her shoulder. To stop being afraid.

There was no way he was here, now. If anything, he'd be scared of her. That's what the cops said.

Abigail realized, suddenly, that she wasn't in San Diego. She shook her head and her vision cleared. The porch. The bread and cheese in front of her. Waiting for Cade.

She reached for her wineglass and watched it tremble in her hand.

Clara whined and stretched. It was getting colder, fast. The sun had set and Abigail was freezing. Where was Cade? She craved seeing him, striding from his house, coming to see her, a grin on his face. She wanted his arms around her again.

She checked her cell phone. Seven twenty. She'd been out here on the porch for twenty minutes already.

At half past seven, she picked up the cheese plate so Clara couldn't indulge. She went inside to check on the food. It was too damn cold out there anyway. Yes, she'd move the whole thing inside. She took the place settings and the glasses and wine inside and set them up at the project table, surrounded by wool.

Nicer in here anyway.

The food had cooled in the pan, and the pasta looked as if it was hardening. If, God forbid, she had to reheat it in her new microwave, she would. But no, Cade would be here any moment, wouldn't he?

Abigail stood by the front door and waited. She saw a light turn on in the hall of the house, and then it went out, and then she saw the light in his room come on. Maybe he was changing.

Thirty minutes later, his light went out.

Ten minutes after that, she admitted to herself that it wasn't just taking him a really long time to come over.

He wasn't coming over.

She took Clara outside. God, it was bitter cold tonight. Freezing. She wrapped her arms around herself, glad for the alpaca sweater she was wearing.

She walked around the side of the house.

The note had been removed from the kitchen door. He'd seen it. He'd seen the invitation, and he hadn't come, hadn't even told her he couldn't.

Or wouldn't.

He would have known she had dinner waiting, must have known she would come to check the door and then walk back, alone, to the cottage. Was he watching her now, from a dark window? She wouldn't look up, wouldn't give him that satisfaction.

She dashed away tears.

The tears burned her cheeks as she threw out the entire dinner. She chewed a crust of the sourdough, but her appetite had disappeared.

She finally poured herself another glass of wine.

"Should have done this hours ago," she said to Clara. "To Eliza. And this store. And to me. And to you, dog. But to no one else." She lifted her glass and drank the wine like water.

Half an hour and two more glasses later, she stumbled tipsily to bed, where she undressed with the curtains closed. Then she lay awake, staring at the ceiling, dry-eyed and heartsick.

Chapter Thirty-two

Sometimes, though, the whole sweater will end up a disaster. When you sew it up and try it on, it doesn't work, doesn't fit, looks like the dog's breakfast. Sometimes that's just the way it goes.

—E.C.

Five or ten grand. Five or ten *thousand* dollars.

Cade stomped around the pasture in the freezing air. First damn night of frost and it had to be the date three of his ewes were due to lamb, the first lambs of the season. He always lambed in November, to make the most of the Easter 4-H rush in spring, but this was the hardest part. Being out here in the cold. He'd hoped they'd birth before he went to bed, but there'd been no sign of lambs when he last checked.

What a shitty day. It had started off well, waking up with Abigail naked next to him. A good start. But then, at the diner, what Bonnie York had said—God, he could still barely get his mind around it.

Bonnie had fiddled with pouring cream in her coffee while she said, "I found spalling on the concrete. It's kind of like a stain, shows where the fire burned the hottest and fastest. A liquid was poured there, and ignited. I can't actually prove malice, so even though it might be arson, it's classified as gross negligence, Cade. I'm sorry." Cade had listened, his heart plummeting.

She went on. "The state will be sending you a bill."

"A bill," he'd said. "For what? I pay my taxes, like everyone else."

"We don't charge if it's accidental. But if it's negligence, and you're in a state resource area, the state will bill for services."

"I've never heard anything so stupid in my whole life. How much is it going to cost me?"

She sighed. "Between five and ten grand, I'd guess. I'm sorry."

Cade had pushed past her and out into the open air outside the diner, where he could breathe.

Shit.

He'd worked all day, as hard as he could.

He should have gone to the cottage for dinner. He knew he should have. But he'd been too upset.

She had moved out. He hadn't needed the invitation to dinner she'd left on the kitchen door to know that she was gone. The house echoed and felt empty. Hollow, like when he was a kid and his mother had gone again.

Cade had held Abigail's invitation in his hands as he went upstairs. He had stared into his closet, and then he'd walked down the hall and stared into the room she'd been sleeping in.

Last night they'd been together.

Now she was too far away, even though the distance was mere steps.

His doubt made her seem even farther away.

He slept a little. A couple hours at the most. Then his alarm went off, the middle-of-the-night, check-the-ewes alarm that would ring almost every night for the next month.

He'd found two of the ewes already, and he'd put them in the barn with their new babies, one single and one pair of lambs. He'd given the babies their vitamin spray that his vet laughed at but Tom swore by, and he'd doused their umbilical cords with iodine.

The freezing air was making his nose and eyes ache. By the end of lambing season, he'd barely feel it, but tonight it hurt.

His first thought when the alarm had gone off had been of her. Then the fire. Then disbelief all over again. Bonnie's words rang in his head. *Spalling. A liquid was poured . . .*

Impossible. He knew Abigail. She wouldn't have any reason to set a fire. None at all. She already had everything she wanted. She had her land, her shop, and now her living space.

And she wasn't crazy.

Or had he been blind this whole time?

What was crazy was this, what he was doing. Out here, in this flock of about a hundred of his sheep—only a fifth of all he owned—he was looking for one that might be giving birth. In the dark. He held a flashlight, cutting its light through the bitter-cold air. Sheep *baa*ed in protest as he moved among them. They didn't like this, didn't like things to be outside their routine. Cade was like them in that way.

He stumbled over a gopher hole. Christ, it was cold. Still no sign of the other new mother.

Setting a fire was a mark of a crazy person, and he'd lived with her for a month. He'd know if she was crazy.

Wouldn't he?

He couldn't be in love with a psycho who set fire to his property.

In love.

Godammit.

He really had the best timing.

But then again, so did she. It was sure a strange coincidence, wasn't it, that she moved out days after the fire was set? And she sure had been quiet while the chief talked to them.

No. There was no way. Not her. He'd dated crazy women in the past, plenty of them. He'd thought for a while he preferred them that way. But Abigail wasn't crazy.

He hated this doubt.

If she hadn't set the fire, then who had? He didn't have enemies. They'd never had problems with arsonists in this valley.

It couldn't be her.

Cade was about to give up. Maybe the other ewe was going to wait until the morning. He'd done his due diligence looking for her out here in this weather. He'd crawl back into bed.

One more place to look, over there, in the shadow of the concrete trough. Something was on the ground, a light-colored lump. Damn, why hadn't he checked over there first?

Cade walked to where a newborn lamb lay on the cold ground. He touched it. Stone cold. He put his finger in the lamb's open mouth. The tongue was hard, dry, and cold. It wasn't breathing.

He shined his flashlight around. Where was the mother ewe? She might have abandoned this one because she was giving birth to another one. There, on the other side . . .

A ewe lay in the shadow of the trough. Blood pooled around her body.

"Oh, hell," said Cade. She must have bled out while giving birth to the lamb that appeared pretty damn dead just feet away.

He left the mother. There was nothing he could do for her now. Focus on the lamb.

He opened his jacket, gasping at the night air. He placed the cold lamb under his clothing, against his skin. He ran out of the pasture and toward the house at a trot.

Once in the house, he filled half the double sink with water. He ran it cooler than tepid, a notch warmer than cold. When the sink was full, he carefully placed the lamb in the water.

No reaction. The lamb didn't breathe. Cade felt no heartbeat.

Shit, he might not get this one back. Sometimes they were just too far gone, too cold, too far in shock.

He checked—it was a boy. A little ram lamb. They weren't good for much, just for selling to the kids at Easter or auctioning off, but it was still a lamb.

"Come on, pal," he said. "You can do it."

After a minute, he ran a little warm water in the sink, raising the temperature slightly.

A few minutes more, another dose of warm water. Still nothing.

After the fourth warming of the water, he felt it. Just a twitch, and he couldn't even say where he'd felt it.

Cade put his finger again into the lamb's mouth. This time it was warm. The tongue was soft again and Cade felt a tiny suckling motion against his finger.

He whooped, and the lamb jerked in his hands.

"Yes! I knew you could do it!"

He took his time, raising the temperature of the water gently until it felt like it was just right. The lamb kicked and jerked and threw its ungainly head around.

"I know, it's not much fun. It'll get better."

Cade wrapped the lamb in towels and carried it into the parlor, where he lit the fire that, thankfully, he'd already laid. In minutes it was roaring. Cade set the lamb down on another dry stack of towels.

"What you need is the hair dryer. Stay there." The lamb wouldn't move much now. It was exhausted from its being-almost-dead ordeal. He raced up the stairs to the bathroom where he kept the hair dryer. It was stupid, really. He never used it for anything but drying lambs. He should keep it in the parlor, but for some reason he always returned it to the bathroom when he was done.

He plugged it in downstairs. He pointed it at the lamb, who was kicking but not walking. There was a snap and a frizzling sound and the hair dryer went dead.

Shit. The fire would work, but it was slow. The faster he got the little guy warm, the better.

Cade didn't have another dryer. But she might.

Chapter Thirty-three

Men are very good for some things, including finding
needles and stitch markers lost in the couch.
—E.C.

When Abigail heard Cade calling her name, she had no idea where she was. This wasn't the right bed. She didn't understand the configuration of the windows. She hardly recognized the curtains when her eyes focused.

In the top room of her cottage. In her new bed.

Why was Cade yelling at her from outside?

The room swung as Abigail stood. She was still a little drunk from the wine, she realized. She pulled the curtain back. Cade was outside, standing below her window.

She tugged up on the window. It was heavy and squeaked as she raised it. She didn't trust that it wouldn't slam shut, so she held it up with one hand as she leaned out in her pajamas. The cold air flooded into her room.

"Do you have a hair dryer?" Cade yelled up at her.

"A hair dryer? What do you need it for?"

"Yes or no?"

It all came flooding back to her. The dinner she'd cooked. How he hadn't come or even called. It would probably hurt again later, like it had before all the wine, but right now Abigail felt cocooned.

"I have one, yes."

He sounded impatient. "Can I borrow it?"

"Oh, all right." She let the window bang down.

She threw a jacket over her pajamas and teetered downstairs to the bathroom. Outside, she handed him her dryer.

"What's it for?"

"Nothing." He walked away from her.

Abigail followed. "No thank you? Tell me. Emergency blow job?" She giggled. It was even funnier when she said it out loud, and it had sounded funny enough when she thought it in her head. Yep, that was the wine.

"Something like that."

Abigail tagged along behind him. The cold air felt good against her flushed cheeks. She gazed up at the stars, which shone clear and bright, but it put her off balance, and she stumbled in the dark.

"I'm okay! I'm okay," she said.

Cade didn't look back.

"Are you really not going to tell me? I *demand* to know."

"I'm not going to tell you," he said over his shoulder.

"You have to."

"If I do, you'll want to come in."

"What's so wrong with that?"

"I'm not in the mood," he said.

"Whatever. Tell me."

"I'm drying a lamb that I brought back from the dead."

Abigail stopped in her tracks. "That is so *awesome*." As Cade opened the door, she pushed past him. "This I have to see."

She heard Cade sigh as he gave up. "Parlor."

Sure enough, a tiny white lamb lay on a pile of blue towels.

"Oh, my God! How much does he weigh?"

"Well, I didn't have my scale out there in the dark, but I'd guess about eight pounds. Not much more."

"She's the size of a small cat! Look at her!"

"Him."

"Him! He's so cute! Can I dry him?"

"I guess so."

Cade plugged the dryer in and handed it to Abigail. "Careful not to get it too close to the wool. You don't want to burn him."

"This is the coolest thing *ever*." She turned the device on and tested it with the back of her hand. Not too hot.

The lamb wriggled when she pointed the warm air, as if he wanted more of it. He squeaked and stretched his legs.

For a long time, she just moved the hair dryer over the lamb. Abigail and Cade didn't speak. The fire crackled, and the low hum of the dryer was soothing. The room smelled of smoke and wet wool. Abigail could taste the wine still on her tongue. Cade stood by the window and looked into the darkness.

Abigail broke the silence.

"Can he walk yet?"

"He could, but it doesn't look like he wants to." Cade's voice was as cold as the air outside.

"Why is he all wet, anyway?"

"I put him in warm water. I found his mother dead. She bled out. He was stiff, not breathing, cold."

"Will another mother take him? Nurse him?"

"Usually one will. I'll put this one in with another that was born tonight. He'll probably suck, if that ewe lets him. If he doesn't, I'll have yet another chore on my hands."

"How did you do it? Bring him back, I mean."

"Warm water in the sink."

"How did you know to do that?"

"Uncle Joshua always had good luck with it. Eliza would stand behind him and say, 'You're not going to save that one, buddy.' He'd do it anyway, running the water, taking his time. When the lamb came back to life, Eliza would say he'd performed another miracle."

Abigail looked up at him. "You performed another miracle!"

Cade looked down at the lamb and shrugged.

As Abigail blew the lamb dry, she watched its curls go soft and curly. It was the newest fiber she'd ever seen in her whole life.

She smiled at Cade. "I wish I'd seen Eliza drying them."

He didn't smile back.

Abigail wished she weren't half tipsy, half hungover, but it was enough that she was sitting here in front of the fire. She pulled the towel and the lamb along with it into her lap.

"Did you get my note?" she asked, not looking at him. She was glad she was past the stage where she might have slurred her words.

"Yeah."

She waited, moving the warm air under the lamb's soft pink belly.

But Cade didn't say anything else; he just stood by the window and watched her.

"I was disappointed when you didn't come to dinner."

"I was disappointed when my shack burned down."

Abigail was surprised. It almost sounded like he was mad at her about it. "Did you find out what caused it?"

"Flammable liquid. Poured and set." He paused. "There may be a ten-thousand-dollar bill coming my way from the state. Is there anything you . . . want to tell me?"

"What?" Abigail's stomach knotted.

"It was arson. They can't prove it, but it obviously was."

"Seriously? Who would have done that? To you?"

Cade just folded his arms and looked at her.

It settled on top of her like a weight, the realization that he doubted her. That he thought she might have had something to do with the fire.

"But I was there putting it out! I could have been hurt, you said that yourself."

"Jesus, move the dryer back, don't burn him. Yeah, like that. You were the first one there, that's true."

Didn't he know her better than that? Abigail's mind raced, thinking of ways she could defend herself. She had no alibi—she'd been alone on the ranch when it started.

Or at least she'd thought she'd been alone.

Samuel.

A stab of terror jolted through her. If he was really here, in the area, if he was after her . . .

She'd fight. She'd fight harder than last time.

Cade still stared at her. Who did he think he was, anyway? Why the hell did she feel like she had to defend herself to him? She hadn't done anything wrong.

She turned off the hair dryer. The lamb was almost perfectly dry now.

She spoke slowly, concentrating on making her words as clear as possible. "I didn't burn down your shack, you moron. I can't believe you'd imply it. I can't believe you'd even *think* it."

She stood and pulled her jacket around her pajamas. Why did she have to be in her sheep pajamas for this? Wearing pink fleece while her heart broke. "I have no idea who started it. But I'm a little worried that it might be the guy I told you about from down south. In which case, I'm terrified. But you thought it was me? That's priceless."

Cade took two steps toward her, holding out a hand. "I didn't mean—" he started.

But Abigail cut him off. "No. That's not cool, Cade." She shook her head. She wished she had bigger, better words to tell him what he'd just done to her heart. "That wasn't cool."

She turned in her slippers and fled, leaving the hair dryer, the mostly dry lamb, and the man she loved behind her.

Chapter Thirty-four

Believe in your skills enough to cast on again, even after failure. The next sweater will look and fit better, I promise.
—E.C.

He knew she'd had customers yesterday, but had she had this many?

Cars were parked haphazardly all over the lower property. There must have been thirty of them down there.

He could practically hear them, all the way up at the barn. He knew what women sounded like when they got together over yarn and fiber. It was like they flipped into speaking a whole different language. Words like draft, and gauge, and colorways, things that didn't make sense to him and that he didn't want to understand.

And the cars kept coming, all day long.

Cade tried to work off the need he had to see her. He chose the farthest fence line, the one that he couldn't get to with the truck, no way, no how. He could have taken the ATV, but instead he rode up on horseback.

He hopped over rocky outcroppings, using his hands to push and pull the lines, making sure a sheep couldn't lean her way out. Lazy things that they were, they usually didn't anyway, but they certainly wouldn't now.

He tried to exhaust himself. But exhaustion was a long time coming. Seemed the harder he worked, the more amped up he got.

Finally, breathing heavily, he stood on a hill. He looked over the oak and eucalyptus below, far down to the gray ocean.

Should he make an appearance today? Would she forgive him for last night?

Cade scratched his nose and pushed back his hat. The thin sunlight wasn't warm but he was working hard and sweating.

He thought about the flame he saw in Abigail's eyes when she was in his bed. He'd never seen anything like that. He loved that.

He loved her.

Oh, hell.

Wasn't love supposed to feel good? Wasn't that what they said?

And no matter how he felt, he'd blown it, totally. He saw to that last night, first by ignoring her invitation and then capping the night off by accusing her of arson.

She hadn't set the fire. He'd known it when her eyes met his last night, after she realized what he was accusing her of. But he should have known before that. He shouldn't have doubted her.

The least he could do was try to apologize. He didn't hold much hope of her buying it, but he could try. He had to try. His heart hurt in a way he'd never known before.

He rode down through his land, down toward the house, past her parking lot, ignoring the stares of women getting in and out of cars and station wagons. Why were they *staring* like that? Like he was a circus freak? It was all he could do not to make rude gestures at them.

He put up his horse and stood at the barn doors. He stared down at the line of cars snaking up from the main road in the late-afternoon sun.

"It's something, isn't it?"

Cade jumped. "Tom! Don't sneak up on me like that."

"I've been standing here for at least a minute, waiting on you to notice me. Looks like you're lost in your own land."

"Not my land I'm lost in."

"Looks like she's having a good start."

"That it does."

"You find out anything else about the fire?" asked Tom.

"Only that she didn't set it."

Tom laughed. Then he looked at Cade. "Oh, hell, are you serious? You actually thought she might have?"

"Why not?"

Tom said, "It's true I haven't spent as much quality time, let's call it, with her as you have, but it's obvious she's a nice little knitter. Smart. Funny. Too good for the likes of you. Doesn't strike me as the arsonist type."

"Shit."

"You actually ask her about it?"

Cade sighed.

Tom said, "You're an idiot sometimes, ain'tcha? All due respect."

"She thinks it might be a stalker-type guy she knew down south."

"Scary. You going to the police?"

"Yeah, I'll add it to my report later. Get her to give them his name."

Tom nodded. "Be careful, boss."

"Hey, I almost totally forgot. That lamb that's in with the twins? The mother ewe died last night over by the trough. I haven't had time to get out there today. Would you mind?"

"No problem. I'll do it tonight before I leave," said Tom.

Cade took a badly needed shower and changed into street clothes. He couldn't wait another minute to see her.

The walk from his house and across the driveway to the cottage seemed the longest he'd ever taken. Women lined the porch, sitting on the swing, on the stairs, chatting and laughing. They stared at him again in that same way.

Cade knew, in their minds, he was cast in the role of the cowboy. They were probably disappointed that he wasn't wearing a six-shooter. He almost wished he was. Might give him a little more courage. His heart was beating so fast he could hear the blood rushing in his ears.

Eliza's. He had to admit the sign was tasteful. Small. No neon as far as he could tell. Just a wooden board with the name in script, no phone number or website listed. It was a good name, he supposed. The right name.

"Ladies," he said, as he started up the steps.

Giggles were all he got in return. They looked like adults but sounded like teenagers.

When had she bought the screen door? Had she installed it herself? It looked like an antique. He pulled it open.

The cottage was completely different.

It was warm, and had bright, yellow walls, bookshelves full of colorful fiber, red couches. A heavy wooden table was covered with skeins of yarn that five or six women were poring over.

It looked homey, and beautiful. It looked like Eliza. And it looked like Abigail, too.

Cade's eyes took in the room at large, but he was really only looking for one thing: Abigail.

She stood across the room, behind an old-fashioned register that was sitting on another long wooden table. Her hair had been pulled up and back somehow, leaving pieces of it hanging around her face. Her cheeks were bright pink, and she looked so . . .

Happy.

She looked happy.

And then she raised her eyes and saw him, and that look went away. The color drained from her face. He could actually see her paling. The smile, which had been natural and real, turned forced. Polite.

Cade felt awful. Her smile was polite, for a stranger. He had made himself a stranger to her. But he moved forward, his own smile plastered in place.

"Abigail. It looks good."

The stricken smile straightened, and he watched her regain control. "Well, thanks. It's not that much yet, but it will be."

"No, it looks great."

"Thanks again." She turned back to the customer she'd been serving. "Here's your receipt, and I expect you back soon to show me what you do with that. It's a wonderful color for you."

The customer, an older woman with short gray hair wearing a heavily cabled blue sweater and motorcycle leathers, said, "I'm so glad you're here. No more riding to San Francisco to feed the addiction. Best of luck to you."

Cade watched Abigail's real smile come back. "Thanks so much."

The customer trotted away. The last group of women followed her outside. He heard them moving toward their cars. Thank God. Now maybe she'd talk to him.

But she seemed to have no interest in doing so.

He watched while she got out paper bags and stamped them with what looked like the same logo as on the outside sign. She didn't look up.

He reached one finger out and touched a bit of prepared fiber.

"Soft," he said, and immediately felt like an idiot. She didn't look up. He heard, rather than saw, the room emptying behind him. The voices moved out to the porch, and he was grateful to them.

"You scared my customers away."

"I didn't mean to."

"I'm sure." That same, thin, fake smile again. It wasn't the smile she should be giving him.

It was no one's fault but his.

"I'm sorry about last night."

"About dinner? You missed a good pasta, but I enjoyed it, and I had the leftovers for lunch, so it all worked out."

BANG. BANG. She stamped the paper bags with such force the register bounced on the wood.

"I wanted to come over."

"Then you should have."

"I couldn't."

She rolled her eyes and went on stamping. "You're an adult. So am I. I was disappointed." She looked at him, no smile this time. "But I'm over it now. I have my business to run, and this sweet dog," Abigail ruffled Clara's ear. "That's all I need."

"Again, I'm really sorry. I don't know what my problem is. Was."

"Are you still apologizing about dinner or about accusing me of arson?"

Cade felt a desperation like none he'd ever felt before. No words were going to fix this, were going to make her eyes light up like they had two nights ago.

Abigail kept stamping her bags. Her breasts swayed ever so slightly under her shirt. In his mind, he saw the bare image of them, the way they had looked two nights ago. The way they had looked cupped in his palms. Trapped under his mouth.

Cade moved to the left, then moved forward, so quickly that he had no time to plan, and she had no time to react. He stood behind the register with her, so close he could smell her perfume. He put both hands to her face and brought his mouth down on hers.

Chapter Thirty-five

Of course, patience is only good to a point in knitting. A decision will have to be made, but you'll know when it's time to make the change that's needed.

—E.C.

Without warning, he was kissing her.

Abigail's heart, which had been racing before he moved the counter, kicked so hard that she thought it might stop working at all.

For one brief moment, she thought about kissing him back. For a moment she knew who he was and why he was kissing her.

Then the fear kicked in.

Abigail brought up her knee sharply into Cade's groin. As he gasped, she swung her closed fist and punched him in the eye.

Cade bent at the waist and then fell over onto the floor.

What had she done? Oh, God, it was Cade. It wasn't Samuel.

But Cade shouldn't have grabbed her like that.

She dropped to the ground next to him. "I'm sorry! Are you okay?"

Cade only groaned.

"What the *hell* were you thinking?" she said.

"I wasn't," he managed to say.

A high-pitched voice pierced the room, "So *there* you both are! I'm so lucky, I wanted a chance at both of you. If you're not too busy."

Abigail leaped away from Cade as if he'd burned her. Which, she thought, he had.

"You do *look* busy. Is there a better time? Should I come back?" The woman's voice was smoothly amused.

Abigail looked at Cade on the floor, took a deep breath, pushed back her hair, and turned around.

The woman who had addressed them was only feet away. Abigail wasn't sure how she had come so close to them so quickly. She tried to still her breathing.

She was striking, to say the least. She was tall, at least six feet, thin but perfectly curved at the bust and hips, with extremely long, red hair, a red that was between auburn and mahogany and looked expensive.

"Trixie Fletcher. Reporter-at-large, the *Independent*." The woman stretched out her hand and Abigail automatically shook it.

"I'll get up in just a minute," said Cade. He groaned again, but then struggled to his feet.

He half smiled at Trixie, and she grinned back at him. Abigail instantly disliked her.

"Cade, you can vouch for my work."

"I haven't been a subject of yours for years." Cade leaned on the counter with both hands. Abigail watched him take a deep breath.

Trixie nodded. "Not since you had that public fight with O'Connor about the water rights. Unless you mean a different *kind* of subject." She laughed, an intimate sound. "Oh, we won't bore you with the details, Abigail." She winked at Cade, one sexy dropped lid.

Abigail never *could* manage that kind of wink. Her head hurt, suddenly, a sharp pain right between her eyes.

"But today, I'm simply here as a member of the press. I'm dying to know about your new little venture, Cade."

He held his hands up. "Not my venture. Ask the lady here. Abigail."

Trixie got out a pen and a small pad of paper. "I do feel like I'm intruding on something though. Do you two need a bit more time?"

Abigail shook her head. "He bet me I didn't know self-defense. But I do, so I showed him."

"Women in this town would have paid good money to see that," said Trixie. "Now tell me about what you're doing here."

"It's a yarn shop. And classroom space." Abigail hoped her face didn't reflect the curtness in her voice.

"Yes, that I know. But it's here! That's the best part, the part I want to capture, it's out here in the heart of sheep country. Selling the wool, teaching people how to knit. Is it just another case of not-your-grandma's knitting? Following the trend? Or is this something more?"

Leading the question, thought Abigail, but she only said, "Oh, it's something more, all right. You, of course, know about Eliza Carpenter."

Trixie nodded. "Cade's aunt, yes."

"You know who she is?"

"To Cade? To you?"

"To the world," said Abigail, and she could feel her eyebrows drawing together. She willed them apart and said, "I don't know how more people in this town aren't aware of what a legend they had living among them. Eliza is the single most important person in the field of knitting. Even deceased, she still is. She was more innovative than anyone else in the last two hundred years." Abigail couldn't keep the passion out of her voice. "She documented her discoveries. She shared them freely. God, her kimono-jacket is something that mathematicians have studied for years—it's like a puzzle that suddenly solves itself."

"You *are* talking about knitting, right?" Trixie laughed again, a tinkling bell that matched the way she tossed her hair.

Abigail was horrified. Had Cade slept with this person?

"I'm talking about art, but if you want to call it knitting, that's fine by me. But it's bigger than that. I'd suggest a little more research if you're writing an article on it."

Trixie flapped a hand, and it landed on Cade's shoulder. He didn't look offended. "So, Cade, my old friend, what's it like, having the artists-slash-knitters converge upon your sacred ground?"

"I guess I'll have to get used to it."

"You really don't mind? I heard through the rumor mill that you were pretty put out by the whole thing."

Cade cleared his throat. "You can't trust everything you hear. You, of all people, should know that, Trix." He reached out and tugged a lock of that long red hair, and Trixie laughed, looking delighted.

"Hey, *Trix*. What exactly did you need from me?" asked Abigail.

"I'm after more of the personal angle. I mean, everyone in the valley is talking about how your shop is going to change the area. People are talking about the expanded retail in the area, and how long it'll be before this is a bedroom community of San Francisco. Strip malls, fast-food joints, big-box stores. And you and Cade are on the forefront of this change, driving it."

Abigail choked, opened her mouth, and then closed it. She looked at Cade. He stepped to the side, and Trixie's hand fell from his shoulder.

She took a breath and straightened the bags she'd been working on. "That can't possibly be what people are talking about."

"You might be surprised what people say."

"I had higher hopes for the intellect of this community."

"People talk. A lot."

"And you write it all down? Share it with your readers? This newspaper, I haven't seen it. It's the local gossip rag?" Abigail's voice was icy.

"It's won many journalistic awards, as have I."

"Awarded by Montel Williams?"

"This isn't getting us anywhere, is it? I apologize to you if it seems like I'm gossiping. I'm only repeating what people in the area are saying, what they're upset about. That's news, and I cover it. So, is an expanded retail base in this area what the two of you are after?"

Cade held up his hand, palm out. "Trixie, first thing you have to understand is that we're not in this together. This is her venture, not mine. It's not what I wanted."

Abigail looked down at the countertop and traced the old wood grain with her fingertips. "But . . ." she started.

Cade interrupted her. "But I'm coming to an acceptance of it."

"You are?" asked Trixie.

"You *are*?" asked Abigail at the same time.

"Well, there's not much I can do. She owns the land, the area is zoned for this. I don't have much to say about it."

"But are you behind it?" asked Trixie.

"What do you mean?"

"You say you accept it," Trixie was scribbling notes into a Moleskine, but she didn't look down at the pen. "But are you in favor of it? Do you want her to succeed?"

"I . . . " Cade's voice trailed off.

Abigail straightened, squaring her shoulders. "He doesn't have to be behind me. I'm a respected author of books in this field. I have my own name, and I'm standing on Eliza Carpenter's land. It's a built-in fan base. People will come."

"Are knitters that serious about what they do?"

"I've had phone calls about the retreats from as far away as Ireland and Germany."

Cade said, "You have?"

Abigail nodded.

He shook his head.

Trixie said, "So how does hearing about the retreats make you feel, Cade?"

"You sound like a shrink."

"Just answer my question, babe."

Babe? Abigail's level of annoyance couldn't go much higher.

Cade tugged at his collar. "How does it make me feel? It makes me want to ride up into the hills to avoid the cars coming up my driveway."

"Our driveway," said Abigail.

Cade shook his head. "Well, technically, the driveway's still mine, but I'm not making a big deal out of it, am I?"

Abigail glared at him, but he was still looking at Trixie. Of course he was.

Trixie made another note. "How much do you think you've lost in terms of the land's worth since this happened?"

Cade frowned, "What do you mean? By her putting a store in?"

"No, by breaking up the parcel. There's an annexed bit in the middle that you don't own."

"I hadn't really . . ."

Abigail said, "The property is still worth the same. Maybe more because of the improvements I've made here."

Trixie held up her pen. "Not to Cade, it isn't. He owns a donut, and you own the middle bit. But if you sold it back to him, the parcel would be complete."

"Why would I sell it back to him? I just started this business."

"That's the question everyone's asking. If you fail, will you sell to him?"

"People are talking about me failing?"

Trixie raised a perfectly manicured eyebrow. "Sam Stephens, who owns the Bar L Ranch up the road, said that not only is he betting on your quick failure, but that he also has a pool going. And that he had a long conversation with Cade about the same thing. Cade, that's hearsay, of course. Will you confirm? Did you discuss Abigail's quick failure?"

Abigail's heart, already constricted into the shape of a small rock, tightened even more. She didn't breathe as she waited for him to answer.

But he didn't. Cade didn't say anything. He looked at the ground.

"Cade?"

After another pause, an unbearably long pause, Cade said, "You know I didn't want the store here at first, Abigail. But it's different now." His voice trailed off.

"How is it different? Will accusing me of arson get me out of here faster?"

"I didn't mean . . . I didn't really think . . ."

Trixie scribbled notes furiously. "Arson . . . So Abigail, California is of course, a joint property state. If you two married, you'd own not just a piece of the land, but half of it. Is that an attractive thought to you, Abigail?"

"Out!" Abigail felt like her head was going to fly off her body. "Get the hell out of my store! You, too, Cade! Clear out!"

Cade said, "But . . ." Nothing else followed.

"Just get out. *Now*!"

Trixie mumbled something that sounded like "hostile" and "combative" while scribbling on her pad, but she allowed Abigail to steer her outside and onto the front porch. Cade followed, his eyes huge. He was pale.

As he reached the edge of the porch he turned to look at her.

"Abigail. I . . ."

His eyes broke her heart.

But he thought she torched his shack.

Abigail slammed the door, shot the lock home, and turned the "Open" sign to "Closed."

Chapter Thirty-six

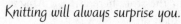

Knitting will always surprise you.
—E.C.

Abigail gripped the steering wheel tightly. She hated this part of the road, this long bridge that seemed to go on forever. But she had to see Janet. She needed a friend's advice. She would take an extra-long lunch break today.

The sky was threatening today, massive dark clouds gathering in the east. A cold front was moving in, she'd heard on the radio. Good. It suited her. She drove with her windows open, the chilly air smelling of the eucalyptus trees she drove past.

It had only been three days since she'd tossed Cade out of the store.

She stood by what she did.

Every time she started to think about how she felt about him, how it had felt being in his arms, how his lips had felt against hers, how she felt when she looked in his eyes, she stopped her thoughts by thinking about the fire at the shack.

He'd doubted her in the most fundamental way. He'd thought that perhaps she might have tried to destroy something of his. The very idea cut into her.

Love did not doubt.

She wasn't sure of much, but she knew that the man who loved her would believe in her, utterly. She'd thought that man was Cade. She loved him, yes. Abigail now freely admitted that to herself.

But he didn't love her.

If he loved her, he'd have believed in her.

Even after she'd told him whom she suspected of setting the blaze, he hadn't followed up on it. Wouldn't he have wanted to know who Samuel was? Whom to watch out for? Whom to protect her from? God knows, Abigail had been watching out for Samuel. She felt constantly on edge, the way she had in San Diego. She'd thought she'd left all that behind.

Last night, she thought she'd heard footsteps on her porch. Creaks, louder than the house settling, had started a staccato rhythm in her heart that hadn't calmed until she'd looked out every single window, Clara at her side. Clara growled once or twice, but then relaxed.

If there had been anything to worry about, Clara would have barked. Abigail slept fitfully, one hand clenching the ruff of Clara's neck.

Even now, Clara sat up on the passenger seat, sticking her nose out the window, sniffing ecstatically. Abigail reached out to scritch Clara's head. It felt good, soft. It reminded her of spinning, something she hadn't had much time for lately. She'd have to change that soon. It would be another thing to keep her mind off Cade.

From behind her, a car approached rapidly in the rearview mirror. It was suddenly much too close.

It was a sports utility vehicle.

A black one.

Abigail's heart sped up. It was too close to her bumper, the cab too high.

She couldn't see who was in it.

Abigail accelerated until she could look back into its front window.

Samuel smiled at her and waved.

"Shit, shit, *shit*." Abigail grabbed her phone and dialed 911. She didn't look again in her rearview mirror. She couldn't. If she saw his face again, she thought her heart might stop altogether.

"A man," she gasped. "A man who tried to kill me. He has a warrant for attempted murder. Following me. I just went over Mills Bridge, heading west. Black SUV, I think it's a Tacoma."

"We're sending officers your way, but don't stop driving. Do you know where the police department is? Drive that direction. I'm going to stay on the line with you as long as I can. You keep telling me where he is, and what he's doing. I have some questions for you to answer, okay?"

Abigail kept her speed constant. He could run her off the road at any time, she knew. There were few other cars out here today. Her body broke into a cold sweat, and the steering wheel slipped in her grasp. The dispatcher's calm voice asking her questions and giving her directions was the only thing that kept her from flying into pieces.

Almost in town, Abigail hit a red light. What was to prevent him from getting out and racing to her door? There was no cross traffic. "I'm running the light."

"As long as it's safe to do so," said the dispatcher.

Samuel ran the light, too.

She told the dispatcher where she was. "Where *are* you guys?"

"Almost with you. Turn right on Main."

As she did, Samuel turned left. Twenty seconds later, three police cars met her, coming from the opposite direction, lights flashing. She hung out her window, yelling and pointing them in the direction he'd gone.

At the Cypress Hollow police station, she made a report.

The officer who helped her, a nice boy not more than twenty-two at the most, listened to the scanner as he entered her information into his laptop. All of the radio talk sounded like gibberish. Abigail held tightly to the Styrofoam cup of water he'd given her.

"Dang," he said earnestly.

"What?"

"Seems like they've lost him. Don't know how he got away. With a felony warrant like that, they gave pursuing him a really good try, and Suthers usually gets his guy. Shoot."

"I wish they had," muttered Abigail. "Are we about done, then?"

"Yep. If you want to press charges on this violation of his restraining order, I'm sure the DA can get the judge to just add another warrant to his sheet."

Abigail wanted to scream. But she kept her voice calm. "How does that protect me?"

"We'll be looking for him, ma'am. He'll be my top priority."

She gave him a thin smile. He really was trying. "Thanks."

It was easy to see Janet coming. Her nod to the approaching storm front was a massive fur coat, white and brown. Under it she wore a short simple black dress that she knew must have cost more than Abigail's entire wardrobe put together.

Abigail waved from the diner booth.

"Darling. I love it." Janet swooped in with a kiss. Then she stood straight and took a good look around. "Tillie's. I've passed it a million times and never even *thought* to come in."

"Why not?"

Janet frowned. "I have no idea. I mean, you know I'm not a *snob*, but . . . Why are you laughing?"

"You're the biggest snob I know. You're wearing couture to a diner."

"What, this old thing?" Janet laughed and removed the coat. She looked around for a coat rack, and then gave up, tossing it on the bench seat. She slid in. "Okay. But it's what I do. What I love." She nodded at Abigail's knitting. "Me without fashion is you without knitting."

"The horror!" Abigail tried to laugh, but it caught in her throat.

"What is it, my lamb?"

"Lamb!" Abigail wailed, and dropped her forehead to the table.

"Are you upset about the article?"

Abigail lifted her head and narrowed her eyes at Janet. "What article?"

"The one in today's *Independent*?"

"Crap. I suppose I should be upset. If you're asking that?"

"It's not the most flattering thing ever." Janet reached into her Birkin bag.

"Go ahead. Let me have it."

Janet took a folded piece of paper from her purse and shook it out. "My favorite part is where she writes, 'Abigail Durant's particular brand of customer service combines a charming old-fashioned blend of forcible ejection and right hooks. If you see Cade MacArthur sporting a black eye, let him tell you he walked into a door. Ranchers need their pride.'"

"Oh, my God."

"The rest is just fluff that says, essentially, writer comes to valley to fulfill dream of yarn store on historic land. Did you really hit him?"

"And kneed him in the nuts. He came at me wrong. He scared me."

"He *scared* you? I'll kick his ass myself. You should see how my Tai Bo has improved. And I'll sic my lawyer on him, you give me the word. I've been paying that man too much, and he doesn't have enough work."

"No, I mean, he shouldn't have kissed me like that, but I was scared about the other guy. I overreacted."

"The other guy?"

"That one I told you about. Samuel. He's back. Actually, he just tried to run me off the road an hour ago. And I'm pretty sure he's the one who torched Cade's shack and started a grass fire on his property." Abigail tried to keep her voice light, but it shook a little.

Janet stopped smiling. "Honey, that's serious."

"I know. I'm scared to death."

"Is Cade taking care of you? When you're not fending off his advances?"

Abigail sighed. Just thinking about Cade made her heart fall to her feet again. For the thousandth time today. "He thought I set the fire."

"Oh, yes, that's just your style, isn't it? I can see where he'd get that. I really *am* going to sic James on him. For something. You let me figure out what. He can go after that Samuel, too, for that matter. Have you filed a police report yet?"

"Yeah. Fat lot of good that'll do. The ranch is pretty secluded, and Cade and Tom aren't always there. At least I have Clara." Abigail looked out at Clara, leashed to a parking meter. She didn't seem to be missing Abigail at all as she made friends with every passerby.

Shirley brought menus to the table. "Hey, hon! Don't leave without waving at the guys in back. They saw you walk by and they want to say hey to you."

"You mean they want to talk about the article," said Abigail.

"They're *dying* to, hon. You punched him? Do you know how many girls in this town would have paid good money to see that? Coffee?"

Abigail looked at Janet, who flipped the plastic menu over and then back again. "Let me order, Janet. We'll have two glasses of wine and two waters. And we'll each have a grilled-cheese sandwich with bacon. On sourdough. Extra pickles on the side. Oh, and fries."

Janet's eyes widened, but she handed her menu to Shirley without protest. "Do you have a wine list, darling?"

"You want red or white?"

Janet gave a single nod. "White it is."

"Me, too," said Abigail. Shirley smiled and went to hang up their order.

"So you punched him, my sweet. Does that mean you love him?"

Abigail laughed. "Is that what it usually means?"

"In my house, always."

"Well, damn. It's all Eliza's fault." Abigail paused, and then went on, "I do wonder if she put me there on purpose. For us to fall in love."

"Which you did."

"I did. He didn't. Eliza got half of it right, at least. I am such an idiot."

"You're not."

"I'm a moron. I went and fell in love, and he thinks I'm a pyromaniac."

Janet didn't say anything. Then she smiled. "You know the last thing Eliza asked me to do, a week before she died? It was twofold, actually."

"What?"

"If anything happened to her, she wanted me to not only watch over you, but to ask Cade's employee to watch over you, too."

"She wanted Tom to keep an eye on me? Why? I never even see him. That doesn't make sense."

"She wanted me to meet Tom."

"Oh, my *God*."

Janet laughed. "She set both of us up on blind dates."

"From the freakin' grave."

"Oh, I loved that woman."

"Me, too," said Abigail.

Janet took Abigail's hand and squeezed it.

"Speaking of Tom," said Abigail, "how goes your love life? Give me something good to think about."

"His boots have been under my bed a lot lately, you could say. And I'm loving it."

"Aargh. The boots that run around on Cade's land."

"Okay, my darling. Let's not think of him. Let's think, instead, of all the lovely money you're going to make on your next book."

"What next book? I haven't been planning a thing."

"You're Eliza's ambassador now. Living in her cottage, living her dream. You know the knitters want that story. They want you to look out the window in the morning when you wake up and describe that landscape. They want you to write about what you're thinking."

"I can't write about that."

"Well, not *that*, exactly. Although a mention of getting some sexy lovin' from her nephew—now, that would sell millions."

"Knitting gossip!"

"Nothing better."

"You know I won't."

"Oh, but wouldn't it drive him crazy if you did?" Janet's smile was wicked.

"But the rest, the store part—oh, it's been wonderful, Janet. I'm so busy during the day that I almost don't have time to think about him. It's only been what, almost a week and a half I've been open? I already have two different knitting groups who've asked if they can move their meeting place to my back room, and I've agreed. So that's two big groups, coming every week. I have three retreats scheduled in the next two months. Their guilds take care of the hotels and food and everything, and I'm hiring teachers to help me. We're going to use Eliza's workbooks to design new takeoffs of her old ideas. I set up that little website last week, you saw it."

"It's genius."

"And it's already getting a ton of hits. All the knit-bloggers are talking about it. I think the UPS guy hates me. I don't think he'd ever come down that road before, unless it was to bring a new harness or whatever it is stupid sheep ranchers need. Now I have him coming down the drive every day, bringing me more stock."

"That's incredible. I'm so proud of you. Oh, and I think you should get a gun."

Landers, one of Cade's rancher friends, passed by their table just as Janet abruptly changed the subject.

"What?" said Abigail.

"A gun?" asked Landers. "What kind you gonna get?"

Janet looked at him. She cocked one perfect eyebrow in withering disdain. This normally stopped men in their tracks.

But not Landers. "I think you should get a Glock. Unless it's for hunting, of course, then you wouldn't need a pistol. But if it's to keep Cade from your door, a Glock'll do the trick. Although you seem to protect yourself just fine."

"Move *along*, old man," hissed Janet.

He grinned and said, "Just offering my advice." He touched his hat and exited.

"This town is crazy," said Janet.

"You were here first," said Abigail.

Chapter Thirty-seven

Protect your knitting like you'd protect anything else you love.
—E.C.

Cade hadn't seen Tom yet this morning. While he waited for him to get back from the feed store, he thought about Abigail. Ostensibly, he was going over books in the office, but his pencil hadn't moved in half an hour.

It didn't help that every time he thought of her he took another punch, this time to the solar plexus, or at least that's where it felt like it was located.

He'd been listening all morning, listening for anything out of the ordinary.

But it had been quiet. Other than the knitters' cars driving up to the store, no one had troubled the ranch.

Why hadn't he asked her more about the guy who was after her? He should have at least insisted that he get the man's description, what he drove . . . If he was the person behind the torched shack, who knew what he might be up to? What if he tried to burn something else? Or hurt her?

Cade would protect her.

She'd never know that though, because he had a pretty good feeling she was never going to talk to him again, let alone trust him. How could she not know how he felt? How could she not feel it?

But she couldn't, and he wouldn't be able to tell her, and even if he found the courage, she'd never believe him.

He'd seen her truck leaving earlier. She hadn't looked in his direction, probably hadn't even seen him standing there, fixing a leaking pipe to one of the freestanding spigots.

She'd looked gorgeous. Like always. His heart ached.

Tom entered the office.

"Nice shiner," Tom said.

"Looking good, huh? Feels good, too."

"You just sitting here pining?"

"Screw you."

"Hey, I tried to find you earlier," Tom said. "That ewe you told me about? The one by the trough, the mother of that ram lamb you saved?"

"Yeah." Cade resharpened his pencil. Again.

"It took me until this morning to notice, since I first moved her last night after it was dark. She was killed, boss."

"Dammit! That's just what I need. The coyotes are back?" He hated coyotes more than any other animal in the world.

Tom's face looked odd. "No. Not a coyote. Her throat was slit."

Cade didn't understand. "What?"

"I don't know. I think it was with a knife, but the cut was jagged. Rough. It took a couple of tries, like the edge was blunt."

"Are you kidding me?"

"When I went back out to where you found her to look around, I found something really weird."

Cade felt the hairs on his arms stand up. "What?"

"Pink roses. Six pink roses on the ground."

Cade dropped the pencil and jammed his hat on his head. He raced out of the barn, running as fast as he could toward her cottage.

He climbed the few steps to the porch. The "Closed for Lunch" sign was visible in the glass of the door. He remembered when she'd first let herself into the cottage for the very first time, and he'd seen her, just after she'd realized what she was up against. She'd looked like she was going to cry, and then she didn't. He'd seen her then for the first time. Strong. Stubborn. Perfect.

The porch swing moved in the breeze, as if someone had just stood up. Cade had watched her surreptitiously from his window that night as she sat right here, that awful night when he didn't come to her. He should have. Cade would have given anything to have that night back: to have had dinner with her, to have loved her that night, to have saved the lamb together, to know he'd done the right thing for the woman he loved. To never have doubted her. To have protected her.

Abigail wasn't going anywhere. He should have known that. He should have trusted her.

A single pink rose lay on the welcome mat.

Cade heard Abigail's voice in his head. That night, in the parlor, when she'd been scared. *Him and his damn pink roses.*

Cade pressed his nose to the window that looked into the main room.

Strewn about the room, on every surface, on top of yarn and books and chairs, were pink roses. There must have been hundreds of them.

He'd find Samuel.

He'd find Samuel, before Samuel found her.

Chapter Thirty-eight

I've known what it's like to hold my needles silently on my lap, unmoved to create. And I've known the liberation that came when I freed myself, when I trusted myself.
—E.C.

Outside Tillie's, Abigail hugged Janet good-bye and went to get Clara where she'd left her tied at the side of the diner. The dog wasn't there.

For a long moment, Abigail considered this. Had she leashed her somewhere else? No, she'd been able to see her from where they were sitting. This was the right post. The leash was gone, too. Clara hadn't accidentally slipped her collar. Someone must have untied her.

"Clara?" Abigail ran to the end of the building and looked around the corner. Nothing.

"Clara!" She tried to suppress the feeling of panic. The worst-case scenario was that she'd have to get her back from the animal shelter. Any second, Clara would come lolloping out from under a parked car or something, trailing her leash.

"Come on, Clara! I don't have time for this!" Abigail went further around Tillie's and peered into the back alley. "Clara!"

A joyous *woof* greeted her, and Clara barreled her way out from behind a trash can.

"There you are! You bad girl! What were you doing back here? You scared me!"

"I could say the same about you."

The voice from behind her sent a spasm of icy fear down Abigail's spine. She couldn't turn around. But she had to.

Samuel. He was well dressed, in a nice gray suit. He looked clean, healthy. He looked sane.

"I've missed you. Standing over you at night isn't quite the same. How've you been, my Abby?"

Abigail shivered. "They're looking for you, you know. They know about your warrant."

"They won't find me, don't worry. I phoned in a shots-fired call on the other side of town. That one-horse police department has every man on duty over there. I won't take up much of your time. I know you have to get back to the ranch. But I've left you a little present, and I hope it will change your mind about how you feel about me. Maybe bring back some of those old feelings."

Abigail's hands shook so much she could barely hold Clara's leash. Clara growled softly, but made no move. "Did you burn something else? Not the cottage. Not the house!"

"That fire was just to get your attention. You did a great job trying to put it out, by the way. I didn't expect that rancher to get back so soon, and I knew slashing his friend's tires would keep the other one out of trouble. I really wanted you to see what a big blast could do. I suppose you could call it a small, a very small, warning. I don't like other men touching you. Just remember that. You've done well this week, keeping the rancher off you. You made me proud."

Abigail put the growling Clara between them, took the deepest breath she could, and screamed. She screamed for all she was worth, and then she took another breath and started again. Samuel turned and ran as doors along the alley were flung open. Two men rounded the corner at a run.

"What's wrong, lady?" one yelled.

"Stop him! He stole my purse!" It was the only thing she could think of, but it worked to set the men into chase mode.

Samuel got away, though. Again.

Abigail spent yet another hour with the young officer, who tripped over his own apologies. "I mean, we thought we had shots fired, so we had to take that super seriously, you know?"

"I know," said Abigail, and signed the second report. She needed to get home. She needed to find what Samuel had left for her.

She longed for Cade.

In her truck, Abigail rolled the windows down and breathed the salt air as she drove along the coast. She headed inland, the radio playing quietly in the background.

It wouldn't be too bad. Right? Whatever it was Samuel had left. Even as she thought it, she didn't believe it.

How the hell was she supposed to get through this? She couldn't do it. She couldn't live here being as scared as she'd been in San Diego.

Oh, God, she wanted Cade.

But things were different now. Abigail was strong. She had her land. Her store. Her dream. She could and would protect what she had. She could do this herself.

She *had* to do this herself.

Abigail distracted herself by thinking about the opening chapters of the book she would write. Janet had been right—it was a great idea. Book. Think about the book.

She'd start the book with driving onto the land, that moment when she first saw her legacy.

The moment she'd seen the cowboy up on the ridge.

Okay, she wouldn't write about that part. She wouldn't write about him.

The road wound through yet another stand of eucalyptus. This was her favorite part of the twenty-five-minute drive back to the ranch, this narrow, swerving bit right before Mills Bridge and its huge curve. This part, before, and the part after, in the live oaks, she loved that.

But now, as she came up on the bridge, she slowed a little. She really hated the next part. There was a tanker truck in front of her, and what looked like a horse trailer behind her. She wanted plenty of room between all of them. People went too damn fast on this road.

Cade went too fast on this road.

No, think of the new book.

She wanted photographs included in it. Pictures of Eliza at home on the ranch—she had a box of them stored somewhere. Lovely pictures of Eliza holding wool, knitting, guffawing at the camera as she always did. Photos of her sweaters, her socks, her mittens. Abigail could replicate the items, make the old sweaters in new colors, sit in the same place, show the students looking out at the same valley. Yes, people would like that.

What *was* that tanker doing? Abigail was in the middle of the long bridge now. She gripped the steering wheel tighter. The tanker swerved a little as if to miss hitting an animal. Then it jerked itself back on course. Up ahead, coming from the other direction, a small car was passing a passenger van over the double yellow line.

Abigail hit her brakes, softly at first, to get the attention of the horse trailer behind her, then harder. But in her rearview mirror, she could see another vehicle passing the horse trailer, dangerously, on the curve.

A black SUV.

It was Samuel.

He passed the trailer and began closing the distance between them fast. He didn't slow down at all.

The small car coming at them in their lane seemed to realize it shouldn't have tried to pass, but by then it was right next to the van. It braked, but it looked as though the van driver was panicking. It slowed as well, both of the vehicles now taking up both lanes.

The tanker hit its brakes and rocked sideways violently.

They reached the second curve of the long bridge. Abigail braked harder, and Samuel's SUV almost hit her rear bumper.

Time slowed down. As if it were a movie shot in slow motion, Abigail saw every detail.

The small car accelerated and shot past the van. It just managed to clear the front end of the tanker in front of her. But the tanker braked so hard that it lost control. Near the end of the bridge where it rejoined the steep cliff and became road again, the tanker jack-knifed. The back cylinder twisted off, rolled, and instantly burst into flames. The van barely cleared the tanker. Abigail had nowhere to go but forward; she'd never stop in time.

She pulled the steering wheel as hard as she could to the left, missing the rear bumper of the van as it passed her. She skidded around the fishtailing, blazing tanker. For one horrifying second, the spinning front cab of the tanker was right in front of her, facing the wrong way, and she looked into the terrified face of the driver.

His mouth was open in a scream. His hands twisted the wheel in vain.

Abigail hit the far left guardrail as she slipped her truck between it and the tanker cab. She corrected her steering, cleared the end of the bridge, and made it to the roadway. Behind her, through the open window, she heard the sickening sounds of metal crashing, shrieking, as the SUV failed to avoid the tanker.

Flames exploded higher in her rearview mirror.

Then, with a noise louder than anything she'd ever heard, the end of the bridge collapsed entirely behind her. It took down with it the fiery tanker, its cab, Samuel's SUV, the horse trailer, the small car, and the van.

Abigail careened to a stop on the shoulder, just off the bridge.

She leaped out of the truck, cell phone in hand. She dialed 911 for the third time that day, and gave the dispatcher all the details she could, as she stood on the edge of the cliff and watched the metal beneath her burn.

"How many people are injured, ma'am?" asked the dispatcher.

"I don't know! At least five. Maybe more! Just hurry! The bridge fell . . ."

"The bridge *fell*? You didn't say that, ma'am! How much of the bridge?"

"The last half, the, uh, eastern half, I guess. Just get out here." Abigail flipped her cell phone closed and closed her eyes, unable to feel anything but the heat rising from below.

Then she heard a scream, followed by another. The flames, fast to rise, were dying down. She could see at least one person—no, there were two—stumbling between vehicles.

She had to help.

She started down the cliff, carefully bracing herself against the slipping rocks.

Almost at the bottom, she called out, "Help is coming! Hold on! They're on their way!" The intensity of the heat terrified her, but she kept going.

A man wearing overalls and bleeding from the head waved her over to a small car. He fell to his knees.

A huge sound, terrible in its volume, came from above her. Abigail looked up.

The whole side of the cliff was coming down. Oh, God, her pickup truck was coming down with it. She saw the back end of it tilting, sliding on the moving rocks, and now the whole hill was moving toward her, carrying the truck, deafening in its roar.

She ran, toward the fire, toward the man, as fast as she could. She'd never make it out of the way in time.

Chapter Thirty-nine

Life is too short to be bothered knitting something you don't love.

—E.C.

On his way up the driveway, Cade tried to slow his breathing. He'd cleared the whole ranch with Tom's help. If Samuel was hiding here, he was invisible. He was out there somewhere, and Cade was going to find him. Tom was in charge of watching for Abigail to return, and Cade had made him swear on his life that he would keep Abigail safe if she beat Cade home. He felt both foolish and dead serious asking Tom to agree.

Cade didn't deserve her. But maybe he could begin to earn her love. Starting right now.

He hit the main road and slammed the gearshift into fourth.

So what if Eliza had some grand plan in place? So what if she'd wanted him to get together with Abigail, to set them up? Eliza had been about love. She had loved Uncle Joshua with every last bit of her heart, and she wouldn't have expected him to be with Abigail unless he loved her.

Which, dammit, he did.

But he'd hurt her, because he was the biggest idiot that had ever lived, and she'd never trust him again. He didn't blame her.

Cade rolled down the window to try to cool his mind.

Wasn't this the way? He finally fell in love, and he couldn't have her, wouldn't ever be with her because he hadn't been able to see who she really was, in time.

He snapped the radio off. He wasn't in the mood for music.

Maybe he'd listen to the scanner. It was good for picking up the fire channels to monitor medicals and house fires, and sometimes he liked to be nosy about what was going on in town. Cops were fun to laugh at when they got hyped up on the radio.

And man, they were hyped right now. So was the dispatcher.

"David-two, David-seven, Adam-four and all other available units, code three for the bridge. Code three for Mills Bridge. Total six ambulances enroute, reports of multiple casualties, MCI initiated, three helos enroute. Proceed with caution, eastern span is out. Repeating, eastern span is *down*. Need road blocked on eastern end. Repeat, road is *not* blocked on eastern end. Four casualties transported by ground so far from western end, unknown status of remaining victims."

Mills Bridge? He was almost to the eastern end of it. He hit the brakes as he came out of the last curve before the bridge started. He knew that doing so had saved his life.

Nothing. A sheer drop into nothing.

He kicked the truck into reverse. He had to set up a roadblock, to set up something. Someone else was going to come around fast and fly off the edge like he almost had.

A hundred yards up the road, he yanked the emergency brake and skidded into a turn that placed his truck squarely across the middle of the road. At least they'd only hit it and not fly over. He grabbed four flares from his tool box, lit them all and threw them up the road as far as he could. Then he turned and raced for the cliff's edge.

It was bad. He could see at least five vehicles down there, some people moving around. Something was on fire, but it looked like it had almost burned out. A fire-patrol rig had four-wheeled down the other side and looked like it was pumping water. At least eight cop cars were flashing their lights on the other side, and he watched as uniforms scrambled down. Two ambulances were loading their crews up the hill on the other side. It looked as if they were carrying patients up on Stokes stretchers.

Thank God the river was low, barely ankle deep at this time of year.

He stood on the edge and tried to ascertain if it was safe to descend. Rocks skittered down, but it looked like the part that had gone down was the shale, and all that was left up here was solid rock. It should be okay.

He started down, his boots slipping immediately. He hit the dirt with his backside and bounced back up.

Then he saw it.

Abigail's truck. At the bottom, halfway covered in rock, a tangled mess. It wasn't near the tanker and the other vehicles—it was closer to the cliff's edge. It was on its side, and he could hear the mangled engine still ticking under the rubble as he got closer.

He stopped breathing.

If she was in that thing when it went down . . .

No.

If she was in that truck . . .

If she had been anywhere *near* that truck when it went over . . . That stupid, little no-good couch-carrying truck.

Still barely breathing, his mind exploding with terror, he went down faster. He wouldn't, couldn't fall.

Everything depended on this.

Everything.

All that he was, depended on her.

"Abigail!" His voice was too quiet. He gathered air into his lungs as he launched himself down the few remaining feet and at the truck. "Abigail!"

He peered into the wrecked cab.

She wasn't there. Thank God, she wasn't there.

But where was she?

"Abigail!" His voice sounded as hysterical as he felt.

Paramedics knelt over someone near a horse trailer that was almost in splinters.

A woman.

They were working on a woman.

Cade tripped and fell to his knees once and he used his hands to scratch at the rocks, to push himself back up so he could run again.

Not her, it couldn't be her. He would die, too.

A startled-looking paramedic, way too young for the job, yelled as Cade pushed between them to look.

The woman they were working on was a blond, not a brunette. Covered in blood. She was breathing: the medics had been positioning her on the board to get her up the other side.

It wasn't her.

"Sorry," Cade mumbled and pushed his hands into his hair.

"Where?" He choked. "Where are the others?"

"The worst were transported first. If you don't see someone here, they've gone to County Hospital. Now get the hell out of the way."

Cade couldn't seem to make his feet respond to his wishes.

"Move!" yelled the paramedic.

He stumbled out of their way, and approached an officer who looked bewildered by the chaos.

"Have you seen a girl? Brown hair that curls at the ends, blue eyes? Slim?"

"Think she went out with the first batch . . ."

"How bad?"

"Don't remember, buddy, we seen a lot in the last half hour. They're all pretty bad. I'm sorry, I didn't notice."

Cade started running.

This was everything.

She was everything.

He ran through the low river, not letting out the sob that threatened to rip from his chest. He ran up the other side of the hill, not allowing himself to fall when he stumbled.

At the top, he saw the officer that had ticketed him.

"John! Have you seen her? Abigail?"

He looked at Cade blankly. Then nodded. "Yes. She's at County."

"How bad is she?"

"I don't know, someone just told me that's where she'd gone, with the driver of the tanker. Don't think he'll make it though."

"Drive me."

"I can't leave!"

"Look, two more of your guys are pulling up, over there. I'm begging you with all that's holy, if I don't get to County—" Cade's voice broke.

John nodded. "All right. I need a report from a medic there anyway. Let me tell the sergeant . . ."

"Tell him later!" Cade roared.

As they raced up the coastal highway, Cade kept his forehead pressed against the glass of the passenger-side window.

If this was love, if this is what fear felt like when you loved someone, he didn't know how so many people made it through life.

What had Aunt Eliza done with this fear, when Uncle Joshua was so sick?

What did anyone do?

He couldn't live without her. It wasn't possible.

At County Hospital, the emergency room was a battlefield. Every nurse and doctor was yelling, every intern racing from bed to bed. Two more ambulances pulled up behind the cop car, but Cade beat them inside.

A nurse yelled at him to stop, but he pulled sheet after sheet aside, looking at bloody faces, bodies. A horribly burned man turned haunted eyes to him as he yanked aside another curtain.

This must be the tanker driver. He looked alert, though, and he was breathing.

"What the hell are you doing?" shouted the nurse. Cade was gone, pulling aside the next curtain.

The sheet was pulled up over the body in the bed, blood staining red against the white. The face was covered. Cade used every ounce of willpower he had. He yanked back the sheet. A man's face. Eyes open, still, staring. The left half of his face was burned to blackness, the skin rippling and charred, peeling back against white skin. The right side of his face looked undamaged, white and pink. The name on the slip of paper next to his head read, "ID: Samuel Collins."

Cade had never prayed before, but he sent something up with all his heart, and he didn't stop to analyze what it was.

He went through the entire emergency room twice. They were too busy to stop him.

She wasn't here.

If she wasn't here . . .

She *had* to be here.

A firm hand grasped his upper arm so hard that it hurt. A small nurse with blood on her scrubs said, "Out. Now. I mean it."

"But . . ."

"Out." She dragged him into a large waiting room. "Stay. If I see you in there again, I'll have you arrested."

Being arrested was the least of his worries, but he couldn't think of a single other thing to do.

Her cell phone. Yes.

Cade dialed.

He waited. It connected.

And then he heard her ring tone play, faintly, around the corner.

He stood. His legs shook, but they bore his weight.

As Abigail answered, he'd already made the turn and was standing in a small hallway.

She sat in a brown plastic chair, the color gone from her face. Her clothes were ripped, and it looked like she was getting a black eye. One to match his.

"Hello?" she repeated into the phone. "Cade? Please?"

Then she looked up at him.

He looked down at her.

Abigail burst into tears.

Cade's arms went around her. He wrapped her up, making sure he cradled every part of her. He kissed her face, her hair, her cheeks.

"You're alive. You're alive." He murmured the words over and over. She said words, too, but he couldn't understand them, at first. They didn't sound like English through her tears, and then she stopped making any noise at all and just shook in his arms.

He hoped she couldn't tell how much he was shaking, too.

After long, long moments, Cade felt her take her first full breath. He released her only enough to look into her face.

"My love," he said.

And he watched that light, that light that he thought he had extinguished, come back on.

"But Samuel . . ."

"Is his last name Collins? Dark-haired? Suit?"

"Yes," she whispered.

"He's dead."

She sagged against him, as if all the air had left her lungs. "I'm not sorry," she said. "It's so awful. But I'm not sorry."

"Nothing matters without you," Cade said against her hair. "Nothing. And I didn't know, I didn't understand that until I thought I lost you." The hot tears that had been threatening finally filled his eyes. "When I saw the truck . . . When I couldn't find you there, or in the ER . . . I thought . . ."

"I was with the tanker driver. No one but me knew CPR before they got there. He was so burned. His lungs were burned. He couldn't breathe. I did CPR until the ambulance got there. I wouldn't leave him, so they took me in the ambulance. But I don't think he'll make it."

"I saw him. He didn't look great. But he was breathing. He was breathing, honey."

Now her eyes were the ones to fill.

"And you're alive," he said. "You're alive. You're here."

She pressed her lips against his, softly. "I'm not going anywhere, cowboy."

He used the back of his hand to swipe away the tears rolling down his cheeks. He wasn't ashamed of them. They were for her.

As gently as he could, he released her from his arms, and set her back on the hard plastic chair. And he slipped off the chair, onto the ground and onto his knee.

"Might not be the best time or place, and I don't have anything to give you, except myself. And some sheep. But Abigail, will you marry me?"

He was startled by her laugh. "Eliza would be so proud of you!"

"But," he said, "is that a yes?"

"Hell, yes, that's a yes. You're my heart." Her smile radiated light—light that he would make sure never dimmed, not for the rest of their lives.

Epilogue

Love through everything.
—E.C.

On a cool Tuesday morning one year later, Abigail turned the "Open" sign to "Closed," and then locked the door of the store. She packed a picnic lunch. She put on her favorite red polka-dot dress and pulled her hair back. She put on lipstick. She put on a new red angora lace cardigan she'd just finished making.

She'd lose money today. Tuesdays were usually good days, customers having missed her on Monday tended to wait impatiently for the next open day. But that would have to be okay.

She got in her blue Nissan pickup truck, the replacement one, and drove up to the barn. Tom and Cade were in the rafters, rigging ropes for something they were doing down below.

"'Lo, boys!"

"Watch out below," hollered Cade, and then he slid down a rope, his gloved hands smoking a little as his legs hit the ground.

"Show-off," she muttered, and kissed him.

"Get a room!" yelled Tom as he slid down the rope. When he got to the bottom, he said, "You should tell Janet I did that. That's cool."

"Tell her yourself tonight, when you go home."

"It's better if you tell her how cool I am. Sliding down a rope."

Abigail raised her eyebrows at him.

Tom grinned, and then asked, "How's the book going?"

"I'm done. I just finished, right now! I just typed 'The End.' And it's time to celebrate with my guy."

Cade smiled, but he said, "Honey, I still have to . . ."

"No, you don't. You get two hours off."

"Who says?"

"Your wife. Come on, I have something to show you."

"This gonna at least be rated R?"

"Cade!"

Tom laughed. "See you later, boss. Have fun."

Abigail drove, Cade complaining good-naturedly the whole way.

"I bet you didn't even bring the turkey sandwich I like."

"Brought it."

"And the Hershey's kisses?"

"You can have my kisses, if you want."

"I always want. They taste better anyway."

He threaded his fingers through the fingers of her non–steering-wheel hand.

"Are we almost there yet? I want some of those kisses."

"Almost," she said.

A few minutes later, "Here."

A beat later, Cade said, "Oh."

The newly reconstructed bridge gleamed in the sun, the long, flat curves angling away from them.

Cade pulled the russet Guernsey on over his head as he got out of the truck. It was the first sweater she'd knit for him, and it was still her favorite on him.

"It's been a year?" he asked.

Abigail nodded. She knew he'd get it. "One year exactly. Come on, let's eat on the edge."

"Doesn't make you nervous?"

"Nothing could today."

She took his hand. God, he was gorgeous. Look at him. He belonged in the movies, on a billboard, advertising saddle soap or something. Instead, he grinned at her, and walked with her, and loved her, every minute of the day. Even in the middle of their infrequent squabbles, she felt his love, all the time.

She was so lucky.

And they were getting luckier by the day.

Abigail led him to the edge of the bridge, to a little metal piece that was wide enough for both of them to sit on. She swung her legs over the edge. The fall sunshine danced on the water below.

They ate their sandwiches, leaning comfortably against each other. He kissed her, and she kissed him back.

"You taste like onions," he said.

"Yep."

They sat in silence, looking down. Most of the metal had been cleared out during construction, but they hadn't removed the bumper from her old pickup truck, and it shone in the sun below.

Cade cleared his throat and pushed his lunch away. He put both arms around her. "Worst day of my life." He kissed her again, and her heart beat faster, as it always did. "And the best day of my life."

"Yeah. Me, too."

Cade held her tighter. The handspun merino was soft under her cheek. "So, you finished the book! Eliza's book?"

"Our book."

"When will I get to read it?"

"Soon."

"Is it about me?"

"No. But you're definitely in it."

"The knitters will love it. Big day! I wish I'd have known, I would have brought champagne."

"I wouldn't have had any."

Cade laughed. "Yeah, right."

"No, I wouldn't."

"You love champagne. And *I* love how giggly it makes you."

"No alcohol for me for a while." Abigail smiled at him, the biggest smile that she'd ever smiled in her whole life.

"I don't get it."

She raised one eyebrow and kept smiling.

"Oh, hot *damn*!" yelled Cade. He scrambled to his feet and whooped, then he grabbed Abigail, and led them both back to solid ground. Then he picked her up and swung her around and around and around.

Abigail's head spun, in a good way.

He kissed her. She kissed him back, and felt him stirring against her.

"We do need to celebrate, though," she purred. "Can you think of any other way we can do it? Champagne aside?"

"Strangely enough, I think I can."

"Back of my truck! Now!" Laughing so hard she almost fell over, Abigail raced for the truck, where she'd already laid out the blankets.

She needed him now. She always did. Always would. She opened her arms, and he held her, and the world spun away, and there was nothing but the two of them, on top of her handspun blanket.

A+

AUTHOR
INSIGHTS,
EXTRAS &
MORE...

FROM

**RACHAEL
HERRON**

AND

AVON A

Love Song Sweater

A Guernsey using raglan construction
Finished Measurements:
Chest: 40 (44, 48, 52) inches
Length: 26 (26½, 27¼, 28¼) inches
Gauge: 18 sts and 26 rows = 4 inches in stockinette stitch
See rachaelherron.com/lovesongsweater for color photos and/
or extras.

Materials:

Worsted-weight wool, 1350 (1500, 1750, 1900) yds.
(Suggested yarn: Lorna's Laces, Shepherd Worsted)
One US #7 (4.5mm) 16-inch circular needle (or size to
get gauge)
One US #7 (4.5mm) 32-inch circular needle (or size to
get gauge)
Yarn needle
Four stitch markers
Stitch holders or scrap yarn
Sleeves—Make two

Sleeves

Using shorter circular needle, cast on 36 (38, 40, 42) sts loosely
enough to join around needle (or use DPNs in correct size).
PM and join to work in the round.

Ribbing Row: * K1tbl, p1; rep from * to end of row.

Repeat this row 8 more times.

Knit one row, increasing 6 (6, 8, 8) sts evenly spaced across row—42 (44, 48, 50) sts.

Row 1: K18 (19, 21, 22), work Row 1 of Chart A, k18 (19, 21, 22).

Row 2: K18 (19, 21, 22), work Row 2 of Chart A, k18 (19, 21, 22).

Continue in this manner for two more rows.

Increase Row: K1f&b, work in pattern to last st, k1f&b—2 sts increased.

Continue to repeat Rows 1–10 of Chart A and work 2 increases as above every 8 (8, 7, 6) rows 10 (11, 12, 14) more times—64 (68, 74, 80) sts.

Work even in pattern until sleeve measures 19½ (20, 20½, 21) inches from beginning. At end of last row, work to 3 (3, 4, 4) sts before marker, slip 6 (6, 8, 8) stitches onto scrap yarn for underarm. Put the rest of the stitches onto stitch holder (or second piece of longer scrap yarn).

Work second sleeve using Chart C instead of Chart A.

Body

Using longer circular needle, cast on 180 (198, 216, 234) stitches. PM and join to work in the round.

Ribbing Row: * K1tbl, p1; rep from * to end of row.

Repeat this row 10 more times.

Work even in stockinette stitch (knit all rows) until piece measures 14 inches from beginning.

Purl one row.

Knit one row, increasing 2 (0, 2, 0) sts evenly across row—182 (198, 218, 234) sts.

Purl one row.

Knit next two rows.

Row 1: PM, k16 (20, 25, 29), p1, work Row 1 of Chart A, p1, work Row 1 of Chart B, p1, work Row 1 of Chart C, p1, k16 (20, 25, 29), PM, k91 (99, 109, 117).

Row 2: Slip marker, k16 (20, 25, 29), p1, work Row 2 of Chart A, p1, work Row 2 of Chart B, p1, work Row 2 of Chart C, p1, k15 (20, 24, 29), slip marker, k91 (99, 109, 117).

Continue in this manner until piece measures 17 inches from beginning.

Join Sleeves to Body

At end of last row, work to 3 (3, 4, 4) sts before marker, slip 6 (6, 8, 8) sts onto scrap yarn for underarm. Continuing to work sleeves and front of body in pattern, PM and work across 58 (62, 66, 72) sts from first sleeve holder, PM, work across front of sweater to 3 (3, 4, 4) sts before next marker, slip 6 (6, 8, 8) sts onto scrap yarn for underarm. PM and work across 58 (62, 66, 72) sts from second sleeve holder, PM, knit across the back of sweater to end of row—286 (310, 334, 362) sts.

Work even for one inch, keeping in patterns as established.

Raglan Decreases

Decrease Row: * K1, ssk, work in pattern to 3 sts before marker, k2tog, k1, slip marker; rep from * to end of row—8 sts decreased.

Repeat Decrease Row every other row 25 (27, 29, 32) more times—78 (86, 94, 98) sts remain. Change to shorter circular needle when necessary.

Back Neck Shaping:

Row 1: Knit 3 sts, wrap next st and turn.

Row 2: Purl 3 sts, slip marker, purl to 3 sts past next marker, wrap next st and turn.

Row 3: Knit to 2 sts before previous wrapped st, wrap next st and turn.

Row 4: Purl to 2 sts before previous wrapped st, wrap next st and turn.

Knit one row, picking up the wraps as you come to them.

Neck

Ribbing Row: * K1tbl, p1; rep from * to end of row.

Repeat this row 7 more times.

Bind off all sts loosely in rib.

Finishing

Graft (kitchener stitch) underarms together. Wet-block and dry.

List of Abbreviations

DPNs—Double-point needles

K—Knit

K1tbl—Knit one through the back loop

K1f&b—Knit one front and back (increase stitch)

K2tog—Knit two together (decrease stitch)

P—Purl

PM—Place marker

Rep—Repeat

Ssk—Slip two stitches as if to knit, then knit those two stitches
   together (decrease stitch)

St(s)– Stitch(es)

Stockinette stitch—in the round, all rows knit.

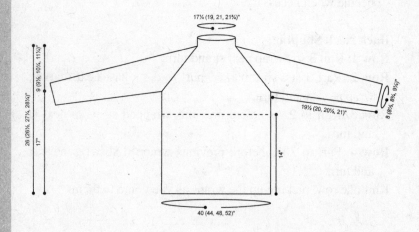

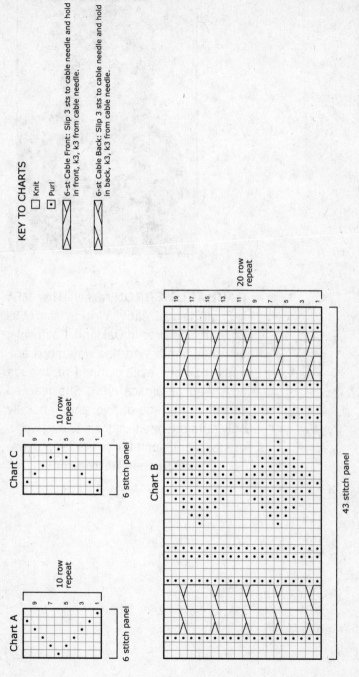

KEY TO CHARTS

□ Knit

• Purl

⬚ 6-st Cable Front: Slip 3 sts to cable needle and hold in front, k3, k3 from cable needle.

⬚ 6-st Cable Back: Slip 3 sts to cable needle and hold in back, k3, k3 from cable needle.

Chart A

10 row repeat

6 stitch panel

Chart C

10 row repeat

6 stitch panel

Chart B

20 row repeat

43 stitch panel

Rachael Herron

Khalli Robinson

RACHAEL HERRON received her MFA in English and Creative Writing from Mills College. She lives in Oakland, California, with her family and has way more animals than she ever planned to, though no sheep or alpaca (yet). She learned to knit at the age of five, and generally only puts the needles down to eat, write, or sleep, and sometimes not even then.
www.RachaelHerron.com